Praise for Karin Rita Gastreich and *Eolyn*

"Gastreich allows her heroes to have flaws—including moments of cowardice—and some victories bring new sorrows. Vigorously told deceptions and battle scenes will satisfy fans of traditional epic fantasy with a romantic thread."

–*Publisher's Weekly*

"Ms. Gastreich's uncanny talent for truly creating a world her readers can become part of is a rare gift, and one she shares abundantly."

–Terri-Lynne DeFino, author of *Finder*

"A book to savor first at great length, and then revisit over and over again."

–Lucy Crowe, author of *Sugarman's Daughter*

"Although rooted in traditional fantasy, *Eolyn* stretches and breaks the bounds in many ways, leading to a read that is fresh and unpredictable."

–Shauna Roberts, author of *Like Mayflies in a Stream*

"Gastreich's *Eolyn* focuses on the emotional, political, and physical conflicts between powerful and three-dimensional characters."

–Carlyle Clark, author of *The Black Song Inside*

"Humour leavens the story...but never becomes intrusive or undermines the strong threads of loss, duty, romance and revenge that permeate the book. And the action is often superb."

–David Hunter, author of *A Road of Blood and Slaughter*

"This story is masterfully written."

–*The Kindle Book Review*

High Maga

A Novel

Karin Rita Gastreich

HADLEY
RILLE
BOOKS

ISBN-13 978-0-9892631-9-1

Edited by Terri-Lynne DeFino

Hadley Rille Books
Eric T. Reynolds, Editor/Publisher
PO Box 25466
Overland Park, KS 66225 USA
www.hrbpress.com
contact@hadleyrillebooks.com

For Loren and Peter

Acknowledgements

Many places, people, and events inspired this story, starting with the forests of Costa Rica, particularly the highlands of Talamanca and the beautiful biological station of Las Cruces. Andrews Experimental Forest in Oregon, through their long-term ecological reflections program, inspired vivid images of East Selen.

From the moment I got it into my head I wanted to write novels, my husband's support has been invaluable. Thank you also to Mom, Dad, Loren, and Peter, and to all my family and friends for never failing to ask how that second book was coming along.

My deepest gratitude goes to my editor and publisher, Eric T. Reynolds, for the way his face lit up the first time I mentioned the possibility of a companion novel to *Eolyn*, and for all the support he has provided in bringing the novel to press. Terri-Lynne DeFino is an amazing editor and good friend; everything that is clean and sparkly about this novel happened thanks to her. Thomas Vandenberg took my breath away with his rendition of Eolyn for the novel's cover. Many thanks to Heather McDougal for the cover design. Tina Black copy edited the manuscript.

I am deeply indebted to David Hunter for undertaking this second journey with me, and tackling the tedious task of thoroughly critiquing each freshly baked (or rather, under-baked) chapter right as it came out of the oven. Thank you also to my beta readers DelSheree Gladden and Cathy Jones. Fellow writers at thenextbigwriter.com and the Dead Horse Society provided important feedback on the early chapters, and Heartland Romance Authors and has been a great source of support and information.

Dollbabies, you know who you are! A heartfelt thanks and many hugs for making me a part of your wonderful writing community. Your compassion and support has been a blessing on so many levels. I hope to join you again in VAB soon.

Most of all, thank you to my readers. For those who are new to Eolyn's world, thank you for choosing this book and giving me the opportunity to share the magic with you. Fans and friends of *Eolyn,* thank you for your patience and enthusiastic support during the completion of *High Maga.* I know you've had a long wait, but I'm confident you will find *High Maga* well worth it. Enjoy!

The Death of the San'iloman

Rishona lay in a fitful sleep, dark hair splayed over silken sheets, agitated moans breaking upon full lips. Placing his hand over hers, Tahmir closed his eyes and tried to capture her dreams, but it was no use. Where once he had seen movement and color, all that remained was stagnation and darkness. His vision had begun fading months before, ebbing even as his sister regained her strength, until nothing remained but a painfully narrow corridor of the present moment.

The future was hidden, the past nothing more than a frozen memory.

Rising abruptly, Tahmir strode across the room to the balcony. Below lay Ech-Nalahm, the jewel of the Syrnte Empire, a broad expanse of rounded roofs and tall spires rising from the dry plains like a coral bed exposed by a retreating sea. Countless oil lamps lined the rooftops, alleyways and doorsteps, a flickering vigil that mirrored the vault of stars above, the people's homage to the last days of Joturi-Nur, San'iloman of the Syrnte.

"Tahmir." Rishona's voice startled him. She stood awake and at his side, a mild frown creasing her features as dark eyes searched his face. "Why do you not sleep?"

He gripped the balustrade, palms damp against the polished wood. "How can you not know?"

"Joturi-Nur will not choose me." She rested her fingers upon his. "He favors our uncle Mechnes, or Paolus-Nur. Mechnes is stronger, Paolus more clever. Either would wield the sword of the San'iloman better than Arbartamor, and our grandfather knows this."

"It does not matter who is strong or clever. Arbartamor is his favored son, and the eldest."

She withdrew. The sudden absence was palpable. "Your pessimism distresses me. What would you have me do? Run and hide?"

"If it will save your life, yes."

"We lost a kingdom once, running and hiding."

He flinched at the rebuke. Years had passed since their defeat in the Battle of Aerunden, and still Rishona had not forgiven him.

"We had no hope that day," he said, "and you know it."

"We had no hope because you ordered our men to abandon the fight. All those to whom we swore our swords, our friendship, our protection, all of them perished because of you."

"Ernan did not know who we are. He would have banished us when the truth came to light."

"We had his sister. She was all we needed."

Tahmir set his jaw and looked away. It had been his task to seduce Ernan's sister and distract her from the Mage King. Once victory was theirs, they would have woven her magic into the fabric of their reign, rendering their hold over Moisehén absolute.

"She would not have stayed," he said. "There was something in her—some part of her spirit—that would not be subdued. She never ceased in her yearning for the Mage King."

"She would have become one with us once he was dead. Heart, body, and soul."

"We cannot be certain of that."

"I was certain." Her sheer gown trembled with the heat of her anger, accentuating the supple contours of her body. "I was always certain."

"Must we argue about this again?" His words came harsher than intended. For a moment he sensed a break in the darkness of his mind, an ephemeral light like the flash of a silver blade.

Her expression softened, and she touched his cheek. "I will not be sacrificed tomorrow. Joturi-Nur will name Mechnes as the new San'iloman, and Mechnes will seal his claim by shedding the blood of his brother Arbartamor. I do not fear this event. I take great joy in it. It is my duty and honor to represent our dead mother, to be called by her name, and to be loved by our grandfather as he once loved her."

Her innocence broke Tahmir's heart. He gathered Rishona in his arms and buried his face in the thick cloud of her hair, breathing in her scent of night and jasmine. "You have become prey to foolish illusions. The only worth you have in Joturi-Nur's eyes is as a sacrifice. You are the one who will die so that all of his sons may live. Let us leave this place, Rishona. Let us escape tonight."

She laughed and shifted inside his embrace."Have your visions abandoned you, my brother?" Her breath fell soft upon his ear. "Is that why you fear tomorrow?"

Tahmir shuddered at the assertion, pressed his lips against her forehead. Had she noticed he was crippled?

Gently she took his hand and guided him to the bed. Beckoning him to recline on the perfumed sheets, she enveloped him with a tender touch. "See what I see, dear brother. Dream my dreams for me."

Tahmir surrendered to the irresistible rush of her Syrnte sight, a rich tapestry of time filling the cold void of his soul. Together they ran with a swarm of soldiers over a ravaged landscape, deafened by the thunderous collapse of stone under the weight of a thousand flames, drenched by the blood of women cut open, unborn children torn from their bellies. Monsters tunneled out of the earth to join their attack, great beasts with long glowing limbs and obsidian claws that ripped through metal, mail, and flesh. Kings cowered and cities fell beneath their onslaught. The orgy of triumph consumed him, until fire exploded from his core and left him with nothing: no thoughts, no anxieties, no fear of the dawn.

* * *

Tahmir woke with a start, Rishona's name upon his lips, sweat breaking on his brow.

The bed was empty.

They must have taken Rishona away before the sun spread its golden rays over the white city, to prepare her for the rituals to come. Tahmir lingered, one hand caressing the place where she had slept, wondering why she had not awakened him when she left.

He spent his day in agitation, wandering aimlessly through the palace halls and gardens, staring without seeing into the sparkling fountains as doom carved a cavern out of his heart.

At sunset he presented himself, along with the rest of the court of Ech'Nalahm, in the expansive bedchamber of the San'iloman. The marble pillars were hung with curtains of dark silk, and the heavy smell of incense impregnated the air.

On the wide bed lay Joturi-Nur, San'iloman of the Syrnte, now a thin old man with clay-colored skin and gray eyes, propped up against voluminous pillows dyed in rich shades of burgundy and gold. To his right sat his First Wife Meanara, tall and stately, hands folded on her lap, a jeweled veil over thin white hair. Though fifteen years his younger, she appeared as aged and wizened as he. At her side sat the Second Wife, Lhandra, taken when Meanara was past her child-bearing years, and his Third Wife, Bheulla. Next to Bheulla knelt the girl Naptari, her shoulders trembling beneath a pale blue veil. A virgin of twelve years, she had been chosen this very day, so that Joturi-Nur might be comforted by her pleasures in the world beyond.

The room filled with courtiers, advisors and nobles from distant provinces, a few engaged in quiet conversation as they took their appointed places. The last to arrive were Joturi-Nur's surviving sons, ten in all. Arbartamor strode at their head, a portly man with heavy-lidded eyes and jowls that sagged on either side of his full lips. The others entered in pairs, with Prince Mechnes sustaining the hand of his niece, Rishona.

Mechnes was an older man but still in his prime, his handsome countenance undiminished by its many scars. Next to him, Rishona glowed like the rising moon, her hair braided and wrapped in an elegant crown. A dark veil adorned with diamonds covered her fine features. Her simple robe of charcoal silk was embroidered with gold threads, and her satin slippers were the color of rubies.

Once the siblings took their places, the high priest, a white-robed man with shaven head and protuberant brow, bent close and whispered in Joturi-Nur's ear. The San'iloman nodded and raised his hand to the assembly as the priest stepped away.

All shifting and murmuring ceased.

A scribe seated next to the brothers bent over his ledger and dipped his pen in ink.

The old man's voice resonated through the chamber. "I, Joturi-Nur, San'iloman of the Syrnte, son of Mahtaron-Feh, and father to seventeen children of royal blood, do hereby declare the end of my reign on this, the last day of the eightieth year of my life."

A sob escaped the virgin Naptari's throat, but no one paid her notice.

"I have served my people with fervor and devotion. I commend my spirit to the Gods, who have prepared a place for me in the hall of my fathers." Joturi paused and looked at each of his sons, until his gaze came to rest on his granddaughter Rishona. "Tamara, my daughter, come to me."

In a sway of silk, Rishona answered to her mother's name, stepping forward to kneel at her grandfather's side.

Tahmir's heart froze.

Joturi-Nur took Rishona's hand. "Tamara, my daughter. You were born of noble blood and granted a kind heart. As a child, you were the delight of my court, as a woman its most precious pearl. I wept the day you left us to follow your foreign prince to a distant land, but I let you go and gave you generous gifts in hopes you would find happiness. On the long road to Moisehén, assassins dishonored our family and murdered you, destroying the sweet dream of your short life. When they brought you to me…"

His voice faltered. Tears escaped his cloudy eyes. "When they brought your body to me, beloved Tamara, I washed you myself. I prepared you to meet our Gods, because no one else was worthy of touching you. Long have I prayed that you would return to me at my death and kneel at my side in the person of your daughter, as you do now. Thank you for the joy you gave me, for your selfless and loving spirit, and for accompanying me on this, the last day of my life."

Joturi reached for the scimitar that lay next to him on the bed. He drew it out of its jewel-encrusted sheath and held it high for all to see. Then he set it in front of Rishona.

Sweat trickled down Tahmir's neck.

"Take my blade, Tamara." The old man pressed his granddaughter's hand to his lips and laid it gently over the hilt of the sword. "Rule my people in my stead."

Arbartamor's plump face twitched in triumph.

Tahmir, sickened by his uncle's eagerness, gripped his dagger and glanced around the room in desperation, but the scribes, the priests, the palace guards, and the many descendants of Joturi-Nur were here to see the last wish of the San'iloman fulfilled. None of them would stand in Arbartamor's path when the time came to butcher the princess.

"Your people are safe with me, Father." Rishona's voice rang steady and clear. "They shall want for nothing as long as I live."

Joturi-Nur drew a breath of satisfaction and leaned back on his pillows. He nodded to the priest, who stepped forward to present the cup of death. The San'iloman drank deep and closed his eyes with a long exhale.

The chalice was then passed to Meanara, who lifted it toward her dying husband. "I have been and always will be your true wife and most faithful servant."

After she drank, the servants helped her to her husband's side, where she laid down, intertwined her fingers in his and set her head on his shoulder. She was followed by the Second Wife and then the Third, who lay close to Meanara, arms wrapped around each other's waists while the gentle poison took effect.

Only young Naptari resisted, pushing the cup away with a frightened wail and spilling the ebony liquid across the marble floor. They caught her gently, for the last virgin of the San'iloman must reach the world beyond unscathed. The priest produced a vial from inside his sleeve and broke it over her lips. At once Naptari's cries were silenced. Her eyes rolled back into her head, and she went limp in their arms. They laid her at Joturi-Nur's feet, curled like a child at rest.

Through all this, Rishona remained by her grandfather's side, hand steady on the jeweled hilt of his broad sword. Her face could not be read behind the veil, and Tahmir no longer had the power to hear her thoughts, to speak words of comfort across the silence, to tell her once more how much he loved her.

Approaching the princess, Arbartamor unsheathed his sword and wet his fleshy lips. "I challenge your claim, Tamara, and send you with my father to the Afterlife."

Rishona spun, hands wrapped around the hilt of the scimitar, and cut through Arbartamor's protruding belly, sending a spray of blood across her shimmering gown. The prince dropped his weapon and staggered back, struggling to stop the spill of entrails, eyes wide with horror, lips quivering in protest.

"What have you done?" he stammered. "A woman? It's not possible . . . not permitted..."

He sat hard on the floor, stared at the mess of viscera like a lost boy, and looked to his brothers in confusion.

Rishona strode forward and drove the scimitar into Arbartamor's neck, laying open muscle and sinew, cleaving head from torso with a few vicious strokes. She removed her veil and leveled the sword at his brothers, eyes glittering with menace. "Who else would challenge me?"

For several moments there was no sound but the gurgle of Arbartamor's blood, pooling around her satin slippers.

Then Paolus-Nur drew his weapon, but Mechnes stayed his hand. "Wait, brother."

Paolus-Nur looked at Mechnes in disbelief. They were cut from the same stone, these two, each with the blue-gray eyes of their mother set in a swarthy face not unlike their father's.

"Surely you cannot expect us to accept the rule of this woman!" Paolus objected. "What she has done is an insult to the tradition of our fathers."

"This is not without precedent." Though Mechnes spoke to his brother, he kept his discerning gaze fixed on Rishona. Behind him Joturi-Nur's sons shifted on their feet and fingered the hilts of their swords, exchanging looks of consternation. "Melani-Naomi defended her claim some five hundred years ago. And before her, there was Shanuri-Pah, in the Time of Fire. Arbartamor knew our niece well. It was foolish of him not to anticipate she would defend her claim."

He turned to his brothers and spoke as one accustomed to his own authority. "Our father has named his heir, and one of our siblings has been offered as sacrifice. The claim is defended. I lay my sword before Tamara-Rishona, San'iloman of the Syrnte. May the Gods keep her wise and fierce."

With that he knelt in front of her. After a few uncertain glances, the brothers followed suit one by one. To Tahmir's astonishment, the entire court went to its knees, all but him. He was too stunned to move, too confused to think.

Rishona caught his eyes and smiled her gentle smile, beckoning him with one hand.

Mesmerized, he obeyed. Relief flooded his heart. When he drew close, she kissed his cheek.

"You see, beloved brother?" she murmured, face infused with happy triumph. "There was nothing to fear."

Stepping away, she raised her bloodied sword and declared to everyone present, “I am Tamara, also called Rishona, San’iloman of the Syrnte. I seal my claim with the blood of my brothers.”

Tahmir fell to his knees like a child before a goddess.

Yet she was not a goddess. She was his sister, his own Rishona.

In the moment Tahmir understood what this meant, it was too late. The San’iloman’s blade flashed toward him, slicing open his throat and leaving his body convulsing in darkness.

Chapter 1

Akmael unsheathed the sword, Kel'Barú, allowing its long silver blade to capture the vermilion flame of the rising sun. Wind lifted his cloak and filled cliffs and crevices with dark whispers of troubling dreams. Behind him he heard the shouts of men and the clatter of tools. Heavy canvas fluttered as they dropped tents in preparation for the next stage of their journey. Far below, the Tarba River roared through the narrow canyon along which the Pass of Aerunden had been cut, a rough road wending precariously over steep descents. Fit for mules, but most unaccommodating to his royal procession.

"My Lord King." Sir Drostan interrupted Akmael's thoughts, pausing at a respectful distance. Though massive in frame, the knight's age had begun to show in the lines around his eyes, in the silver streaks of his red beard. "Our preparations are complete. We depart at your command."

Akmael nodded and beckoned him to approach. "What do you know of this place? Of the people who built it?"

They had camped among the crumbled foundations of an old fortress, its remains little more than intersecting trails of stone smothered by dense brambles. A single tower struggled against the unforgiving passage of time, leaning precipitously toward the gorge below. The keystone that guarded its arched doorway was weakened by a fracture through its heart, dooming the structure to imminent collapse.

"I am not certain," Drostan admitted. "Judging by the workmanship, I would say the tower was built by the early Kings of Vortingen, perhaps during the conquest of Moehn. Or before that, even, in the great battles against the People of Thunder. Whatever its history, it has long since been lost."

The gusts picked up again, and Kel'Barú responded with an unusual hum, a bright tone layered over its typically mournful cadence.

Eolyn, it murmured. *Eolyn, Eolyn, Eolyn.*

Drostan raised his brow. "It would seem the sword knows its destiny."

Akmael frowned, shook his head in doubt. For years he had tried to divine Kel'Baru's song without success, frustrating as he had never encountered a weapon he could not understand. "Even a mage cannot see into the future. How then can a sword? No, I do not believe Kel'Barú suspects our destination. It only repeats her name, as it has from the time they were separated."

Like an echo of his own heart.

Drostan said quietly, "The Maga Eolyn will not want this sword."

"It was her brother's weapon."

"That is why."

"This is the only sword that has ever spoken to her. It belongs with Maga Eolyn, though I have long tried to convince it otherwise."

"She has no interest in tools of death," insisted Drostan. "Even if she did, this is a Galian sword, infused with strange wizardry. Such weapons have no place in our traditions. They are unpredictable. Suspect. Leaving it with the maga could invoke dangers unknown."

Akmael drew a breath and sheathed the weapon. He had thought through this matter at length, and despite his own misgivings, would not be dissuaded. "This sword is her inheritance. What to do with it will be her decision."

They walked down the slope to the entourage that waited, a milling party of robed ladies, armored knights and attentive servants. The banners of Vortingen snapped high over their heads, silver dragons dancing against a purple night. In their midst waited the Queen Taesara, pale and slender, erect as a summer lily. She greeted her King with a gracious smile and deep bow. Together they mounted their horses and spurred the procession forward, descending from Falon's Ridge onto the high fertile plains of Moehn.

Two more days they rode through a rough-hewn landscape, the villages mere clusters of earthen homes, the people humble in dress and aspect. Cultivated fields were thrown haphazardly across the rolling hills. Wheat and lentils grew among scattered saplings as if in constant battle against an ever-encroaching forest. Deer grazed amidst the sheep. Pigs and chickens ran unfettered across the road, squealing and squawking. Dogs barked and snapped at the horses. Barefoot children stared at the royal couple, wide eyed and bold. The whistling wind carried rich aromas of rain, tall grass, aged oaks, and fresh manure.

"This is an unkempt place." Queen Taesara wrinkled her nose. "Half wild, and most unwelcoming."

Her displeasure distracted the King from his thoughts, which had once again drifted to Eolyn. He glanced at his young Queen, small chin held high, wheat-colored hair tucked carefully under a delicate veil and jeweled cap.

"There is a certain beauty to it." He responded more out of courtesy than a real desire to engage her in conversation. "An unrestrained spirit, reminiscent of East Selen."

"It is ragged," she replied. "And dirty."

She noticed him watching her, offered a thin smile.

He said nothing and looked away.

At last the Town of Moehn appeared, crouched low over brooding hills. Horns sounded from the ramparts to greet them. Akmael's trumpets responded with prolonged blasts. A crowd of people gathered outside the gates, commoners mixing freely with nobility. Children threw wildflowers in their path. Peasants sang and danced in improvised circles. The reception was heartfelt, though it bore none of the pageantry offered by the wealthier provinces. As they approached, Akmael observed the dilapidated state of the town walls with consternation.

"Gods be praised!" Lord Felton, a portly man with a generous white beard and bushy eyebrows stepped forward, greeting the King with a jovial smile. "Our Lord King has arrived! Long live the King! Long live King Akmael!"

The people echoed Felton while he and his family knelt. Akmael dismounted. At the King's bidding, Felton rose with some difficulty, favoring his left leg. They embraced heartily, for the old man could not contain his excitement.

Then Eolyn appeared among a group of ladies just behind the patriarch, and Akmael was distracted from Felton's enthusiastic banter. Dark red curls tumbled over her shoulders, a refreshing display of sensual beauty among so many caps and veils. The cut of her burgundy gown accentuated the fine curve of her breasts; a golden sash embroidered with emerald leaves adorned her slim waist. She held a staff of polished oak crowned with water crystal. A lovely smile spread through her dark eyes when they met his, an honest expression of joy and long-remembered friendship.

The moment ignited a painful shift inside his soul, an avalanche of lost possibilities exposing a rugged landscape of forgotten hope.

"My Lord King." The Queen called to him, her voice a shade unsteady.

He turned as if awakened from a dream, and then glanced back toward Eolyn, but the maga was distracted by a flaxen-haired woman who leaned close to speak in her ear.

Akmael assisted Taesara as she dismounted. Despite her regal bearing, the wear of their journey showed in the Queen's stiff shoulders and drawn face. She offered the King a strained smile and summoned her lady-in-waiting Sonia, who brought forth the Princess Eliasara. The Queen took the rosy-cheeked baby in her arms, and Akmael presented them both to Lord Felton and his retinue. Much fuss was made over Eliasara's great beauty and good health, and many wishes expressed that the Gods soon grant them a son.

With a sweep of his arm, Lord Felton invited them to enter the city. They passed through the gates amidst trumpets, song, and dance. Eolyn disappeared in the milling crowd. To Akmael's disappointment, she did not arrive at Felton's table for the evening meal. He considered asking after her, but decided to hold his peace.

He had waited three long years. He could wait one more night.

* * *

"They're coming! They're coming!" Ghemena burst through the kitchen door, cheeks soiled, ash-brown hair disheveled, and eyes bright with excitement.

"Child!" Maga Renate caught the girl firmly by the arm, a fierce scowl on her hawk-nosed face. "Can you not remain presentable for at least one hour on this one day?"

Ghemena grimaced as Renate yanked her locks out of their tattered braids and began combing her hair again. "I saw them.

Twenty-five riders under the King's banner. Sir Borten had me count them all!"

The activity around the hearth halted, and everyone turned expectant gazes toward Eolyn. The maga's breath came up short. She rubbed damp palms on her apron. "Very well. We are done here, for the moment. Everyone assemble in the courtyard as planned."

Eolyn's students darted out in a flurry of giggles and excitement, Maga Renate quick on their heels with sharp rebukes and calls to order. Adiana, however, waited for Eolyn at the door, smoothing her flaxen hair and pinning it in a loose knot.

"All this fuss," the musician from Selkynsen muttered, "and for what? A few ordinary men on fancy horses."

"Not ordinary men." Eolyn refreshed her face with water from the basin. "Our King. Our liege and benefactor."

"Benefactor?" Adiana laughed as if Eolyn had made a fine joke. "I like that very much. A fitting name for a royal lover, our *benefactor*."

"He is not my lover," the maga responded tersely. "That time is long past. We have not even seen each other since—"

"He saw you well enough yesterday. That man may have a face of stone, but I know desire when I see it."

"Hush, Adiana!" Eolyn stepped close and lowered her voice. "I can tolerate your gossiping about many things, but on this matter you must be circumspect. The walls whisper what they hear. The nobles and mages of Moisehén hold us in enough suspicion without you declaring me the King's mistress."

Adiana's pale brow furrowed. After a moment, she took Eolyn's hand in hers. "The nobles and mages need not listen to me, or to your whispering walls. What happened at the gates of Moehn was plain for everyone to see. That man is still fond of you, and you, I daresay, of him."

Eolyn felt a tremor in her heart, like the ring of crystal in the instant before it breaks. She buried the sensation and forced a laugh through her lips. "Of course we are still fond of each other. He has long been my friend, and I will always be his."

Eolyn ignored Adiana's deepening frown and tugged at her hand. They continued with haste to the courtyard, where Renate and their five students stood beside a young fir at the center of a circle of neatly kept houses. Beside them, Sir Borten had gathered with the guards. Eolyn and Adiana took their places just as the King and his escort rode through the open gateway, the whinny of horses filling the air as the royal guard assumed formation. Eolyn recognized the mage warrior Sir Drostan, his carriage still imposing despite his many years. The diplomat High Mage Tzetobar also accompanied them, as did Lord Felton, their plump faces flushed over thick white beards.

Eolyn stepped forward while the Mage King dismounted, words of welcome hovering on her lips. She intended to bow in respect, but the intensity of his presence arrested her. She stood like a deer caught in his gaze as he strode forward then stopped at arm's length.

"My Lord King," she murmured, disconcerted by his searching stare. "Thank you for honoring us with your presence."

He made no reply. His countenance had changed little, save for the beard that now marked the line of his jaw. His familiar aroma of polished stone and timeless magic made her heart ache with nostalgia. Wind sifted through his dark hair, bringing forth visions of the South Woods: the song of the river, the whisper of trees, the heat of the sun rising off Lynx's ridge. For the briefest of moments the Mage King faded, and the boy by the river appeared. The tension in Akmael's eyes released. Eolyn lifted a hand to touch his cheek.

"Where's the Queen?" Ghemena's demand shattered the moment. Shoving herself between them, the girl thrust a bouquet of wildflowers in Akmael's face. "I was supposed to give these to her. Where is she?"

"Ghemena, hush!" Eolyn took the child in hand and pulled her back a few steps, embarrassed not so much by Ghemena's impertinence as by the fact that she herself had not noticed the Queen's absence. "You must not address the King so!"

"But where is she?" the girl insisted.

"She is indisposed, my Lady Ghemena." Akmael bent on one knee and beckoned her. "But you may entrust me with the gift you have prepared for the good Queen Taesara."

The girl stayed put, suspicion in her hazel eyes, a scowl fixed upon her round face. "I'm not a lady."

"Ghemena!" Eolyn scolded, but Akmael was smiling. It was rare to see him smile, or at least it had been in times past.

"Then what shall I call you?" the Mage King asked. "Maga Ghemena?"

"Yes, that's right!" Ghemena's eyes brightened. "Except, I'm not a maga. Not yet. But I will be someday. And it's much better to be a maga than a lady. That's what Mistress Adiana says. She says magas are glorious and ladies are *impsipid*. Mistress Adiana says Maga Eolyn could have been a lady once, but she refused because she knew better!"

Stunned by this unbidden reference to her past, Eolyn looked to Renate, who shot a furious glance at Adiana, who simply rolled her eyes and shrugged.

Akmael lost his smile. A shadow darkened his brow. Years ago, when Eolyn had refused the crown following her brother's defeat, the King's fury had been terrible. She had hoped by now the flame of his anger would have faded, imagined it so given all the support he had provided for her coven. But she could not be certain, and this was not the moment in which she wished to find out.

"Your Mistress Adiana has an interesting perspective," the Mage King said. "Come then, Maga Ghemena. Tell us what you have prepared for our Queen."

It was a fragrant bouquet, carefully crafted for long life and fertility. The girl pointed out each herb and explained its properties. Clove, ginger, and summer savory to bring passion to Taesara's nights. Chamomile and lady's mantle to preserve her beauty; juniper and rosemary to protect her children. And at the center, a long stem of purple carorose, that she might soon be granted a son.

"But it won't work now," Ghemena said in disappointment, "because I was supposed to give it to her, and teach her the spells besides."

"I will see she receives your present," he assured her, "and that she knows how to use it."

The King stood. Eolyn responded to his expectant stance with an invitation to see the grounds. Renate and Adiana ushered the girls back to the kitchen, while Sir Borten accompanied Eolyn and Akmael through lush gardens and past humble buildings.

Knight and King spoke at length while they inspected the wall being built at Akmael's behest. Eolyn bristled at their discussion. She had never seen any need to fortify her *Aekelahr*, nestled as it was in the peaceful and sparsely populated highlands of Moehn, but all her vigorous objections had been ignored. This was one decision from which Akmael would not be dissuaded. So she held her tongue while the men talked their foolish talk, and breathed an inward sigh of relief when Ghemena ran up to announce the midday meal was ready.

They had secured venison with the help of Lord Felton's hunters, and ordered wine weeks before from Selkynsen. Despite these luxuries, Eolyn felt the sting of inadequacy when she saw the food laid out. All their preparations seemed a poor show in comparison to the sumptuous feasts she remembered from the King's City. If the meager fare troubled Akmael, he did not show it, but ate heartily and expressed appreciation for the meat and wine, for the garden vegetables dressed with herbs from the South Woods, and for Renate's dark and flavorful bread.

Following the meal, each of Eolyn's students stood before the King to recite stories from the history of Moisehén, demonstrate their magic, and answer his questions regarding the practice of their craft. This was Eolyn's finest moment, for hers were well-educated and talented students, ranging in age from Mariel and Sirena at fourteen, to Ghemena, who had seen but nine summers.

By the time they finished, the sun was descending in the west. The Mage King rose and bade his escort to ready their horses for the ride back into the town of Moehn. Then he turned to Eolyn and requested a word in private.

It seemed too great a demand somehow. Eolyn hesitated, keenly aware that Adiana and the girls had paused in their task of clearing the tables to watch her and the Mage King. After a moment, she nodded and led Akmael to her study.

The room was simple but clean, with wide windows facing north and south. When they entered, Akmael paused at the bookshelves lining the eastern wall. He took a tome from its place and leafed through its pages.

"These must have belonged to your tutor, the Doyenne Ghemena," he said.

"Yes, my Lord King. She salvaged them from the library at Berlingen. I have brought almost all her books back from the South Woods."

"A small collection, but quite valuable." He replaced the book with care. "When we return to the City, I will have additional volumes sent from the royal library, to complement these works."

"Thank you, my Lord King. That is most generous."

Akmael gave a slight shrug. "An *Aekelahr* should have a proper library."

Eolyn had taken her stance on the other side of the room, behind a polished oak table that served as her desk. It was disconcerting, being alone with him like this. She drew a breath and forced her hands to be still by setting her fingers upon the table.

A trace of annoyance flitted across his features. He strode forward and stopped just short of the desk. "You look well, Eolyn."

The maga saw more than these words reflected in his eyes. A tightness filled her belly and extended its provocative grip toward more intimate places, bringing a flush to her cheeks.

"Thank you, my Lord King. I am most glad to see you and the Queen in good health, and your daughter, the Princess Eliasara." The thought that his child could have been hers surfaced unbidden, making her blink and glance away. "She must bring you great happiness."

"She will be entrusted to you when she is of age."

"My Lord King?"

"I want her to learn the ways of magic."

"Don't you think…?" Eolyn bit her lip. One did not simply accept students at the will of their parents. Eliasara would have to prove her abilities and disposition, and even if she had an aptitude, the decision to take her on would be complicated. There were still many in Moisehén who did not wish to see magic wielded by the Royal House of Vortingen, and Eolyn struggled with the question of whether their concerns were well-founded. "The Queen has no knowledge of our traditions. She might not approve."

"It does not matter whether she approves. It is my will that Eliasara become a maga."

"I see." Eolyn frowned. How could Taesara's opinion not matter in decisions regarding the education of their daughter?

There was a knock at the door, followed by Sir Drostan's muffled baritone. Akmael bade the knight to enter, and kept his gaze steady upon Eolyn as Drostan crossed the room and laid a long package wrapped in well-oiled leather on the table. The knight paused and cleared his throat, looking from High Maga to Mage King as if to say something, but then he merely bowed and took his leave.

Akmael removed the leather wrapping, unsheathed the sword therein and set it before Eolyn. The hilt was inlaid with ivory, the blade shone silver-white. Her throat went dry when she recognized it.

"This? Where did you get this?" she asked.

"I have had it since the Battle of Aerunden."

Eolyn sat down, so great was her shock. "Kel'Barú. My brother's sword. All this time you have had it?"

"I wanted to keep it," he confessed. "It is a fine weapon, and you seemed to have little use for tools of war. But the Galian wizards gave this sword a will of its own, and it has done nothing these past years but weep for you."

She stood and lifted the sword, one hand sustaining the ivory hilt, the flat of the blade resting on her long fingers.

Eolyn, it sang in the quiet hum of metals. *Eolyn, Eolyn, Eolyn.*

"I want you to learn how to use it," Akmael said.

At once she set it down. "No."

"I will not argue this with you."

"Stop it!" Every fiber of her body ignited with anger. "Stop it, Akmael. Why are you doing this?"

A moment passed before she realized her transgression. She lowered her eyes. "Forgive me, my Lord King. I didn't intend—"

"Do not apologize. It pleases me, to hear you say my name. I would have you say it more often."

There was such unexpected kindness to his tone that the rage slipped through her fingers. She managed a hesitant smile. "Thank you. I mean no insult by questioning your gift, but you know my feelings on this matter. We have no use for knights and walls and swords. This is an *Aekelahr,* not a military outpost."

"This is a fragile community of magas cultivating seeds of great power. You are not to go unprotected."

"Moehn is a peaceful province. That is why I chose it. We are well received here. No one wishes us harm."

"It is not Moehn I worry about."

"Who, then? There won't be any armies emerging from the South Woods, and no one can get through the Pass of Aerunden without crossing the kingdom and defeating you first."

Akmael let go a slow breath. The turmoil that stirred behind his dark eyes disturbed her; as if there were something of importance he could not bring himself to reveal. He picked up Kel'Baru and proffered it to her.

Eolyn shook her head, hands clenched stubbornly at her sides. "We tried this, a long time ago. You know I have no gift for weaponry."

"You are not the frightened girl you were then. You have strength, balance and speed. And you have a sword that loves you. Borten can teach you how to use it."

"I've seen how your men fight. I could never hope to—"

"No, you could not!" He struck his fist against the table and gestured angrily toward the courtyard where his guards waited. "One of those men—trained from the time they were children—one of them could kill you in a heartbeat. But with this blade in your hand, it might take them two heartbeats. Or three. Or fifteen. And that might be enough for someone to come to your aid before it is too late."

"I am not without defenses. I have my magic and my staff. I can invoke almost every manner of flame known to our people. I have even cast the curse of Ahmad-kupt, though I hope never to use it again."

"Your magic will not be enough."

"For what?"

He glanced away, set his jaw. "I want you to have every tool at your disposal, for whatever may come."

She lifted her chin. "I will accept this sword, Akmael, because it is a most generous and thoughtful gift. I will keep it and honor it, but I cannot wield it."

"For the love of the Gods! Why not?"

"Because this is the weapon that betrayed my brother!"

Her fingers flew to her lips, but it was too late. The memory of Aerunden coalesced around them, a roiling cloud pounding against the walls of her heart: wretched screams and torn bodies, scorched air and bloodied earth. Devastation, loss, the black pit of the Underworld sucking them toward oblivion.

"What do you mean, *betrayed your brother*?" Akmael had the look of a serpent startled from its sleep.

Eolyn placed a hand on her breast to steady her heart. Not once had they spoken of that day. The fate of her brother Ernan and his rebellion had been buried in silence, hidden by mutual consent beneath the kinder fabric of their renewed love.

The past is always with us, Doyenne Ghemena had once said, *and it grows more insidious when it remains unspoken.*

"On the morning of that battle," Eolyn spoke with hesitation, "before the fighting began, the curse of Ahmad-melan was invoked against my brother."

"That was the work of Tzeremond." Akmael's response was emphatic, defensive. "The wizard acted without my knowledge or permission."

"I know." Though hearing him say it lifted a burden from her heart. "I suppose I have always known. In his madness, my brother tried to kill me. I broke the curse, but Kel'Barú did not understand what had happened. The sword resented Ernan and no longer wished to protect him. I *knew* this, Akmael."

She faltered. So much time had passed, and still that day weighed like a stone chained to her spirit. It seemed unreal, unthinkable, what she had done, what she had failed to do. "I heard and understood Kel'Barú. I tried to warn Ernan, but he didn't listen and then I simply let him go. I allowed my brother to ride into battle with this weapon, knowing it would fail him. Gods help me. Sometimes I think I did it because I wanted…"

What had she wanted? For Akmael to live? For Ernan to die? And if the desire of her heart had invoked her brother's doom, was this not a fitting fate: to be without either of them in the life that followed, Ernan stolen away by death, Akmael by his crown.

"It was all so wrong. I should have stopped him, but I didn't." Grief surged anew, choking back her words. "I couldn't."

Eolyn hid her face as tears began to sting her eyes.

Shoving the table aside, Akmael drew the maga into his arms. His lips rested warm upon her forehead, his breath fell tender against her ear. "You must not blame yourself for your brother's death, Eolyn. Ernan chose his own fate."

She clung to the Mage King and wept, realizing how the absence of his embrace had followed her all these years, a deep and abiding ache that could not be cured, only ignored. She cursed the Gods for breaking open her sorrows on this of all days, for reclaiming what small happiness had blossomed with their brief reunion.

"Perhaps you will remember that I offered him a truce," Akmael continued in soothing tones, "which you counseled him to accept. He did not listen to you then, either. It was not you who closed Ernan's ears in Aerunden. From what little I knew of your brother, he was not inclined to acknowledge his sister's wisdom. This was what cost him his life, not your neglect, nor the anger of Kel'Barú."

Her sobs faded under the spell of his words. Eolyn withdrew from his embrace, wiped tears from her cheeks, and forced a laugh. "You must think me of fragile constitution. It is just a passing melancholy, I assure you. These have been days of great agitation, and they have brought back many memories."

He brushed a stray lock of hair from her face, let his fingers linger a moment beneath her chin. Desire flared in the hidden places of her soul. Eolyn wanted to kiss him, but stepped away instead.

"Fond memories as well as difficult ones, I hope," he said.

"Oh, yes." She smiled through bitter tears. "Many fond memories, indeed."

Chapter 2

Eolyn retired early that evening, leaving Adiana and Renate laughing in their cups as they celebrated the success of the King's visit. The air was cool, the grass soothing and damp beneath bare feet. A guard greeted her as she walked to her quarters. She inquired after Sir Borten, but the knight had already sought solitude and rest. For weeks Borten had goaded the builders from dawn until dusk, coercing the wall into its half-finished state in preparation for the King's arrival. The incessant clatter of stone and tools had given Eolyn a constant headache, making the silence of this night particularly welcome.

She paused a moment in front of her students' quarters, listening to Mariel's soft snore, the quiet song of crickets, the occasional rustle of a field mouse. No other sound came to her ears. The girls had long since surrendered to the world of their dreams.

Eolyn expected to fall fast asleep as well, but she lay awake in bed a long while, nestled beneath fresh linen sheets, running her fingers absently over the soft wool blanket. A storm building somewhere along the eastern flank of the South Woods sent low rumbles across the hills. Yet here the night was clear, illuminated by a waning moon. The aroma of sage, mint, and rosemary drifted from the garden.

Eolyn sighed and shifted her position.

In spite of everything, the visit had gone well. She should feel grateful for that. Akmael—the King—appeared satisfied as he surveyed the grounds and spoke with her students. The memory of her outburst still embarrassed her, crying in front of him like a foolish child. He was kind about it though, and now she thought her shame a small price to pay for the feel of his arms around her, for the steady strength of his embrace.

If only he had not ridden away after that.

If only this day had not ended.

Pushing the covers aside, she got up and went to Kel'Baru, left leaning against the stone wall close to her bed. The weapon had a way of gathering light into itself even when sheathed, and it glowed like the moon caught behind translucent clouds. The blade emitted a constant, contented hum, as if in the middle of some pleasant dream.

She sat on the cool floor in front of it and gathered her knees to her chest, wondering if she could ever acquire the skills to use such a weapon. She remembered some of what Akmael had taught her years ago, like how to grip the hilt. And there were eight angles, if she recalled correctly, through which one could sweep the blade. Whenever she swung she had to think about which side was left open, except she would never have time to think. Not in a real fight.

Eolyn puffed her cheeks in frustration, let her chin rest on folded arms.

Curse him. Why did Akmael always insist on this foolishness? He knew her distaste for such weapons.

Yet how could she refuse his will, after all that he had done for her, after everything he had forgiven.

"Do you forgive me too, Ernan?" She spoke out loud, as if Kel'Barú might hold the answer.

Her brother would know by now of her love for the Mage King. The Doyenne Ghemena had taught her that a soul perceives everything through the lens of the Afterlife. Ernan would see she deceived him from the beginning, that she hid the secrets of her childhood and lied about the yearnings of her heart. But surely he would also realize he had made it impossible for her to confide in him. Anything that had exposed her bond to the Mage King, and all the uncertainties surrounding it, would have condemned her in Ernan's eyes.

The more she thought about Akmael's words, the more she realized he spoke the truth. Ernan had loved her, treasured and protected her, but not once did he listen to her, or try to understand her.

Why was her instinct of so little consequence to him?

Perhaps he thought her too naïve and inexperienced—which was true, but that did not mean she was wrong. His campaign might have played out differently, had he considered her counsel. He might be alive now, and she in a different place altogether.

But then Akmael would have perished, for Ernan was bent upon slaying him, and nothing would have stayed his hand had the Gods given him the opportunity.

Tears burned in her eyes. She clenched her jaw and wiped them away, angered by the inability to leave this heartache behind. A single day in Akmael's presence, and all her barriers had been hopelessly unraveled, her heart laid open, his to take or leave as he pleased.

Did he notice? She prayed he did not. She wanted the Mage King to go away, to return to the City without looking back at her or her *Aekelahr*. She wanted to be left alone with her magic, so she could heal and forget once again.

A hush of wings on the windowsill caught her attention.

Eolyn looked up to see a Great River Owl, its proud silhouette outlined by moonlight. She rose to her feet in surprise, keenly aware of its penetrating gaze, though she could not see its round eyes in the dark. A breeze ruffled its feathers. Its aura was impossibly familiar: intense shades of gold, burgundy and forest green, shot through with streaks of deepest indigo.

She held her breath and let it go in a whisper. "Akmael?"

More than a question, it was a hope, a fear, an invocation.

A shimmer passed through the owl, followed by a flash of white light, and suddenly he was with her, the heat of his hand upon her throat, the strength of his fingers intertwining in her hair, the demand of his lips upon hers, so warm and full of passion. He kissed her until she had no more breath to give. Then he paused and held her close, their foreheads touching as her fingers traced the prominence of his cheekbone, the line of his jaw, the curve of his full lips.

All she could hear was his desire, carried on the rhythm of his heart. She dared not speak, for if she did, she might stumble upon words of caution or prudence or common sense, and none of that had any place here. Not when he was so near, nearer than he had been in such a painfully long time, closer than he might ever be again.

The magic of the South Woods rose from the fragrant earth and blew through the window in a humid gust, swirling about them, begging her to remember who they were and what they once meant to each other.

"Eolyn, I—"

She hushed him with a kiss.

Elation filled her heart as he responded. Her nightshift slipped away at his touch, his tunic disappeared at her insistence, the bed cushions shifted beneath their weight. Her hands explored the familiar contours of his torso, solid like the living trunk of some great tree. His kisses flowed over her like water let loose from a dam, leaving burning rivers across her shivering skin.

"Akmael," she murmured. "My love, please."

He interlaced his fingers with hers, and she pulled him close, delighting in the burden of his weight. Then he found her and entered her, and all at once everything that had gone wrong with their world was set right. Eolyn understood there was no greater truth than this, no expanse of time or conflict that could ever erase their unity.

They made love late into the night, pausing at intervals to rest in each other's arms, conversing in a silent language of tender caresses, until the Spirit of the Forest beckoned them again toward ecstasy. When the first light of dawn crept through the window, Akmael departed in the shape of the Great River Owl.

Filled with the sweet ache of their spent desire, Eolyn pulled her pillow close, breathed in his lingering aroma of earth, stone, and brine, and let her satiated body drift into a peaceful sleep.

* * *

Adiana awoke late, with stiff limbs and a queasy stomach, glad this business with the King was over for another year or two—more if they were lucky. It was far too much fuss in her opinion, for just another man on a horse. Eolyn had set them to scrubbing every building from floor to ceiling, dusting furniture, cleaning linens, weeding the gardens, sweeping the stables a dozen times over, until even the sweet and hard working Tasha had complained.

Of course, Adiana had put on a good face and given the whole ordeal her best, because she knew what the Mage King's visit meant to her good friend Eolyn. At least the occasion had inspired the maga to buy some decent wine, something Adiana had not enjoyed since she moved to this forsaken province. When at last the King had departed, there was still half a barrel to spare, so she and Renate had finished off as much as they could to celebrate the success, and most especially the end, of the King's visit.

Now Adiana had a royal headache.

She shielded her eyes against the mid-morning sun as she crossed the gardens to the herbarium. The building was cool inside, with a well swept dirt floor. Fragrant bundles of plants hung from the ceiling and lined the plain wooden shelves, along with a variety of forest and garden products such as nuts, mushrooms, spider silks, and dried fruit. Eolyn stood at a small table, mortar and pestle in hand, her expression an odd mixture of intense happiness and mild preoccupation.

Scanning the herbs on the table, Adiana closed the door behind her and leaned against it, arms folded across her chest. "I'll wager you have a story to tell."

Eolyn glanced up from her task, a flush rising to her cheeks. "This is not as it seems."

"Oh no?" Adiana crossed to the table and picked up each plant in turn. "Angelica, coltsfoot, hemlock, and fickle bloodswort. I know this recipe well, Eolyn. It's the first one you taught me. What did you do, take Borten as a lover?"

Eolyn selected a short stem of hemlock and removed all the leaves with one sure sweep of her fingers, letting them fall into the mortar. "Don't be coarse, Adiana."

"Why not? It's what I'm best at."

A bitter sting hit Adiana's nose, causing her to sneeze. She snatched the mortar from Eolyn's grasp, sniffed and sneezed again. "For the love of the Gods! How much bloodswort did you put into this? You'll be sick for a month if you drink it. Or worse."

The maga blinked and looked at Adiana as if seeing her for the first time. "It's just as Doyenne Ghemena taught me. Equal parts of angelica, coltsfoot and hemlock, with a pinch of bloodswort, to be brewed by midday and taken before the next moon rises."

Her voice faltered. Stepping away, Eolyn sat on a stool and rubbed her forehead with one hand as if trying to collect her thoughts. Adiana watched her friend with some concern. It was not in Eolyn's nature to be distracted.

"I'll take care of this," Adiana said, tossing the foul mixture onto the coals of the hearth and rinsing the mortar and pestle.

Several minutes passed in silence as Adiana worked, measuring the amount of each plant and grinding them together into a fine mass. She filled a small pot with water, emptied the ingredients into it and set it over the hearth. Once the brew was ready, she strained it into a cup and served it to Eolyn. Then she pulled up a stool and sat next to her friend. "It was the King, then?"

Eolyn nodded as she swirled her cup.

"Well, go on. Tell me about it."

The maga let go an impatient sigh. "Adiana, please. I can't bear to have you treat this as your next piece of gossip."

"You know I keep the secrets that are meant to be kept. You need to talk to someone, and the Gods brought me here this morning, with a splitting headache and a queasy stomach, both of which have now mysteriously disappeared. I'd say that's a sign that you should talk to me."

"There's not much to say, really. Nothing that could be captured in words. It was…"

"Divine?"

"Yes. And now it's over. Again." Eolyn stood and set the cup on the table, not having taken a drop.

"He might come back, you know. I heard they'll be a week or more in Moehn."

"Perhaps." Eolyn paced the room, fingering the jewel around her neck, a finely woven net of silver encrusted with crystal and hung on a long chain, a gift given her long ago by the King. "But then he'll return to the City with his Queen, and I'll stay here with my coven and this life I've come to love. It'll be a year or two or more before we're brought together again, and then if anything happens at all, it will be just another moment, a night." She stopped and looked at her friend, dark eyes haunted with regret. "What have I done, Adiana? I turned away the man I love, and for what? I keep telling myself there were so many reasons, and they all seemed so important at the time, but now I can't recall any of them. Not a one."

"You refused him because you are one of the few women in the kingdom with the wisdom and courage to say 'no' to a king. You're a maga, Eolyn. You're not meant to walk in the shadow of any man. Did you not see the Queen when they arrived in Moehn? She's pretty enough, but drawn tight around the edges, with those stiff shoulders and that peaked face and tense eyes. Not even twenty, and already she's growing old. Is that the life you wanted for yourself? To follow him like a well-dressed mouse, your worth measured by the sons you bear?"

"Akmael would have never—"

"It doesn't matter what he would have done. It's the nature of nobility. Even he can't change that." Adiana nodded at the tea. "You'd better drink that before it gets cold. I don't want to spend what's left of my morning mixing potions."

Eolyn stared at the cup and shook her head.

Foreboding crept into Adiana's heart. "Oh, no. Don't you dare even consider it."

"I can't drink this. The thought of rejecting his seed is repulsive to me."

"Why?" Adiana threw up her hands, perplexed. "You've used this potion a hundred times, when you were with the King after your brother's defeat, and prior to that, with your lover Tahmir—"

"It doesn't matter. It was right then. It feels wrong now." Eolyn rested one hand protectively over her abdomen, as if a child of the Mage King had already taken root there.

With an audible groan, Adiana pulled her friend to a stool and sat her down. She took a place in front of the maga and looked hard into her eyes.

"Eolyn, let me tell you something about nobility, speaking as a dear friend who has watched those vipers from the time she was very young. They are just like merchants, only more ruthless and arrogant, convinced the Gods have given them license to do whatever they please. If a child of the King should grow in your womb, all the nobles of the realm will set their eyes on Moehn, to see what meat they can take from this situation, what marrow they can suck from its bones."

"No one need know who the father is."

"How will they not know? The King himself will claim this child. It's not as if you're some village wench in whom he has taken a passing fancy. You are a High Maga, the only one left in the kingdom. You are also his first love, and everyone knows it, though no one speaks of it."

Eolyn bit her lip and glanced away, fingers clutched tight around the silver pendant. "I must have some part of him, Adiana, something that can stay with me, someone I can love and protect. I would not ask for anything from the King. Nothing. You know that."

Adiana extricated Eolyn's fingers from the jewel and held the maga's hands in hers, tone gentle yet resolute. "But the King would ask much of you. He might let a daughter stay here, grow up among us, and learn the ways of the magas like any other student. But if you have a son, the Mage King will claim him, because that child will have sprung from the womb of a maga, and this is the one thing his insipid Princess of Roenfyn cannot give him. Before your son has seen five summers, they will take him to the City, where they will teach him the sordid ways of princes and kings. And the Queen and all her offspring, and all those loyal to them, will hate your son, and wish him dead, and see it done before he is old enough to understand his own power. This is what you ask for, Eolyn, when you refuse that cup. Love the Mage King if you must, be his maga and his mistress, but do not bear his children, for it will only destroy you with grief."

Eolyn withdrew from Adiana, pressed her palms against her forehead. Curls cascaded over her face like a cloud of fire. Her shoulders shivered under the burden of unspoken thoughts.

After a long period of contemplation, the maga straightened. Her eyes were dry, her lips set in a firm line. She stood and retrieved the cup from the table, then cradled it in her hands and studied its depths as if she could see all possible futures bound inside the dark liquid.

"Leave me, Adiana, for I must do this alone."

Adiana hesitated under a momentary premonition in which she saw Eolyn pouring that bitter liquid onto the steaming hearth. Yet she was not about to force the issue like some overbearing mother with an unruly child. Eolyn deserved more respect than that.

So Adiana rose, embraced her friend, and departed, closing the door quietly behind her.

Chapter 3

Ever since childhood, Prince Mechnes had found ceremony insufferable.

He despised the idle time it imposed upon him, and had invented all manner of strategies to avoid it, except for certain rites of sacrifice and pleasure during the brief period when he came of age. Even that grew wearisome; the invigorating smell of blood, sex, and incense proved insufficient compensation for the tedious hours spent in prayer and song. What was the point of so much chanting if he could simply walk down to the stables, slaughter a lamb, and put the meat on his own table instead of burning it for the silent Gods? And why all that fuss around taking a woman if with a single word Mechnes could have a servant or a slave—indeed, several when it pleased him—delivered to his bedchamber?

No, he had no use for ceremony. Not when there were battles to be fought and cities to be won. Not when there were so many appetites to be satisfied, and but one short life to indulge them.

So when Joturi-Nur surrendered his worn-out body to the world of the dead, Mechnes considered simply burning the old man in the inner courtyard, along with his headless son Abartamor and Rishona's witless brother Tahmir. Yet the Syrnte prince knew his family well, and understood he was unique in his intolerance of ceremonial excess. So he held his tongue and ground his teeth, hiding his impatience behind a carefully maintained façade of respect on the long road to Urq'Namahan, the silent city of royal mausoleums that sprawled over the foothills of the southeast flank of the Paramen Mountains.

The procession lasted two interminable days along a sun-parched road. At its head rode the sarcophagus of his father Joturi-Nur, encrusted with precious stones and born on the shoulders of a dozen slaves whose muscled torsos glistened in the luminous heat.

Others carried Joturi's three dead wives, the first in a sarcophagus inlaid with gold, the second with silver, the third with bronze.

Mechnes could have raised a thousand armored horsemen and paid them for a year using the gems and metals they were about to commit to a dank hole in the indolent earth.

As for the virgin Naptari, she was the greatest tragedy of all, in her casket of turtlewood and lapis lazuli. An attractive girl with a budding figure, slaughtered before she could discover the power of her own appeal. Had not the last virgin of Joturi-Nur been under such heavy guard—and the consequences of violating the prohibition so grim—Mechnes would have taken it upon himself to unleash her womanhood, giving her a taste of life before they wasted her beauty on worms.

Mechnes glanced up at his niece Rishona, who sat in a sparkling howdah on the back of an armored elephant. He and his brothers flanked the San'iloman on horseback. Their families and households trailed behind in a long snaking column that stretched back toward Ech'Naláhm. The new queen wore voluminous robes of red and gold, and a red mask hid her face. On her lap lay her grandfather's sword encased in its jeweled scabbard. Mechnes could feel the current of her power like a river of molten rock, indomitable and all-consuming. He wondered whether his brothers perceived this fiery energy, whether it aroused them as it did him.

The first time Mechnes's had laid eyes on Rishona, she was a squalling babe rescued from the murderous wild lands of Moisehén. Orphans of his slain sister Tamara, she and her brother Tahmir were entrusted to a much younger Mechnes by Joturi-Nur, to be raised by the prince's new wife Salome. Within a year of the adoption, however, Salome's womb bore fruit and she had abandoned her charges, giving them little more than food, shelter and an occasional moment of distracted attention. Rishona became an unruly child, running free through Mechnes's household and making herself seen in places where girls were generally not allowed. The Syrnte lord did not concern himself with the situation. It was Salome's task to tame the girl, and if she failed it would then fall to Rishona's future husband to discipline her.

During her sixth year, Rishona took to appearing in the east atrium where the men gathered to practice weaponry. She watched them without pause, her hair falling in ebony ringlets against her rounded cheeks, lower lip protruding in a frown of concentration. After they finished, she would follow Mechnes toward the baths, running to keep up with his stride as she tugged on his cloak and begged to learn how to use the sword. Every morning he laughed and sent her away. This game continued for about a month, her pleading and him refusing, until one day his amusement provoked her tears, and without warning she sank against the pale stone wall, weeping as if the world were about to come to an end.

Moved by his niece's distress, Mechnes knelt beside to her and explained in very clear terms why she had no need for weaponry. She was a girl after all, and a princess besides, and therefore destined to have many armed men at her disposal—not the least of whom would be her husband—who could fight and die for her.

Rishona's sobs only intensified.

"But you must teach me!" she insisted. "The Ones Who Speak told me so! It must be you, or I will never—"

She stopped wide-eyed and clapped her hands over her mouth. An unfamiliar chill settled in Mechnes's heart. It was heresy, the worst possible crime, for a child to claim she could hear the Ones Who Speak. The Syrnte were not granted the gift of visions until the age of thirteen, when those chosen by the Gods were cleansed of all shadows by the hot breath of Saefira. Children who insisted on lying about such things were removed from this life, sacrificed to the hungry goddess Mikata, that she might teach them obedience in the world beyond. Rishona knew this, and she watched him now in terror.

"That's not what I meant," she whispered. "It wasn't them at all."

Mechnes took her small hands in his, noting they were icy cold. "Tell me what they said, Rishona. I promise I will not reveal your secret to anyone."

She swallowed hard, eyes wary yet expressing a need for his complicity and protection. It was the first time, he remembered now, that the sweet curve of her face had touched his heart. "They said I am going to avenge my mother and my father, and that I will be queen of two kingdoms. But none of it will come to pass if you do not teach me."

Rishona was an undisciplined child, but she was not prone to lying. Mechnes heard the conviction in her voice, and understood she spoke the truth. That same day he took her back to the atrium and put a wooden sword in her hand. For seven years he taught her, until one morning during her thirteenth summer, after having returned from a campaign in the east, he noticed the blossoming of her figure, the heady scent of her sweat, the way she flushed during her lessons when he stood too close.

Giving rest to their sword play, he sent her with his servants to be bathed and perfumed. Afterwards they delivered her to his chambers, where he taught her the ways of a man with a woman.

Joturi-Nur's funeral procession drew to a halt, interrupting some of Mechnes's more pleasant memories, much to his annoyance. The priest and his attendants waited in flowing white robes on the steps of the new tomb. On either side of the entrance, smoky flames of the grassland herb mara'luni rose from large copper plates sustained on stone pedestals. After droning through a lengthy incantation, the balding priest summoned Joturi-Nur to his final resting place. The old man's sarcophagus was carried up the steep steps, followed by his faithful wives and the hapless virgin Naptari. Then the servants chosen to accompany them were brought forward, and all the members of Joturi-Nur's eternal household disappeared into the dark hole of the crypt.

Time dragged as the last rites were conducted inside the mausoleum. A relentless sun drifted overhead. Sweat trickled down Mechnes back and dampened his silk robe. His thoughts wandered again, this time to Moisehén. He could picture the map of that kingdom in his mind: the Wastes of Faernvort in the northwest, the citadel of the King's City, the wealthy province of Selkynsen with the newly acquired Port of Linfeln in the south. On the eastern frontier were Selen and Moehn, along with the mountains and forests that gave texture to their landscape. Layered over this image of ink upon parchment were the countless minute details Rishona had shared with him, the location of small ravines and minor passes, places where the open plains were studded with quiet woodlands, hamlets, and minor towns the scribes had not bothered to draw.

Three years ago, Mechnes had looked upon that rich land from across the wide expanse of the Furma River, having arrived on the western border of Moisehén to deliver Rishona's ransom. His caravan had skirted the Paramen Mountains and traversed Antaria. They had hired ships to carry them over the Sea of Rabeln, and gained entry to the primitive realm of Roenfyn. Even now the taste of the Mage King's territory lingered upon his tongue, fertile fields and dense forests, iron hills and precious stones, constant rivers of earth-bound magic. A kingdom that invited conquest.

At last the priest emerged from the tomb and ordered the door sealed. He gave a long ululating cry, both arms raised toward Rishona. Steps were positioned next to the elephant. Mechnes's niece descended from her perch and with elegant strides, approached the tomb of her grandfather, shoulders set and head held high. The priest received her, removed her mask and revealed her true countenance to the people. As she raised the scimitar of the San'iloman with both hands, a great roar rose from all assembled, evoking a smile of satisfaction from Mechnes. Joturi-Nur was dead, but the San'iloman lived among them. A woman, no less. A warrior princess of his making.

They stayed the night in Urq'Namahan, the camps of the different houses spread in a flickering carpet of firelight outside the walls of the dead city. A feast was organized in the temple, attended by Joturi-Nur's sons and their closest kin. Rishona sat on an ivory throne at the head of the hall, back straight and expression regal, her table laid with flatbread, spiced meats and fresh fruit. Food and wine flowed in abundance. Musicians hand-picked by Prince Mechnes filled the hall with song and melody. The people ate and drank, engaged in jovial conversation.

When the dancers arrived, lithe girls draped in translucent veils, Mechnes took his cup in hand and strolled restless about the hall, observing the drunken revelry with a keen and sober eye.

Meanara's surviving offspring, three in all, sat closest to the San'iloman. Gluttonous men, they were now fat and useless with age. Already they had expressed opposition to the campaign for Moisehén, and as the eldest sons of Joturi-Nur, they could yet stir up unrest over the circumstances of Rishona's succession. Mechnes gave them a month, at most, before Rishona's poisons found a way into their households.

The other brothers would be less inclined to oppose her, at least for the moment. The two sons of Joturi's third wife carried little political weight among the Syrnte. All those born to the Second Wife Lhandra, including Mechnes and Paolus-Nur, respected Rishona, having witnessed her passion for weaponry during the years in which she trained with Mechnes. She had earned their admiration in a way no other woman could, though mere admiration, Mechnes knew, was not enough to keep her on the throne.

"Brother." Paolus-Nur appeared at his side, one hand holding his cup, the other coming to rest on Mechnes's shoulder. "Why that scowl upon your face?"

Mechnes grunted and nodded toward a fair-headed man who played the dulcimer. "That new musician is careless; his instrument is not well-tuned, and he strays ahead of the rhythm."

Paolus-Nur shrugged. "None will notice with the wine we've had."

"I notice."

"Dismiss him, then."

"I will. Tonight. In a most unceremonious fashion."

Paolus-Nur chuckled, drew close, and lowered his voice. "You never hesitate to dispose of that which is useless. It makes me wonder what witchcraft kept you from taking our niece's head?"

Mechnes did not return Paolus's questioning gaze but continued to study his musicians with a critical eye. "Who is asking?"

"All your brothers, including those born by the second wife of Joturi-Nur."

"There was no witchcraft at work. Our father named her, and she defended her claim. Custom demands the blood of but one sibling, and with good reason. Had you cut her down, another might have challenged you, and then another would have challenged him. By the end of it, all Joturi-Nur's sons would have drowned in their own blood, except me of course." He shot Paolus-Nur a sharp glance, assessing his brother's stance, the set of his jaw, the placement of his hand on the hilt of his knife. "Indeed, now that I reflect on the matter, perhaps it would have served me better to be rid of the whole brood at once."

Paolus smiled and drank from his wine. He was three years Mechnes's senior, but looked the younger, when one compared his lean figure to Mechnes's stocky build and battle-worn face. "You did not answer my question. You could have challenged her yourself, and none would have opposed you. Why did you not spill her blood?"

Mechnes let his gaze settle on Rishona. She had shed her mourning robes before the feast, donning a more provocative gown of gold, scarlet, cerulean, and ivory. The silky folds clung to the curves of her torso and hinted at the length of her legs. Bracelets adorned her bare arms and shapely ankles. Her black hair fell in voluptuous waves to her waist. A simple diadem sat on her forehead, accentuating the magnetic pull of her kohl-darkened eyes.

"Because it pleases me to see her alive," he replied. "Rishona is of my household. She is like a daughter to me, and I am as her father. She may carry Joturi-Nur's sword, but I am the one who wields its power."

Paolus narrowed his blue-gray eyes. "Then it is your wish, not hers, that we invade Moisehén?"

"It is my wish, and hers. Moisehén is a worthy conquest, and it is Rishona's kingdom, by right of birth."

"The people of Moisehén know nothing of her or her heritage."

"That is hardly relevant. Even if they did, the Mage King would not simply step aside and hand her the crown."

"This is a dangerous undertaking, Mechnes. They've forged a new alliance with Roenfyn."

"Roenfyn is a backward kingdom with an inconsequential army. Whatever pathetic levies he can coax from their incompetent king will be trampled by our warriors."

"Still, the army of Moisehén will not fall so easily. It is said that the class of mage warriors has been resurrected. We understand too little of their magic to—"

"And they understand nothing of ours. The Mage King's effort to revive the tradition of Caedmon is yet in its infancy."

"He wields a wizard's staff."

"But he is young and inexperienced in war."

"The rebellion Rishona supported was crushed by his inexperienced hand."

"A ragged band of mercenaries. He has other enemies of greater skill and power, enemies that seek our support and will not be put down."

"I have heard of no kingdom anxious to declare war on the son of Kedehen."

Mechnes paused before responding, uncertain whether this was the moment to speak of the creatures Rishona had befriended, of what they wanted and how she thought to aid them.

"I've never seen you so reluctant to wage a war, Paolus-Nur," he said.

"I've never been asked to wage it through three kingdoms and across a stormy sea."

"You will remain in Ech'Naláhm. I need someone here I can trust."

"I do not press this issue out of concern for myself. The journey alone would tear our army to shreds. How do you expect to secure safe passage through Antaria, Galia, and Roenfyn?"

"We will open up the pass of Fehren-vey and attack Moisehén from the east."

"Fehren-vey." Paolus-Nur let go a low whistle. "That ancient route? But it's impassible."

"The work to restore the road began weeks ago."

The older prince shook his head, a bemused smile touching his lips. "Once again your scheme takes root before anyone can object. You always were the clever one, little brother. Clever, but mad."

Mechnes laughed at this, and caught Rishona's eye through the frenzied swirl of veiled dancers. She greeted his gaze with a slight lift of the chin, a subtle smile upon her full lips, dark eyes sparkling with beguile and menace. The Syrnte lord raised his cup to her and drank. "Mad, perhaps. But always victorious."

Chapter 4

Akmael set the bread down on his plate and studied Taesara's lady-in-waiting, Sonia, who stood in the narrow doorway, hands folded and shoulders erect. This was the third time since their arrival that the Queen had spurned Lord Felton's hospitality, sending word she was too ill to breakfast with them.

"What ails her?" he asked, though he could well guess the answer: lack of comfort, cramped quarters, and all too common food. The patriarch of Moehn provided them the best of everything he had, but his generosity failed miserably when compared to the luxury to which Taesara was accustomed.

"I am certain I do not know, my Lord King." The Lady Sonia had a small nose and puffy freckled cheeks. Her uninviting lips were drawn in a tight line, and her hazel eyes carried a bitter bite. "My Lady Queen grows weaker with every day we spend in Moehn. She has lost her color, is beset with fatigue, and cannot keep down food or drink."

At once Akmael suspected what the problem might be, the realization hitting him like cold water in the face. His irritation gave way to an odd mix of surprise, hope, and dismay.

"Perhaps we should send for Maga Eolyn," Lord Felton volunteered.

"The witch of Moehn?" Sonia's laugh was haughty, derisive. "I doubt our Lady Queen would receive her."

"She is not a common witch," countered Sir Drostan, his tone severe. "The Lady Eolyn is a High Maga, trained in the tradition of Aithne and Caradoc."

"She is a wench who dabbles in potions and poisons—"

"Enough!" Akmael silenced the dispute. "You may not understand our traditions, Lady Sonia, but you are now a subject of Moisehén, and you will respect them. Lord Felton, yours is a worthy suggestion. Have one of my messengers fetch Maga Eolyn."

Felton nodded to his steward, who hurried off to see the King's will done.

The Lady Sonia pursed her lips and gave a curt bow. "Forgive me, my Lord King. It was not my intention to offend you or your people."

"In the future, watch your tongue." Akmael dismissed her with a wave of his hand. "And do not frighten our Queen with your foolish talk of potions and poisons."

Drostan grunted after she left. "We should send Lady Sonia back to Roenfyn. She is steeped in the prejudices of her people, and she has far too much influence over the Queen."

"The Queen is entitled to appoint a portion of her own attendants," Akmael reminded him. "Lady Sonia has been her most constant companion, the only woman of Roenfyn who has remained at her side since our marriage. I will not take that away from her. Besides it is only talk, and women's talk at that."

The old knight frowned. "The silver blade of a woman's lie cuts deeper than any knife."

Lord Felton let go a hearty laugh and clapped Sir Drostan on the shoulder, a gesture that did not appear to please the mage warrior. "Oh, that's a good one, dear knight. A silver blade cuts deeper than a woman's lie, is it? No. What was that you said again?"

Drostan shook his head and returned to his meal in silence.

"You're right, of course." Felton leaned toward him with a conspiratorial smile. "It's best I not remember lest I repeat your jest in the presence of the good Lady Gwen. She'd have a few choice words to say in response, I'll wager."

Akmael smiled, but his sense of levity was short-lived. In truth, it troubled him to bring Eolyn here under these circumstances, to ask his mistress to attend his Queen.

His mistress.

The words left a bitter taste in his mouth. This was not the fate he had intended for Eolyn, yet this was what he had made her in recent nights of burning need. Every kiss they shared tasted of destiny; every caress was an expression of truth. Eolyn—not Taesara—should have been his Queen, her magic envied and revered by all the people of Moisehén, not hidden away in this remote province, misunderstood and ridiculed by the women of his own court.

The food lost its flavor, the wine its body.

Pushing aside his breakfast, Akmael announced he wished to survey the city wall. Lord Felton and Sir Drostan stood at once, leaving their meals unfinished in order to accompany him.

The day was overcast and damp. From the ramparts Akmael could see the narrow streets of the small town, bustling with farmers peddling vegetables, grains, livestock, and wool. Barefoot children ran through the alleyways, lighthearted and mischievous, stealing an occasional apple or roll, then scampering off amidst shouts and rebukes from outraged vendors. The guards who patrolled the wall were scant in number, and they spent more time watching inconsequential dramas in the streets below than scanning the terrain that surrounded their home. Drostan said nothing of their distraction, but Akmael could detect the knight's consternation at the lack of order and discipline.

How Sir Borten had become such a formidable soldier among these idle men was a mystery to both of them.

"It was my understanding you would begin repairs on the wall at once, Lord Felton." Akmael did not bother to conceal his annoyance. Numerous areas were weak or crumbling. Whole sections would have to be torn down and rebuilt if the town hoped to have functional defenses. Akmael had returned to this topic repeatedly since his arrival, and Felton's continued delay was unacceptable.

"My apologies, my Lord King, but we have a limited number of masons in Moehn, and it would seem Sir Borten has hired all of them to finish the wall of the new *Aekelahr*."

Now there was a fine dilemma: which wall to finish first. In truth, Akmael would rather abandon all the walls of Moehn and take Eolyn back to the City, where he could put his own fortress and army to the task of keeping her safe.

"I see," he said. "I will speak to Sir Borten about it, and have additional stoneworkers sent from Selkynsen or Moisehén to assist you both."

"That is most generous of you, my Lord King, although…" Felton's words drifted into an uncomfortable silence. He scanned the wall with quick, nervous eyes, and rubbed the palms of his meaty hands. "It just that, masons from Selkynsen…"

Akmael let go an inward sigh of frustration. Of course, he thought. Selkynsen craftsmen would charge three times as much as their counterparts in Moehn. "The Crown will cover the additional cost, Lord Felton. This wall is a priority. It must be completed with all haste."

"As you wish, my Lord King." He gave a congenial nod. "Though in truth, it is too generous of you. Moehn has avoided war for centuries now, and all our noble houses live in peace. The repair of this wall is an exorbitant and unnecessary investment. I must counsel you once again to reconsider. Surely the kingdom has more pressing needs."

Nothing was more pressing than Eolyn's protection.

"I appreciate your frankness, Lord Felton, but it is my responsibility to determine the priorities of Moisehén. Moehn has long been overlooked, yet your people feed the kingdom, and now you have given a new home to the Magas. Yours is a humble but noble province. I will not allow it to drift in neglect any longer."

Felton appeared pleased by these words, and drew a breath as if to speak, but a boy racing toward them along the ramparts distracted him. The child stopped several paces away, eyes wide and uncertain as he stared at the King. Akmael recognized him as one of Felton's family, a grandson perhaps or a nephew, though he looked little more than street waif with his simple clothes, smudged cheeks, and unkempt mop of brown hair.

"Come, come, Markl. Don't be shy." Felton beckoned the boy. Markl approached and stood close to the patriarch, who set a firm hand on his shoulder. "What news do you bring?"

"The Lady Gwen said to tell you Maga Eolyn has arrived." Markl looked at Felton as he spoke, then glanced at Akmael and Sir Drostan.

"Ah well, then." Felton ruffled his hair, leaving it standing on end. "We must go in all haste, to see that our Queen is made well. Why don't you stay on the wall, Markl, and accompany Sir Drostan? You've a sharp eye and a good memory. You can make me a list of what needs to be repaired."

Markl glanced around the ramparts and shrugged. "Everything needs to be repaired. I can climb over the wall in a dozen places, and through it in half a dozen more."

Drostan cleared his throat, and Akmael caught the amusement in his eyes.

"It would seem you've found a worthy assistant, Sir Drostan," he said.

"It would seem so, my Lord King. Very well, Markl. Why don't we start with the easiest climb?"

"If it pleases you, Sir Drostan," the boy replied, "I think it might be better to start with the biggest hole."

Akmael and Felton returned to the lord's home, a half-timber manor that loomed a haphazard three stories over the central square of Moehn. The largest edifice in the town—indeed, in the entire province—its windows were adorned with painted shutters, and lush blossoms grew in boxes suspended beneath the sills. The whole structure would burn in an hour, Akmael had often thought, were someone to scale the tattered city wall and throw flaming torches through its windows.

He drew a breath to steady his pulse before striding through the heavy oak doors, carved with images of wheat, barley, fruit, and cattle. Confusion plagued his heart, the desire to see Eolyn tempered by the dread of asking her to confirm the news he most wanted to hear and least wanted to confront: that Taesara was with child, that his Queen might at last be carrying the son who would one day wear the Crown of Vortingen.

In the small receiving hall, Eolyn stood in quiet conversation with Maga Renate and Lady Gwen. The High Maga wore her burgundy robes, while Renate was clothed in the sapphire blue colors of a Middle Maga. Upon the King's entrance, all three looked up. Joy and desire flared through Eolyn's aura. Her gracious smile made his heart ache. She stepped toward him then stopped short, the happy expression fading into a slight frown. As if remembering herself, she lowered her gaze and bowed alongside the other women.

"Lady Gwen, Maga Eolyn." He beckoned them to rise, resenting the formality required. "Maga Renate."

"My Lord King," they responded in unison.

Eolyn continued, "We came as quickly as we could. Your messenger said the Queen has taken ill."

"She has not risen for breakfast these past days." He faltered, surprised at his sudden inability to continue. "If you would see her, Maga Eolyn, I would be most grateful."

"Of course, my Lord King." She studied him carefully now, a puzzled look on her face. "We are here at your service."

They climbed two sets of steep and narrow stairs to the small apartments that comprised the Queen's quarters. The polished oak floor was warped in places and creaked beneath their feet, the door to Taesara's room opened on hinges that required oil. The Queen lay in bed, her flaxen hair brushed and braided, complexion as white as the linens. Dark rings had settled under her tired blue eyes. Upon seeing Akmael, she smiled and bade the Lady Sonia to help her with the pillows that she might sit up to receive him.

"My Lord King," she reached out to him. "It is good of you to come."

Akmael approached and took her delicate hand in his. Her touch had always been fragile, and today her fingers were cold. The shadow of his guilt spread heavy across his shoulders. In the week since they had arrived he had dedicated all waking thoughts to Eolyn, while the Queen of Moisehén languished in this sorry state, forgotten and neglected.

"We have brought healers to see you, Taesara," he said. "High Maga Eolyn and Maga Renate."

She cast a nervous glance at both. "You bring these witches into my chambers?"

"My Lady Queen." Felton's cheeks reddened. "Forgive my boldness in speaking so directly, but High Maga Eolyn is the finest healer in our province, and Maga Renate is second in skill only to her."

Taesara lifted her chin, indignant. "Then it is no wonder Moehn remains mired in its backward ways."

"Taesara." Akmael's tone was harsh.

The Queen responded with an expression he had come to know well, that of a confused child who could not understand what she had done wrong. After a moment, she lowered her eyes and reached for the Lady Sonia, gripping her hand tight. "As you wish, my Lord King."

Akmael and Felton left the women to their task and waited outside the Queen's room. As Felton paced the antechamber, the

King took a stance by one of the narrow windows and stared unseeing into the courtyard below, one hand resting idly upon the hilt of his sword. He considered the possible futures that might unfold, depending on what truth emerged in the next few moments. If Taesara were with child, it would be glorious and terrible news, a bond of duty that would secure the future of his kingdom yet end his stay in Moehn and separate him from Eolyn, once and for all.

Yet if Taesara were not pregnant…

The thought provoked a sharp intake of breath.

If she were not pregnant, there might yet be an opportunity to set right what he had allowed to go wrong: to dissolve the contract with Roenfyn, bring Eolyn to the City, and fulfill the destiny envisioned by his father.

Convince her to bear your sons, Kedehen had urged with his last breath. *Do as I did. Only then will your power be complete.*

Even now, Akmael doubted that Eolyn could ever be convinced. Time after time she had turned him away—out of fear, anger, or a sense of betrayal. In all the years they had known each other, how often had she truly been his? There was one brief kiss in the South Woods, another years later in the forests of East Selen. After the defeat of her brother Ernan, the Gods granted them a few short months of intimacy, lulling Akmael into the belief that she would at last remain at his side. Yet once again she had abandoned him, this time for the dream of founding a new coven in Moehn. Dragon had called her to a different destiny, she claimed. A woman could not be both Queen and High Maga.

So he had let her go, and married this dull and delicate princess of Roenfyn, who for all her beauty did not inspire the passion ignited by a single glance from his beloved Eolyn.

A squeak of rusted hinges interrupted his thoughts. Eolyn and Renate appeared, closing the door to the Queen's room as quietly as they could. Entrusting her staff to Renate, Eolyn approached Akmael.

"I have given her an infusion of chamomile and mint to calm her stomach and restore her appetite." She drew a shaky breath, but kept her dark eyes steady upon his. "It would seem the damp climate does not agree with her, and she… Well, my Lord King, it appears that the Queen…"

Eolyn's words drifted into silence. She bit her lip and looked away.

"The Queen is with child." Renate stepped forward, her sharp tone a fine match for that hawkish face. "She is about two months along, my Lord King. This is the primary reason for her indisposition."

Felton clapped his hands in joy. "Praise the Gods!"

Akmael watched Eolyn. She did not return his gaze but instead studied her hands, working restlessly against each other. The memory of their recent nights stirred inside him, like wind through the high branches of an ancient fir, beautiful and poignant. Ephemeral in time, enduring in the imagination.

"We would recommend the Queen return to the King's City as soon as possible," continued Renate, shoulders stiff and back as straight as an arrow. "Preferably by litter. She should not mount a horse again, not until the baby comes to term. Do you not agree, Maga Eolyn?"

Eolyn blinked at the sound of her name and nodded. "Yes, of course. She requires a warmer climate and the comfort of her home, if the baby is to come to term successfully."

Akmael turned to Felton. "Have a litter readied by morning, and send a messenger at once to the City to advise High Mage Rezlyn. He is to meet us in Rhiemsaven. We will send her by royal barge from there to Moisehén."

"As you wish, my Lord King."

"The Lady Gwen is to assist Lady Sonia in readying the Queen and her attendants," Akmael continued. "Advise Sir Drostan to inform the rest of our party. We will depart at dawn."

Felton bowed and started down the hall, muttering his list of tasks and marking them on chubby fingers.

"Lord Felton."

He turned and looked at Akmael as if caught in the middle of a very important thought.

"I hope you will understand my decision to cut short our visit is no reflection on the hospitality shown by you and Lady Gwen, which has been generous and most appreciated from our first day here. We will visit Moehn again, as soon as circumstances permit."

"Yes, of course, my Lord King." He grinned and bowed low. "It has been our greatest honor to receive you, and to be the first to hear this most glorious news. May the Gods grant you a son, a fine and healthy baby boy!"

Akmael turned his attention back to Eolyn and Renate. The High Maga had retreated to her own thoughts, while the older woman watched him with arched brows and an unabashed stare.

"It would seem the Queen disposed of the herbs we sent the other day," Renate said, "an unfortunate decision as they would have been of great help to her now."

"We will gather additional medicines this afternoon and have a fresh bundle sent by evening." Eolyn spoke as if measuring her words to soften Renate's accusatory tone. "The Queen must make use of them, otherwise it will be a hard journey from here to Rhiemsaven."

"I will see it done," Akmael replied.

Eolyn nodded. Her hand drifted to her throat and found the silver web at its base, a jewel of magic that he had given to her long ago. "I suppose we are finished here, then. If it pleases you, my Lord King, Renate and I will take our leave."

"Maga Renate is dismissed. I would have a word with you alone, Maga Eolyn, before you depart."

Renate set her lips in a firm line, and directed a questioning gaze at her companion.

Eolyn's shoulders deflated, but she laid a hand on the old maga's arm and said, "Find Sir Borten and have him prepare the horses, would you, Renate? You can wait for me in the courtyard. I won't be a moment."

Renate gave a stiff bow and departed.

Akmael drew close to Eolyn and invoked a sound ward about them. She did not retreat, nor did she move to touch him. In her fingers she cradled the jewel woven by his mother, the silver web that had brought them together as children in the South Woods. It seemed a lifetime ago, a world forever lost.

A quiet sob broke on her lips. "I have been such a fool."

"I was the one who overstepped my bounds. Forgive me, Eolyn. It was not my intention—"

"I am not speaking of these nights, recently passed." Her hand found his, their fingers intertwined. Such tenderness to her touch, such sadness in her eyes. "I walked away from you, my love. I turned my back on this gift the Gods had given us, because I was frightened—so very terrified—and of what? Of you? All you ever did was love me. "

"I was not so perfect in my affection."

"You were my only Caradoc. I see that now, and it is too late."

Her words felt small inside the growing void of his soul, though they would have filled him with pleasure just a few years before. He touched her cheek then drew her into his embrace, inhaling the honey-and-wood scent of her hair. A verse came to mind from his childhood days, a song his mother had sung, and he recited it now as he held Eolyn close. "Caradoc waited for his one true love, withstanding the tides of tempest and sun. Caradoc defied the cruel threats of time, and received his Aithne when her journey was done."

Eolyn laughed into his chest, a bright sound that invoked images of the sun-flecked woods. She withdrew and looked at him, a mischievous glint in her brown eyes. "That mage had no crown upon his fair head. A King needs an heir before he is dead."

The improvised verse amused him, but even as he allowed himself a smile the merriment drained from her features.

Her eyes drifted toward Taesara's room, and she murmured, "I would have born your children with love. Just as she will do, I could have done—that, and so much more."

Akmael felt something rupture inside, an old wound he now knew would never heal.

"I should leave," she said, but her lips met his instead.

Their kiss was impassioned yet brief. Abruptly she withdrew and held him at arms length. Recovering her breath, she straightened her shoulders and pulled away entirely. When she spoke, her tone was formal though the emotion in her eyes communicated a message much deeper and more heartfelt.

"May the Gods grant you a son, my Lord King. May they see you safely back to the City, and give you, the Queen, and all your children a long and happy life."

"Eolyn, please—" He stepped toward her.

"Don't." She lifted a hand to halt him. In a rustle of burgundy skirts she was gone, light footsteps echoing down the oak paneled stairs. Only her essence lingered behind, wrapping misty tendrils around memories that could not be forgotten and dreams that would never be fulfilled.

Chapter 5

"How will I recognize Dragon, when the time comes for my fast?" Sirena kept her gaze fixed upon their path as she spoke. The spring breeze lifted the fine tendrils of her hair, shining gold beneath the afternoon sun. "You say she can shapeshift in any form, but there are so many creatures in the forest. How will I know which one is she?"

Eolyn smiled, remembering her own uncertainty when she was young, in the days before she petitioned for a staff of High Magic.

"You will sense something akin what a High Maga sees when she recognizes a practitioner who has shapeshifted." The cool grass pricked at her feet, and the air felt fresh in her lungs. The baskets strapped to their backs were laden with fragrant herbs, fresh mushrooms, and other treasures gathered from the surrounding hills and woodlands. Eolyn found comfort in the familiarity of the burden. It distracted her from the persistent ache of her heart. "The energy of the animal will be different: grander, more all-encompassing than Owl or Lynx or Spider alone. There will be a spirit inside its skin that is not of its essence."

"But what if more than one creature appears, and what if all of them seem different in their essence? How will I know which one is she?" Sirena gave Eolyn a pleading look. "How did you know?"

A vision of glittering scales and silver eyes flashed through Eolyn's mind. A great expanse of wings, a tremendous gust of wind. "I prefer not to speak of the days of my fast, Sirena. I have given that memory to a sacred place inside my heart, that place we all must guard in silence and keep as a refuge and source of strength."

"But why?"

Because it would be dangerous to claim the Gods had granted her a privilege not witnessed since ancient times. "Perhaps you will understand, once you have had the experience."

"Must I not talk about it, then?"

"You may speak of it as often or as little as you wish. That is your choice."

"And what if Messenger does not appear at all? What then?"

"If the Gods do not grant your petition, it is not because you are unworthy." Doyenne Ghemena's words echoed in Eolyn's heart, bringing with them memories of a kind and ancient face, the aroma of burning candles, the sweet bite of hot berry-and-primrose wine. "It simply means they have a different plan for you, one that will bring you even greater happiness. One that will be of better service to our people."

Sirena frowned, glanced away. "Will you send me away if Dragon does not appear?"

"No, of course not. Why would you think such a thing?"

"But if I can't be a maga—"

"You are a maga. You are a Middle Maga, and you can continue your studies of Middle Magic for the rest of your life, if you desire. Some of the greatest healers of Moisehén were Middle Magas. Our dear Renate is a Middle Maga, and she is just as much a daughter of Aithne as any of us."

"I can stay with the coven no matter what, then? I can stay forever if I want?"

"You can stay forever, Sirena. I hope that you do."

Sirena grinned and added a skip to her step. Their home came into view, a humble collection of buildings nestled inside the unfinished wall. Eolyn looked upon her *Aekelahr* with the same mixture of pride and melancholy that had filled the days since Akmael's departure. She had accomplished so much, and yet at times it seemed so little.

Next to the kitchen, Mariel and Ghemena were busy skinning rabbits, while Tasha and Catarina sat peeling parsnips. Eolyn and Sirena left a bundle of fresh herbs in their care before proceeding to the herbarium. There they set their baskets on the floor and opened the windows to let in the last of the afternoon light. While they worked, Sirena recited the use and preparation of each plant as if drawn from a poem deep inside her heart: the white flowers of the Elder tree could reduce a fever; the stems and roots of cat's claw eased the aching of joints; Felian's rose relieved the pain of a woman's monthly cycle.

Of all Eolyn's students, Sirena was the most gifted when it came to the language of plants. She would spend hours in the herbarium listening to the brittle whispers of their collection, removing specimens whose magic had faded and replacing them with fresh herbs. In the forest, Sirena could detect voices so quiet they were beyond even Eolyn's ear, and so had discovered hidden mushrooms and the tiniest of plants, all of which had turned out to have medicinal uses.

They had not yet finished sorting the collection when Sir Borten appeared, filling the doorway with his broad frame, steady blue eyes set in a sober countenance. "Pardon my intrusion, Maga Eolyn, Maga Sirena."

"Good evening, Sir Borten." Sirena flushed, a slight tremor invaded her voice. Eolyn had come to suspect that all of her girls were somewhat infatuated with the King's knight.

"How may I help you, Sir Borten?" she said.

"I received word you had returned, and I thought we might resume your lessons."

Eolyn sighed. In truth, she would much rather stay with her plants. "I'm afraid we have quite a lot of work to do here—"

"Oh, don't worry about this, Maga Eolyn," Sirena intervened brightly. "Do go with Sir Borten. I can take care of the plants."

Eolyn met Borten's gaze. The amusement in his expression made her bristle.

"Very well." She set down the stems and shoved past the knight into the afternoon light.

Sir Borten matched her impatient gait, and waited respectfully outside her quarters while she retrieved Kel'Barú.

"You should carry the sword with you always," he said as they resumed their walk toward the inner courtyard.

"I hardly know how to use it. I'd sooner cut off my own nose than injure an opponent."

"That is not true. Even if it were, simply to carry the sword serves as a deterrent."

"A deterrent for what?" She met him with a defiant gaze. "What is it that everyone is so worried about in this province of farmers where the greatest threat I might encounter is a violent gust from a summer storm?"

Sir Borten drew a slow breath. "It is not my intention to upset you, Maga Eolyn. The King has asked me to teach you, and that is all I am trying to do."

The patience in his tone deflated her anger. Her quarrel was with Akmael, not with Borten.

Or perhaps it was with herself.

"Pardon my temper, Sir Borten. I am, perhaps, still fatigued from the King's visit."

For a while the silence between them was broken only by the rhythmic fall of their feet.

"Markl and his boys were here today," Borten said.

This had become a weekly ritual, for Felton's grandson and his street urchins to make the journey from Moehn in order to spy on the mysterious girls of the *Aekelahr*. Catarina had made a game of it, imagining she was a maiden about to be rescued by the handsome Lord Markl and his brave knights, but young Ghemena despised them all. "I suppose you ran them off as usual."

"A straight charge into their ranks never fails. Ghemena was quite amused."

"I'm certain she was. It is a harmless game, Sir Borten. You really shouldn't trouble yourself to—"

"Harmless now, perhaps, but the whims of boys soon become the desires of men. I will not have this place treated with disrespect by anyone of any age."

Eolyn absorbed these words, struck by the realization that his commitment to the *Aekelahr* ran deeper than mere duty.

"With any luck, one of those miscreants will stand his ground one day against my horse," he added in a lighter tone. "When that happens, I will recruit that boy and train him."

Eolyn laughed. Levity felt unfamiliar in Borten's presence.

"Of course, I would only do so with your permission, Maga Eolyn."

"You would have it, Sir Borten," she assured him. "You would have it."

They arrived at circle of compacted dirt where the men practiced daily, and where Eolyn now trained every morning and every evening. The maga drew her sword, reflexes awakened by the compelling ring of Kel'Baru.

"Where shall we begin?" she asked.

Borten opened his mouth and then closed it again, a troubled frown creasing his brow. He shifted on his feet and spoke in careful tones. "This is very important, what you are doing."

The awkward delivery of his words confused her. "To learn the sword? I understand that, Sir Borten, it's simply that I—"

"No. I mean, yes. But that is not what I am talking about." He cleared his throat. "It is important, the home that you have given to these girls. The life you are teaching them to live."

Eolyn blinked, taken aback by the declaration.

She looked from him to the buildings that comprised the *Aekelahr*, their shadows cast long by the setting sun. Sirena appeared at the doorway to the herbarium and skipped across the dense garden to join Mariel, Ghemena, and Tasha. Giggles and lively chatter marked their reunion, until Renate called them all inside with a typically sharp rebuke.

Each of these beautiful and gifted girls had come from backgrounds plagued by poverty, violence, and neglect. Their families had seen the *Aekelahr* not as the birthplace of a new era of magic, but as a way to rid themselves of unwanted daughters. Even Renate and Adiana, grown women with extraordinary talents, had joined Eolyn's coven because there was nowhere else for them to go.

"None of us have a place in this world as it was given to us." A knot took hold in her stomach, a need to share with him this dream nestled deep in her heart. A dream that had cost her the man she loved. "I believe the Gods have brought us together here, so that we might build a new world of our own."

She returned her gaze to Borten, wary of what she might find, relieved to discover understanding and companionship.

The knight drew his sword and assumed a low guard.

"Come, then, Maga Eolyn," he said. "Let us see what you remember."

Chapter 6

The trunk gave way with a loud snap. Men shouted and scrambled out from under the giant fir, axes in hand. The tree shifted then hovered at an angle, viridian branches wavering against the gray sky as if caught by surprise and reluctant to fall. From one moment to the next, its balance was lost. Wind hissed through the needles, a quiet rush gathering into a thunderous roar until the fir hit the ground with a deafening crash, sending up a splatter of mud and a fragrant cloud of wet needles, branches heaving then settling like the final expiration of some great beast.

Silence followed, broken by triumphant cries as the men set upon their quarry and began dismembering it, limb by verdant limb.

Mounted on his horse, Mechnes nodded with approval and turned to Rishona, who sat next to him on her ebony destrier, reins held steady between hands gloved in red suede. The San'iloman had closed her eyes as if in prayer. Charcoal lashes rested over cheeks that looked pale in contrast to the richly embroidered midnight blue cloak that covered her head. She drew a sharp breath through parted lips and opened her eyes. "That must be the last one. There can be no more."

"Of course, San'iloman. Your instructions were very explicit."

"I mean it must be the last tree to fall in all the forest along this road." She embellished the statement with an expansive gesture of her arm.

Mechnes puffed out his cheeks in a slow exhale, looking east and west along the winding path they were trying to navigate. In places the abandoned route was still intact, and they had ridden quiet hours over flat stones placed centuries ago by the slaves of some long forgotten civilization. But for the most part the ancient pass had degraded into a muddy trench overgrown with trees and vines. Every half day he had left crews along the route to finish breaking open this backdoor into Moisehén.

"We have five thousand men to get up this road," he said. "We cannot bring them single file, trudging knee-deep in muck."

"We do not need five thousand to take Moehn," she countered. "We don't even need five hundred."

"We will require five thousand—and more—to defend it and to finish our conquest, if this Mage King is everything you say he is."

Anger flickered behind her dark eyes.

"We are done here until evening," she said to the overseer, a tall man with wiry build. "Have everything ready, just as I requested, by sunset."

"As you wish, San'iloman." He bowed low as she spurred her horse past.

Mechnes fell in line beside her, their personal guard close behind. He could taste the salty heat of her well-concealed anger, its bristling aroma a welcome change in the bland climate of this mountain pass. The sodden ground sucked against the horses' hooves, and Mechnes cursed when his animal stumbled. The terrain reminded him of the steamy jungles of Jhiroco. He had lost many good men in that hellish war, though in the end they had succeeded in subjugating the barbarous Vurduren and subsuming their mines of gold and precious ores into the growing territories of the Syrnte.

At least these forests were not plagued by the same stifling heat. Nor did he expect anything comparable to the fierce resistance of the Vurduren from the peasants of Moehn.

They arrived at camp a short distance away. Rishona dismounted amidst the red and gold tents. Her tone was authoritative, her smile pleasant as she bade Mechnes to follow and the others to remain outside.

Raised on a platform of wood, the pavilion of the San'iloman was large and richly furnished. At its center stood an oval table spread with maps of their homeland and of Moisehén. To the back of the tent was her bed, concealed by a misty curtain of silk and adorned with colorful pillows. Blue flames flickered inside large copper plates, providing much needed heat. Her servants and slaves waited with food, drink and dry clothing, but they scattered upon her orders.

Once they were alone, Rishona unclasped her cloak and flung it to the floor at Mechnes's feet. "You are not to question my wisdom or my will in public. Ever."

Mechnes could not help but smile at the sight of his niece, now a grown woman pretending to give him orders. "With all due respect, San'iloman, I am your military advisor. It is my duty to speak my mind when the weight of my experience contradicts your rather naïve instincts."

She moved to strike him, but he caught her wrist and forced her arm until she gasped. "It is a little early in the day to start with these games, my Queen. But if you desire a spark of conflict to brighten this weary morning, I am more than willing to please you."

Rishona kept her eyes hard as stone and her voice taut with menace. "Speak your mind, Mechnes, but do so with discretion. I will not have our disagreements heard by those who would use them to spread malicious rumors against me. Nor will I have our men, who have struggled long and hard up this wretched pass, fall victim to any suspicion that our unity of purpose is wavering."

He brought her body tight against his, let his breath fall upon her silky skin until he felt a shiver pass through her, followed by the softening of her shoulders and the almost imperceptible tilt of her face that always preceded that ardent kiss.

Before their lips met, he released her. "We must open up this road if we hope to bring a proper army through it."

"We cannot bring down any more trees," she insisted. "We are undermining the power of this forest. We need its magic for everything that is to come."

"This is a very big forest." He drew out one of their maps, passing his hand over the moss green crescent of impenetrable woodland that swept north toward East Selen and south along the foothills of the Paramen Mountains. "And a very small pass."

Rishona stared at the map, lips protruding in that familiar charming frown. She rubbed her arms to ward off the damp chill. Noting her discomfort, Mechnes retrieved a dry cloak and placed it about her shoulders.

"I hope you are right," she said. "It is just that every time we bring down one of those trees, I feel strength torn out of the earth. I fear I went too far by clearing the valley where my parents died."

"You are Syrnte, Rishona. Your magic derives from the air."

"Yes, but these creatures were not banished to the Underworld by Syrnte magic. They were imprisoned by the mages and magas of Moisehén, and they must be summoned by the same powers. I will need the air to anchor my spirit when I summon them, but without the earth I cannot control them."

Mechnes narrowed his eyes. "If you have doubts regarding your ability to manage these beasts, you should have mentioned them before now."

"I have no doubts." She looked up at him, defiant. "I know how to gratify the Naether Demons and bring them into our service. But there are many elements involved, and they must be integrated carefully. No one has attempted this before, uncle. Or if they have, they failed miserably, and hence we know nothing of their fate."

"Are you ready to summon these beasts or not?" He did not bother to hide the threat in his tone. Already he had poured tremendous resources into this conquest. He would show no mercy if she had deceived him.

Rishona straightened her shoulders, expression resolute. "Yes, I am ready. For tonight, I am most ready. And for what is to come, I have time to prepare."

* * *

By late afternoon the clouds had cleared, exposing the vermilion face of a sun that seemed anxious to hide behind the western hills. Rishona emerged from her tent in a splendid ivory robe lined with ermine, diamonds sparkling in her ebony hair. Mechnes assisted her as she mounted her horse. At their side rode Donatya, priestess of Mikata, and an elegant hag if there ever was one. Gold circlets adorned her white hair and wrinkled throat, rubies hung from her flaccid earlobes. The most trusted men of Rishona's personal guard followed them.

Toward the rear of the small procession came the servant Merina, a woman with a swarthy and somewhat flattened countenance, whose small body was ripening with child. Long a favorite of Rishona's, the servant rode in a litter with instruments needed for the summoning: an obsidian knife wrapped in silk, a white screech owl in a small wooden cage, flasks of fa'hin wine and armen oil, caskets of mara'luni, winter sage, white albanett, and nightshade mushrooms.

Mechnes posted guards on the road with orders to let no one pass. They arrived at the modest valley now cleared of trees, the place where Mechnes's sister Tamara and her beloved prince, Feroden of Moisehén, had perished in an ambush a generation ago.

Their deaths had paved the way for the Mage Prince Kedehen to assume the throne of his fathers, an event that plunged the kingdom into civil war. By the end of it, the Magas were destroyed, the Mage King unopposed, and the fates of Feroden, Tamara, and their two young children all but forgotten.

Sober of countenance, Rishona dismounted and approached the site where she had forced herself out of Tamara's dying womb, a babe who refused to follow her mother into the Afterlife, a girl destined to wield the scimitar no woman had dared to claim for more than five centuries. The trees towered over them, immense shadows shifting in the deepening twilight. Wind whispered through dense branches. An involuntary shiver travelled up Mechnes's spine as the past wrapped around his senses. He heard his sister's cries of terror and agony, the echoes of metal hacking through flesh, the desperate squall of a newborn child. The salty taste of fresh blood and bitter afterbirth settled upon his tongue.

Rishona knelt, gathered the earth in her fine strong hands, pressed the soft loam against her face, and wept.

When at last the San'iloman's sobs faded, she returned the tear-drenched earth to its place, stood and commanded the priestess Donatya to bring the tools of sacrifice. Using traditional herbs of Moisehén, they marked the four cardinal points at twelve paces from the place where Tamara had perished and Rishona was born. Branches of the dried herb mara'luni were intercalated with these, also at twelve paces, yielding an eight-point circle. As Rishona and Donatya poured wine and oil along the rim, Mechnes placed his guards at the periphery.

Rishona began to chant, her rich voice calling upon all the Gods of the Syrnte, ancient and young, forgotten and remembered. She took a place at the center of the circle, hands extended toward the earth, face lifted to the heavens, her hair a dusky cloud of sensuous night. The fine fabric of her dress billowed in the mountain breeze and caught the faint light of flickering stars. Awe spread through Mechnes's chest, and his loins tightened with desire. This was his beloved niece, his Rishona, San'iloman of the Syrnte, a goddess come to earth on this moonless night.

Donatya led Merina toward the circle. The servant hummed an absent tune, white owl cradled between her swollen breasts, gaze unfocussed. She walked on unsteady feet, supported at the elbow by Donatya's gentle touch as she knelt before Rishona.

The San'iloman took the owl in a flutter of wings, calmed it, stroked it, kissed the miniature head, and pressed its shivering body over her heart. Accepting the obsidian blade from Donatya, the San'iloman closed her eyes, and murmured a prayer of sacrifice. In a single motion, she swept the knife and released the owl. Merina looked up as the bird fluttered away on silent wings. A gasp escaped her lips. Her hands came to her throat and clutched at a fresh river of blood. The San'iloman took hold of the servant and held her close.

"I am sorry, sweet Merina," she murmured. "This had to be done. Today the Gods will write your name in the books of the immortals, for you have made a great sacrifice for the glory of the Syrnte."

Merina's blood spilled dark upon Rishona's ivory dress. She beat helplessly against the firm hold of the queen, squirming like a rabbit ensnared, passing one hand over her belly in desperate, rapid strokes as her knees slipped against damp earth.

Donatya retreated to the edge of the circle.

Achme talam nu. Bechnem ahraht neme. Salahm machne du.

The rim ignited in a high blue flame. A muffled scream sounded from beneath the mountain, and a tremor passed through the earth. Mechnes's heart accelerated. He sucked in his breath and signaled the men to ready their arms.

Mechahne
Mechahne achnam
Talam nu ahram

Merina seized the ivory gown of her mistress in a soundless plea for mercy.

Rishona paused and set her black eyes on the frantic servant. She bent low, stroked Merina's hair, murmured in her ear. The servant's struggles diminished, then ceased. Rishona wiped Merina's bloodstained cheeks and placed a comforting hand upon her swollen belly. Her lips met the servant's in a tender kiss. Then she laid Merina on the wet ground, where the pregnant woman twitched as gurgling whimpers escaped her lips.

Talam nu ahram
Merina

An inky shadow bloomed beneath them. The trees shivered. The earth moaned. Rishona stood and retreated across the periphery of the circle, pace calm, slender back erect. The wall of flame left no mark upon her. She turned to observe her dying servant, and the world grew silent.

Merina's body convulsed. Her eyes closed, and the tension left her limbs. Mechnes held his breath, hands gripping the hilt of his sword, eyes darting between the circle and his men, who watched with weapons drawn and shields raised. It was here, upon the threshold of death for Merina and her unborn child, that the Naether Demon had to find its way to the world of the living. Mechnes had waited long for this moment. All their dreams of conquering Moisehén depended on it. Yet as the ground beneath them groaned and shifted once again, a cold knot took hold of his belly, and he found himself hoping the creature would not appear.

A hollow scream shattered the silence. Inside the circle, the ground twisted, flowed into a vortex of soil and rock, dragging the slave's limp body down toward the heart of the mountain. Merina disappeared amidst unearthly howls and the sounds of tearing flesh. The earth exploded upward, bathing Mechnes and his men in a shower of dirt and gravel. Inside the ring of fire, a creature swayed on long glowing limbs, its predatory eyes lost in gaping hollows, its mouth an open pit dripping with blackened saliva. One ebon-clawed limb grasped Merina's corpse by the ankle. The slave's belly had been ripped open, her ribcage torn apart.

Merolim

Matue

Rishona lifted her palms in a gesture of supplication, speaking a smooth cadence of motherly love and reassurance.

Hem alouim natue

The creature roared and lunged at her, hitting the wall of fire with an agonized shriek. Mechnes rushed toward Rishona's side, but stopped short when she raised her hand in warning. The Naether Demon stumbled backwards and rocked on oversized limbs, the murky pits of its eyes steady on the San'iloman as it drew Merina's corpse into a glowing embrace. Its head jerked around, seeming to focus on each of Mechnes's men before turning toward the sky, the forest, the ground at its feet. It dragged one long claw through the upturned earth, gathered the loam and crumbled the rotting leaves in its pulsing grasp. Then it returned its empty gaze to Rishona.

Merolim, Matue. She stepped into the ring of fire. *Hem alouim natue.*

Merina's corpse slipped from the Naether Demon's grasp. Shuffling forward, the beast pressed its flat muzzle against the palm of Rishona's hand. Her breasts rose with a sudden intake of breath, a smile graced her lips.

Natue, she murmured. *Alouim natue.*

The Naether Demon nuzzled the places where Merina's blood had soaked the ivory dress. A deep shudder passed through it, melting into a constant echoing purr. It lowered itself on lengthy limbs and released the weight of its body to the ground, reclining at her feet, resting its naked head against her soiled skirt, mouth yawning then closing again. Rishona stroked its glowing skin, a quiet hum upon her lips. When at last the creature closed its eyes, she looked at Mechnes, her expression one of triumph, passion, and joy.

"It is ours," she said.

Chapter 7

A crash jolted Eolyn out of her sleep. The door flung open and Ghemena burst into the room, throwing herself at the maga and wrapping her arms tight around Eolyn's neck.

"Don't leave, don't leave, don't leave!" she cried.

"Ghemena, what has gotten into you?"

"You can't go to the South Woods!" Ghemena could barely speak between choking sobs. "You mustn't."

"The South Woods?"

There was a knock at the doorway and one of the guards appeared, a black figure silhouetted against the starry night. "Maga Eolyn. We heard a disturbance—"

"It's just one of the girls." Eolyn ignited her bedside candle with a short spell, casting a tenuous light across the shadow-filled room. "She's had a nightmare. You may go. I will call if I need you."

The man nodded and disappeared, closing the door behind him.

"Come now, Ghemena." Eolyn extracted herself from the girl's hold. "We've already talked about this. It will be a short trip—a quarter moon, perhaps. A fortnight at the most. I'll return before you even notice I'm gone."

"You can't go!" Ghemena wailed.

Eolyn wiped her tears away with a troubled frown. "You must tell me what this is all about."

"I had a feeling."

"A feeling?"

"Not a feeling. I saw something. Shadows and flame."

"You had a dream?"

"No, not a dream! It saw it happen."

"Magas cannot see the future, Ghemena. Dreams are simply dreams, and divination—"

"Is a reckless form of magic, I know." Ghemena recited the truism with exasperation. "But I saw something. Something bad."

Eolyn smoothed down the stray locks of the girl's hair. "Nothing will happen to you while Mariel, Sirena, and I are away. You're living in the most peaceful province of the kingdom, protected by some of the finest knights of the King's guard."

Ghemena frowned. After a moment, she offered tentatively, "Sir Borten is very brave."

"That he is."

"He led a battle against invaders from the north, just a few days ago."

"Yes." Eolyn smiled. "I heard about that."

"He charged them on his destrier and swung his sword like this, and this." Ghemena's arms carved clean arcs through the air. Her voice gathered enthusiasm. "They ran off in terror, and they'll never come back again."

"There, you see? With a knight like him to protect us, we need not worry about our enemies."

"But it wasn't the boys from the village that I saw just now. . ." Ghemena bit her lip, brow furrowed in concentration. "It was something worse . . . something awful."

Eolyn gathered the girl into a comforting embrace. Ghemena's father had been a brutal man, and her brothers inclined to abusing their baby sister and locking her in the cellar. The child was prone to nightmares, though several months had passed since the last incident.

"I have an idea." Eolyn searched the neckline of her gown and pulled a jewel out from hiding. "Can you keep a very important secret?"

Instantly, Ghemena's eyes were alert with curiosity. She nodded emphatically.

"Show me your hand."

The girl obeyed, and Eolyn placed the silver web carefully in her palm. The pendant, small but exquisite, was made of tiny quartz crystals woven into silver threads.

"This is very old magic, women's magic," Eolyn said. "The ways of weaving it have been lost to us, so you must take very good care of it. If you misuse this, or damage or lose it, we will never have another one again."

"What does it do?"

"It allows you to find a friend. It can take you to wherever I am in a blink of an eye."

Ghemena whistled through her teeth. "Even all the way to the South Woods?"

"All the way across the kingdom, if necessary. All you have to do is spin it, and say the spell I will teach you, and keep all your heart and all your spirit focused on me."

"I can come to you any time at all?"

"No. Not any time at all. You may invoke this magic only if you or one of your sisters are in grave danger. You must promise me you will not use it otherwise. Do you understand?"

Ghemena nodded, wrapping her fingers around the pendant and pressing it close to her heart. "Where did you get it?"

"King Akmael gave it to me a long time ago."

"The Mage King? But you said it's women's magic."

"It was woven by his mother, Briana of East Selen. She gifted it to him when he was a child, shortly before she died. Then one day he discovered how to use it. The silver web took him to the South Woods, and that was how we met. Years later, after my brother's rebellion, when the King pardoned me and let me return to Moehn, he gave it to me."

"Why?"

"The jewel carries the essence of us both. As long as I have it, I can find him in the same way you will be able to find me."

"Yes, but why would he want you to find him?"

"It is difficult to explain, Ghemena. It's just that the King and I…"

A lump caught in Eolyn's throat. She drew Ghemena close again, pressing her lips against the girl's silky hair, breathing in her wonderful aroma of honey and warm bread. "I suppose King Akmael gave this to me because he did not want me to be afraid, just like I don't want you to be afraid, ever again."

"Did you ever use it to go to him?"

"No. Never."

Should she have?

"I'm glad." Ghemena tightened her hold. "I'm glad you never went to him, because if you had, he might never have let you come back."

Ghemena slept with Eolyn that night. When the maga awoke, her ward had already risen and disappeared. Dawn illuminated the windows and the birds were welcoming the morning sun.

Eolyn found Ghemena in the kitchen along with the rest of the coven, all of them absorbed in vivacious chatter.

The three youngest sat on high stools, legs swinging while they tore apart dark bread and took down gulps of Renate's hearty morning tea. They teased and poked at each other even as the old maga admonished them to be still. Mariel and Sirena sat a little apart, heads bent together in quiet conversation. Adiana hovered over them all, refreshing supplies of bread, fruit, and Berenben cheese. She glanced up as Eolyn set down her satchel, winked and said, "Well, don't you look like the maga warrior this morning, with a sword on your hip and a staff in your hand!"

There were gasps of delight and giggles from the girls, but Ghemena's disappointed moan rose over it all. "You're taking Kel'Baru?"

"Of course she is, child," replied Renate. "It's her weapon, isn't it? She can take it wherever she pleases."

Ghemena pushed out her lower lip in a frown.

"You should get yourself some chain mail, too," said Adiana, "and a nice shiny helmet. And a pair of a fancy gauntlets like the ones Sir Borten had delivered from Moisehén."

"I'd lose myself under so much metal." Eolyn took a place at the table and accepted the tea Renate poured for her. "I wouldn't be able to hear anything, not the trees or the animals. Not the plants whispering on the wind, or the earth pulsing beneath them."

"Doesn't matter." Adiana helped herself to a generous portion of Berenben cheese, and served Eolyn as well. "You don't need to hear anything if you've got a plate of metal over your chest and a sword in your hand. That's why men don't bother listening. Once they're armed, all they really need to settle an argument is a few good blows."

"Adiana." Eolyn's reproach was quiet, held in the tone of her voice. She had come to accept her friend's cynicism regarding men, and to understand its origins, but she worried the girls might pick up the musician's constant disparaging banter. "Sometimes there are moments when a few good blows are necessary."

Adiana arched a brow. "Never thought I'd hear you say that."

"If you're taking Kel'Baru, you should take all of us!" Ghemena blurted. "Catarina and Tasha want to go, too."

At once the three youngest sprang upon Eolyn with wide suffering eyes.

"She's right, Maga Eolyn. Please take us along!"

"There'll be nothing to do here when you're gone."

"What do you mean there'll be nothing to do?" Eolyn threw up her hands in mock irritation. "All of you have spells I expect you to master before we return. Maga Renate and Mistress Adiana will have plenty of lessons and chores for you. Your days will be very full, and a maga is never bored, because her joy—"

"—Comes from the endless renewal of the earth itself," they recited in unison, before breaking into exaggerated groans.

"We're going to make pies, breads, and jellies." Adiana draped her arms around the young girls' shoulders and spoke into their ears with a mischievous grin. "We'll eat all the sweets we want while Maga Eolyn's away."

"That's not true." Ghemena shrugged her off, indignant. "You said that the last time she left, and it wasn't true then, either."

"Well you caught me in the act, didn't you? Clever girl!" Adiana seized Ghemena and tickled her without mercy. "Now you know not to listen to my promises. And it's a good lesson that one, *never* believe a promise."

Squealing, the girl wriggled out of Adiana's grasp and darted around the table, taking shelter beside Eolyn. Her small body heaved with breathless laughter as the maga pulled her close.

"I want to go with you to the South Woods," she said, wrapping her arms around Eolyn's waist.

Eolyn's heart wavered, overtaken by a sudden nostalgia, the intense joy of companionship intermingled with the haunting sense that everything she most loved in life was constantly slipping away.

"You will." She looked at all of them as she spoke. "When Mariel, Sirena, and I return, we will organize another trip for everyone. We will journey to the South Woods together, and we will dance with the trees under the light of the next full moon."

They cheered and clapped and set to work clearing the table.

Eolyn had expected three horses prepared for them, but much to her chagrin Sir Borten and Delric waited with five mounts. Delric was a new member of the guard, having stayed behind with a few others after the King's visit. Short and stocky, with a swarthy face and unkempt look, he gave Eolyn a curt nod before busying himself with the horses.

The maga turned to confront Borten, her tone sharp and final. "I told you we have no need of an escort."

Borten finished adjusting the girth strap, jaw set and gaze focused inward. "That is for me to decide, Maga Eolyn."

"We are only travelling to the South Woods. There is no place in this kingdom I know better, no terrain more secure for me and my students." Indeed, the South Woods was her last refuge from men-at-arms like these two, and Eolyn wished to keep it that way. "I need you to stay here with Renate, Adiana, and the children. You are sworn to protect this school, Sir Borten."

"My men are sworn to protect this school." He turned to face her, expression resolute. "I am sworn to protect you."

The challenge in his eyes gave Eolyn pause. Borten had dedicated three years of his life to this lonely outpost on the edge of the kingdom. During that time she had worked with him, argued with him, and yet never truly come to know him. He had family somewhere in Moehn, parents and siblings to the north if she remembered correctly. Years ago he had killed Akmael's father in a jousting accident, an error that would have cost him his life were it not for the last command of the old King, to see young knight pardoned. Akmael had honored this wish and restored Borten to knighthood in the first act of mercy of his reign. It was said Borten had fought valiantly in the Battle of Aerunden, and that he had saved Akmael's life. But Eolyn knew little else about him. For her, he had simply been an unwelcome burden forced upon her by the King. His vigilance was a constant thorn in her side, and she never let him forget it.

Perhaps just this once, she could allow him to fulfill his duty in peace.

"Very well," she decided. "You may accompany us, Sir Borten. I presume you and Delric have set aside additional supplies? Mariel, Sirena, and I packed food only for three. We can't have our protectors going hungry."

"We have what we need, Maga Eolyn." Borten's shoulders relaxed, and he gave her a satisfied nod. "Thank you."

They rode southeast along the Tarba River, fording its minor tributaries and making camp at night along the banks. The river was high and murky with recent rains, and in the morning the damp earth expired a thick haze that painted the landscape in muted shades of rose and gold. Reeds wavered in the changing currents, and silver blue herons watched them from partially hidden places along the river's edge, necks long and graceful, gaits slow and stately.

On their second day of travel, Eolyn took advantage of the herons' presence by shapeshifting Mariel and Sirena, so they might learn something of the waterfowls' magic. She followed barefoot along the grassy banks, quiet so as not to disturb the animals, yet never too far from the transformed girls.

The river's happy riffle renewed the ache in her heart, for it reminded her of the day she and Akmael first played as children in the headwaters of the Tarba, deep in the heart of the South Woods. They had searched its crystalline depths for the rainbow snail, and encountered other wonders instead. Her laughter rang high and carefree, his demeanor had been serious and attentive. It was strange how those days could be gone forever and yet so very present.

She wrapped her arms around herself and lifted her face to the breeze, inhaling the fresh aromas of silt, sedges and rotting leaves. On a low hill nearby the men waited with the horses, Delric scanning the landscape, Borten's gaze fixed upon Eolyn and her students, silent sentinels under the midday sun.

Late in the afternoon of the third day, the South Woods came into view, a dark smudge of tall oaks and giant pines looming over abandoned fields, thickets and loose stands of birch and alder. Mariel clapped her hands when she caught sight of it, and challenged Eolyn and Sirena to a race. The maga laughed and spurred her horse. Leaning forward, she connected her spirit with the animal, bringing hooves into synchrony with the pulse of the ancient forest. In a moment, she had left the girls behind. Wind tore the ribbons out of her hair, the smell of horse hide and summer sweat saturated her senses. The high branches reached toward her, and she closed her eyes, opening them just in time to see the forest whip around with its sudden embrace.

Eolyn reigned in her steed, breath coming in short gasps, cheeks flushed and hair spun into wild curls.

Dense foliage and heavy trunks shut out the sun, erasing all traces of the world left behind. The maga dismounted and inhaled the rich aroma of pine, loam and summer herbs. She knelt to caress the leaves and the stems of young shrubs. The whisper of a mighty black oak brought her back to her feet. Approaching the ancient tree, Eolyn spread her palms upon its coarse bark and pressed her body against the solid pillar of its trunk. Directing her senses toward the river of life within, she wove tendrils of her spirit around its constant current, drawn from the depths of the earth and delivered in invisible clouds to the sky, pulling trunk and branches taut between two worlds.

"It's me, dear friend," she murmured, content inside the quiet embrace. "I've come home at last."

The oak sighed and swayed. The tree's leathery leaves hissed in the mounting wind. Branches creaked and clattered against each other, shuddering with the incongruous voice of winter. Fingers of ice spread along the forest floor, trapping tender herbs in their adamantine grasp, winding around the oak like a slitherwort vine, crushing and twisting the trunk until with a long terrible groan, an immense fissure ran down its length and rent the ancient tree in two. The earth opened up beneath Eolyn, a yawning cavern of absolute night, dragging her toward nameless terror.

She cried out, released the tree and stumbled backwards into the light of day. A hand wrapped vise-like around her arm. Eolyn's quick spell sent a blue spark crackling into the assailant. He released her and found the tip of her sword at his throat.

Borten watched her like a hawk, his expression a strange mixture of surprise, concern, and approval.

Eolyn blinked and stepped away, lowering Kel'Baru and looking around her in confusion. Delric stood with a scowl on his face and knife in hand, his firm stance setting him like a wall between her and the girls, who—eyes wide with astonishment—remained mounted a short distance away.

The grove had returned to its original state, the black oak as solid and upright as ever. The summer sun filtered through the verdant canopy, spreading warmth across the forest floor. But the cold terror stayed with her, unnamable yet familiar, its aftertaste harsh and rancid.

She had felt this same fear before, during the Battle of Aerunden, when her brother had clashed swords with Akmael, and the wizard Tzeremond had banished her spirit into the Underworld.

Eolyn sheathed her sword, returned to the oak and placed an unsteady hand on its surface.

Borten came up next to her, his tone quiet and direct. "What happened?"

He rubbed the arm that had received the brunt of her curse, flexed it, and clenched his injured fist.

"I'm sorry." She took his wrist in one hand and ran her fingers from his shoulder down the length of the limb to restore circulation. "I didn't know it was you. The pain will pass shortly. It was a mild spell."

"Mild?"

His quizzical expression made her laugh. "Yes. This was nothing. You should have seen the curse I cast upon Tzeremond."

Eolyn realized her fingers still lingered upon his wrist. She released him, feeling oddly unsettled. For the first time since they had met, she was grateful to have him at her side.

"The trees have seen something they don't understand," she said, "something that has caused them great anxiety. Not this tree, but its cousins, living toward the north, I think . . . and the east. Word is traveling on the wind, but they have no way to describe it. It is like an echo of death and birth intertwined, something hideous and indefinable dragged from the bowels of the earth . . . I've never felt anything like it in this forest. All I could capture was hunger, and fury."

Borten scanned the dense stand of trees, hand ready upon the hilt of his sword. "This danger is nearby?"

"I don't think so."

"We should return to Moehn at once."

Her heart caved in at the words, though she knew he was right. Every instinct was urging her to make haste for the school, to ensure the girls' protection and send word to Akmael, even if she was not quite sure what she would tell him.

Eolyn looked over at Mariel and Sirena who had already dismounted and were moving through the underbrush like a happy pair of flame throated warblers. They gathered herbs and berries and searched the leaf litter for mushrooms, their chatter interweaving with the vivid life of the South Woods.

"There is a spring nearby where we can camp for the night," she said.

"We should not linger."

"We have an hour, two at most, before sunset. If we leave now, we would be forced to camp on open fields. Quite frankly, Sir Borten, I feel safer here. I know this may contradict your thinking, but the tighter the cloak of the forest, the greater my power. We can depart before dawn, and travel as far and fast as daylight will allow tomorrow."

Borten studied her in silence. She had learned to recognize that particular flicker behind his eyes, when his thoughts began to gather in preparation for their next argument.

"The trees here were not witnesses to the event they tried to show me," she hastened to add. "Whatever happened, it was far away from here. They have only shared what they heard. Indeed, with a little more time spent listening to them, I might be able to gather information that would be helpful, if whatever the forest saw is a true threat to us."

There was doubt on his countenance, but after a moment he nodded. "As you wish, Maga Eolyn."

Chapter 8

Mage Corey squinted as he scanned the sodden heath, a vast plain that stretched north and west toward uncharted lands. Pools of water reflected a lackluster sky. Shrubs and grasses grew in motley patches of sage and russet. The solitary keen of a mud kite rose off the bog then sank into desolation. Nearby, sheep grazed in a silence broken by the occasional dull clang of their bells.

"Curse it all," Corey muttered, and strode heavily down the short slope.

For days he had roamed this landscape like some mad hermit, chased by elusive dreams and meaningless visions to this abandoned corner of the kingdom. His path had taken him along the northern reaches of Moisehén, from the forests of Selen to the ruins of Berlingen, then across the foothills of the Eastern Surmaeg to Tor Binder, where he had received a tepid welcome from bored and indifferent guards—a matter he planned to bring to Sir Drostan's attention during his next visit to the City.

Binder was not meant as an outpost for common soldiers. It required mages of the highest order, men who could recognize the slightest breach between the world of the living and the world of the dead. Already Corey had a few names in mind, Sir Galison of the King's guard, along with a dozen of the new mage warriors if Akmael would see fit to spare them. Echior of Moehn, perhaps; not particularly experienced in High Magic, but keen of mind and sharp in perception. It might also be a useful opportunity to move Melthian off the Council. Melthian was well intentioned, but difficult at times, and Corey could offer many sound and flattering arguments as to why he would be the most appropriate man to oversee a renewed watch on the edge of the wilderness. This would solve several problems at once without provoking undue resentment.

The thought made Corey smile.

A restless hum invaded the mage's staff, and its malachite crystal droned like a hive of bees. Erratic bursts of magic were to be expected on the edge of these wastes, but Corey could not shake the sensation that something of great importance was eluding him. A shadow had trailed him these past days, clinging like smoke to the horizon. At night, it slipped into his dreams, billowed and coalesced into a faceless witch with ebony hair. At first, he had thought her to be his cousin Briana, Kedehen's Queen and Akmael's mother, the last witch of East Selen. Now, he suspected differently.

"Boy!" he called.

A sheep herder jumped and spun around as if he had not expected to see another human soul, though they had arrived here together not more than an hour ago.

"Show me what you told me about this morning," Corey said.

The lad nodded and whistled to his dog. The scruffy mutt padded at their heels as mage and youth hiked to the next rise, from which they could see a long line of granite monoliths. This was Ahmad-fuhraen, a centuries old barrier of magic that bordered the rim of the wastes, bridging the gap between the Eastern and Western Surmaeg, separating the world of the living from the realm of the dead. Corey's staff connected to the energy of the stones and crackled. The voice of his dreams returned unbidden, a sudden hiss upon the wind.

Corey, she whispered. *Friend.*

The mage shivered against the lure. He closed his eyes and invoked an ancient ward.

The phantom's grasp receded like an icy mist.

"That one, and that one." The boy's rough accent called Corey back to the waking world. "They weren't like that last week. Straight as an arrow, they were. Looking up at the heavens, just like my Pa says they should."

Corey frowned at the leaning pillars. It was not unreasonable for the ground to shift. The earth beneath the bog was treacherous, apt to swallow these monoliths whole as it was to allow them to waver and lean.

"Is it true what my Pa says?" The boy's boney fingers worked against his crooked staff. "Pa says there's a demon in the wastes, and the only thing that keeps him there is the stones. If the stones start moving, it means we have to run, and run far away, to Roenfyn, or

Galia, or maybe even to the Paramen Mountains, because it'll hunt us down and kill us sure as wolf can kill rabbits. That's what he says. But he's just a sheep herder, see? Like me. What do we know about demons? You're a mage, though, so I bet you know what all those rocks are for."

"There are no demons in these wastes." Corey's eyes followed the line of granite until it faded in the distance. "Nor have there ever been. The creatures of which your father speaks were flesh and blood, like us. Predators of the most vicious kind. This is where they left our world, a long time ago."

"Where'd they go?"

"They were banished to the realm of the dead, by the Mages and Magas of Old. When they sank into the bowels of the earth, they dragged the mountains down with them, dividing the Surmaeg into East and West, and leaving the wastes in their wake."

"Can they come back?"

"No." Corey responded without hesitation, though a knot of uncertainty had settled in his stomach. "The curse cast against them was irreversible."

"Then who put the stones there? What're they for?"

"My predecessors left them behind. As a remembrance, perhaps. Or a precaution."

A promise of sanctuary, meant to last a thousand years.

Mage Corey did not linger in the wastes. Leaving the sheepherder and his family with a gift of food and blessing, he turned back toward the King's City, enduring many days of dusty travel before reaching the western gates, fatigued and grateful for the journey's end. The guards recognized him at once, and without delay he was granted passage through the shadow of the great stone arch. He found their ready welcome oddly disappointing. Many times he had confronted death within these walls, walking on a knife's edge between conflicting and powerful interests. He had called the castle's highest towers and its deepest dungeons home. Now, even as he enjoyed brighter streets and fairer times, the mage missed the anticipation of games of wit against Tzeremond, the tension of an uncertain future, the freedom of his Circle, of living outside the rigid world of mages and royals.

Where were his beautiful dancers now, his temperamental musicians, his occasional lovers? The ragged crew of happy rebels that had made up Corey's Circle was scattered and lost, like so many leaves on an autumn wind. And the most valued member of them all, hidden away in the province of Moehn, like a dormouse in wintertime.

His horse's hooves clattered against cobblestones as Corey followed the winding streets. The well-remembered smells of the city assaulted his senses: sweat and urine, fresh meat and rotting vegetables, wet wool and stale manure, perfumed whores and bitter ale. Children scampered at his side, calling him by name and begging for sweets, which he granted to those who could answer his riddles or give him a rhyme.

Under the reign of Akmael's father Kedehen, the King's City had been a somber place of nervous whispers and restrained passions. But now, the Gods had breathed life into this town. Every passage was awash with merchants and craftsmen, artists and musicians, countrymen and foreigners engaged in a boisterous exchange of words and goods.

At last the alleys widened into proper avenues, indicating his arrival at the Mages' Quarter. Situated on the lower slopes of the mountain that housed the Fortress of Vortingen, this was a neighborhood of broad promenades adorned by graceful saplings and fragrant herbs. The stone buildings boasted tall windows and impressive archways attended by stiff-postured guards. The unpleasant smells of the lower quarters faded for the most part, and the scamper of street urchins was replaced by the unhurried pace of long-robed mages engaged in reflection or quiet conversation. Several looked up as Corey rode past, and recognizing him, nodded with respect.

The mage paused at the portal of the residence of High Mage Thelyn who, as befit a long standing member of the King's Council, occupied one of the more impressive buildings of the Quarter. Two stone effigies marked the entrance to his outer courtyard, one of a mage and the other, commissioned shortly after the prohibition was lifted, of a maga. Thelyn had been the first to welcome the return of women's magic to Moisehén with this gesture. Since then statues of Aithne had sprung up all over the City, often with fresh lilies and flickering candles at their feet. Mage Corey scowled as he passed between the twin images.

"Much good it does us," he muttered, and not for the first time, "to have only magas cast in stone."

Thelyn greeted him with a hearty embrace, a leather-bound tome cradled in one arm. The mage, tall and lean, had seen some sun since their last encounter. His dark beard marked a thin line along an angular jaw, and his keen black eyes sparked with curiosity.

"How good it is to see you," he said. "We had begun to wonder what kept you so long in East Selen."

"It proved a more arduous journey than expected," Corey replied, voice bright but aspect grim. "Arduous and lonely. A cup of wine would be most welcome now, as well as some conversation with an old friend."

Thelyn furrowed his brow but said nothing. He led Corey to a spacious receiving room that overlooked the city square, a place Corey knew well. Since the days of the Circle, Thelyn had protected it with a sound ward, which he invoked using a brief spell as they passed the threshold.

Tapestries and paintings covered the walls. Tables and shelves housed all manner of artifacts, a visible testimony to Thelyn's admiration of diverse and primitive arts. Corey passed one hand over the stone figure of some ancient god, and examined an uncut crystal of amethyst.

Years ago he had attended an event here with Eolyn. Those had been amusing nights, in the days before the great festival of Bel-Aethne, when she was no more than a peasant dancer with an elusive past and a disquieting gift. He had introduced her as his consort, and on occasion had secretly wished it so. But Rishona's charming if vacuous brother had distracted her first, and then the Mage King claimed her heart forever after—a turn of events that Corey would not have minded so much, if only Eolyn had demonstrated the wits to make use of the opportunity.

"What news of the maga?" Corey asked as Thelyn served wine.

"It is said she has two girls who will petition for staves next spring, and three more behind them."

"The King and Queen visited the new *Aekelahr*?"

"They spent nearly two weeks in Moehn, before being forced to return, due to the Queen's pregnancy."

Corey nearly choked on his wine. "She's with child? Again?"

"Have you not heard?" Thelyn set down his cup with a look of mild surprise. "The King's messengers should have reached you along the road to Selen."

"I did not come by direct route from Selen. I made a pilgrimage to the Wastes of Faernvorn, traveling from Berlingen across the iron range to Tor Binder."

"Tor Binder?" The mage raised his brow in astonishment. "What in the name of the Gods took you there?"

"A whim." Corey shrugged. "So the Queen is with child. I suppose this is the moment I am obliged to say, 'May the Gods grant her a son.'"

"May the Gods make it so."

"And what of her lady, the sweet and ever-gracious Sonia?"

"There is little to tell. She insulted Maga Eolyn once in the King's presence. Other than that, she's been extraordinarily quiet, reluctant to cause any further stir with her words."

"Is that so?" Corey had no love for the lady of Roenfyn, not so much because of her open disdain for magic, but because of the taut thread of fury he sensed buried deep inside her soul. He knew not from whence the rage came, but it worried him, just as her silence worried him, more than her words. "You have found nothing else?"

"I have set our best mages to studying her aura, but it is as clean as new fallen snow. If she uses a ward, it is the finest yet crafted. Not a seam to be found."

"Perhaps we were wrong about her, then."

"Perhaps," conceded Thelyn. "Whatever the truth, she despises us and has far too much influence on the Queen. We must continue to treat her with caution."

The wine tasted sweet upon Corey's tongue, though it soured in his stomach.

"What little power of East Selen was preserved through the sacrifice of my cousin Briana will be lost because of this queen," he said. "Taesara's people repudiate magic, and she carries nothing of the Spirit of the Forest in her blood."

"There are those who say this is a good thing," Thelyn replied, "that magic has no place in the royal lineage, and that the King made a wise choice for the future of our people."

"Good for Moisehén, perhaps. Not for East Selen."

"East Selen is not the King's concern. You could always sire an heir of your own, you know."

There was a bitter edge to Corey's chuckle. "I might have by now, if the woman of my choosing had received me. As the case is, she's occupied her heart with less worthy men, and I have yet to find another to whom I would entrust the burden of my Clan's future."

"Ah." The mage set his wine aside, leveled a questioning gaze at Corey. "And this woman is…?"

"None of your concern, my friend, and in the end, a story not worth telling. That path was lost to me before she and I even met. Let us return to the topic of Maga Eolyn. Any sign of her coming out of the hole she dug for herself in that wretched province of peasants?"

"No."

"She wastes her talents in Moehn. We should bring her back to the City."

"So you have said, many times. It is rumored the King agrees, and has requested she return."

"Requested or demanded?"

Thelyn lifted his hands in a gesture of appeasement.

"He is too lax with her," said Corey. "She was spared after her brother's rebellion in order for her magic to serve this kingdom. She belongs in the City, so that the memory of the Old Orders can be kept alive with more than useless stone effigies."

"By all reports, she has been very successful, earning the respect of the province, and recruiting excellent students."

"She has but five girls in Moehn. She would have twenty here, and all of them under our watchful eyes."

An amused frown crossed Thelyn's face. "Old Tzeremond has been visiting your dreams of late, hasn't he? I daresay I hear his thoughts slipping into your words."

"Even his approach would be more astute than this utter lack of oversight. The King does not understand the maga's worth, much less how to make use of her power. If we do not secure Eolyn's place among us, as an integral part of this Order, the decision to allow women's magic to return to Moisehen will end in disaster."

"It was you who argued—passionately, as I remember—for the lifting of the prohibition after Ernan's defeat."

"The intention was to cultivate the flame of women's magic, not to let it languish in neglect, or burn out of control. However I look at this situation, it does not bode well. Eolyn and her paltry collection of students will either finish the slow death of the Magas on the high plains of Moehn, or they will gather strength in an environment of unprecedented freedom. And we all know what happened the last time the magas had that kind of power."

Thelyn refreshed their wine, dark eyes narrowed in doubt. "How did the Wastes of Faernvorn inspire this renewed concern for vigilance of the magas?"

This was Thelyn's gift, at once indispensable and unsettling: to see past any debate to the heart of Corey's concerns. It was the price of a friendship that had lasted too many years.

Corey set aside his cup and stalked a few paces away, hands clasped behind his back. An old tapestry caught his eye, interwoven threads portraying a woman bound to a barren tree, her ashen face twisted in sadness, her thin white shift torn at the hip. A unicorn lay at her feet, sliced open from throat to belly, entrails floating in a river of blood that had faded to pale orange with the passing of time. The image ignited a burning in the pit of his stomach, followed by a sudden rise of bile that he forced down with a hard swallow. The foul taste lingered on his tongue.

"The stones of Faernvorn are moving."

Corey could sense the tension that took hold of his comrade. The air in the room thickened, Thelyn stepped close.

"Impossible," the mage said, but his tone was wary. "That barrier was bound for a thousand years."

"At least two of them lean north, toward the interior of the wastes."

"It does not matter." Thelyn laid a hand on Corey's shoulder. "Those creatures have no way of returning."

"We cannot be certain of that."

"Centuries have passed since the Naether Demons were banished. Even if they persist in the Underworld, their earth-bound bodies have been reclaimed by the wild lands, shredded by crows and scattered by wolves. The tethers are broken, their spirits have faded. They would not have the strength to come back."

"They would if someone were to assist them."

Several moments passed before Thelyn spoke again. "Who would do such a thing?"

"A maga, perhaps. A woman, most certainly. Someone of formidable powers, seeking vengeance, or conquest. Do not ask me how I know, for I could not tell you."

"You speak of the Maga Eolyn?"

"Eolyn is capable. She journeyed to the Underworld, and brought its magic back with her. I doubt, however, that she would turn her gifts to such purposes, though someone close to her might. Someone . . . inspired by her accomplishments."

Thelyn drew a slow breath. "And you believe that by bringing her here, we would be able to decipher this threat."

"Or draw out the culprit, perhaps. We could at least come to an understanding of any true danger." Corey returned to his wine. "It is, in any case, but one of many reasons to bring her to the City."

"You have a difficult argument ahead, my friend. I am inclined to trust your instinct, but the King—and his Council—may not be so easily convinced."

"The significance of Faernvorn might be lost upon them, but the Council bowed before Tzeremond's influence before, and many still favor his legacy of prudence. They will understand the need for vigilance, and will be most pleased to insist upon it."

"Their insistence will do little good if the King sees no need to rein her in. He has long favored the maga in ways that defy common sense."

"His affection for her occasionally clouds his judgment," Corey agreed, "yet that same desire can be turned to our advantage, depending on how we present our case. The Council can be motivated by concerns for stability, but other considerations will move the King to action, as surely as a wolf acts to defend his mate."

"Then we will bring our case before the Council, and bring the weight of the Council's opinion to bear upon the King. If everything is as you say, we could have the Maga Eolyn and her coven brought to the City in short order, perhaps even in time for Summer Solstice."

Corey smiled, as this was precisely his plan. "I knew I could count on you, old friend, to listen to reason."

Chapter 9

There was no darkness more comforting than night in the South Woods, no shade of ebony more absolute. Eolyn wrapped it around herself like a familiar cloak that evoked memories of her childhood with Doyenne Ghemena: smoke from the hearth and bread in the oven, soft woolen blankets and hardened dirt floors, insects buzzing through the garden in spring, and trees rattling in fall. In wintertime, Eolyn would huddle with Ghemena in front of the fire. The old maga's embrace had been much like this summer evening, affectionate and soothing, filled with aromas of age and wisdom.

Crickets chirped in the shadows. The open fire coughed, crackled and sent a sudden shower of sparks toward the sky. Mariel and Sirena sat close together, resting after their lessons in magic, sharing a melody of whispers and giggles about some youth they had seen during their last visit to Moehn. Watching them, Eolyn wondered whether Doyenne Ghemena had felt these same emotions as her ward approach womanhood, this mix of sweet joy and deep nostalgia that melted into sadness if she let it linger too long.

Eolyn stood and stepped away from the fire, one hand resting idly on the smooth hilt of Kel'Baru. As she wandered between the trees, her thoughts lingered behind like an afternoon shadow. Next spring, her two eldest students would become women in magic. Like Eolyn had done, they would fast here in the South Woods, and petition for a staff. According to the traditions of the Old Orders, they would also be ready for the High Ceremony of Bel-Aethne, the consecration of *aen-lasati*, the awakening of passion and desire.

But the Old Orders had vanished, and with them the numbers that conferred anonymity upon the women undergoing initiation. Masks would be meaningless with only two girls, and in any case what mage could she trust to assist her with such a sacred event?

Corey of East Selen came to mind unbidden, and Eolyn stifled a laugh. No doubt he would undertake the project with great enthusiasm, but as well as Eolyn knew the mage, she did not trust him. Nor could she, after the manner in which he had betrayed her brother.

She paused at the edge of another circle of light, realizing she had walked toward Borten and Delric's fire, set several paces from her own. The knight stood, his gaze shooting past her shoulder into the gloom of the forest, then settling again upon her face.

"Maga Eolyn," he said. "Is something amiss?"

"No." She looked from him to Delric, who paused in the middle of tearing a bite off a piece of dried meat. "Nothing is wrong at all, Sir Borten. It's just… Well, the girls are caught up in their own conversation, and I thought I might sit at your fire, yours and Delric's, if you would have me."

Delric shrugged and continued gnawing on his meal. Sir Borten studied her with a puzzled frown. The awkward silence left Eolyn nonplussed. She stepped away, uneasy. "I'm sorry, Sir Borten. I did not mean to disturb your evening. If you'll excuse me—"

"No." He jumped as if waking from a trance. "Please, Maga Eolyn, join us. Forgive my rudeness. I simply wasn't expecting…"

His words drifted into renewed silence. A smile rose from the depths of Eolyn's spirit and spread warm across her lips. "You weren't expecting me to appear unless there was a problem."

Borten laughed, a short deep bark that ended with an expression of respect. He gestured toward a log by the fire, and took a seat next to her. Eolyn could not help but notice his musk, heavy after the long day, impregnated with traces of loam and freshly crushed leaves. He smelled like the forests and hills of Moehn.

Borten picked up a long branch and stoked the fire. Delric finished his meat and took a swig from his wine. He wiped his sleeve across a dripping beard and proffered the skin to Eolyn. She accepted with gratitude.

"I was thinking, Sir Borten." She took a mouthful of the bittersweet liquid. "Seeing as you are teaching me how to handle the sword and all, perhaps I could return the favor. I would like to teach you some magic."

Delric guffawed and stood abruptly. He stretched his arms then set one hand on the hilt of his sword, searching the shadows with narrowed eyes. "Guess I'll be taking the first watch, then."

He spat before tramping into the bush, where he cursed over some errant root that tripped him on his way.

"Have I offended him somehow?" Eolyn asked, watching him go.

"No, not in the least, Maga Eolyn."

"He hasn't directed a word to me since we left the school."

"Delric prefers to listen rather than speak. None of my men have keener ears. That is why I had him accompany us."

"I see." She set down the wineskin, folded her hands in her lap, and returned her gaze to Borten. "What do you say to my proposal, then?"

A smile touched his lips. "I am grateful for your generous offer, Maga Eolyn. But I would think I'm too old to become a mage."

Eolyn laughed. "I was too much of a girl once, to learn magic. And Kedehen too much of a prince. It is up to the Gods to decide who is too much of one thing, or another, to receive their gifts. I, for one, believe Dragon intends for you to learn magic. Otherwise, why would the Gods have compelled the King to appoint you to my *Aekelahr*, here in Moehn?"

Borten's expression became obscure. "Perhaps the Gods intend for men to repay their debts."

"Debts?" The response took her by surprise. "What debts?"

Borten did not reply, but clenched his jaw and directed his gaze toward the flickering flames.

"Your debt to the King? For the accident at Eostar in which his father perished?"

Still he did not speak, and Eolyn understood she was venturing into forbidden territory.

"Well, no matter." She brightened her voice, turning away from the wall of silence. "Let's just say, then, that learning magic will be part of repaying your debts. Do you have a cup, Sir Borten? Any small vessel will do, with some water."

He nodded as if relieved to have a task to distract him from his thoughts, and produced a simple wooden mug from his pack. Eolyn withdrew some fresh mint from her belt, set it in the water, and returned the cup to him.

"I'm going to show you the first trick Doyenne Ghemena taught me. We will make a cup of tea." There was a spirit in her voice that she had not felt in a long time, as if she were young again and playing without a care under the golden green canopy of this great forest. "You must hold the cup with both hands and stand, pressing your feet firmly against the earth, as if—" She searched for a metaphor he might understand. "As if you are about to go into battle, with all your senses open to the space around you, and all your spirit focused on the task at hand."

Borten rose, and for the first time Eolyn noticed just how tall he was. She stepped behind him and placed her hands against his back, fingers spreading over his linen tunic. His shoulders tensed.

"Close your eyes," she said, "and breathe."

She sensed the expansion of his lungs beneath her palms.

"What do you feel at your feet, Sir Borten?"

"The ground."

"Yes, the earth. And inside the earth? What do you feel there?"

"The foundation of my strength."

Not what one of her girls might have said, but the words rang true.

"Now take another breath and tell me," she continued, "what do you feel in the air?"

Again, that wonderful expansion beneath the strong muscles of his back. For a moment she was reminded of Akmael.

"The air is an anchor to life, to this world, to the people I . . . to the people I love."

Eolyn closed her eyes, moved by how well he understood the exercise, how readily he was molding the magic with his own spirit. "Now, the water in your cup, Sir Borten. Tell me about it."

"It is calm. A small reservoir of great power."

Eolyn's hands moved to his shoulders. She pressed her ear to his back and listened to the deep steady rhythm of his core. "And your heart, Sir Borten? What do you feel in your heart?"

"A flame." His voice was subdued, and with it all the sounds of the night faded. "An unending fire."

The energy of the forest pulsed at their feet, poised to respond to his bidding. "There is your magic, Sir Borten. Now here is what you must do. Bring together all the elements you just told me about, the earth beneath you, the air in your lungs, the water in your cup, and the fire in your heart. Imagine all of it coming together into a single brilliant point of light, and when you see that light, repeat these words: *Ehekahtu naeom tzefur. Ehukae.*"

The night thickened with his effort. After a moment, magic coursed up from the ground through his legs, filling his torso, wrapping around his heart. The strength of the vortex pulled a second current from Eolyn, and her magic tingled as it passed from her hands into his back. He drew a steady breath and exhaled the verse.

Eolyn withdrew.

Borten turned to face her. Steam rose from the water. His expression was incredulous, jubilant.

Eolyn clapped her hands in joy. "You see, Sir Borten? It is not so difficult after—"

Agonized screams ripped through her words. With a frightened cry, Eolyn took off toward the girls. She burst into the adjacent clearing and stopped short at the sight of a beast that swayed on long glowing limbs, a set of gaping pits where the eyes and mouth should have been. In one ebony-clawed hand it held Sirena, her chest torn open from throat to sternum, the shredded bodice black with blood.

Eolyn's vision blurred. Her heart imploded. She clutched at her ribs, breath reduced to ragged gasps, knees buckling beneath her. Borten caught one arm and hauled her to her feet. Their eyes met.

All your senses open.

The knight released her and approached the monster with sword drawn.

Eolyn forced back the grief that had scattered her thoughts.

All your spirit focused on the task at hand.

Mariel crouched in the shadows, clutching Eolyn's staff. Tears streamed down the girl's face. Her shoulders shook like leaves on the wind.

"Mariel." Eolyn's voice was calm. "Set down my staff and climb the beech behind you, as quick and high as you can."

"But Maga Eolyn—"

"Do as I say. If this goes badly, you are not to come down until dawn."

With a sob the young maga fled up the tree. Eolyn called the staff to her. The water crystal ignited, casting an ivory light over the dwindling fire, illuminating the creature in full. The beast groaned, a needy howl born of insatiable hunger.

Eolyn stepped forward, coming around to Borten's left.

"Stay behind me," he ordered.

"Your sword may not be enough," she replied.

Delric crashed out of the woods with a warrior's cry. Borten sprang forward and they attacked as one, blades flashing in the silvery light. The creature reared up on its hind legs and caught Delric in its clawed arms, ripping the stocky man's throat open and tossing him aside.

Borten stumbled back, fear and confusion on his face.

"The swords," he gasped. "The swords do nothing."

With horror Eolyn realized truth of his words. Their blades had left no mark, though they had cut through its flesh many times.

The animal lifted its flattened face toward the sky, letting go a hollow scream. It charged Borten, who scrambled backwards, reduced to dodging blow after blow.

Ehekaht, faeom dumae!

Energy exploded from Eolyn's staff. The creature stumbled away from the knight, shaking its bald head, striking at the empty air.

Naeom aenre!

Fire burst from her palm and consumed the animal in red flame. It fell to its knees, emitting an ear-piercing, torturous scream. The pressure upon Eolyn's ears became intolerable. Her breath failed her. The magic slipped from her control. The flames dried up, and the creature struggled to its feet unscathed, its jade skin as luminous as ever.

The ebony maw worked in a slow and rhythmic fashion. The charcoal eyes closed then opened again before turning toward her. Its deep haunting moan sent a shudder through the maga.

Dropping on all fours, it approached.

"No!" Borten sprang upon it, useless sword in hand. The creature knocked him into the trunk of a nearby tree with an audible crack. His body fell limp to the ground.

Eolyn was paralyzed with terror. She could not move, she could not think as the animal drew close. The staff slipped from her fingers. The crystal light was extinguished. Darkness veiled the forest. The beast's terrible purr droned in her ears.

Eolyn.

That was her father's voice, she thought, or her brother's, calling across the wastes of the dead, anticipating her return to their embrace.

Eolyn!

She blinked, and understood. In an instant Kel'Baru was released from its sheath. The metal rang as she swung. Kel'Baru sliced into the creature's torso. Viscous flesh parted then recoiled from the weapon.

Finish it.

Kel'Baru's voice was infused with Akmael's, the boy who tried to teach her how to fight, how to kill. Both hands firm upon the hilt, Eolyn dragged the Galian sword through the creature's stomach, releasing a foul river of inky blood.

The animal cried out and fell, clutching at the wound.

Never leave an opponent half dead.

She bore down upon the beast and struck again, and again, driving the blade into its chest, cleaving the shoulder, hacking off its head, severing its limbs, reducing the corpse to as many pieces as she could, until Borten appeared at her side, called her name, and wrenched her away.

Eolyn let go a terrible wail, like the fierce howl of a deranged wolf, and flung Kel'Barú deep into the forest.

Borten caught her and wrapped his arms tight around her even as she beat her fists against his chest. He urged her to be still, kissing her forehead between hushed words of comfort, waiting with fortitude until her rage gave way to inconsolable sobs.

Chapter 10

Charging out of the shadowy woods, Akmael leapt upon his enemy. He trapped the assailant with his bare hands and rent the monster limb from limb. The beast howled and flailed until at last it went limp, melting into linen sheets that remained clutched in Akmael's fists. The trees of the forest flattened into long stone walls. Sounds of a peaceful summer night floated through open shutters. The aroma of fresh cut rushes filled the air.

Disconcerted, the King searched his dimly lit room, the terrible vision clinging to his awareness. For months now these dreams had plagued him, each more vivid than the last: of violent creatures breaking through the earth, murderous fires sweeping down from the sky, the woman he loved trapped inside the chaos and covered with her own blood.

He had told no one, for it seemed a kind of madness, an unpredictable and sinister form of magic that had no place in the traditions of his people.

The change of the guard sounded from the west tower; a clattering of hooves floated up from the stables. The birds lifted their voices in the first tentative songs of the day.

Akmael drew a cloak about his shoulders and strode across the room, seeking a view of the southern hills. He half expected to find the landscape cast in darkness, but torches dotted the battlements of his fortress, and lamps flickered in the city below. A pale gray light was just beginning to creep into the sky, extinguishing the stars in preparation for the sun's arrival. The plains extending south were lost in gloom, bisected by a glistening obsidian river, the Furma. In the distance, the ridge of Moehn was no more than a charcoal smudge on the horizon.

"Eolyn," he whispered, as if she might hear and respond.

The bitter taste of her death, still fresh from the dream, lingered upon his tongue.

His fingers drifted absently to his throat, where the medallion of his mother once rested. He had entrusted the jewel of magic to Eolyn on the night of his wedding. In all the years since, she had never used it to find him.

Would she invoke its magic now, if death stood at her doorstep? Would the silver web respond swiftly enough to bear her to safety?

Akmael hit his fist against the wall.

He should have brought her back from Moehn. Eolyn was too important—her magic too unique—to leave her alone and unprotected in that forsaken corner of the kingdom. Even his Council understood this, and now they clamored for her return.

The only person who did not want Eolyn inside the walls of this city was Eolyn.

The torches of his chambers flickered to life, ignited by a wave of his hand. The presence of the dream faded, though it did not disappear. Drawing a decisive breath, Akmael refreshed his face with water from the basin before calling the servants and asking his steward to summon Sir Drostan.

A short time later, the King found the knight waiting as instructed, at a small wooden door on the northern flank of the castle, a portion of the fortress that dated back to the time of the warrior chief Vortingen. Akmael bade Drostan to follow while his other guards remained behind. The wall was thick, and the passage narrow. The King could feel the slow pulse of ancient stone beneath his palm, its resonance tied intimately to the heart of the mountain.

They emerged from the cool passage onto a grassy knoll that ended at some fifty paces in the sudden descent of sharp cliffs. Scattered trees twisted by time and exposure guarded the precipice. Monoliths stood in a wide circle, at the center of which sat an outcrop of granite that bore in its natural contours a map of the four provinces. Akmael closed his eyes and laid his hands upon the stone slab. This was the Foundation of Vortingen, where Dragon first appeared to the ancient warrior chief and charged him with founding a line of kings. The spirit of Messenger still lived in this stone, his fiery breath caught inside the rose-colored mountains and valleys, his silver-black scales scattered in glittering fragments across its face.

There was no site more sacred to Akmael's family, no sanctuary that allowed him to hear with greater clarity the wisdom of his fathers. Kedehen and Briana had consecrated their bond of marriage in this place, and Akmael would have done the same had his bride been a woman of magic, a High Maga worthy of the Mage King.

"What do you make of Mage Corey's tale of Faernvorn?" Akmael opened his eyes and set his gaze upon Sir Drostan.

The warrior's brow furrowed. "Mage Corey has told us the truth regarding what he saw, though I believe he has not told us everything he knows about the matter."

"This would not be the first time my cousin from East Selen has kept secrets."

"His concern about the lack of vigilance at Tor Binder is genuine, and well founded. It is a post that has been ignored for too many generations."

"Perhaps." Akmael remembered the monsters of his dreams, glowing creatures with long limbs and gaping eyes. He wondered how Drostan would respond if he were to speak of them. In the tradition of Caradoc and Caedmon, only fools and charlatans gave credence to the uncertain paths of divination. The future lay not in ambiguous visions of the night, but in thought and desire transformed step by deliberate step into action. "How likely do you think it is those beasts will return?"

"Not very. The annals surviving from that time are clear. The curse of Ahmad-dur is irreversible."

"Ahmad-dur was cast upon the Maga Eolyn," Akmael reminded him, "and she returned."

"You brought her back from the Underworld, my Lord King," Drostan acknowledged with a respectful nod, "but not without extraordinary magic, and at great risk to your own person. Moreover, she was not asleep for long, and Tzeremond's power was greatly compromised in the moment he tried to banish her."

Akmael nodded. "Nonetheless, you prefer not to leave the wastes unguarded."

"It is best not to take our safety for granted, lest the Gods decide to punish our complacency."

Complacency. The word sank to Akmael's core and lodged there like a heavy stone. That was what he had been. Complacent.

"And the magas, Sir Drostan? What do you think of the Council's recommendation regarding their *Aekelahr*?"

"Maga Eolyn and all her coven should return to the City as soon as possible."

Akmael let go a quiet breath of satisfaction. The knight's judgment was never compromised by sentiment.

"Although," Drostan added, "not for the reasons put forward by the Council."

"What reason, then?"

The knight hesitated.

"Speak freely, Drostan. There are none to hear us here, and I require your wisdom in this matter."

"There is no 'lingering threat' to be found in the work of Maga Eolyn. No desire on her part—or the part of her students—to return to the conflicts of the past. The concerns of the Council in this respect are unfounded."

"I quite agree. Yet you also insist they return to the City?"

"The Gods intended men and women to walk the path of magic together. That is how our heritage began, and that is how it must continue. All the great victories of our past—the discoveries of Aithne and Caradoc, the defeat of the Thunder People, the banishment of the Naether Demons—depended on the integration of male and female magic. If we wish to restore that legacy, we must keep Maga Eolyn and her students with us, here." He paused, eyes shifting away for a moment before adding quietly. "The Mage King Kedehen understood this, in his own way, when he spared and wedded Briana."

Akmael studied Drostan for a long moment, but the knight did not meet his eyes. This was the first time he had ever compared Akmael to his father and found the younger King wanting. "As you may recall, Drostan, I did offer Maga Eolyn the crown. It was she who refused."

"Forgive me, my Lord King. I did not mean to imply—"

"What would you have me do, imprison her as my father imprisoned Briana?"

"No, my Lord King." His words came with haste. "You acted well in this, as you have in all things since the day the Gods made you King. I merely meant to say that I find it regrettable that Maga Eolyn did not see the wisdom in your intentions."

"I see. I, too, find it regrettable Sir Drostan, but she made her choice, and now we must chart a new path accordingly."

"As you say, my Lord King. What would you have me do?"

"Send a messenger out today." Eolyn would not be pleased when he plucked her from the wild lands of Moehn, but her desires were subordinate to the interests of the kingdom and the needs of the Crown. Sooner or later she would learn to accept that. "Maga Eolyn is to ready her students and her person for immediate transfer to the City. Send her escort tomorrow at dawn, twenty men . . . no, thirty. The best we have. You are to lead them, Drostan. I want the magas safely delivered to Moisehén by Summer Solstice."

"As you wish. And the men posted at the school?"

"Half a dozen soldiers of Borten's choosing are to remain with him in Moehn, under his command. They are charged with maintaining and protecting the grounds until they receive further instructions from me."

"I will see it done, my Lord King." With a respectful bow, the knight took his leave.

Akmael lingered a few moments, ran one hand through his thick black hair. A weight had slipped from his shoulders. His heart was less troubled now that the choice was made. Soon Eolyn would return to his world, resentful perhaps, but Akmael loved the maga even in her anger. With time she would understand the wisdom of this decision and find comfort in the renewal of their love. He would, of course, permit her to return to the South Woods as often as the seasons allowed. Perhaps they could travel there together.

The eastern horizon had grown brighter. Overhead, salmon colored clouds heralded the arrival of the waking sun. Mindful of the hour, Akmael departed the Foundation and began the long walk across multiple courtyards, up twisting stairs and through winding corridors, until he arrived at the Queen's apartments, where Taesara was expecting him for their morning meal.

The young Queen greeted her King with an ebullient smile and deep curtsy. Pale blue silks complemented her figure; her golden hair was neatly plaited beneath a chiffon veil. She took his hand in hers and led him to a table spread with bread, meats, fruit and wine. Shooing her ladies away, she insisted on serving him herself.

"It is good of you to come, my Lord King," she said, taking her seat across from him.

"You look well, Taesara." Akmael spoke the truth. The Queen had recovered quickly, once delivered to the comforts of the City and the care of High Mage Rezlyn,

"Thank you." She blushed and lowered her gaze, then looked up again, eyes bright with excitement. "I have heard the most wonderful news, my Lord King. Is it true that my father has appointed my uncle Lord Penamor as the new ambassador to Moisehén? I understand he is expected to arrive in the coming days."

Akmael nodded, tore at his bread and drank from his cup. "That is the word we have from Roenfyn."

"He will be most well received here, I am certain. He is a good man, careful in his judgments, noble of heart."

"It pleases me that you are pleased."

She beamed at this, and picked at her fruit. They ate for a while in silence. Taesara's quarters were always perfectly kept, brightly illuminated with fresh flowers on every available table. She herself was the rose of his court, with her lithe figure, pink lips and glowing complexion. Not for the first time Akmael wondered why her beauty had failed to ignite his passion.

Seeming to sense his attention, she glanced up. Her lips parted in a needy smile, a sweet child-like expression that should have charmed him, but he had tired of it long ago.

"Rezlyn says the baby is in the best of health." One of her hands settled upon her belly. She reached across the table and sought his fingers, gripping them tight as she confided with great excitement, "It will be a son, my Lord King. I am certain of it."

Akmael nodded and withdrew his hand, thoughts occupied by another woman with auburn hair and earth brown eyes, a maga of extraordinary power who might yet give him a true Prince of Vortingen.

"May the Gods make it so," he said.

Chapter 11

"I speak in earnest, Renate." Adiana's words were slurred by drink. "Borten would be an excellent suitor for her. He's good man, a considerate lover—"

Wine escaped Renate's lips in a sputtering laugh. "How would you know Borten's a considerate lover?"

Adiana shrugged. "I can see it in his face."

Renate let go a high pitched cackle and shook her head. "See it in his face? I'll wager you've seen more than his face. You've been restless as a lynx in heat since Eostar."

Adiana gave a mock cry of protest and struck Renate playfully on the shoulder. "How dare you! One does not have to be a maga to see into the hearts of men. I learned a few things working the taverns in Selkynsen, you know. I can read a man as surely as Eolyn reads her books."

"As surely as Eolyn reads her books in *bed*," Renate replied in crisp tones.

Adiana flopped back on the blanket with an indignant harrumph. They had settled in the courtyard for an evening of wine and companionship, after having tucked the girls into bed. Days had passed since Eolyn departed for the South Woods, and the week would likely see its end before she returned.

"And you accuse me of inventing stories and gossip!" Adiana complained. "Even if I had 'read Borten in bed', what would it matter? The magas always had untamed teachings with respect to that sort of thing. Isn't *aen-lasati* the source of a woman's greatest magic? I swear to the Gods, Renate, sometimes you seem too much of a prude to be a maga."

A prude. Renate rolled the word over her tongue as she swirled the wine in her cup. Yes, that's what she was. Tight inside, dry as autumn leaves underfoot. Forever bound by the failures and disillusions of her past. "The Magas of the Old Orders were disciplined women, not harlots at a summer festival. To lay claim to their understanding of *aen-lasati* while ignoring all their other teachings does their memory a disservice. It's precisely that sort of myth that led us to the pyres in the first place."

"Oh, Renate." Adiana groaned, sat up, and reached for the wine skin. "Why must you take everything so seriously? It's finished, remember? The war, the purges, the rebellion, the prohibition. We're free now. The magas have been restored to their rightful place in Moisehén. We've got a proper *Aekelahr*, aspiring young magas, the protection of the Mage King, and a nice little regiment of handsome guards. Even you could have some fun, you know."

The thought of her tired old body wrapped around one of the King's men made Renate giggle until the giddiness shook her ribs and broke upon her lips.

"That's the spirit!" said Adiana. "Here, have some more wine. And tell me, which one of the guards do you like the most?"

"Oh, for the love of the Gods, Adiana!" Renate was laughing uncontrollably now, tears streaming down her cheeks. "I am an old woman."

"Age is meaningless for a true maga. That's what Eolyn says." Adiana rested her head on Renate's shoulder.

The older woman returned her warm embrace, inhaling the sweet smells of night mingled with Adiana's vibrant aroma, of primrose and summer winds, of the riverside city that had once been her home. She envied her friend in that moment, not so much for her youth and beauty, but for her continued faith in the possibility that anything could be *finished*. Someday time and experience would break that faith. Desire and loss, terror and death, treachery and abandonment, all of it stayed with a person until the end of her days, animating the shadows at night, invading dreams, stealing away tranquility in the lonely hours before dawn.

Adiana sighed and lifted her cup to the sky. "I love this moment, when the wine makes the stars shine brighter than ever. Gods bless the vineyards of Selkynsen! Look at the fir, Renate. See how it dances in the torch light?"

Was the young tree dancing, Renate wondered, or trembling with the knowledge of some hardship yet to come?

"This is but a momentary truce with the Gods," the maga murmured into her cup. "Three years they have left us in peace; it cannot last much longer."

"Hah! There you go again." Adiana took Renate's hand in hers. "What's wrong, Renate? Are you having bad dreams?"

Renate bit her lip and looked away, took another sip from her cup. "Last night I was in the wastes of the dead. The Magas came after me with clawed hands and hateful screams."

"Gods, that's awful!" Adiana withdrew from their embrace and studied Renate in the dark. "You burden yourself with far too much guilt, dear friend. It wasn't your fault what happened."

"It was my fault, Adiana." There was no sadness in her voice, no regret, only the cold acknowledgment of truth. "I could blame my youth or my fear and innocence. I could say circumstances went beyond my control, but I would only be hiding inside my own myth. I made my choices. I understood their consequences, and many of my sisters burned because of it."

Adiana sent a slow whistle through her teeth. "You've never said it quite like that before."

Renate shrugged and stared absently into the darkness.

"Does Eolyn know you feel that way?"

"She thinks the Gods have a different way of judging our transgressions, that they interpret our acts across a grander expanse of time and consequence." Renate shivered as the memory of Eolyn's words echoed inside her head. "She believes I survived then in order to serve a greater purpose now."

"Well, she's right, isn't she? You're here after all, helping to rebuild the legacy of the Magas. I bet all your dead sisters are happy about that."

Renate frowned. How to explain to Adiana that this would not be enough? Dragon was waiting to exact a greater payment, a harsher sacrifice. The old maga had left everything behind and followed Eolyn to Moehn in anticipation of this.

"Do you know what I dream about, Renate?" Adiana's voice became bright again, washing the away the shadows of doom, as was her gift. "The Circle. Now those are good dreams, about singing with Rishona, making music with Nathan and Kahlil after the show. I miss those times, all our friends from those far-flung kingdoms, travelling from one end of Moisehén to the other."

Renate gave a short mocking laugh. "Corey had us on a knife's edge with that show of his. Not a day passed when I didn't think the next magistrate would throw us all on the pyre."

"But we laughed about it didn't we? And we created like happy fools. So much defiance in our art! So much beauty. Do you think Corey will ever organize something like that again?"

"I don't know." Renate had cared deeply for Corey. She might have loved him once, had she not been such an old crone and he such a young fool. "He might. But I don't think it would be the same, if he did."

"No, I suppose not. I used to think Corey would be the perfect match for Eolyn."

"Corey and Eolyn?" Renate's tone was doubtful. "Adiana, you have many gifts, but matchmaking is not one of them."

"What would have been so wrong about that? He is a mage, and she is a maga."

"Corey is like a vine growing in the dark. Eolyn is a flower open to the sun."

"Very well, so he turned out to be a treacherous bastard. But none of us saw that coming back then."

"I thought you could read a man like a book."

"I can tell if a man's a considerate lover. It's much harder picking out the treacherous bastards."

"Corey was not so bad." Renate swirled her cup and took another drink. "He only did what he thought he had to do."

"Well, she'll never trust him again, not after the way he betrayed her brother."

The sound of heavy footfalls distracted them from their conversation. One of the men approached, torch in hand.

"Maga Renate," he said, "Mistress Adiana. Sir Malrec requests that you meet him at the north wall at once."

Something in the man's tone extinguished the heat of the wine. Renate's bones creaked as she rose to her feet, and she gripped Adiana's hand for help. They fastened their cloaks and followed the soldier between the stone buildings, across the gardens. There were no voices to be heard, no soldiers engaged in idle conversation. Crickets and frogs filled the silence with their insistent song. The nervous whinny of horses drifted toward them from the stable. When they approached the half-built wall, their escort brought the torch low. Malrec greeted them in subdued tones and beckoned them to his side.

"There toward the north." He indicated with a nod.

Renate peered over the half-finished wall. In the distance she spotted a luminous mist that wavered, faded then flared again. A memory stirred inside her, nebulous in form, as if she had lived this moment before though she could not quite capture when.

"What is it?" she asked, not certain she wanted to hear the answer.

"Fire," he replied. "The fields around Moehn are burning. Or worse, the town itself."

Renate gripped Adiana's arm. "We must go to them. We'll need marigold, yellow carowort, and fire-of-aethne, among other herbs and ointments. Adiana, come with me to the herbarium. Malrec, see the horses are readied at once."

"No." The finality of his response caught Renate off guard.

"No?" she replied. "What do you mean, no?"

"I have readied the horses, but not to take you to Moehn. At least, not until we have some idea of what is happening there."

"Are you mad? We can see what is happening. Those people are suffering! As a maga, I am sworn to help them."

"As a Knight of Vortingen, I am sworn to protect you. You and the Mistress Adiana are not to depart until I give you leave to do so. I have sent a scout to assess the situation. We should have word from him within the hour."

"I will not sit here a prisoner in my own home while people's lives are in danger."

"The town may be under attack."

"Moehn under siege?" Renate threw up her hands in disbelief. "Oh, for Gods' sake. Who would attack Moehn? Some drunken imbecile kicked over a lantern, or a torch fell from its rusted sconce."

"We cannot be certain of that."

A shout from one of the men perched on the wall silenced them both. All eyes turned north once again. The nightwent still. The crickets stopped singing. Renate scanned the darkness, conscious of the unnatural silence. She could hear Malrec's breath, low and steady. A charge filled the air, as if lightning were poised to rip through the starry heavens.

"What is it?" she whispered. "What did they see?"

Malrec hushed her, raising one hand as he searched the obscure terrain. Once, a lifetime ago, Renate had been a High Maga, and she could change into an owl and see the night world with clarity. But she had long since abandoned those powers, and now the hills so familiar by daylight were amorphous, the distances impossible to judge.

Was that movement she saw along the nearby ridge? A lynx, perhaps, taking advantage of the moonless night to scurry across open fields. But then a flame ignited in its wake, followed by a discontinuous arc of light that spread point by point over the low hill, like a line of small torches. On sudden impulse, the string of flames rose high into the air, slowed against the ebony firmament, then fell toward the school in a hissing rain of fire.

Malrec took hold of Renate and crushed her against the wall, knocking the wind out of her as the arrows fell behind them, some embedding in the earth, others landing on nearby roofs and igniting the thatch in an instant.

"The children!" Adiana cried, and she tore away from the soldier who had shielded her, disappearing into the flickering shadows.

Renate moved to follow, but Malrec caught her by the arm and yanked her back.

"The horses are ready," he said. She had never seen his face so close, so vivid. The rounded cheeks, the rough curls of his beard, the fine spittle that rode on his rapid words. "Take them and head south. Do not look back, do not stop, until you reach the forest. Three of the men will accompany you. Go!"

He shoved her away. Renate's feet moved of their own volition, carrying her toward the girls' room even as a second volley of flames descended from the heavens. Behind her raged the shouts of desperate men, followed by the ring of metal upon metal, sudden cries of anguish. Already the assailants were topping the half-finished wall.

Her truce with the Gods had ended, suddenly and without warning as was their pleasure.

Adiana was ushering the girls out of their room, bleary eyed and confused with summer cloaks thrown over their nightshifts. The soldiers met them with five steeds. One of the men hauled Catarina up to ride with him, Adiana mounted with Tasha, and Ghemena was given to Renate. As they turned the horses toward the south gate, Renate caught site of Eolyn's study. The roof was ablaze with golden flames, bright as the sun come to earth.

"The annals," she cried in panic and spurred her horse toward the fire.

The animal whinnied and pulled back before they reached the building. Leaving the reins with Ghemena, Renate dropped to the ground. Ignoring the shock of pain in her legs, she raced to the study and burst through the door. Smoke lodged in her throat and stung her eyes. The room itself was not yet aflame, but the roof roared and burning ash fluttered on the air like black snow.

Renate blinked back tears. Was this what her sisters had seen, as the flames rose up around them? The world aglow with scalding heat, the cold realm of the dead their only promise of escape. Shaking the image from her mind, she spotted the books on the corner shelves. She threw her cloak down in front of them and piled all the volumes she could before tying the corners into a makeshift sack and dragging it back to the entrance. By the time she emerged from the study, every muscle in her body ached.

"For the love of the Gods, old woman!" One of the men scolded. "You kept us waiting for this?"

"The horses will never run with such a load on their backs," objected another.

"We cannot leave this behind! It is all that is left of our heritage." She looked from one man to another, and finding no sympathy in their faces, turned to her friend. "Adiana, please! Help me."

After a moment of hesitation, the young woman dismounted and removed her cloak. They divided the tomes between the two of them. Renate heaved her burden into Ghemena's arms and bade the child to hold it tight. Then she swung herself up behind the girl and spurred the horse into a canter. In moments they were through the south entrance and racing over open fields, hooves pounding against the earth. The horses snorted and drew labored breaths, straining under their loads. Renate leaned forward, molding her body to Ghemena's back, eyes focused on the black hills ahead.

"Help me, Ghemena. Speak to the horse." she urged as the girl's fine hair whipped in her face. "Tell it to run faster!"

"I am." The child's voice was desperate, panicked. "She's trying as hard as she can."

The horse to their right whinnied then reared. Metal clashed against metal, the taunts of men in battle overtook their flight. Attackers closed in on both sides, swords drawn and tipped with blue flames. One assailant met the guard ahead of them, his blade a glowing arc. The animal screamed; the guard was unhorsed.

Panicked, Renate reined in her own steed to avoid riding into the fray. To her left, Adiana and Tasha slipped toward the shadows at full gallop. Digging her heels into the flanks of her mount, Renate veered in the opposite direction, heading west away from the melee. Only when the cries and whinnies began to fade did Renate remember Catarina had been left behind. The girl was riding with one of the guards, and all three of the men were engaged with their pursuers. The realization sent a knife through her heart. Renate halted their flight and looked behind, uncertain whether to risk returning.

A rider appeared as if emerging from the portals of the Underworld, cloaked by shadows, carried upon an ominous melody of hooves and mail. His blow was blunt and brutal, tearing her off the horse. Pain shot through her ribs and shoulders as Renate hit the ground. She staggered to her feet, head spinning. Ghemena also toppled from her seat with a sharp cry, the books tumbling out of her embrace and scattering over the earth.

"Come, child!" Renate reached toward the girl, but the shadow of a horse stepped between them, tall and heavy, restless upon the earth. The rider's face was hidden by the night, his sword a shaft of cobalt flame. Before Renate could think to run, another man appeared behind her, chest to her back, knife at her throat.

"Let the child go." Her voice sounded weak, ineffectual. "I beg you."

If they heard, they gave no indication. Renate was shoved in the direction from which they came, and Ghemena dragged kicking and screaming after her. They were taken to a circle lit by torches, where Adiana stood ashen-faced with Catarina and Tasha clinging to her skirts. The King's knights were nowhere to be seen. Renate's throat was released from the bite of her captor's blade. She straightened her shoulders and walked with deliberate calm to Adiana's side. Ghemena was thrown at their feet with such force her enraged cries were silenced. Renate helped her up, wiped the tears of anger from the girl's cheeks and took tight hold of her hand.

Men-at-arms surrounded them—too many, it seemed to Renate, for raiding a school and capturing a handful of women and children. The colors they wore were indiscernible in the dark. Swords were drawn and trained upon them, bolts cocked at close range. The pungent scent of sulfur hung in the air, coupled with an odor of sweet spices that tugged at Renate's memory with disturbing familiarity. One of the men stepped forward. His long nose, straight brow and chiseled features reminded Renate of Tahmir, the Syrnte Prince who had worked with Corey's Circle and collaborated in Ernan's rebellion.

"Which one of you is the Maga Eolyn?"

Renate pursed her lips. Catarina and Tasha whimpered, wrapping their arms tighter around Adiana's waist.

"Which one is the maga? Speak now, or all will die."

A cold stillness settled in Renate's stomach, a deep awareness of the inevitable. She looked down at her hands and noticed how aged they had become, papery skin stretched over brittle bones and dark veins.

Ghemena broke away from her grip sprang forward. "She's not here, you fool! If she were, you'd all be turned into toads by now."

"Hold your tongue, child!" Renate scolded. "Or these men may well cut it out."

Ghemena drew a breath to respond, but upon seeing Renate's stony countenance she bit her lip and lowered her chin. The maga smoothed her skirt and drew a deep breath. She caught Adiana's gaze, noting the terror and uncertainty in the young woman's eyes, and gave her a reassuring smile.

Then she lifted her chin and announced, "I am the Maga Eolyn."

Adiana gasped. "What are you doing?"

Renate stepped forward, speaking quickly to prevent Adiana from exposing the deception. "I am the one you seek. This woman is my scullery maid, the girls her helpers. Let them go. They are worth nothing to you."

She was but a couple paces from the soldier now, and could see the harsh lines of his face, the mean intensity of his eyes. A satisfied smile touched his full lips. He gave her a nod of respect. "Maga Eolyn. The San'iloman will be pleased."

With that he drove his sword into her stomach, hard metal ripping through soft flesh, violating her entrails with the searing kiss of death. The metal point emerged from her back, releasing a hot river of blood. Renate doubled over. She heard the girls scream as if from the bottom of a well. A red mist hovered in front of her eyes and she struggled to recover her focus.

The man withdrew his weapon. After a moment, Renate regained her breath and pulled herself erect, facing him with fierce determination, fingers pressed against her abdomen and sticky with blood. Her torso was a mass of throbbing pain, but she understood the meaning of this moment and refused to cower in front of her assassin.

Again he ran her through.

"Stop!" cried Adiana. "Oh, for the love of the Gods, please stop!"

Renate stumbled back, inky stains spreading over her bodice as the sword released her once more. She clutched at her stomach with both hands, but the blood flowed in torrents now. Burdened by an unbearable weight, she sank to the ground, first on one knee, then on the other.

The night wavered around her.

Ghemena stood close by, fists clenched at her sides, watching her with unblinking eyes and set jaw.

"Child," she murmured. "Remember what I have taught you."

The sword plunged into her ribcage, snapping bone and cartilage, bursting open her heart. Renate slid away from the blade and crumpled to the ground. Shadows descended on the world of the living, warm and soothing in their embrace. At last the Gods had exacted their price. Her crimes were paid, her burden released. Renate surrendered to the abyss, hopeful the dead Magas would soon call her home.

Chapter 12

Adiana's nostrils flared at the smell of charred wood and floating ash, punctuated by the occasional stench of burnt flesh. Sounds of lament rose from hidden places, terrified wails and tortured sobs that made her wince and turn away. Moehn had always been a ramshackle town, but now it was little more than a disordered pile of stone and rubble. The wall had crumbled, entire buildings were destroyed. On the edge of the remains, there were shouts and movement, the flutter of starched canvas and the rhythmic fall of hammers upon stakes. The soldiers who had laid their claim were now setting up residence. They were Syrnte, all of them, yet Adiana could make no sense of their presence in this mountain-bound province.

Their captors stopped and began to dismount. Some of the men threw the children over their shoulders, hauling them off like sacks of grain. Tasha's and Catarina's screams were muffled, their small feet flailing in useless kicks. Ghemena, remarkably, did not resist, but lifted her face and watched Adiana with an intense gaze, her brow furrowed as if immersed in some difficult thought. Her lower lip protruded in that stubborn frown Adiana had so come to love, and as the shadows threatened to conceal her retreating figure, Adiana cried out and lurched after her.

The men stopped her, their steely grip sending fresh pain through her shoulder and ribs.

"Where are you taking them?" she demanded, struggling as best she could against their hold, for her hands were bound and her teeth could not cut through mail.

They shoved her in the opposite direction.

She was escorted to a broad pavilion surrounded by guards whose immobility contrasted sharply with the energetic activity of the camp. Inside the tent was filled with movement and conversation. Servants set out food, poured wine, carried water basins and even assembled furniture. At the center was a long table overlaid with maps under scrutiny by a group of men in armor. Upon Adiana's entrance, one of them fixed his gaze upon her. His blue eyes were set in a swarthy face, handsome though scarred and marked with the fine lines of age. Adiana shivered under his cold assessment, feeling like a fawn among a pack of wolves.

"Lord Mechnes," her captor saluted the blue-eyed man. "The maga's stronghold is destroyed. I bring you two women." He held up the blood-stained bundle that contained Renate's head. "This one claimed to be the Maga Eolyn, and said her companion was a scullery maid. Three children were with them and are now under guard. All the others are dead, just as you ordered."

"This is all you found?" The Syrnte commander's brow lifted. There was doubt in his voice.

"Yes, my Lord. I assure you no one could have escaped. We had the site surrounded well before the attack. All routes were cut off. They were taken completely by surprise."

Mechnes nodded. His eyes flicked toward the bundle in the soldier's hand. "Leave that here, and the woman. I will send for you shortly."

The soldier departed with a brief bow. Lord Mechnes turned back to his men. There was something deeply familiar about his stance, the set of his shoulders, the dark vigor of his presence. Adiana's breath caught in her throat when she realized what it was. Mechnes reminded her of Kedehen. She had seen the old King, Akmael's father, on a few occasions during the days of Corey's Circle, when they were invited to perform in the City. Kedehen's physical appearance was very different, having had chestnut brown hair, eyes black as night, and somewhat more angular features, but the ease with which he wore his authority and the hint of ruthlessness that hovered about him were almost identical.

"You have your orders," Lord Mechnes was saying. "Go now. You've earned your rest. Find some drink, and some women. We will continue this conversation at dawn."

Their departure filled Adiana with an unnerving sense of invisibility, for not one of them glanced her way when they left the tent. Four guards remained inside, their gazes fixed on some empty point in front of them. The servants continued oblivious to her, engrossed in their business of clearing, cleaning, assembling, arranging. Lord Mechnes lingered at the table with his maps, took a leisurely drink from his cup, and wiped his beard absently on his sleeve.

Sweat trickled down Adiana's back, though a chill had penetrated her bones. Her arms ached from being bound. The cords were cutting into her wrists, and her fingers were falling asleep. Without looking at her, the Syrnte commander strode to the table on which the soldier had left Renate's head. His demeanor was quiet, contemplative. He took his time unwrapping the bundle, exposing Renate's matted tresses, the ragged edge of severed flesh, the face—oh, Renate's face! Stiff, gray, and lifeless. Never again would she laugh, drink wine, cast a spell, or heal a friend.

Adiana's stomach contracted, and she fought against the surge of bile in her throat.

Calm, she told herself. She must remain calm, just as Renate had, just like Eolyn would, without so much as a change in the rhythm of her breath.

"Who is this woman?" Mechnes's voice hit Adiana like a spear, and she nearly stumbled backwards with the force of it.

"It is…" Her throat closed around the words. Every breath sent sharp needles of pain through her ribs. "…*was* the Maga Eolyn."

Mechnes grunted, glanced at the gruesome package, then set his hard gaze on Adiana. "And who are you?"

"My name is Adiana."

"You are this woman's scullery maid?"

She swallowed, bit her lip. She had learned how to lie during her youth in Selkynsen, after her parents were killed and she fled to the piers. Lies must be presented on a bed of truth, or they lose their seductive power. "No, I am not a servant. I am a musician from Selkynsen. Maga Eolyn brought me to Moehn to teach music to her students."

"Music?" An amused smirk broke upon the commander's face. He seemed genuinely surprised by the response. "What interest do magas have in music?"

She searched for her breath. "Music is also magic, according to the traditions of Moisehén. Eolyn says . . . used to say . . . that it's a form of Primitive Magic, the oldest and most sacred of all. Magas and mages use music in their ceremonies, their spells, sometimes even in their healing."

"So you are a maga?"

"No, I'm not a maga." The thought came, terrible and unbidden, that now she would never be. "I simply play music."

"Then Maga Eolyn was trying to protect you by saying you were a scullery maid? How curious." He draped one end of the bloodied cloth over Renate's disfigured face. "I can assure you a musician will find a much better place among the Syrnte than a scullery maid."

"I don't intend to find a place among the Syrnte." Her breath stalled under the look he gave her, a strange mixture of amusement and menace. "What I mean is, my home is here, in Moisehén, not with the Syrnte."

"It's all one kingdom now. Or perhaps better stated, will be soon." He nodded to the guards. "Unbind this woman."

In an instant, the cords that secured her wrists were removed. Adiana cradled her hands, rubbing places where the leather straps had left her skin raw.

Mechnes closed the distance between them in two strides.

"You will have to find a place among us, Adiana, or you will perish. That is the way of conquest." He took her hands in his and studied them carefully, strong fingers tracing the fine delicate length of her own. "What do you play?"

Adiana's skin crawled at the intimacy of his touch. His aroma was sharp, like coals on the hearth, and laced with the smell of blood. She wanted desperately to look elsewhere, but could not. Mechnes's massive frame filled her vision; his presence, at once sinister and magnetic, demanded all her attention.

"The cornamuse." Her voice had dropped to a nervous whisper. "The dulcimer, and the lute, the short wood, as well. Among others."

He pressed her hands between his. Adiana was visited by the sudden image of him snapping her fingers one by one, as if they were nothing more than dry twigs.

"I see you are telling the truth, in this much at least," he said. "You have beautiful hands, Adiana. We must be grateful they were not damaged during the attack on Maga Eolyn's *Aekelahr*. And we must also hope they will come to no harm here, under my care."

A heavy silence followed. Adiana understood the unspoken threat that hovered between them. Who else would he ask? The children, the survivors of the siege, the members of Lord Felton's household, if any of them still lived. There were untold numbers of people in Moehn who could recognize Renate's face. What would Adiana's deception gain for Eolyn in the end—fifteen minutes? Half an hour? It did not matter. Every additional moment could mean the difference between Eolyn's escape and her death. Adiana had already lost one friend tonight. She would not betray the other.

She lowered her eyes and held her tongue.

Mechnes lingered close for what seemed an endless moment before releasing her.

"Bring Felton back," he said to the guards, and two of the men departed.

The Syrnte commander moved a few paces away. He studied her in silence, as if judging the wares of a street merchant. Presently, the guards returned, towing Lord Felton between them. Adiana stifled a sob at the appearance of the old patriarch, who had treated Eolyn, Adiana, and all their companions with only kindness and generosity. His face was bruised and swollen, his white beard encrusted with blood. All laughter had vanished from his once jovial expression. He kept his eyes downcast, his shoulders slumped in defeat. Adiana was not even certain whether he saw her.

"Lord Felton," Mechnes said, "I'm pleased you could join us. I need your assistance with a new prisoner that has been brought into my camp."

Felton looked up then, and when Mechnes nodded in Adiana's direction, turned his head toward her. His gaze seemed distracted, his spirit hollowed out by the weight of unbearable losses. Where was his wife, she wondered. His children and grandchildren?

"Please, Felton, tell me who this woman is."

Felton blinked, cleared his throat, stared at the floor again. "That is the Mistress Adiana, my Lord Mechnes. She teaches music at the maga's school."

Mechnes nodded, a satisfied smile touching his lips. "I cannot tell you how much it pleases me to hear this, Lord Felton. Now one more question and you may go." He removed the cloth that had concealed Renate's head, exposing her ghastly countenance once more. "Who is this?"

Adiana could hear every beat of her heart in the silence that followed. When Lord Felton's eyes focused on Renate, he gasped and lost his balance. He would have fallen to the floor had not the guards caught him and pulled him upright.

"I am waiting, Lord Felton," Mechnes prompted.

The poor man was trembling. He looked from the severed head to Adiana, then back again, eyes wide with terror and uncertainty. Moments passed, and he did not speak.

Mechnes approached him, his tone quiet and tense. "Lord Felton?"

"M-my Lord." He looked past Mechnes at Renate's head, once again averted his gaze to the floor. "That is the one you seek . . . the Maga Eolyn."

Adiana lowered her face, hoping the intense relief that flooded her heart did not show in her eyes. Praise the Gods for granting Felton such a fine instinct! She wanted to dance and laugh and hug the old man, but she held as still as a mouse under the eyes of a cat.

"Could it be that the humble citizens of Moehn have acquired Syrnte powers of speaking to each other through thought?" Mechnes returned to Renate's head and lifted it up by a fistful of hair. "I was led to believe the Maga Eolyn has hair the color of fire. That she is young and beautiful—beautiful enough to seduce a king."

"The magas can change the color of their hair with the seasons," retorted Adiana, emboldened by this small success. "And nobody is beautiful when they're dead."

Mechnes threw his head back with a rich and throaty laugh.

"Well spoken, Mistress Adiana." He let go Renate's head, and it landed with a thud on the table. "I hope your music is as sharp as your wit. Take Felton away. I'm done with him, for the moment."

The old patriarch was dragged off, and Adiana left alone once again with Lord Mechnes. The activity in his tent had died down considerably. Only two of the guards remained, and all of the servants had disappeared, except for one who was arranging the covers and pillows on his bed.

"My sleeping quarters are quite comfortable," Mechnes said, "and always open to beautiful women like yourself."

She looked away, embarrassed and sickened by the fact that he had noticed the direction of her gaze.

"Where are the children being held?" she asked. "Can I go to them now?"

"They are no longer your concern."

"They are always my concern." Her cheeks flushed with anger, and she raised her voice. "They are as my own daughters to me. What your men did to their tutor—the way they cut her down in front of them—they will never recover from that. They are innocents, miserable and terrified, suffering through no fault of their own. They require my comfort and my support. I must be allowed to see them. Now."

"You are in a fine position to make demands," he said with a shrewd smile. "But if you must know, I have entrusted them to the care of my men."

"Entrusted them to your—?" Adiana lost her voice, so horrifying was the thought inspired by his words. "But they are only little girls!"

"How old are they?"

"Eleven, twelve. Ghemena has seen but nine summers."

"Old enough for our needs. Indeed, not too old, fortunately. You see, Mistress Adiana, our allies have . . . special appetites that the students of Maga Eolyn will serve quite well."

Adiana flung herself at him, fingers extended to claw out his eyes. She did not feel his blow until she hit the ground, palms stinging from their impact against the swept dirt, her cheek swelling, hot with pain. She spat out the blood that pooled on her lips, and beat back the burn of tears, vowing in that moment to never ever let him see her weep.

When her vision cleared, his booted feet were inches from her face.

"They are only children," she said fiercely. "For the love of the Gods, let them go."

He bent down next to her, ran his fingers over her golden tresses. "What would you give me, Mistress Adiana, in exchange for their freedom? The hiding place of the Maga Eolyn, perhaps? In the event, of course, that it turns out she is not entirely dead."

"I..." Adiana's heart broke under the weight of her fate. She had left this life behind, hadn't she? Years ago, when her father's steward rescued her from the taverns. She had left it all behind, forgotten it, and after a long journey, had found her freedom, her peace. Here, with Eolyn in the highlands of Moehn. "Lord Mechnes, I . . . know things, because I worked on the piers of Selkynsen as a girl, during a time when I had no other choice. So I can please you. You and all your men, if that's what you want. It may not mean much to you, but it's what I have to offer. Set the girls free. Take me in their stead."

For a long while, he said nothing. When at last she gathered the courage to lift her face, his expression caught her by surprise; it was thoughtful, bordering on compassionate. Lord Mechnes drew a breath and stood up.

"I see this thing you offer would mean a great sacrifice for you, Mistress Adiana. It moves me to witness such generosity." He stroked his beard.

Hope flickered like a weak flame in her heart.

"I do not negotiate with prisoners."

The guards grasped her arms and jerked her to her feet, sending another shaft of pain through her ribs.

"Clean her up," Lord Mechnes said. "I would see this one again, perhaps before the night has ended."

Chapter 13

Ghemena awoke cramped and shivering, huddled against Tasha and Catarina. Outside she heard the shouts of men broken by occasional laughter, heavy footsteps and the whinny of horses. Her tongue felt like it was covered with sand, and her arms were numb from being bound. She tried to move her hands, but found a sickly sensation of nothingness where her fingers should have been.

Sitting up, she looked around the bare tent, illuminated by a thin shaft of light streaming through a break in the canvas. Catarina and Tasha slept, bodies curled side by side on the hard dirt floor, faces swollen from the many tears they had shed. With growing dread, Ghemena realized Mistress Adiana was not with them. She shuddered at the memory of Renate's headless corpse and closed her eyes to shut the image out.

Tasha whimpered and stirred. She lifted her head, tangled dark tresses hanging in her rounded face, and stared with bleary eyes at their grim surroundings before focusing on Ghemena.

"Where's Mistress Adiana?" she asked.

A painful lump in Ghemena's throat would not let her speak. She bit her lip, working her arms and wrists against each other, trying to get the blood to return to her fingers.

Tasha moaned and hid her face against Catarina's shoulder. "This was supposed to be a dream. I was going to wake up, and have it all be a very bad dream."

"We've no time to cry," Ghemena replied sharply. "We have to get out of here as fast as we can."

Tasha dragged herself away from Catarina's sleeping figure and sat up. She pointed to her bound arms with her chin. "How are we supposed to escape tied up like this? And where would we go if we did? You saw the town last night. Nothing's left of it, and those horrible men are everywhere."

"I have a way to find Maga Eolyn, but I have to free my hands first." A burning sensation moved through her palms, followed by the prick of a thousand pins on her fingers. Ghemena knew this was a good sign.

"What way?" asked Tasha.

"A magic way. She showed it to me before she left. I'm going find her and tell her what's happened, and then she'll come to rescue you."

"You mean we can't go with you?" Tasha's brow furrowed and she glanced nervously at Catarina. "Don't leave us alone here. Please."

Ghemena stopped fidgeting and gave Tasha a worried frown. "I don't think it'll work with more than one of us."

"Why not?"

"Maga Eolyn never said anything about taking more than one person."

"That doesn't mean it's not possible."

"No," Ghemena conceded doubtfully. "I guess we can try."

"Promise me you'll try, Ghemena." Tasha's eyes were wide beneath her dark brows. "Promise me you won't leave without us."

Ghemena looked at her friend. Tasha had always been the quiet one, happy in the company of her friends, forever trying to make peace between Ghemena and Catarina.

"We're sisters," Ghemena said. "We must be loyal to each other, right?"

Tasha grinned and nodded.

"So you see, I won't leave you alone. I can't."

"How does the spell work?" Tasha asked.

"Well first, I have to get my hands free." Ghemena scooted around on her rump to show Tasha her back. "Can you see the knots? Maybe you can chew through them."

Tasha wrinkled her freckled nose. "Chew through them? What kind of an idea is that?"

"Well, I don't have a knife. Do you?"

"It'd take me days to chew through those chords, and I'd have no teeth left at the end of it."

"Tasha, just do it. Please."

Tasha scowled, but she eased over toward Ghemena, then fell heavy on her side behind the girl's back.

"Ow!" Ghemena winced. "You're supposed to bite the chords, not my wrists!"

"Well it all looks the same in the dark. Hold still, will you? You're only making it harder."

A sudden flood of harsh light interrupted their efforts. Tasha gasped and Ghemena looked up, squinting, at three figures silhouetted in the tent entrance.

"By the graces of Mikata, what is this?" The voice was lilting and feminine. As Ghemena's eyes adjusted, she saw the slight figure of a woman not much older than Mariel, clothed in a simple rose colored dress. She had fine brown skin and hair the color of wheat, neatly braided and coiled. Her expression was kind, with a knowing smile and soft eyes set in an oval face. "Our little mice are trying to escape!"

The men behind her stepped forward, bent low, and cut loose their bindings. Ghemena rubbed her wrists as they hauled Catarina out of her sleep. The drowsy girl whimpered, looked around with a troubled frown and began to weep.

"Oh come, my love." The woman approached Catarina, knelt and gathered the girl in her arms. "I know it was a difficult night for all of you, but that's over now. You'll have a new life from this day forward, and a very pretty one at that." She took Catarina's small chin in her fingers, wiped the tears from her cheeks. "My name is Pashnari, and I have special orders from Lord Mechnes. You're to be cleaned up, given food and new clothes. The San'iloman will arrive soon, and she would make you her own."

"What's a San'iloman?" Catarina sniffled and wiped her nose on her tattered cloak.

"She's the Queen of all the Syrnte, and soon of all Moisehén. And you," Pashnari touched Catarina's nose with the tip of her finger, "will be her lady-in-waiting."

"Me? A lady?" Catarina's eyes were wide and hopeful. Ghemena had never thought her more stupid than in that moment.

"Where is Mistress Adiana?" Ghemena demanded.

Pashnari's eyes pinned her quick as a hawk's, that sweet smile fixed upon her face. "Mistress Adiana? Who is that?"

"She's our music teacher," said Tasha. "She came with us last night, but then the soldiers took her somewhere else."

"I see." Uncertainty flickered through Pashnari's expression. She shrugged and gave a light shake of her head. "I will ask after her, but you must understand I am a mere servant here. I am not always privy to the fate of Lord Mechnes's prisoners."

"Liar!" Ghemena sprang at Pashnari with clenched fists, hoping to beat that pretty face until it bled, but one of the guards caught the girl and held her fast, so she tried to kick his shins instead. "You know where she is! You just aren't telling us."

Pashnari withdrew from Catarina and approached Ghemena. She ran her fingers over the girl's disheveled hair, then took a fistful and yanked it back, making Ghemena cry out. "I do not lie, little one, nor will I ever lie to you. But you will find the Syrnte do not tolerate ill-behaved children. Be still, or I will have you bound and thrown to the fires of Mikata, whether the San'iloman approves or not."

Ghemena ceased her thrashing, her fury checked not by Pashnari's tone, but by the thought of having her hands bound.

"That's better." Pashnari released the girl's hair and turned to Tasha and Catarina. She spread her arms wide in a welcoming gesture. "Come then, all of you. We've a grand day ahead of us."

Catarina accepted Pashnari's hand and clung to her side as they walked. Ghemena and Tasha followed a step behind, herded by the guards, fingers interlaced and eyes wide as they surveyed the camp. Ghemena had never seen so many men in one place. Her ears rang with the pounding of hammers, the clatter of wood, stone, and metal. The air smelled of sweat and horses, of charred wood and smoke.

"Why are you here?" asked Ghemena.

Pashnari looked over her shoulder. "To bring peace to Moisehén."

"We were at peace," retorted Ghemena, "until you came. Why are you really here?"

The servant responded with laughter, clear and high-pitched. "Because the San'iloman is your rightful queen."

Ghemena frowned in confusion. "That's not true. Taesara is our rightful queen. The San'iloman is queen of the Syrnte. You just said so yourself."

Tasha elbowed her in the ribs.

"Don't make her mad again," the girl whispered. "There's something mean about that woman. I think she *likes* hurting you."

Pashnari stopped and turned around. Ghemena and Tasha froze beneath her needled gaze.

"There will be no whispering in my presence," the woman said.

Tasha swallowed hard. When she spoke it sounded as if she were squeezing her voice through a very tiny hole. "I'm sorry, Mistress Pashnari. I won't do it again."

Pashnari assessed them with arched brows Before continuing their march in silence.

They arrived at a tent striped in colors of sand and burgundy. The inside was well furnished, and the girls were seated at a table spread with fruit, bread, sausage, and cheese. Pashnari bade them to eat all they wanted. Tasha picked nervously at a piece of bread, while Catarina sat with her back straight, taking fruit in dainty but obedient bites. Ghemena kept her hands clenched at her sides, fighting the impulse to finger the silver web that lay hidden beneath her nightshift.

She looked from the girls to Pashnari, then glanced furtively at the guards who accompanied them. What Ghemena required was a moment alone, hidden from everyone, in order to spin the jewel and sing the incantation Maga Eolyn had taught her. Trying to take Catarina and Tasha along would complicate matters, for she did not know if the medallion would carry more than one person, and if the spell failed on the first attempt, there might not be another opportunity. But try she must, for she had promised Tasha she would, and in truth she did not like the thought of leaving her friends alone with this unpleasant woman and these cruel men.

They had not been eating long when several servants brought in a large shallow basin that they filled with water and then covered with blossoms of lily and primrose. Pashnari bade Catarina to leave the table and shed her soiled nightshift, which she did without protest. The girl kept her eyes downcast as she stepped into the basin, where Pashnari scrubbed her pale skin with a soft sponge, cleaning arms, legs, back and tummy before pouring the perfumed water in clear streams through her blond tresses. It was not until one of the servants wrapped a towel around Catarina's shivering body, and Pashnari called Tasha to the wash basin, that Ghemena realized her plan for escape was about to crumble. If she undressed, they would discover the jewel and seize it. Perhaps they would even recognize its use, find Maga Eolyn, and kill her just like they had killed Renate.

Panicked, Ghemena pushed the chair back and stood, one hand pressed against her breastbone, where she felt the fine silver threads of the medallion beneath the thin folds of her linen gown.

"Child, you will sit until I call for you," scolded Pashnari.

Ghemena glanced at the woman, then at the guards on either side of the tent door.

"Tasha…" she began, but the sight of her friend standing in that pool of lilies, naked and vulnerable, stole away her words. Ghemena blinked against the burning sensation in her eyes. A black shadow coiled around her heart, threatening to cut off her breath. She had to go now, she told herself. It was the best way. The only way. Otherwise none of them would ever be rescued. Ghemena connected her spirit to the earth, like Maga Eolyn had taught her, and steadied her pulse. "I'm sorry, Tasha."

With that, she sprang between the guards and rushed into the light of day. Feet pounding against the dirt, Ghemena dodged carts and leapt over discarded campfires, swerved around hobbled horses and ducked from the meaty grasp of shouting soldiers. Her haphazard path brought her to the town wall, where she ran along the edge until she spotted a collapsed portion that she had scaled countless times with Markl. Rough stones scraped her hands and knees as she scrambled upward. At last, she reached the top, leapt, and landed breathless on the other side.

Her heart sank in disappointment. Ghemena had known every hiding place in the town of Moehn, but this landscape of blackened timber skeletons was unrecognizable.

Where was she to go? How could she escape long enough to invoke the magic of the silver web?

Behind, she heard the throaty shouts of men and the sound of loose rocks giving way beneath heavy feet.

Gripped by fear, Ghemena charged down the remains of an alley, feet tripping over scattered stones and rubble. At last she found a wall still standing. She slipped behind it, taking shelter under the remains of a stairwell, and pulled the silver web from its hiding place.

Sunlight caught in the crystals, causing them to dance inside the web. The instrument hummed like a mother singing her child to sleep. Focusing all her thoughts on Maga Eolyn, Ghemena spun the jewel on its axis.

Ehekaht, she murmured, *Elaeom enem.*

The shout of a man nearby startled her out of the spell. Ghemena heard their footsteps on the other side of the wall and bit her lip, uncertain whether to run or start the spell anew. She closed her eyes.

Eleaom enem, elaeom enem

"I have you now, you little wench."

Ghemena's eyes flew open. A man towered over her, a satisfied grin on his scarred face and a curved knife in his hand. The web spun between them, a fine silver orb that gathered all light, all form, all sensation toward a single tiny vortex.

Renoenem mae, Ghemena begged as the guard reached toward her.

Ehukae.

Chapter 14

At midmorning, trumpets sounded from the western wall.

King Akmael glanced up from the table where he was engrossed in discussion with Lords Herensen and Langerhans, and representatives from the merchant guilds of Selkynsen. When the trumpets sounded a second time, the King rose and all the men in attendance followed suit. "It would seem our new ambassador from Roenfyn has arrived," Akmael announced. "Let us adjourn this meeting."

Herensen, a tall man of angular features, allowed his disappointment to show. Already the debate over port tariffs had dragged on for hours, with no clear resolution in sight.

"We will continue this audience tomorrow," he assured the lord and his companions. They departed with respectful bows and quiet murmurs.

Akmael strode to the southern windows while one of the servants brought his riding cloak. It was a fine summer day, with a bold sun in a cloudless sky. High over the slate roofs of the city, almost at eye level with the balcony, hovered a Stone Hawk, a large raptor with mottled gray wings, black legs and an ebony-tipped beak. Its cry was a low-pitched wail, more ominous than the sharp keen of its lesser brothers.

"Odd," Akmael murmured as the servant placed the cloak about his shoulders and fitted the clasp, a dragon finely wrought in silver. Stone Hawks inhabited the Eastern Surmaeg. It was unusual, though not entirely unheard of, to see them this far south.

The servant stepped away, eyes lowered in deference. Akmael departed the receiving room and proceeded down the long halls of the fortress, accompanied by his guards. They descended a series of winding steps that led them to the outer courtyard, where horses waited attended by grooms. The silver and purple colors of the House of Vortingen fluttered over the gathering. Those appointed to the royal procession were engaged in a lively chatter that quieted upon the King's entrance as all turned to pay their respects.

Taesara arrived shortly after the King, appearing from one of the opposite towers with six of her ladies and escorted by Mage Corey of East Selen. She wore an elegant summer gown of pale green, cut in voluminous folds that hid the demure rise of her belly. Her golden hair was bound in a jeweled net that sparkled under the midmorning sun, and her laughter rang like the song of a thrush. She approached Akmael, one hand upon Corey's arm. Both bowed low before him.

"My Lord King," she said. "The Gods bring me joy with your presence."

"My Queen." Akmael responded. "High Mage Corey."

Corey straightened at the King's acknowledgment and met Akmael's gaze, his expression at once respectful yet indecipherable. "My Lord King. It has been a great honor to spend these days at court, and to serve you in person once again."

"I always find it reassuring when you are close at hand," Akmael replied.

Amusement sparked in Corey's silver-green eyes then vanished under the cover of neutrality. He bowed again. "It humbles me to hear you say so. If you would excuse me, my Lord King, I would speak with High Mage Tzetobar before we get underway."

Akmael nodded his assent. Once Corey had departed, he turned to Taesara. "You look as lovely as this fine day, my good Queen."

She blushed and lowered her eyes. "You are too kind, my Lord King."

"To what purpose did Mage Corey seek an audience with you this morning?"

She gave a short laugh and shrugged. "I assure you, my King, I still do not know. Half the morning passed us by, and not a single petition or grievance on his part."

"What then did he speak about?"

She lowered her voice in an amused whisper. "Your cousin has the boldest stories, my Lord King, of the days before your coronation, when he traveled the kingdom with a group of troubadours, drunken musicians and wanton dancers who caused all manner of scandals from one village to the next."

Akmael's brow furrowed. Corey was speaking of the Circle, no doubt, but why would he share such tales with the Queen?

Hesitation clouded Taesara's smile. "Is something wrong, my Lord King?"

Akmael shook his head, thoughtful. "I am not certain."

"Perhaps it was unwise of me to let him carry on so," she conceded, "but truly my ladies have not been so well entertained since we returned from Moehn. Sonia laughed so hard, I feared her bodice might split at the seams."

The image of that unattractive and tight-lipped woman surrendering to a fit of laughter amused Akmael, and he allowed a smile to touch his lips.

Taesara's shoulders relaxed. She gestured toward the procession being assembled. "Shall we, my Lord King? I do not wish to keep my uncle waiting."

"Your litter is not here." Akmael scanned the courtyard in consternation, seeing no sign of the Queen's transport. "It should have been ready by now."

"I had the grooms prepare my mare, Kaeva, that I might ride at your side to the docks."

"Impossible." Annoyance rose inside of him. "I will not have it."

"But my Lord King—"

"You are with child, a Prince of Vortingen entrusted to your womb. And you have been ill."

"It is a short ride on cobbled streets, and Kaeva is a docile mare. I have already consulted with High Mage Rezlyn, and he says I am well enough."

"Rezlyn!" Akmael's summons thundered across the courtyard, silencing all conversation. The old physician scurried to his side. "My Lord King?"

"Why do you counsel my Queen to ride?"

The mage frowned, shifting his eyes from Akmael to Taesara and back again. His long dark beard, streaked with red and silver, quivered as he stroked it. "I'm sorry, my Lord King, my Lady Queen, but I do not recall—"

"Taesara, are you trying to deceive me?"

"I am not lying, my Lord King. Rezlyn assured me I am fully recovered from my illness."

"That is not the same as being fit to ride."

They glared at each other, then at the physician. High Mage Rezlyn took a step back.

"My Lord King, my Lady Queen, It is true the Queen Taesara has recovered from the ailment that beset her in Moehn, but she is with child and I would not recommend—"

"I will not hear it!" Taesara's face flushed with anger. "My mother rode from Merolyn to Reonahn to Fahlvort, from the moment she conceived to the day she gave birth. I, my brother and sisters, all of us were riding horses before we were born. I am a Daughter of Roenfyn, and I will not receive my kinsmen lying on my side like some helpless old woman. I suffered quite enough from that sort of humiliation in Moehn."

Her blue eyes flashed in defiance, her jaw was set.

In that moment, she reminded Akmael of Eolyn. The similarity of their ire softened his heart. He touched her cheek, an inadvertent and rare gesture on his part. Her eyes widened in response and she lowered her gaze, uncertain.

"Please, my Lord King," she said, "I meant no disrespect. If you will not allow me to ride, I would rather wait to receive Lord Penamor here, than be carted down to the river on that accursed litter."

Akmael placed his fingers beneath her chin and brought her gaze back to his. Truly she had a beautiful face, and in the years they had known each other, she had never failed in her gentleness and obedience. "Very well, my Lady Queen. You will ride today to greet your uncle."

Relief and gratitude shone plain upon her countenance. "Thank you, my Lord King. You are most generous."

Trumpets sounded as the castle gates opened. They descended along the single long road that wound from the Fortress of Vortingen toward the city square. From there, the procession bore south along a broad promenade toward the banks of the Furma River. News of the King's passing rippled before them, carried on the shouts of excited adults and scampering children. The people flocked to witness their progress, crowding the streets and hanging from windows, wishing the King long life and throwing blossoms in the path of Taesara's horse.

"A son!" they cried. "A son! Gods grant our beautiful Queen a son."

Taesara glowed at their attention and reached out to touch the hands of the commoners. In a few short years she had garnered the love of this city, with her beauty, sweet demeanor, and her gentle attentions to the cause of the poor and the sick.

The horses plodded over the cobblestones at a tedious pace as befit the occasion, taking them slowly along the street as it sloped downward and veered right. Rounding a bend, Akmael could see the sparkle of the Furma, its turbid jade waters stretching wide toward the opposite shore. The fore of Penamor's barge was just visible beyond the last of the stone buildings, the sage-colored flags of Roenfyn fluttering over its wooden deck. Though the ambassador had already docked, protocol obligated him to wait until the King and his entourage arrived before disembarking.

"My Lady," Akmael turned to his Queen, curious about this uncle she appeared so fond of, "tell me once again how—"

A terrified scream interrupted his question, followed by shouts and the ring of swords pulled from their scabbards. Gasps pulsed through the crowd as people scattered away from the King and Queen, crushing hapless onlookers against the walls and forcing street urchins up the sides of buildings. Taesara's horse whinnied and reared, eyes wide and nostrils flaring. Coming down on all four hooves, it scuffled backwards until Akmael caught the bridle and forced the animal to be still. The Queen clung breathless to her saddle, face pinched and pale.

"Are you hurt?" Akmael asked.

She shook her head, though her blue eyes were wide and she trembled like a mouse in wintertime.

"Are you certain?" he insisted.

"Yes, my Lord King, I was just . . . Kaeva has never . . . I thought I saw . . ." Her words faltered into a startled cry, gaze fixed upon the road just ahead of them.

Akmael turned to see several of his guards had dismounted, swords drawn around a barefoot girl. Her eyes were reddened, her cheeks and sandy brown hair smudged with soot. Beneath her russet cloak she wore a soiled nightshift. Her lower lip trembled, tears welled in her eyes. She let out long terrible wail.

"No!" she cried, looking frantically around her. "This isn't how it's supposed to work! Where is she? Where is she?"

To his shock, Akmael recognized the child. He dismounted and strode toward her.

"With care, my Lord King," counseled one of the guards.

"She's a child, Galison."

"Not a child, my Lord King. Some sort of demon, perhaps. Did you not see? She appeared out of thin air."

Silence had descended upon the crowd, and the guards watched Ghemena with wary expressions, as if she were the dead come to walk among them.

"I know this girl," Akmael said. "She is a student of the Maga Eolyn. Lower your swords."

"But my Lord—"

"Do as I say."

The moment they sheathed their weapons, Ghemena bolted, but one of the guards anticipated her impulse and caught her. She kicked and punched and screamed even as he set her in front of the King.

"Ghemena," Akmael said sternly, but she was too engaged in the battle with her captor to pay him heed. "Maga Ghemena."

At this she quieted, looked around and then up at him with a puzzled expression. "Who are you?"

There was a low chuckle behind him. Akmael glanced back to see Mage Corey, who had dismounted and pushed his way to the front of the column.

"Oh, I remember now," Ghemena said. "You're the King. But I wasn't supposed to come to you. Where's Maga Eolyn?"

Akmael knelt on one knee in front of her. "Ghemena, how did you get here?"

She bit her lip. After a moment of hesitation, she held up the silver web crafted by Akmael's mother. Its fine crystals glittered in the bright sun. "With this."

Akmael's heart turned cold under the harrowing sense that a nightmare was about to unfold. "How did you come by it? Did you take it?"

She frowned in indignation. "I'm a maga, not a thief!"

"How did you come by this jewel, Ghemena?"

An agonized expression broke across her face. She stumbled backwards and sank to the ground, hugging her knees to her chest. "She said I could use it to find her, if something bad happened. She said…"

Her small shoulders began to shake.

Akmael drew a breath to steady his apprehension. Placing a hand upon her shoulder, he asked with forced calm, "What bad thing, Ghemena? What has happened?"

"They burned everything! They attacked the school and killed Maga Renate and took Mistress Adiana away, and I was going to find Maga Eolyn so she could rescue everyone, but the web didn't work! She promised it would! She did! Did I do it wrong? Is she dead, too?" The child hid her face and succumbed to a fit of weeping.

Akmael stood abruptly. His muscles were taut, his abdomen clenched in a deep and primitive rage. "Who attacked the school, Ghemena?"

"I don't know!" She scrambled to her feet, face puckered and crimson, eyes wild and angry. "But I left Tasha and Catarina alone. I have to go back. I have to go back now!"

She raised the jewel and spun it, but Akmael snatched it out of her hand before she could invoke the spell. With an angry cry, Ghemena sprang upon him, clutching after the silver web, hissing, biting, and spitting like a rabid wolverine. One of the guards dragged her off the King, but when the man lifted a hand to strike her Akmael stopped him. "She will not be mistreated."

"My Lord King." Corey stepped forward, eyes focused upon the girl, his tone subdued yet assertive. "If you would allow me, I know an invocation that may calm her."

Akmael nodded his consent. Corey approached the girl, set one palm upon her forehead and murmured a quiet spell. Ghemena ceased thrashing and closed her eyes, legs buckling beneath her. Corey caught her, removed his cloak and wrapped it around her slight figure.

"She is overwrought," he said, "traumatized by whatever has happened, and desperate to find the maga. I suggest we ask no more questions of her until she is rested and has had some proper food."

How long would that be? Akmael studied the jewel of his mother, cradled in the palm of his hand. He could be with Eolyn in a moment, in the space of a single breath.

"My Lord King, if I may ask," Corey's tone was wary, "what is that device?"

"It was crafted by the Queen Briana. It has the power to take me to the maga."

"Just as it took the child?" The mage's expression was doubtful, cautious.

"Perhaps she did not invoke the spell correctly."

"If Maga Eolyn entrusted her with this magic, she must have been certain the child would use it as intended. There is a reason it brought her to us instead, though I hesitate to guess what that reason might be." Corey's voice broke momentarily, an odd contrast to his otherwise imperturbable demeanor. Akmael noted the tension around the mage's eyes and realized that he, too, feared the worst. "Until we understand what dangers have befallen Moehn, it is too great a risk, my Lord King, for you to try to find her alone."

Sage words, yet unacceptable. Akmael closed a fist around his mother's heirloom.

A single breath, he thought. A short spell.

Mage Corey stepped close. "My Lord King, if we are to aid Maga Eolyn we must first understand what she faces. I will take the girl back to the keep, look after her, and question her when she awakes. By the time you return with the ambassador of Roenfyn, we will have the answers we need in order to act."

Akmael studied his cousin's face. Though they were bound by the blood of East Selen, Corey was not what Akmael would call a trustworthy man. The mage was loyal only to his own interests, at times as difficult to decipher as a maga's heart. Still, Corey's assistance had proven invaluable in the defeat of Ernan's rebellion, and in truth the mage had not yet failed to put his knowledge to the King's service.

Most importantly, he was the only person among Akmael's subjects who valued Eolyn's life above all else. If the girl Ghemena carried any knowledge pertinent to Eolyn's whereabouts, Corey would not rest until he found it.

"Very well," the King decided. "The girl is in your care. Report to me as soon as we return to the castle."

Corey nodded, and Akmael returned to his steed, only to find his Queen doubled over on her brown mare, breath coming in short gasps. Akmael rushed to her side and took her hand. Her delicate fingers dug into his gloves like the talons of a hawk.

"Oh, my beloved King." She sought his eyes, tears spilling onto her pallid cheeks. "My Liege . . . forgive me."

Eyes rolling back into her head, she slipped from the saddle and into his arms.

Chapter 15

Mechnes sent immediate word of the child's escape to the San'iloman, still about a day's march from Moehn with a few thousand men.

Rishona's arrival could not come soon enough. Mechnes hungered for their untamed nights, the delirium of her passion, the heady aroma of her skin flushed and damp from exertion. The vision of his niece naked and ravenous drove the Syrnte Lord to such distraction that he spent his need on the servant Pashnari, even as he punished the woman's carelessness in letting the child run free. It was a satisfying release achieved through vicious blows and brutal thrusts that evoked wails of remorse and pleas for mercy.

When he finished with Pashnari, Mechnes summoned the guards and told them to bring Mistress Adiana.

After a thought he added, "Fetch one of those waifs that were caught at the school, as well. Whichever one has the sweetest face. Secure her in the usual manner. I want her out of sight, but ready to appear on my signal."

Mechnes paced the pavilion as he waited, restless and impatient. At times even the best of his men seemed slow at their task. When he realized Pashnari had not moved from where he had left her, crumpled and shivering on the floor, he kicked her in the ribs.

"Get up," he growled. "Make yourself presentable. I may yet have use for you."

She struggled to her feet, shoulders bent and eyes downcast, and did her best to smooth her torn robes and disheveled hair.

"Over there," Mechnes nodded to a nearby corner. "Wait until I call for you."

Bruised and repentant, Pashnari obeyed in silence.

Still his guards did not return.

Mechnes drummed his fingers against the polished wood table and opened one of several tomes brought by his men from the maga's *Aekelahr*. It was a heavy volume, beautiful in script and illustrations, written in a language unrecognizable to him. He reached for another, then another, and found they all contained the same mysterious calligraphy.

"Curse it all," he muttered. "What use are these if we cannot read them?"

At last the guards appeared with the woman Adiana. Mechnes did not acknowledge her arrival, choosing instead to give the appearance of studying the books while he assessed her out of the corner of his eye.

She was a pretty one, this Adiana, though that fair face was swollen and discolored from the admonishment he had given her the previous night. Her hair fell straight like the fine roots of the Silky Orchid, and was of a shade almost as pale and luminous. As he watched, she assumed a peculiar stance, setting her feet slightly apart, lowering her head and closing her eyes. She reminded him of the virgin priestesses of Eirayna, attempting their futile communion with the Gods just before his men had taken them all. The memory brought a smile to his lips.

Curiosity piqued, Mechnes approached the prisoner, keeping his footsteps quiet so as not to disturb her trance. He stopped a couple paces away. The steady rhythm of her shallow breath ignited something unexpected inside of him, a sense of tranquility. His pulse slowed, his gaze lingered on those dark lashes resting against pale cheeks. Without warning she opened her eyes, blue as the Sea of Rabeln and calm as its most quiet shores. The woman focused on him, and dread chased away her composure.

Mechnes would never tire of this moment, or the surge of satisfaction it brought him.

"Did you not sleep well last night, Mistress Adiana?"

The woman averted her gaze. He noted the tremor in her hands, and imagined her shivering beneath his weight.

"Or perhaps my company has already bored you? It's not every day I have a prisoner fall asleep on her feet."

"I slept well enough, Lord Mechnes," she murmured. "May I see the children now?"

"No you may not. Though it is a fine coincidence you should mention them. I have brought you here to inform you that they are quite well."

"Well?" Adiana looked at him. Doubt clouded those striking eyes. "How can they be well when you left them—"

"If you would remember the details of our conversation, Mistress Adiana, I made no claims as to the fate of your precious waifs. It was you who presumed. Though I do confess, I played with your presumption rather cruelly."

"And you do not play with me now? How am I to know when you tell the truth and when you do not?"

"You cannot know." He strode back to the table and ran his fingers over the leather bindings of the tomes, enjoying the scent of Adiana's agitation. "However, the question is not whether I am telling the truth. The question is what risk you wish to assume. If I'm lying the girls are beyond your aid, and nothing you do or say will change that. If I'm telling the truth, on the other hand, then their well-being is in your exquisite hands, Mistress Adiana. And that is something for you to keep in mind."

The woman's brow furrowed.

He beckoned her. "Come, we have much to talk about."

She glanced around the pavilion, first at his guards, then at Pashnari. When at last she approached, it was with timid steps. He drew her close, one hand upon the small of her back, and opened a tome in front of her.

"What language is this?" he asked.

"It is a sacred script of the Old Orders."

There was a refreshing aroma about her beneath all that ash and soot, a smell of primrose and summer winds. "Can you read it?"

"No, I cannot."

Not a shade of hesitation in her answer. "Why then do you value it?"

"I . . . I don't understand, Lord Mechnes."

"You chose to save these books from the fire, and perhaps forfeited your own escape because of it. Why?"

"I know what they meant to Eolyn."

As soft as the finest silk, her hair. Like a feather to his touch.

"What did they mean to her?" he asked.

She clenched her jaw and managed an admirable look of defiance. "Why do you want to know?"

"You are not the one to be asking questions. Answer me, Mistress Adiana, and tell me the truth, as I know many ways to make you suffer."

Adiana bit her lip, and an image slipped from her mind into his awareness: three girls frightened and alone.

Mechnes drew a quiet breath and stepped closer, seeking to strengthen the connection.

"She valued them because they are all that is left," Adiana was saying. "Most of the annals of the magas were burned in the purges under Kedehen. Only three small collections remain, one in the royal library, another in East Selen, and this one that belonged to Eolyn."

"I see. Can her students read it?"

Adiana shook her head. "Catarina and Tasha joined us last fall. Ghemena has been with us longer, but she is still very young. They were all just learning to read when your men put an end to everything. They might be able to interpret some of it, but it would be risky to have them try."

"Risky?"

"The spells, especially. If they are pronounced incorrectly or invoked without proper focus, anything could happen."

Mechnes stood behind her now, close enough to feel the heat rising from her back. He touched her wrist, delighting in her rapid pulse, and let his breath fall upon her ear. "Where is the maga hiding?"

"She's not hiding." The calm in her voice was unexpected. The tenuous connection he had just forged with her mind snapped. "She is dead. Your men saw to that last night."

Mechnes withdrew, chuckling to mask his disappointment. He circled the table to face her. "You are a poor liar, Mistress Adiana." Then gesturing toward a nearby chair, he asked, "Do you know this instrument?"

Adiana frowned as her gaze settled on the lute. "Yes."

"Play it for me."

She blinked, took a step backwards.

"I would hear your music before we continue our conversation."

"Why?"

He let go a patient breath. "Play for me. I will not ask again."

She walked over to the chair, picked up the lute, then ran her hands over its curved back and polished neck. There was grace in her movement, Mechnes observed. A sense of self-assurance that set her apart from peasants but did not carry the haughty overtones so often found in women of nobility. A merchant's daughter, he concluded, or something of that sort. He wondered how a woman of her station could have succumbed to the fate she confessed last night. He found it difficult to imagine this Mistress Adiana as a whore on the piers of Selkynsen, although the thought was not unpleasant.

Adiana settled in the chair, wincing in her shoulder as she found a position to sustain the lute. She reached for the pegs, but the strings were perfectly tuned. Mechnes had seen to that. He had chosen a superior instrument for her. The soundboard was of pale spruce polished to a golden sheen, the rose at its center intricately carved. The back was crafted from dark cherry wood and the neck finished with an ebony veneer. Closing her eyes, Adiana drew a long shallow breath, asking no melody of the lute just yet, but rather playing a single note at a time so that the resonance of each one was felt.

"It's a lovely instrument," she murmured, keeping her head down. "Where did you find it?"

It pleased him to hear her say that. "The Syrnte have a great fondness for music. I travel with musicians wherever I go."

Adiana nodded, and another image slipped into his awareness: a humble room, filled with instruments gathered from many countries. Her place of joy and intimacy, consumed in its entirety by flames. The vision took him aback. So she had abandoned her own treasures attempting to save the maga's books. It was the second time in as many meetings this woman's selflessness had given him pause.

"I've worked with Syrnte musicians," she said. "They were fine artists, flawless in their technique. Among the best I've ever played with."

"Perhaps you will play with them again."

She let go a harsh laugh. "You've toyed with me quite enough, Lord Mechnes. Do not torment me in this." She lifted her countenance and met his gaze with a fine mix of courage and resignation. "What shall I play for you?"

Mechnes took a seat in front of her and signaled the guards to shift their positions, so that one stood on either side of Adiana. "Whatever your heart desires."

The woman turned her focus toward the lute. Music rose through her body, emerged upon her fingers, and filled the room with subtle protest. Mechnes closed his eyes, allowing the melody to carry him on haunting waves. It washed him up on the shores of her resentful heart, where she beat against the walls of an invisible prison, the limitations of her sex, the confines of her vulnerability. The notes twisted away from each other, then wove back together, tightening their embrace even as they strained to diverge once again, breaking into a sharp crescendo, a dance of war upon the strings, the rhythm against the soundboard like a distant drum, the rumble of thunder from a storm not yet fully manifest. Three times she took the melody to its summit, three times she descended from that peak, and on the third she let the music fade, fingers trembling as the melody abandoned her, face contorted in anguish, eyes damp with the fear of impending loss.

She faltered on a discordant note and stopped altogether.

Wrapping her arms around the instrument, Adiana clutched it tightly to her chest, as if it were a lost child returned to her. Tears spilled unrestrained down her cheeks.

An odd disappointment needled Mechnes's sense of satisfaction. He saw now that it would not be necessary to mangle those children Rishona so dearly wanted whole. Crippling this woman's hands would be more than sufficient.

"Do you also sing, Adiana?"

She wiped away tears, her breath coming in short shallow gasps, cheek pressed tight against the lute's dark neck. "I cannot draw enough air. I took a fall last night and my ribs are badly bruised."

"I see. But you do sing?"

"Yes," she whispered. "I have heard it said that I sing well."

"What a pity." He spoke with sincerity. "I would have liked to have heard you sing while playing."

At Mechnes signal, one of the guards wrested the lute from her embrace.

"No!" she cried and lunged after it, but the other guard caught the woman and pinned her arms, immobilizing her as Mechnes approached.

The Syrnte commander took one of her hands with great care and turned it palm upward. He traced each finger, admiring their length and elegance. "Where is the Maga Eolyn?"

"She's dead. I told you."

"You lie, Mistress Adiana." Mechnes bent one of her fingers back, just short of the breaking point.

Her cry was loud, satisfactory in its desperation.

"Where is she?"

"I don't know."

Mechnes struck her full in the face. A sob broke through her bloodied lips. He thrust his hand under her chin, putting pressure on her throat until he felt the staccato beat of her terrified pulse. "Do you understand what it is I intend to take from you, Mistress Adiana?"

"I tell you the truth, Lord Mechnes," she gasped. "I do not know."

"Pashnari." He spoke without raising his voice. In a moment, the servant was at his side, head bowed and contrite. He grasped the woman's wrist, held her hand in front of Adiana and snapped three fingers in quick succession. Pashnari's sudden screams he silenced with a blow that sent her to the floor. Horror was plain upon Adiana's face, and she struggled against the guard's firm grip. Mechnes took her hand in his once again. "Which finger do you value least, Mistress Adiana? Perhaps we should start with the smallest?"

"Gods, no!" she begged. "Please, it's all I have! The music—"

"It is not my desire to hurt you, much less put an end to that extraordinary talent of yours. But you have information I need. I would hear it now."

"I do not know where she is!"

Mechnes gripped her hand, wrapped his fist around her finger. Her body shook, her eyes begged him to stop, and Mechnes, upon feeling the delicate strength of her music at his mercy, was confronted by a sickening realization.

He could not destroy this.

Infuriated, he struck her again.

Pacing in front of her, he considered his next move, then nodded to one of the guards. "Bring me the child."

Rishona would not be pleased to have one of her toys damaged, but no matter. He would deal with that when the time came.

The girl was delivered bound hand and foot, dark of hair and with a spray of freckles across her small nose. Her brown eyes were wide with terror.

"Tasha!" Adiana moaned. The child responded with a muffled whimper, as his men had stuffed a rag in her mouth.

Mechnes ordered the bindings around her feet cut. Taking her by a fistful of hair, he dragged Tasha to the table and threw her face down upon it, ripping open the skirt to reveal her pale thighs and frail buttocks.

"Stop," Adiana wailed. "Oh, for the love of the Gods, please stop! I tell you the truth, Lord Mechnes. I beg you, don't hurt the child. Ask me something else, anything. I will answer whatever I can. Please. Don't do this."

The child was immobile beneath Mechnes's tight grip, eyes open and alert, like a young rabbit in the clutches of a hawk.

"Where was the maga when we attacked the school?" He kept his gaze fixed on the girl. The desire to break something burned hard in Mechnes's loins, and this little one would shatter so easily.

"In . . . In the South Woods."

"Alone?"

"No."

"How many were with her?"

Adiana hesitated. Mechnes grabbed the girl by the hair and struck her head against the table, eliciting a cry of horror from Adiana.

"How many?" he repeated.

"Two guards and two students."

There were more of these young magas, then. That was useful knowledge to have.

"What will she do, when she returns?" he asked.

"Do?"

"Will she try to rescue you? The girls?"

Adiana frowned.

"Answer me."

"I . . . I'm not certain. I think she would fist try to..."

"Warn the King?"

The woman looked away. Mechnes abandoned the child and took Adiana by the throat. "How?"

"I don't know." Tears filled her eyes. "She might fly."

He caught an image of the maga pacing in agitation, fingers lingering on a jewel around her neck, a silver web with fine crystals suspended on a simple chain.

"That." Mechnes tightened his grip. "That object. What it is?"

"Object?" She stared at him in confusion.

"The jewel she wears."

"How did you—?"

"Tell me!"

"It was a gift." She forced each word through frantic gasps. "A gift from the King."

"What power does it have?"

"It . . . binds them somehow. I don't know. She never told me."

Mechnes released her, and she wilted coughing and wheezing against the guard.

He had recognized that jewel. It matched perfectly the description of the device used by the girl to escape that very morning.

It binds them, he thought. The child to the maga, the maga to the King.

"The Mage King has been informed," he concluded out loud. "Or at least, we must assume that is the case."

It was disappointing news. He had planned to move his army as far north as Rhiemsaven before word of their invasion reached the King's City. That might not be possible now, and Mechnes did not care to get bogged down in a conflict over the Pass of Aerunden. Still, the advantage remained with the Syrnte, and there was yet time to secure the pass if they moved quickly. He nodded to his men. "That's enough, for the moment. Take the girl away, leave the woman with me. Send for my officers and bring me one of the Queen's messengers."

The guards shoved Adiana into a chair and departed. Pashnari remained huddled on the ground, cradling her mutilated hand. Mechnes kicked her once more.

"Get out," he said.

She scurried away like a rat.

The Syrnte Prince returned his attention to Adiana, who had curled into herself and was overcome with wretched sobs. He drew close, took her hands from her face and wiped her tears away. His rage was spent now. Indeed, he was very satisfied with how everything had turned out. He had the information he needed, Rishona's toys could yet be delivered whole, and Adiana's exceptional music was still his to enjoy.

He lifted a cup of wine to her lips, and she accepted it with desperate gulps. Her fine golden hair hung ragged over bruised cheeks. The tremble on her bloodied lips was most inviting. Mechnes considered taking her by force in that moment, as had often pleased him, but it occurred to him it might be more entertaining to indulge in a game of seduction with this musician, merchant's daughter and whore from Selkynsen.

She sputtered in the middle of a swallow and shoved the cup away, a shudder running through her shoulders as she sank into another round of weeping.

"You mustn't take it so hard, Mistress Adiana," Mechnes said quietly, brushing a lock of hair from her face and taking her chin tenderly in hand. "That is a rare gift, the music that resides in your soul. I am most pleased you did not see fit to surrender it."

Chapter 16

"What was that creature?" Borten's voice, stern and direct, jolted Eolyn out of her reverie.

The knight had waited two days before confronting her with the question. Still, Eolyn did not feel ready to answer. She averted her gaze to where Mariel stood with her skirts hitched up, arms wrapped tight around her slender body. The quiet waters of the Tarba lapped at her ankles. The summer sky glowed with a deep sapphire hue that under any other circumstances would have instilled joy in a girl's heart. Yet Mariel did not smile, nor did she move, save for a subtle rocking of her body in synchrony with the swaying reeds.

"I'm worried about her," Eolyn said. "She hasn't spoken a word since we scattered their ashes."

They had burned the bodies of Sirena and Delric in accordance with the old rites, on a pyre of Beech to preserve the old, Alder to protect the new, and Ash for wisdom during times of loss. As Eolyn had lifted her voice to mourn their passing, the smoke had twisted toward the heavens in black billows and drifted in a charcoal haze over the rim of the South Woods.

I sing for the passing of this witch, this warrior,
These wise and beautiful friends
Who brought joy to our days and laughter to our nights…

"Eolyn." Borten laid a hand on her arm, calling her back to the present. "Answer my question."

She studied his face, the strength behind those clear blue eyes. His touch ignited a dull ache inside her, a longing to wrap herself in his arms and never come out again.

Even so, every time she looked at him she felt as if she were searching for someone else.

"I am not certain, Borten. If I knew, I would have spoken to you about it by now." Her voice was constricted. She cleared her throat and called to her student. "Mariel, come! We have delayed long enough."

For a moment, the girl showed no signs of having heard. Then she withdrew from the water, retrieved her boots and came up the steep bank to join them. Her gait was heavy and her gaze vacant. Eolyn put one arm around her waist and pulled her close in a gentle embrace.

"We've but half a day of travel left," she said in quiet encouragement. "Then we'll be home again, eating Renate's soup and Adiana's bread, playing games with the girls, sleeping in our own beds."

Eolyn touched her student's chin. Mariel responded with a hesitant smile, though her eyes remained shadowed with sorrow.

"I'll need you to be strong for the young ones, Mariel," Eolyn continued. "It'll be difficult news for everyone."

The girl nodded, but her shoulders sagged.

Troubled, Eolyn bit her lip and withdrew. "Perhaps we could walk for a little while, give the horses a rest and take in some of this fine day. What do you say, Sir Borten?"

His scowl rendered any response unnecessary. Borten wanted them to return to the school with all haste. Though Eolyn shared his sense of urgency, she also saw that Mariel's spirit could not be rushed. The girl needed time, fresh air, warm days, and quiet nights.

Most of all, she needed quiet nights.

"There are things you and I must discuss, Sir Borten," Eolyn insisted. "It will be easier, if we walk."

This seemed to appease him, though his nod was stiff. Leading the horses by the reins, they started downriver once more, Eolyn falling in step beside Sir Borten, Mariel lagging behind.

"That monster in the South Woods…" Eolyn's heart spasmed, and her voice failed her. She yearned to share her fears and doubts, yet every time she drew a breath to speak of the attack, some inexplicable force silenced her. She paused, connected her spirit to the earth, and tried again. "I have seen it before, or something very much like it, when Tzeremond banished my spirit to the Underworld. I believe it was a Naether Demon."

For a long moment, Borten did not reply. Their feet sounded against the grass, accompanied by the rhythmic plod of the horses behind them. A fresh wind blew across the rolling hills, muffling the songs of warblers and thrushes.

"I know something of those legends," he said. "It would make sense. All the beast took from Sirena was her heart."

"But it does not make sense, Sir Borten. The Naether Demons were trapped in the Underworld, banished for all ages. How could it have escaped, and why here in the South Woods? The curse of Ahmad-dur has been reversed only once that I know of, when it was cast upon me. Akmael . . .I mean the King, was able to bring me back because very little time had passed, and my earthly body was still intact. My spirit had a home to which it could return. The Naether Demons have no earthly bodies left, and even if they did those vessels would be on the other side of the kingdom, in the Wastes of Faernvorn. Not here in Moehn."

"That beast was not made of flesh and blood. You saw how our swords passed through it. Only the weapon of the Galian sorcerers could cut it open." He nodded toward Kel'Baru, now hanging on his belt.

She rubbed her forehead, troubled by the nagging sense that she had all the pieces necessary to solve this puzzle, if only she could put them in proper order. Pausing in her gait, she closed her eyes and focused on the darkness within.

"Corey." The sound of his name on her breath surprised her. "Corey might know."

"The mage of East Selen? Why?"

Indeed, why? Eolyn's pace quickened, as if every step could bring her closer to an answer. "Something he said once. If I could only remember…"

Borten stopped in his tracks, eyes fixed on the horizon. A frown filled his face.

"What is it?" she asked, following the direction of his gaze.

Two dark lines twisted against the sky, one toward the west and the other further north, as if some great hand had drawn a line of watery ink from the earth to the heavens.

"Moehn," he murmured, "and the *Aekelahr*."

In a flash of horror, Eolyn dropped the reins and ran, feet pounding hard against the earth until she reached the top of the next ridge and stood breathless, one hand shielding her eyes from the bright sun, trying to see what distance refused to reveal.

Borten came up beside her.

"Burning?" she said in disbelief. "Both of them? How can that be? Gods help us . . . the children!"

Energy coursed through her as she invoked the shape of Hawk.

"What are you doing?" demanded Borten, but already she had left him, soaring high toward the heavens. "Eolyn, stop!"

She keened while catching an updraft, letting his figure fall away. The landscape billowed into broad rolling plain of golden green, dark patches of forest nestled inside shallow ravines, the Tarba a silver ribbon winding between low hills. With the pulse of the wind beneath her wings, Eolyn veered west toward the school. At last it came into view, and her worst fear was realized.

Eolyn alighted on the western wall, clinging to the form of Hawk, too stunned to think beyond the burnt out hulls that confronted her. She ruffled her feathers, flapped her wings, and settled again on her perch, restless and uncertain, eyes darting between the blackened stone ruins that had once been the kitchen, the herbarium, the study, her quarters. A strident cry escaped her, repeating in a string of staccato notes as grief beat relentless through her breast, excruciating and implacable.

Was this all that was left after years of labor and a lifetime of hope?

Was this the reward of the Gods for the many sacrifices of her heart?

With a stroke of her powerful wings, Eolyn soared upward and circled the complex, seeking some sign of Adiana, Renate, or the girls, but the place was deserted. Gardens, medicines, books, all her greatest treasures reduced to ash.

A flutter of black wings drew her gaze south, alerting her to a flock of ravens beyond a nearby ridge. Eolyn flew toward them. At their center she saw a forsaken corpse, a flash of cloth dyed midnight blue, the color of a Middle Maga.

She charged into the ravens screaming, wings spread and talons extended, clawing at their black eyes and snapping at their sharp beaks. In moments, the lesser birds scattered, hissing their fury but respecting her dominance. When they had retreated she resumed her human form, and knelt trembling beside what was left of Renate.

The maga's head had disappeared. Her gut was torn open, emptied by a scavenger in the night. The rest of her ragged remains were being picked to pieces by the ravens.

"Oh, my dear, sweet sister." Eolyn covered her face and wept.

The sun continued its slow arc toward the western sky. The ravens cawed, impatient, a few paces away. Eolyn lifted her face to the breeze, drew a shuddering breath, and wiped the tears from her cheeks though they had not yet ceased to flow.

The grass was whispering, *You cannot stay.*

Borten would be sick with worry, and furious. Even now he might be galloping toward the school, Mariel dragging in his wake. She had to stop them before they came too close, for whoever did this might yet be wandering the hills.

"You there!"

Eolyn jumped, and scrambled to her feet. Three men-at-arms were approaching, one on foot with bow drawn, the others mounted behind. They were too far away to recognize their faces, but Eolyn could see their colors. These were not the King's soldiers.

"What business have you here?" one of them called.

Eolyn took a few steps backwards.

"Answer me!"

She turned and ran.

An arrow hissed past her, and she leapt forward, plunging into the shape of Wolf, bounding over the hill as fast as four legs could take her. Shouts pursued her, followed by the whinny and prance of horses. Panic nipped at her heels. She did not dare look back.

Already fatigued from grief and flight, Eolyn did not know how long she could run, much less hold the shape of Wolf. Another arrow shot past, grazing her back with its heat. She yelped and began a desperate run, dodging arrows as she followed the ravines, hoping the ridges would conceal the path of her retreat, keeping head and tail low while her pursuers fanned out behind her. Her breath came in harsh pants, her tongue hung steaming from her jowls, her muscles ached with every movement.

Suddenly her snout caught the peppery green scent of woodlands. Lifting her head Eolyn spotted a small patch of forest nestled between two hills. She hurtled toward the cover and crashed into the underbrush, thorny branches scraping her flanks as she sought refuge under the shifting shadows of the bushes.

Once inside, she crouched low and froze, peering through the dense branches, every muscle taut. She heard the horses' thunder before she saw them rush by in a blur of color. The leaves rattled in their wake. When the hoof beats faded, Eolyn crept further into the forest, scooting along the ground until the thorn bushes gave way to an open understory.

She stood and shook out her fur.

Every breath burned in her lungs, and pain shot up her foreleg when she put weight on it. Limping toward the broad trunk of an old beech, she settled exhausted at its base. Her belly felt hot upon the cool dirt, blood pounded through her veins. She rested her muzzle on her paws, eyes open and ears alert, burdened with sorrow and angst, fearing with all her heart that the soldiers would recognize their mistake and return before she recovered her strength.

Chapter 17

A mournful wail rose from the Queen's chambers, a bitter melody of loss and death that crescendoed then faded, leaving Akmael and the others who kept vigil outside burdened by a heavy silence.

Presently the door to Taesara's room opened and High Mage Rezlyn appeared. The physician's aspect was worn. He had cleaned his hands meticulously, but blood stained his sleeves, and a grave mood clouded his aged eyes. He paused for moment and glanced around the room, as if taking stock of those present, Taesara's ladies and the new ambassador of Roenfyn among them.

Approaching Akmael, Rezlyn bowed and announced in subdued tones, "I believe the worst has passed, my Lord King. The Queen will recover, though she requires much rest. I am most sorry to inform you, however, that it is too late for the child."

"Too late?" The words felt out of place somehow.

Time has no meaning for a mage, Tzeremond had often told him.

How, then, could it be too late?

"She bleeds heavily, my Lord King, and no remedy known to me has been able to slow the hemorrhaging. The Prince will not be saved."

Akmael set his jaw, channeling the surge of grief and anger deep into his core.

Rage is not to be directed at the Gods, but held within and used for a greater purpose. The Gods take from us to incite our anger. They incite our anger to unleash the full potential of our power.

"The Queen is weak," continued Rezlyn, "and sick with remorse. She must be confined to her bed for the coming days, until the bleeding stops."

"And her womb?"

"Intact, thank the Gods. She will bear children again."

"I would see her at once."

"As you wish, my Lord King." Rezlyn stepped to one side.

"King Akmael, if it pleases you, I would also see my niece." Lord Penamor, the new ambassador from Roenfyn, spoke. A lean man with a long face and gray eyes, he had in the end been escorted from the piers by High Mage Tzetobar.

Akmael nodded. "I will advise the Queen that you are here."

"I would prefer to accompany you now."

The King stiffened. It was an impertinent request for a recently arrived guest of his court. "You will see the Queen at her command, Lord Penamor."

The ambassador's lips twitched, but he indicated his acquiescence with a respectful bow.

Inside the Queen's chambers, the Lady Sonia attended Taesara, refreshing her pallid face with a damp cloth. Noting the King's entrance, Sonia threw a fresh coverlet over the Queen's lap to hide the damp and soiled sheets.

At the foot of the bed, a small table had been set with midnight blue candles and burning sage. The sight brought a surge of grief, and Akmael checked his emotions at the loss of his son. He paused over the candles and sang the songs of passage, sending what magic he could into the Underworld, that the child's fragile soul might survive the dark maze and enter the halls of his ancestors.

Taesara's remorse hung over the room like a bitter mist, carrying with it the unpleasant smell of blood and salt. She hid her face behind trembling hands and refused to show her countenance even as Akmael took a place at her side. For many moments no words were exchanged between them, the silence of the room broken only by the Queen's stifled sobs.

"Leave us," Akmael said to the Lady Sonia. The woman cast a nervous glance at the Queen then curtsied and departed, taking the servants and other ladies with her.

Akmael sat on the bed and extracted Taesara's hands from her face. They were clammy, her grip limp and without strength, her cheeks splotched as if by a fever. She directed her gaze toward some empty place in front of her.

"I am much grieved by this news," he said.

"Forgive me, my Lord King." Her voice was surprisingly steady given the tremor in her shoulders.

"There is nothing to forgive. It was I who permitted you to ride. You are not to carry this burden, nor will we speak of it again."

She blinked and nodded, but did not meet his gaze.

"High Mage Rezlyn has assured me you suffered no injury and will soon be able bear more children."

"If it please my Lord King." She bit her lip, choked back a sob. "Then it will be so."

"It would please me." Akmael brought her listless fingers to his lips. In truth, he doubted his own words. Taesara's bed was a place of stark duty and little pleasure. He suspected he would not be inclined to seek it once Eolyn was returned to him. "I cannot linger, my Queen. Moehn may be under siege, and I must speak with Mage Corey to see what else he has learned from the girl."

She withdrew her hand and looked at him, her expression sad and uncertain. "Stay with me a little while longer."

"High Mage Rezlyn will see you are well cared for."

She swallowed, drew an unsteady breath, took his hand once more. "My Lord King, do you not think it is curious how that girl arrived, in that moment and precisely that place?"

He found the comment puzzling. "We are uncertain how it came about. The device should have taken her to the Maga Eolyn."

"Yet she appeared in front of me, and sent my horse—a creature that has always been gentle in nature—into panic."

Akmael withdrew from her touch and hardened his expression. "Speak plainly, Taesara. What is your concern?"

She pursed her lips and held her silence for a moment. "Forgive me, my Lord King, for what I am about to say. I am a woman of discretion, but I am not without ears. I have heard the rumors of your youth, how you once meant something to that woman, the witch from Moehn."

"Taesara, it is not your place—"

"I know, my Lord King. I have never questioned the events of the past, nor have I ever doubted your loyalty to me, my house and my people. But that witch is dangerous. I cannot help but suspect my illness in Moehn was her doing, and the loss of this child as well."

"Impossible." Akmael's tone was resolute, final.

"There was witchcraft at work today. I am certain of it."

"A maga of Moisehén would not put her powers to such foul use."

"I grew up listening to stories of your magas. They declared war against your father, and brought this kingdom to near ruin. It would be a little thing for them to kill a prince."

Akmael rose in anger. "Enough of these accusations."

"My Lord King, I only want—"

"You want nothing but to deny your own failure, Taesara. I intended to relieve you of the burden of that guilt, as I thought the pain of our loss was punishment enough. But my mercy has been ill-received."

"Please, my Lord King!" A sob broke through her words. "Do not speak such cruelties. Remember that I bore our first child without any difficulties. I am neither weak nor unskilled as a rider. You must at least consider—"

"I will consider none of this foolishness."

"I speak only out of concern for our future, the future of our sons, of your kingdom!"

He took hold of her arm, his grip so harsh she cried out. "You accuse an innocent woman—and a mere child—of high treason. Maga Eolyn and her students are faithful servants of the Crown. If you ever utter such lies again, you will suffer far worse than my wrath."

Akmael released her as suddenly as he had taken hold of her. Taesara collapsed into a fit of tears, but her distress only magnified his distaste. Without further word, he abandoned her.

In the antechamber, a steward waited with word from Mage Corey, who was requesting an immediate audience. Akmael gave instructions to have the mage wait for him in the Council room, along with Sir Galison. Lord Penamor stepped forward with yet another petition to see the Queen, but Akmael denied his request and informed High Mage Rezlyn that Taesara was not to receive any visitors except by his leave.

When Akmael arrived at the Council room, Corey and Galison stood at the long oak table, maps of the eastern territories laid out before them. The bright and breezy morning had given away to a stifling afternoon heat. Though the southern windows were flung open, perspiration beaded everyone's brow, the faint smell of sweat like a silent herald of battles to come.

"My Lord King," Corey greeted Akmael with a respectful bow, his expression one of pronounced concern, his tone deferential. "What news of your son?"

"The Prince is lost." Akmael's voice was terse, his heart already hardened.

Corey studied him a moment, brow furrowed. "I am most grieved to hear it. And the Queen?"

"She will recover soon enough."

"May the Gods make it so," said Sir Galison.

The King acknowledged their condolences with a brief nod. "What have you gathered from the girl, Mage Corey?"

"If I interpret her testimony correctly, it would seem Moehn has been taken by a band of Syrnte raiders. They destroyed the school, burned the town, and have camped outside what remains of the walls."

The useless walls of Moehn, Akmael thought bitterly. Too long had he waited to attend to the reinforcement of that province. The Gods were indeed punishing his complacency.

"They must have come from the east." Akmael drew forth one of the maps. "Here, around the flank of the Paramen Mountains. An ancient trade route, perhaps. Or a path known only to the foresters that wander the region."

"An army cannot be brought up a forester's path," said Galison.

"They would not have required many men to take Moehn, and for all we know they have opened the path into a proper road. Mage Corey, what of the maga? Does the girl know anything of her whereabouts?"

"Eolyn departed for the South Woods a few days before the attack, accompanied by Sir Borten, Delric and two of her students. The night the school was taken, she had not yet returned."

Akmael expressed his relief with a slow exhale. There was hope, then, for no one knew the South Woods better or could find safer refuge within its corridors than Eolyn. "How many men among the Syrnte?"

"Impossible to tell," Corey said. "If I were to believe the child, I would say thousands. But she has never seen an army, and did not—I think—see this one very well, so what appeared an infinite horde to her may be no more than a few hundred men."

"An army of significant size cannot traverse such rugged terrain," insisted Galison.

"We would be unwise to rest on that assumption. The rebel Ernan amassed a formidable army in the forests of East Selen, man by man and weapon by weapon over many months. We have always assumed his followers passed unnoticed in small groups through the western territories, but they may have had other routes of entry about which we were never informed." Akmael cast an acerbic gaze toward Mage Corey. "What say you, who knew that failed movement all too well?"

Corey set his jaw under the King's assessment, his silver green eyes calm as a serpent in the summer sun. "Their routes of entry were just as I informed you, my Lord King. Ernan's men came from Galia across the Sea of Rabeln, and Khelia's warriors descended from the Paramen Mountains into Selkynsen. Both travelled along the northern hills of the Taeschel range to meet Ernan in East Selen. Additional rebels were gathered from the peasant classes of Moisehén, and when Ernan forged his alliance with Selen he called upon the levies of those treacherous lords."

"And the Syrnte?" prompted Galison. "It was said they, too, were party to the rebellion."

The mage let go an impatient breath. "The Syrnte were always enigmatic participants in Ernan's movement. Rishona and Tahmir, for the most part, worked on their own, intent upon their pact of vengeance against Tzeremond, with only a handful of guards at their disposal. But Ernan was promised a hundred or so Syrnte cavalry, which at the time I departed his company had not yet appeared. Nor, as the King well knows, did these mounted soldiers materialize during the Battle of Aerunden. It was never revealed to me how Rishona and Tahmir's men were expected to enter the kingdom unnoticed, and until this day I had assumed they never did."

Akmael studied his cousin in wary contempt, frustrated once more by the capriciousness of the Gods, who had seen fit to take away so fine and straightforward an advisor as Tzeremond and leave this man—who never once lied and yet had proven a master of deception—as the highest ranking mage of the kingdom. "Mage Corey, when we finish here, you will accompany Sir Galison to speak with our mage warriors. You will tell them all you know of the Syrnte and the magic that is at their disposal. If I should discover at any time that you have withheld information of importance, I will have you drawn and quartered, and your remains thrown to the wolves."

The mage bowed, apparently undaunted by the King's threat. "As you wish, my Lord King."

"Galison, once Corey has finished his task, you are to send a hundred additional men—twenty mage warriors among them—to Rhiemsaven. They will communicate all we know about the Syrnte to Sir Drostan and be placed under his command."

"I will see it done, my Lord King."

"If I may be so bold, my Lord King." Corey directed their attention to yet another map of the eastern provinces that displayed Selen to the north and Moehn to the south. "History and habit compel us to think of East Selen and the South Woods as separate entities, when in fact they comprise a single swath of dense forest, separated in only the most minimal sense by the low ridges of the Taeschel Mountains. If the Syrnte have come from the east into Moehn, they may also find passage directly into Selen."

"We should consider sending reinforcements to that province as well," said Galison.

The knight's conclusion, however well founded, did not please Akmael. Selen was almost as ill-prepared as Moehn to defend itself. Governance had become weak and disorganized after Ernan's uprising, when the King had purged the province of its most rebellious lords. In all of Selen, Corey was the most reliable man Akmael had, a sobering thought if there ever was one.

"In addition to our effort to protect the eastern border," the mage continued, "I would also counsel that we not forget the sorry state of Tor Binder. We need to resume our vigilance of the Wastes of Faernvort—a recent proposal that was endorsed, as you may remember, by Sir Drostan himself."

Akmael clenched his jaw. "How thin would you have me spread my army, Mage Corey?"

The man paused as if considering the question carefully. "My Lord King, the Syrnte have powers beyond our understanding. They allowed me very little insight to their ways during their time with the Circle. But we know Princess Rishona summoned a Naether Demon when she slew Tzeremond. I would not put it past her to bring those creatures into her service now."

"From the Wastes of Faernvort?" Galison expressed his skepticism with a sardonic smile. "She'd need a spell that reaches clear across the kingdom."

"There are spells that conquer great expanses of place and time," Corey replied. "They may be uncommon, rare even in legend, and difficult to weave. But they exist. It was just such a spell that brought the girl to us today."

"I will take your advice under consideration, Mage Corey," Akmael conceded, "but for the moment we must prioritize the known threats. We will first secure the Pass of Aerunden, and then proceed from there. That will be all, both of you, until we meet again this afternoon in full Council."

Sir Galison turned to take his leave, but Corey said, "One more question, if you would permit me, my Lord King. The device that brought the child here. I presume it remains in your possession?"

"Yes."

"I would counsel you not to use it."

Akmael studied the mage, remembering their meeting on the eve of Ernan's rebellion, when Corey was bound and beaten deep inside the dungeons of Vortingen. Even then his swollen and discolored face had failed to diminish the imperturbable authority with which he always spoke.

"Galison, you may retire to the antechamber until I have finished with Mage Corey."

The knight departed with a brief bow. When the heavy oak doors shut behind him, Akmael turned on his cousin with a harsh tone. "Speak and speak plainly. I have no patience today for your riddles."

"Mine is a simple concern, my Lord King. We do not know the fate of the maga, and therefore have no manner of anticipating where the device will take you. Should the jewel land you in the middle of a Syrnte camp, we will have lost Moisehén in a single blow."

"I have considered this possibility, and will await Drostan's assessment of the situation in Moehn before taking any action to retrieve her."

Corey shook his head. "While we wait, she may be at the mercy of those invaders. Forgive my presumption, my Lord King, but I do not have the heart to abandon Eolyn to such a fate, and neither do you."

"Our first duty lies with the kingdom." Akmael spoke with more conviction than he felt. "We cannot risk the future of Moisehén for the sake of one woman."

"Eolyn is the key to our future. Her magic is just as important to this kingdom as the bloodline of Vortingen." Corey drew a slow breath and set his silver-green eyes upon Akmael's. "Send me to find her."

"I am to trust you with such a task?"

"You entrusted her to me once before, and I did not fail you."

"You delivered Maga Eolyn to the rebels."

"I put her in the safest place imaginable, under the guardianship of her brother, and thus kept her alive. You have no other subject who sets a higher priority upon Eolyn's fate than I do. You know this." Corey stepped close and lowered his voice. "You saw her in Moehn, my Lord King. Does she still wear the serpent upon her arm?"

Corey referred to a bracelet wrought in silver, etched with images of Dragon, an heirloom of the Clan of East Selen. "Yes."

"Then she is one of us, and I am sworn to protect her. Send me to Moehn. I will find the maga and deliver her to you whole, or may Dragon in his wisdom destroy me and all my magic."

Chapter 18

Eolyn found Borten and Mariel where she had left them on the banks of the Tarba. Mariel sat grim faced and silent. Borten paced restlessly, hand on the hilt of his sword, eyes scanning the western horizon.

She fluttered down as Hawk, her descent more of a fall than a proper landing. The muscles in her chest and back burned with fatigue. Her legs failed to hold her weight, and her feathered stomach hit the ground with a thud, forcing a squawk from her throat. Using what strength remained to her, she recaptured her human form and lay panting on the grass, hair undone and falling about her shoulders in ragged tresses, wrist throbbing from the injury she had sustained as Wolf.

Uttering a guttural curse, Borten marched over, grabbed her by the arm and hauled her to her feet. Eolyn cried out in pain, her body revolting against the sudden movement, but the knight paid no heed. He dragged her away from Mariel, his long stride indifferent to Eolyn's awkward stumble as she struggled to keep pace. At last Borten released Eolyn with a harsh shove that landed her at his feet.

"If you ever run off like that again, I swear to the Gods I will kill you myself!"

Eolyn lifted a hand to ward off his anger. "I'm sorry, Sir Borten. I did not think—"

"No, you did not." His face was red with fury, veins bulged at his neck. "You had best learn how to think, Maga Eolyn, or that fool's impulse of yours will be the death of us all."

She nodded, unable to find the breath for more words. The earth was lurching beneath her like an angry river. Her shoulders sagged, her stomach contracted violently, and she spewed bile upon the grass. Gasping, she dragged herself away from the pool of vomit, sat weary upon her heels and hid her face in her hands.

"It's gone," she moaned. "All of it. The kitchen, the dormitory, the stables, the herbarium, my study. All burned to the ground. Renate is dead. Adiana and the girls have disappeared."

Borten paced in front of her, feet falling heavy against the grass. After a moment, he stopped and let go a long exhale. Kneeling next to her, he offered a flask of minted water that she used to rinse the bile from her mouth.

"And Moehn?" he asked, his voice taking on a gentler tone.

"I did not go to Moehn." She managed a weak smile. "I am foolish, but not that foolish."

Borten's expression softened. He reached forward, drew a few unruly tresses away from her face, brushed a tear off her cheek.

"Any indication of who did this?"

Eolyn nodded, her heart sinking into despondency. "I saw their colors, a burgundy flame against a sand-colored field. They are Syrnte warriors."

"The Syrnte?" Borten's brow furrowed. "How? They would have to march through Antaria and Roenfyn before crossing Selkynsen, where they would have met with the Mage King. We should have, at the very least, heard about this invasion long before they arrived."

Eolyn shook her head. "There's another way. An old route that runs along the northwest flank of the Paramen Mountains."

"I've never heard of such a road," Borten said doubtfully. "How did you come by this knowledge?"

"Ernan intended for me to escape that way with his Syrnte allies, in event his rebellion failed."

Borten studied her, curiosity flickering behind his eyes. "Your brother's rebellion did fail. Why, then, did you not flee with his allies?"

The blood was returning to her cheeks now, and the midday sun warmed her skin. "Because—as you have well learned Sir Borten—I am rarely inclined to listen to men-at-arms."

He rolled his eyes and looked away, but a grin broke upon his countenance. Borten stood and proffered his hand to help her up. Eolyn steadied herself on her feet and brushed the soil from her skirt. Still dizzy and slightly nauseous, she took hold of Borten's arm as they started back toward Mariel.

"I ignored my brother's wishes because my place is here, among our people. When I received the staff of High Magic, I promised Dragon I would restore the tradition of the Magas to Moisehén. I could hardly succeed in that task were I living on the other side of the Paramen Mountains. I would never flee this kingdom, even if it meant facing death on the pyre." She stopped, brought her fingers to her lips. "Borten, we must find out what has happened to Adiana and the girls."

He shook his head. "It is too late for those left behind at the *Aekelahr*. Even if Adiana and the girls were taken alive, they are likely dead by now. At best, they have been badly used and are beyond our aid."

"Surely you are not suggesting we leave their fates to the whims of those marauders?"

Borten turned to face her, set his hands on her shoulders. "Their fates are already decided. We are only two people, you and I, with a young and confused girl as our ward. We have our own survival to think about. There is nothing we can do for Mistress Adiana or your students."

She stared back at him in disbelief. "How can you possibly expect me to—?"

"Our task is a greater one now." Each word was spoken with a great intensity of purpose. "Eolyn, if you listen to me only once in your life, then let it be in this moment. You must escape Moehn and get word to the King."

"Well, I can get word to the King right away. All I have to do is—"

Her hand went instinctively to her breast, where she had worn Akmael's gift close to her heart for so long.

"Ghemena," she whispered. What hope was left for her students crumbled into a void of certainty.

"What about Ghemena?" Borten asked.

"I gave her a device before we left, an amulet crafted by Queen Briana that would have allowed her to come to us on a moment's notice. Nothing would have kept her from using it . . . nothing except death itself."

The silence that followed was long and bleak. Wind blew hard across the rolling plains, shaking the folds of Eolyn's skirt, whipping through her loose tresses. High overhead, white clouds chased each other toward the east

"Tell me I am wrong." Eolyn searched Borten's face. Her heart threatened to shatter under the weight of her grief. "Tell me that Ghemena, at least, might still be alive."

"Those men who have claimed Moehn, will make for the Pass of Aerunden with all haste." Borten pronounced each word with care. "They will take control of the pass, and kill or turn back any peasant they find along the way. It could be days before the merchants of Rhiemsaven realize the oxcarts are no longer arriving from Moehn. Even if they send word to the King at once, it will be yet another two days before their fastest messenger reaches the City. By then, the Syrnte may well have an army assembled in the valley below the pass."

The full horror of their situation enveloped her like a black fog. "You think they mean to take the entire kingdom."

"They did not break open that ancient pass to raid a handful of peasant farmers and go home. Moehn is but a stepping stone to the precious mines of Selkynsen, the iron hills of Moisehén, the wells of magic that spring from East Selen."

"So we are at war once again." The grim irony of the situation was not lost on her. "What should we do?"

"You must take flight."

"Flight?"

"Like you did now. As a hawk or an eagle. Go to the King's City and warn our liege."

"It's not that easy. Shape shifting requires a great deal of magic. I could not sustain the illusion for that long."

"What about your staff? Can you fly on that, as the High Mages do?"

"Yes." She responded with a thoughtful nod. "But I would have to go by night, and even then it could be dangerous. The Syrnte may be able to detect my aura in the dark."

"How long would it take for us to reach the pass if we flew?"

"About a day. A night, rather. Two, at most. But Borten, I could not take you or Mariel along." The words stuck like burrs on her tongue. "My staff will carry only me."

His face fell. He took a few paces away from her and stopped, hand on the hilt of his sword, eyes fixed on the rolling clouds. After a moment Eolyn approached him and set a tentative hand upon his arm.

"I don't want to leave either of you here," she said, "not with that army and those creatures lurking about. Mariel is the only student I have left. Her life is my own. And you…" A lump rose in her throat. She blinked and looked away. "I won't go like this, unless you tell me there is no better way."

He drew a deep breath and cast her a sideways glance. "I don't suppose you can turn us both into owls that we might fly at your side?"

She shook her head.

"Or mice, and take us along in your pocket?" A faint smile played upon his lips.

"No, Sir Borten. Mariel is in no state to undertake shape shifting, and you know far too little of the language of plants and animals. If I change either of you into another creature, I would lose you to their world."

"I see." He studied her a moment. "I cannot have you cross the province alone and without protection."

"It would only be one night, perhaps two, before I reach the border."

"It does not matter. I will not abide any uncertainty as to whether you've escaped alive. We will travel together to the western arm of the Taeschel Mountains, and find a place south of the pass where you can make the flight into Selkynsen safely."

She nodded her acquiescence, torn between the urgency that tugged at her spirit and the relief that she could rely upon Borten's steadfast presence for a few more precious days.

Chapter 19

Mechnes took the evening meal with his officers. He sent for Adiana that she might play with the musicians who had traveled with him from the city of Ech'Nalahm. One of these, named Kahlil, a dark skinned young man who hailed from the southern reaches of the Syrnte Empire, rose to his feet when Adiana entered flanked by guards. The force of his astonishment hit Mechnes like the raw wind of a desert storm. Adept at concealing his thoughts from Syrnte magic, the musician buried the impact of Adiana's appearance deep in his interior before the Syrnte Lord could capture it with clarity. Adiana's memories of Kahlil, however, spilled forth like jewels from a merchant's purse. Mechnes gathered them up one by one, and examined each with great curiosity.

Thus he learned that Adiana had known Kahlil some years before, when the Syrnte musician followed Rishona and Tahmir into the heart of Moisehén. Her memories of him were disturbing in their vibrance, full of laughter and song. The two had forged a strong bond of mutual admiration through their artistic endeavors, though there was no evidence of romance, as Mechnes was pleased to note.

Still, the tightness around Kahlil's lips and the determined effort he made not to let his gaze linger on Adiana's bruises was enough to arouse Mechnes's concern. His years in the company of musicians had taught the Syrnte Lord something of the workings of their hearts—irrational in motivation, unpredictable in action. Within moments the threads of Kahlil's possible futures coalesced in Mechnes's mind, causing him to frown. He did not relish the idea of sentencing his best composer to a miserable death because of some foolish act of heroism.

Mechnes resolved to speak with Kahlil regarding Adiana before allowing them to meet again.

Their music did not disappoint, providing lively accompaniment to the banter of his officers. Toward the end of the last course, the mournful tones of Idahm's flute invoked the melody of *Ihm mah'lid,* a classic Syrnte ballad of love and loss. Kahlil's voice rose rich and sorrowful; Adiana's accompaniment on the psaltery was passionate, impeccable. She understood this song, Mechnes realized, and had played it before. He wondered what other Syrnte ballads Kahlil had taught her. Under the spell of their interpretation, his men fell silent, hands growing idle at their cups, gazes drifting toward private thoughts, until only the sound of sweet longing filled the tent. A moment after the last chords were played, the officers broke into hearty applause.

The conversation spent and the hour grown late, Mechnes sent them all away save Adiana. She set aside the psaltery and remained in her chair, back erect, hands folded on her lap, eyes refusing to meet his. As if with this simple trick she could make him disappear. The thought amused Mechnes. He refilled his wine and drew up a chair to sit in front of her.

"You played well, with your old friend Kahlil."

She looked at him, startled. "He's told you about the Circle?"

"He has told me nothing. He did not know you were in my possession until this evening. But I have ways of knowing, Adiana. The gift of *Saefira* was given to me when I was a boy. It allows me to see the thoughts, desires, memories, and futures of those with whom I have established a close bond."

"You saw into his thoughts?"

"I saw into yours."

Such a beautiful pallor to her skin, when fear surged inside her breast.

"There is no bond between us," she said.

"In that you are mistaken. I broke open your spirit this afternoon, and made it mine."

"I am not broken."

"You are not ready to surrender to your new life; that is a different thing. But I can see into your heart now. I know what you want to do, and what you likely will do, in your attempts to escape the inevitable. Your place is with me now. You had best accept it. Look forward to your future, and forget the past. There are worse fates, after all, than being the favored musician of a Syrnte Prince."

He stood and approached her, ran his fingers over her feather-soft tresses. Producing a cloth of dark silk, he covered her eyes and secured the mask with a knot. "Play for me."

She obeyed, accepting the lute he gave her and invoking a melody that was simple but skillfully executed. Mechnes was glad for it. He needed a way to maim her—to prevent any attempt at escape—without compromising her beauty, grace or talent. Blinding could be a simple solution. A few drops of venom from the midnight *naja*, and her world would be cast in darkness. Though it might destroy the stunning color of her eyes, a sacrifice Mechnes preferred to avoid. Come morning, he would consult with his physician Xhoremy about the matter.

Adiana finished her song, set aside the instrument, and tried to remove the blindfold.

Mechnes stayed her hand. "No."

She stiffened as he enclosed her delicate fingers with his grip. Her stillness reminded him of the hermit crabs on the shores of Antaria, hiding from the sun inside their colorful shells. A fisherman's boy had shown him how to draw them out, blowing until their spiny forelegs and bulbous eyes unfolded like chitinous flowers.

Would Adiana blossom in the same way, he wondered, with one warm breath?

He pressed her fingers to his lips, studied the rise and fall of her bosom. Her breath quickened as he kissed the palm of her hand, and stopped when he tasted the satin-smooth skin of her wrist. With a choked sob she pulled away, stumbling as she fumbled with her blindfold. She managed to tear it off before reaching the table, where she sagged ashen-faced, one hand clutching her abdomen.

"Please," she gasped, "let me go to the children."

"We made an agreement, Adiana," he approached with a conciliatory tone. "You were to please me—and all my men—if I set your girls free."

She recovered her breath and straightened her shoulders, confronting him with clear blue eyes. "Then let me see them free."

"You will," he said, noting her surreptitious reach for a stray knife. "Tomorrow, when the San'iloman arrives, they are to be entrusted to her."

"From one gaoler to another? That is not freedom."

"What greater freedom can there be for a child, than to be made the ward of a queen?"

"They are not meant to be wards, they are meant to be magas. Free women, bound to no one, living in the tradition of Aithne and Caradoc."

Mechnes chuckled. No wonder Kedehen had done away with the magas and all their allies. No king in his right mind would tolerate such nonsense. "Who is to say they will not learn magic from the San'iloman? Those girls are merely trading one teacher for another, and advancing their station for it. Not only is their new mistress more richly appointed, she has a much greater chance of surviving this war."

Adiana lunged at him, blade flashing in the torchlight. Mechnes caught her with ease, forcing the knife from her grip and turning her hard against the table. Plates and cups clattered as she hit the surface with a sharp cry. Immobilizing her with one hand, he indulged in a generous exploration the curve of her back and the satisfying rise of her rump. The smell of her fear added a provocative spice to that aroma of summer winds and wild roses. Mechnes pressed tight against her, that she might feel the threat of his manhood through the ineffective shield of her russet skirts.

"I want no more violence between us," he said quietly. "Do you understand?"

She responded with sullen silence that he decided to accept as a yes.

He released her. "Get up."

Adiana dragged herself away from the table. Bits of food clung to her flaxen hair, and wine stained her dress. Hatred smoldered in her eyes, but this did not concern Mechnes. He had seen the brief flare of her desire when caressing her fingers with his lips, before she fled that moment of truth and buried it under a dutiful sense of revulsion. It was only a matter of time before he invoked her passion again and fanned it into an insatiable fire.

"Tomorrow you will be bathed and given fresh clothes," he said. "You are to meet the San'iloman. Just as you recognized Kahlil, you will recognize your new queen. You knew her once, as a fellow artist named Rishona."

"Rishona?" Adiana frowned. "Tahmir's sister, Rishona? She is the Queen of the Syrnte?"

"And of Moisehén."

"And she allows all of this?" Adiana opened her arm in a low sweeping gesture. There was such honest confusion in her tone that Mechnes could not help but smile.

"Allows it, and commands it."

"If her intention is to finish what Ernan started, there is no longer any need. We live in peace with the Mage King; the magas are being restored to Moisehén—"

"The San'iloman is the daughter of Ferien, the third son of Uriel. She is Queen of Moisehén by right of birth, and has come to claim her crown."

Mechnes allowed Adiana a few moments to assimilate his words.

"I must speak with her," she murmured.

"If you try, it will be your death. She is not the person you once called friend. Her guards are quick and ruthless. Any action in her presence that violates protocol will be met with their blades. I am warning you, Adiana: do not address her directly. If she speaks to you, you may respond, but do not meet her gaze. And for the love of any Gods you care to worship, never attempt to touch her."

"She will recognize me." Her voice was resolute, her gaze steady as a lake on a windless day. "She will remember our friendship."

"Yes, she will." He shrugged, and signaled for his guards, that they might return his prisoner to the cold solitude of her cell. "But you are a fool if you believe that will have any influence on your fate."

Chapter 20

"What will become of me?"

Eolyn started at the sound of Mariel's voice, so accustomed had she become to her silence. The girl had not spoken since the death of Sirena. She lay upon her cloak as if contemplating a fire. Above them, tenebrous clouds shrouded a waxing moon.

"When you leave us to find the King," she said, "what will happen to me?"

Eolyn, unable to sleep, had been sitting with her back against an isolated tree. Now she moved to lie next to her student, wrapping an arm around Mariel's waist.

"You're cold," she said. This worried her, as the night was very warm. "You should eat more, Mariel. You must maintain your strength."

"Why do you not answer my question?"

Eolyn sighed. Her body ached from the day's long journey through abandoned pastures and remnant woodlands. Her arms and shoulders were stiff from having spent the twilight hours practicing sword play with Borten. At nightfall, the knight had taken a position a few paces away to keep the first watch, Kel'Barú at his side. Eolyn's keen ears picked up a shift in his position, as if he had turned to give greater attention to their words.

"Because I, too, am uncertain about the future," she confessed.

"Will I be torn apart by one of those things that killed Sirena? Is that how I am going to die?"

"No, Mariel. That will never happen. Not if we can help it."

"You won't be able to help if you go to the King. You'll be too far away."

Eolyn's heart constricted at this truth.

"And you're taking your sword with you," Mariel continued, agitation coloring her words. "That sword's the only thing that will kill them."

"We have not seen another Naether Demon since we left the South Woods," Eolyn said. "Perhaps that was the only one that escaped the Underworld."

"There are more. I am certain of it. Such evil cannot walk this world alone."

Eolyn paused at Mariel's comment, sobered by the idea that evil might seek companionship. "The Doyenne Ghemena often told me there is no evil in this world except that which we create by our own choices."

"Then whoever created that monster must be very evil, and must have much company."

Eolyn snuggled closer to Mariel. The night was indeed taking on a chill. "Let us imagine you are right, Mariel, and that there are other Naether Demons let loose in the living world. We must then assume the wards I cast every evening have kept them away. So if you learn those wards and use them after I fly north, then you will be safe."

Mariel shivered and choked back a sob. "How long must Sir Borten and I continue like this? Wandering in the wilderness?"

"Only a few more days. He intends to take you north to the lands of his father, where he will hide you among the servants of his household. You will be safe there until the King comes to the aid of Moehn, or until I return. In the meantime, you must always do as Sir Borten says. Promise me that."

"You don't do as he says."

"No." Eolyn allowed a hint of amusement in her tone. "But I am a lucky fool, for the Gods have kept me safe in spite of it. They may not have as much patience with you."

Something between a sob and a laugh escaped Mariel's throat. Her shoulders shook, and she drew a sniffling breath. "They're all dead, aren't they? All our sisters are gone."

"Sir Borten insists they are dead to us, and in this he is right, Mariel. We cannot think about them anymore. Our first concern is the good of the kingdom, and the future of our magic. Even so, in my heart I believe the Gods have not yet called them home. I am hopeful we will one day be reunited."

"I miss them. I want them back." Tears spilled down Mariel's cheeks, and the girl surrendered to a fit of weeping. The outburst brought great relief to Eolyn. At last her student's wall of silence had crumbled. The girl would be better off for it, more able to look after herself in Borten's company after Eolyn's departure.

She held Mariel a long while, whispering words of comfort until the mourning gave way to exhaustion and then to sleep. She kissed the girl's forehead and tucked her cloak close around her shoulders. Then she rose and sought Sir Borten's company.

"You, too, should sleep," he said as she approached, though the admonishment was filled with gentle concern.

Her eyes had long since adjusted to the intermittent moonlight, and she could see his profile as he scanned the shadowy landscape. He did not allow as much as a glance to stray toward her as she sat next to him.

"I cannot sleep. Every time I close my eyes I am visited by horrible visions, of Adiana. The girls. The men who destroyed the school."

"You must keep your mind on the future, and have faith in the coming of the King's justice."

Eolyn had suffered the power of the King's justice when she was a small girl. Kedehen's wrath had left nothing in its wake, leveling her village, murdering the innocent, destroying all she had known and loved. She had loathed the King's justice in those times, and had dreamed of a world where such cruelty would cease to exist.

Now she longed to have that same terror executed on her behalf, to see all those who had caused this misery suffer under Akmael's most brutal retribution.

She raised her hands to cover her face. "Gods help me. I fear I am learning to hate."

Eolyn heard Borten shift his position, and felt the solid weight of his hand upon her shoulder. What an extraordinary gift the Gods had given to men, that they could communicate such strength in a single touch.

"Hate, well tempered," he said, "can be a powerful weapon."

She nodded, finding comfort in his words, and drew a sharp breath as she straightened her back. "The Doyenne Ghemena would have a few things to say about that, were she still here."

The impulse for revenge has no place in this household, the old maga had scolded her more than once, *much less in your lessons.*

"The struggles you face are your own, not hers," Borten replied.

Eolyn knew not whether it was his words or the cadence of his voice, but her tutor's specter faded into the shadows. Borten returned to his surveillance of the fields, and Eolyn remained at his side in companionable silence. A humid wind rustled through the leaves and grass; the contented songs of crickets and frogs filled the air with a rhythmic pulse.

"They expect rain," she said.

"Rain?" Borten's puzzlement was plain in his voice. "Who expects rain?"

"The frogs. They expect rain, and are most glad for it. It is a good night to…" She paused, having been on the verge of saying *to find a mate*, and finished instead with, "To sing."

Borten chuckled, a low sound beneath his breath that she had heard often in recent days, despite the many trials they had endured. "Your conversation is strange at times, Maga Eolyn. Do you always pay so much heed to the small creatures of the fields?"

"Of course. Sometimes we find the greatest wisdom in the smallest of creatures, Sir Borten."

"So you are much inclined to listen to frogs, yet disinclined to listen to men-at-arms?"

The question was put forward with humor, and Eolyn smiled. "Yes, I suppose I am."

"And what else do the frogs tell you, Maga Eolyn?"

He had taken her chin in his hand, though Eolyn had not noticed when, so natural was his touch. Borten's face was outlined by the shadows of the night. His musk of loam and crushed leaves wrapped around her and settled upon her shoulders like an old familiar cloak.

"I don't know," she stammered. "Just what I said . . . about the rain, and the song."

He kissed her without preamble, a brief and gentle touch that receded, then returned with greater need. Eolyn released herself to his desire, even as uncertainty overwhelmed her heart, for had she not just a fortnight before professed her love for Akmael?

Yet that seemed another world to her now, a different age inhabited by an unfamiliar Eolyn, an illusion on the other side of a chasm created by devastating and irreversible loss. And Borten, who had walked with her through the fires of these past days, who had sustained her in moments of unimaginable terror, was now washing away even the pain of her impossible love for the King, making her dreams of Akmael seem distant and small, like the stars destined to surrender their nighttime brilliance upon the arrival of the sun.

"Sleep, Eolyn," he murmured, gathering her against his chest. "I will call you when it is time."

"You can hardly expect her to sleep after a kiss like that."

The man's voice, bold and sarcastic, had Borten on his feet in an instant, with Kel'Barú unsheathed.

Eolyn rose as well, heart pounding in her chest. She cursed herself silently for having left her staff at Mariel's side. Indeed, for having left Mariel at all.

"Nor should you let her sleep," the intruder continued, "for a maga's passion is quick, but her heart is fickle."

In that moment Eolyn recognized the voice, and she placed a restraining hand on Borten's arm.

"Mage Corey," she demanded, "show yourself."

A few paces away, a flame ignited inside a malachite crystal set upon a long staff. The virescent glow illuminated Corey's face in eerie shades. His eyes sparked with a dry amusement that Eolyn had come to know all too well.

"Why are you here?" she asked warily.

"I was sent by our revered King, who having had news of events in Moehn is sick with worry over his beloved maga, as was I until this moment. I can see now we had no reason to fear. At least, not for the maga's life."

Eolyn sensed Borten's uncertainty at the strange and unexpected appearance of the King's cousin. The knight did not lower his weapon, and Eolyn stepped away that he might have room to use it.

"How did you find us?" Borten's words came sharp and settled like a blade at Corey's throat.

The mage regarded him like a sleepy cat assessing whether this particular field mouse was worth the trouble of a chase. He held his free hand close to the glow of his staff and let dangle from it a jewel of fine silver threads and glittering crystals. "With this."

Crying out, Eolyn sprang forward and snatched the silver web from him.

"Ghemena." She clutched the medallion to her heart, her breath caught between fear and hope. "Where is she? What have you done with her?"

"She is in the King's City, enjoying all the comforts of the Fortress of Vortingen."

"Impossible."

"This device brought her to us."

"It was meant to bring her to me!"

"So I understand."

Eolyn bit her lip, tormented by doubt, the memory of her brother's betrayal opening like a fresh wound in her heart. "Syrnte warriors have invaded Moehn."

"I know, as does the King. Young Ghemena shared everything she saw."

"What did she say of Catarina and Tasha? Of Adiana?"

"The girls were with her and unharmed when she used the device. She was not certain about Adiana."

"Not certain?"

"She had not seen her for many hours."

"You lie!"

"Lie?" Corey seemed truly taken aback by the accusation.

"Always, you have deceived me. Why should I believe you now?"

"I do not lie, Eolyn. Certainly not to you."

"You have friends among the Syrnte," she insisted. "Old friends in powerful positions. How am I to know you were not with them when they took Moehn, when they burned my school? How am I to know they did not send you to me now?"

"You have friends among the Syrnte as well." He responded in crisp tones. "Indeed, you had a lover among their princes, if I remember correctly. Am I then to suspect you of treason?"

"Enough of your insults!" Borten lunged at the mage.

Corey raised his staff to deflect the blow, but Kel'Barú cut through the magically cured walnut as if it were butter. Astonished, the mage sprang backwards and invoked a swift ward that halted the blade's descent, throwing Borten off balance. Corey hurled a yellow flame at the knight, but Eolyn intercepted it with a searing blue arc of her own. Their flames exploded upon contact, then fizzled in a shower of sparks, leaving a smell of sulfur and charred grass.

The frogs and crickets ceased their song.

Maga, knight, and mage watched each other in tense silence.

After a moment, Mariel's voice wafted toward them, anxious and uncertain.

"Maga Eolyn?" she said. "Is everything all right?"

"Stay where you are, Mariel," Eolyn replied. She strode toward Corey, her anger fueled by years of unspoken resentment. "Leave us. We do not want or need your assistance."

"Akmael will be most disappointed if you refuse my aid."

"I care not who sent you or why. Go back to the rancid hole you crawled out of."

"I cannot go anywhere now. The silver web that brought me here is in your possession, and your vile knight has broken my staff."

"Then shape shift into the snake you are and slither away!" she retorted. "With any luck, Owl will make a meal of you before dawn."

Corey studied her with narrowed eyes, a percipient smile playing upon his lips.

"What a strange fate the Gods have woven for you, Maga Eolyn. Here you are, on the high plains of Moehn, lost in the night, dogged by Syrnte invaders, robbed of your school and your nascent coven. Alone and with only two men to whom you can turn: I, who betrayed your brother." The mage's eyes flicked toward the knight, his words piercing the air like small daggers. "And Sir Borten, who killed him."

Eolyn gasped, disbelief curdling under a wave of dread. "What?"

She looked toward Borten, hoping he would deny the accusation. But the knight said nothing. His face lost all expression, save for eyes that hardened like granite and remained fixed on the mage.

The earth wavered, and she struggled to maintain her balance. It should not matter, she told herself, though her inner voice was desperate and small. They did not know each other in those times, and Borten had only acted to protect his liege.

Yet her stomach churned at the thought of the pleasure she had just taken from his kiss, and her throat burned with bile. Ernan's cruel accusations thundered forth from her memories, pounding against her head.

Will you betray your kin, Eolyn, as Briana betrayed hers?

What had she done, giving her heart and body to these men who, one by one, had brought about her brother's doom?

"Ah." Mage Corey's quiet voice cut through her thoughts. "I see the lovers have not yet had the opportunity to discuss this particular piece of their history."

Eolyn had never despised Corey more than in this moment.

"You are not welcome here," she said. "You cannot stay."

"I have sworn an oath to the King to return you safely to the City," Corey replied. "We can depart now, if you like, you with the jewel and I on your staff. Or you can endure my company for as long as necessary while we hide in this wilderness."

"If you remain," Borten informed him tersely, "you will not live through this night."

"Do not try to take me again with that insipid blade of yours," the mage shot back, "or I will send you to the Underworld in half a breath. You have already slain one friend of Eolyn's. I would counsel you against slaying another."

"You are no friend of mine!" Eolyn countered.

"Oh, but I am." He held his gaze steady against the heat of her rage. "I am the most valuable friend you have, Eolyn, though you have long refused to see it."

Chapter 21

Adiana woke with a start. The smell of dirt and straw greeted her, followed by the more acrid sting of human waste. She registered the shouts of men, stamps of horses, the sounds of metal and wood. Beneath it all, a rhythmic tremor in the earth reminded her of the day Ernan's troops had emerged from the forests of East Selen.

Trumpets sounded in the distance.

The San'iloman,Rishona, was marching into Moehn.

Adiana rolled onto her back, winced at the pain in her ribs. The dirt floor was hard and unyielding; her prison dark and plagued by strange rustlings in shadowy corners. There was not a muscle in her body that did not ache, except perhaps the most intimate part of her, the heart of her womanhood. She knew that would not be spared much longer.

If only he would let her see Tasha, Catarina, and Ghemena. Just that much would make everything else bearable.

Oh, Eolyn. What have the Gods done to us?

Presently a wash basin was brought to her, along with the fresh robes Lord Mechnes had promised. She turned her back on the guards and servant who watched her with curious eyes while she shed her old dress, hopelessly impregnated with the stench of fear and torture. The water was cool, scented with wild lilies. It refreshed her exhausted spirit, and seemed somehow the most luxurious bath she had ever taken despite the mean circumstances. The new undergarment and frock were simple but made of finely woven cotton. When she had nearly finished dressing the servant stepped forward to help her lace the bodice, and insisted on combing and plaiting her hair. They bound her hands and left her alone, bolting the door behind them.

Adiana remained standing in the dim light. She had not felt this clean in days and was reluctant to sit down in the dirt or lean against the soiled walls.

Moans and soft weeping came from the neighboring cells. Adiana had recognized the building where they were housed as the remains of a small brothel, the existence of which had been willfully ignored by the majority of the good citizens of Moehn. Yet the Maga Eolyn had visited it on occasion and with Adiana's assistance, tended to the girls who worked there. Adiana wondered where those girls were now, alive or dead, imprisoned or plying their trade freely with a host of new and eager clients.

In their place were captive women and children. Adiana had glimpsed a few members of the noble families of Moehn, others she could not see or recognize, but she had deduced from listening that she was the only prisoner with a cell to herself. The others were crowded like dogs in a kennel. Sometimes at night the whispers and weeping of her neighbors pitched into wails and terrible screams, accompanied by the laughter and satisfied grunts of the guards who came to have their way.

There are worse fates, Lord Mechnes's words returned unbidden, *than to be the favored musician of a Syrnte Prince.*

Adiana laughed out loud, giddy from exhaustion and lack of proper food, overwhelmed by the cruel irony of her situation. If only Renate or Eolyn were here to share the joke.

"No common soldier's rape for me," she announced to the shadows, lifting her chin in mock arrogance. "I have earned the favor of a Syrnte Prince, and therefore am to be granted a *royal* raping."

Renate's mocking laughter echoed back to her.

"Do you think princes have jeweled members, Renate? Perhaps their seed tastes like sweet spice, perhaps their blood runs with gold."

All men are common when they are naked, the old maga retorted. *All of them are just common men.*

"I want to see him dead," Adiana confessed. "I want to feel his royal blood running hot through my fingers."

Each blow returned fresh to her memory, every humiliating reminder of his dominance. What a foolish and desperate impulse that had been, to attack him. The only task Adiana had ever used a knife for was chopping vegetables. Even the preparation of pheasants, rabbits and other small game was beyond her sensibilities.

She had always left the bloodier kitchen endeavors to the girls, who had a much stronger stomach for such things than she.

"Is it true what he said?" she murmured. "Can he see my thoughts and desires, everything that I intend to do?"

Music is your magic, Renate reminded her. *Melody is your spell.*

The door sounded, jolting Adiana out of her thoughts. As the guards led her outside, Adiana squinted in the harsh light, searching the beige and burgundy tents for any sign of the girls. Already she knew this path well, and imagined she could walk it in the dark if ever the need arose.

Soon Lord Mechnes's pavilion came into view. His men had gathered in front of it, mounted soldiers and infantry forming long lines on either side of a straight path that led to the entrance. Adiana had not yet seen the Syrnte forces assembled in this fashion, and the solid wall of armor and mail, adorned by long spears and raised swords, brought renewed trepidation to her heart.

One of the guards shoved her in a harsh signal to quicken her pace. She stumbled and hurried to keep up as they took her behind the lines and through a side opening apparently meant for servants. Inside an old matron barked orders to a dozen servants who ran in as many directions as they tidied the tent and laid the table with abundant food and drink. Off to one side Kahlil and his companions prepared their own space. Adiana's heart leapt upon seeing him again. She forgot the presence of her guards even as they loosened her bonds. Though it hurt to smile she did so as she approached Kahlil and called his name.

The musician turned to greet her, though his acknowledgment was solemn and his gaze somewhat distracted. With a slight nod he indicated the seat next to him. Once she took her place he paid her no notice, but returned to his conversation with the others.

The silence hit her harder than any blow she had yet suffered at Mechnes's hands. It was incomprehensible, given the hope of friendship Kahlil had offered the previous night. She felt invisible, unwanted, inconsequential. Not since her days on the piers of Selkynsen, where she had sought work as a singer following her parents' death, had she found herself so alone in such a cruel world.

Retrieving the psaltery, she clung to it, trembling and fighting fresh tears.

"They're here!" barked the matron. "The San'iloman has arrived. Out, everyone. Out!"

All but three of the servants scattered. Trumpets and drums thundered outside the tent, followed by the unified shouts of hundreds of men.

The musicians readied their instruments. Kahlil took his seat next to Adiana.

"Don't do this," she whispered fiercely.

Kahlil shifted uncomfortably on his chair, but did not reply.

"Do not abandon me. We were friends once. Does that mean nothing to you now?"

He set his jaw and said in a low voice. "I have not forgotten our friendship, Adiana, but circumstances have changed. You are a prize of war, and I have seen how Lord Mechnes covets his prizes."

"I am not fool enough to ask you to protect me from him. But nor must you let him or his madness stand between you and me, and the friendship we once shared."

Kahlil let out a slow breath, glanced at his companions, one a red-haired youth with a face burnished by the sun, the other an older man with skin as dark as the night. Both seemed intently focused on tuning their instruments. He turned back to Adiana, touched her bruised cheek. His hazel eyes were imbued a sense of resignation that unsettled her.

"The Syrnte's vision depends on strong emotions," he said. "Fear, anger, hatred, desire—these are the tools he can use to open the windows to your past and your possible futures. If you are able control the intensity of your emotions, you may find some refuge from his games." He withdrew his touch, and picked up a flute. "That is all I can give you, Adiana."

Voices were approaching the tent, Lord Mechnes's imposing baritone among them, followed by what Adiana reluctantly recognized as Rishona's rich laughter.

She reached forward and placed a hand upon her friend's arm.

"It is enough," she said. "Thank you."

Chapter 22

Rain fell in the hours before dawn, a brief but intense shower that hummed against leaves and branches of scattered trees, and grumbled a quiet thunder. By the time the first hint of daylight crept into the sky, the deluge had ended. Clothes and gear were soaked, the campsite transformed into muddy puddles. The horses snorted restlessly, steam rising from their damp backs. Eolyn, Borten, Corey, and Mariel took their breakfast without conversation, the maga keenly aware of Borten's silence, and saddened by the awkwardness she now felt in his presence.

She watched Corey with a wary eye. Wrapped in a sodden cloak and huddled over his tea, the mage seemed far less imposing than he had the night before. She remembered when they first met, she a vulnerable girl, uncertain of the future and fearful of the pyres of Moisehén; he the master of his own small world. During her time with the Circle, the mage had guarded her and kept her under his wing, despite his knowledge of her forbidden magic. After the disaster at Bel-Aethne, he had risked his life to defend her against the Mage King and Tzeremond; and then delivered her swift and sure to the protection of her brother Ernan.

It was odd, in view of all this, how she had come to distrust him so. Though perhaps it was not distrust she felt, so much as an uneasy sense of security. While she believed Mage Corey would never allow harm to come to her person, but she also understood he would not hesitate to sacrifice those she loved if he thought it necessary. He had proven this when he betrayed her brother and all those who fought beside him. One day he might prove it again.

Corey set aside his cup and retrieved the pieces of his staff, which he examined with an irritated scowl.

"That was a foolish act, destroying this," he said to Borten. "We may regret its absence in the coming days."

"You managed quite well without a staff during your years with the Circle," Eolyn snapped. "I don't see why you should need one now."

Corey had allowed all the members of the Circle to believe he had never completed his training, yet as soon as Ernan's rebellion had ended his staff reappeared, exposing him as a master of High Magic, and a true student of Tzeremond.

"I was just getting accustomed to having this instrument in hand again. Is there anything else that accursed Galian sword can do that I should be aware of?"

Eolyn and Borten exchanged a glance. The knight gave a slight shake of his head, but Eolyn drew a breath and said, "It will kill a Naether Demon."

The mage looked at her in surprise.

"Eolyn," Borten said in rebuke.

"It is better to tell him. Perhaps he can help us understand why the creature appeared, whether it might return."

"Now I know the highlands of Moehn have driven you mad," said Corey, though his tone betrayed uncertainty. "Naether Demons are already dead; they cannot be killed again."

"Not by normal weapons," Eolyn replied. "We were attacked in the South Woods. Borten, Mariel, and I survived because of Kel'Baru."

"The South Woods is home to many strange and magical creatures. How can you be certain what attacked you was a Naether Demon?"

"I know what I saw. The beast consumed Sirena's heart—only her heart—before it turned on us. Borten's and Delric's weapons were of no use against it, but Kel'Baru could pierce the substance one might call its flesh. It was not a creature of true flesh and blood, but rather made of something luminescent, at once solid and ephemeral."

Corey sank into a brooding silence. Water from last night's rain dripped from the leaves. The horses whinnied and stamped their impatience. When the mage spoke again, his voice was subdued. "The stones of Faernvorn are moving."

Dread crept like a winter fog into Eolyn's heart. "How do you know?"

"I was there, less than a fortnight ago. Two monoliths were leaning toward the center of the wastes."

"Then the demons have escaped to the plains of Moisehén?"

"Not that I know of. Indeed, you are the first to tell me you have seen one."

"This makes no sense," said Eolyn. "The Naether Demons were banished from Faernvorn; if they found a way to return at all, it should be through Faernvorn, not here on the other side of the kingdom. Not in the South Woods."

"Perhaps the Syrnte have brought them here," suggested Borten.

"This knight of yours can be astute when he makes the effort," said Corey. "There are many passages that lead toward the Underworld. Any place in which souls were torn from their bodies through violence is a potential point of entry or exit, unless the door has been properly closed with magic. Moehn has a relatively peaceful history, but that does not mean it is without portals that the Syrnte could put to use, if they know how."

The maga rose and paced the campsite, mud sloshing underfoot. A question burned upon her tongue, though she felt a great reluctance to voice it. She stopped and scanned the low hills, back turned to her companions, apprehensive of what she might see.

Akmael's description of Tzeremond's death returned fresh to her memory. *A muffled scream sounded from the heart of the mountain, a tremor passed through the earth.* The creature had risen toward the surface without ever showing its face and plucked Tzeremond's soul from his body, dooming the wizard's magic to obliteration.

"Rishona called the Naether Demons to finish Tzeremond," said Eolyn. "She was our ally then. I cannot imagine her allowing this magic to be used against us."

"Perhaps she has no control over events recently come to pass," said Corey. "Though there is another possibility. The death of Tzeremond may not have been the last act of a desperate ally, but rather the first strike of a clever enemy."

"What do you mean?"

"Tzeremond was the oldest mage left to our people, unsurpassed in skill and knowledge. Even you must recognize this, though he made your life quite miserable. You and I will be stumbling in the dark if we are to confront an army of these monsters. Tzeremond could have shown us the way."

"Rishona slew Tzeremond so that Ernan might defeat Akmael."

"And to this day she probably wishes your brother had achieved victory. With the Mage King defeated, Tzeremond dead and his mages scattered, who would have been left to defend Moisehén against Syrnte ambitions?"

"She killed the wizard that I might live," Eolyn insisted.

"If Rishona had been concerned for your survival, she would have struck before Tzeremond cast the curse of Ahmad-dur, not after."

"But she and Tahmir…" Eolyn's voice faltered.

"Distracted you," Corey finished for her. "Yes, the Syrnte charmer was very good at that."

"Who are these people you speak of?" Borten intervened. "Rishona? Tahmir?"

Eolyn shook her head sadly. "Friends of times long past. Or so I would like to believe."

"They were members of the Circle," said Corey. "Syrnte royalty who negotiated an alliance with Eolyn's brother, but never delivered on their promises. Tahmir disappeared after the rebellion, Rishona was taken prisoner and ransomed back to her people."

"I see," said Borten, and the pensive tone of his voice led Eolyn to believe he understood much more than she desired.

"There will be more of those beasts, then," Mariel said quietly.

"Will be, and perhaps already are," agreed Corey.

Borten stood and approached the maga. "You have the silver web, Eolyn. Take Kel'Baru, and deliver it now to the King. Tell him everything that we have seen and spoken of."

"And leave you?" She responded, though her heart buckled under the force of her doubts. "Abandon Mariel, now that I know more of those creatures are out there? Their greatest hunger is for the magic of Moisehén. They will not rest until they devour her, and you can do nothing to stop them without the Galian sword."

"I will find a way to protect her. I will keep her well hidden."

"No. It won't work to leave her in Moehn. I see that now. I was a fool to ever imagine otherwise."

"The man who needs that sword is Sir Drostan," said Corey. "He is Rhiemsaven, under orders to secure the pass. He will expect Syrnte warriors with swords of flame, not Naether Demons."

"Then I will go first to Rhiemsaven, but otherwise our plan is unchanged. We will ride together to the foothills of the Taeschel Mountains. From there, I will fly into Selkynsen by night, and Mariel can use the amulet to follow me in the morning."

Borten took Eolyn's arm in a gentle but firm hold, compelling her to meet his gaze. "It is unwise of you to linger in Moehn, now that you have the means to escape."

"It would be heartless to escape on my own now that I can take Mariel with me."

"Do not let sentiment cloud your judgment. Mariel is but one girl. Every moment you delay puts an entire kingdom at risk."

Eolyn blinked against the sting of tears. "How can you say that? She is my world. All I have left. None of my students remain, don't you see? Just Mariel and Ghemena. Ghemena is safe, if we are to believe Corey. Mariel must be made safe as well. Otherwise all the work I have done these past two years—every sacrifice of my life—becomes meaningless."

Sadness invaded his eyes, and his expression softened. "Nothing about you is meaningless, Eolyn."

He left her to ready the horses.

The sun warmed the morning mist with golden hues as they broke camp. Sir Borten assigned the horse Sirena had ridden to Corey, and though the mage expressed his preference for Delric's sturdier animal, he accepted the lithe brown gelding without argument.

They departed with Borten leading the way, marking a path that led roughly west through abandoned fields and remnant woodlands. Mariel lingered behind, as had become her habit, and Mage Corey took a place beside her, occupying the girl with his carefree banter until midmorning, when her shy laughter began to mingle with the songs of thrushes and warblers. The intermittent patches of fog burned away, leaving a clear sky in its wake, though a shadow darkened the eastern horizon.

"She is a fine young maga," Corey remarked, appearing unannounced at Eolyn's side and distracting the maga from her contemplation of the strangely colored sky. "An excellent testimony to your gifts as a teacher. We are lucky the Gods saw fit to spare her the fate of the others."

Eolyn made no response.

"I gather she will be in her fifteenth year next spring." He continued lighthearted, as if oblivious to her silence. "Time to petition for her staff, if I understand the traditions of the magas correctly."

Eolyn nodded stiffly. "The fifteenth spring was my time. It will also be hers."

"And afterwards, of course, there will be the awakening of *aen-lasati* at Bel-Aethne. . ." Corey paused, allowing the words to hang in the air between them. "If you're in need of a mage to assist with the ceremony, I'd be happy to—"

"You can be most certain I will not call upon you."

An amused grin spread across his face, and Eolyn sighed in frustration.

"Why do you bait me so?" she demanded, her tone more one of resignation than anger.

"Because you always bite." He scanned the landscape before contemplating her. "I've missed you, Eolyn. I'd convinced the King to bring you back to the City, you know, before news of the Syrnte reached us. You were to be with us in time for Summer Solstice. I had hoped we would be reunited under kinder circumstances."

"I am beginning to fear there are no kind circumstances left in this world."

"Perhaps you are right," he said. "Although your friendship with the King is a kind circumstance—one you appear determined to ignore."

"My friendship with the King is not your concern."

"Everything about you concerns me." His tone became severe, patronizing. "Do you know what I thought when you refused the Crown yet attended Akmael's wedding? *Now there is a woman with political instinct,* I told myself. *For all her apparent innocence, my sweet Eolyn understands that the only woman more powerful than a queen is the king's mistress.*"

"I despise your vulgarity, Corey."

"I'm not vulgar, I'm honest. And you have disappointed me. Why do you waste your affections on that peasant-turned-knight from the backwoods of Moehn?"

Eolyn winced at his words, mortified that Borten might have overheard. "There is nothing unworthy about Moehn or its people. This is my home you insult with your arrogance."

"You are no daughter of Moehn. You are a High Maga, heiress to East Selen, and a woman most favored by the King. You may not be able to trace your ancestors to the line of Vortingen, but your blood is just as precious and your power just as formidable as any nobleman's. You could have been a mother of kings."

Eolyn laughed, shook her head. "I'd rather be a teacher of magas. Let the good Queen Taesara be a mother of kings. She is prepared for that duty, much better than I."

"Prepared or not, the Gods may have other plans," Corey replied under his breath. "Taesara has lost her child."

Eolyn reined in her steed, an icy flutter settling in the pit of her stomach. Her hand went inadvertently to her abdomen. She remembered with some trepidation that her blood was due in these days, but had not yet come.

"How awful," she murmured, imagining the heavy shadow of the Queen's grief. "How terrible for her. And Akmael, is he…?"

Her words drifted into silence, for she was not quite certain what she wanted to ask, or whether she wished to hear the answer. Corey had stopped at her side, but waited until Mariel caught up with them, and bade the girl to ride ahead with Sir Borten.

"The King is as stony-faced as any Prince of Vortingen ever was," he said, "though I imagine he is much affected by the news. We are four years into his reign after all, and no heir to speak of."

Eolyn spurred her horse forward. Corey followed.

"Miscarriages are regrettable, but not uncommon," she said. Indeed, they were much more common than most men cared to acknowledge. She and Renate had attended many failed pregnancies during their short time in Moehn. "The Queen will recover and conceive again."

"High Mage Rezlyn, it seems, would agree with you. As for myself, I am not so certain."

Eolyn cast him a sideways glance. "What would you know that Rezlyn does not?"

He shrugged and looked away. "Not nearly enough. But I suspect the Queen has enemies, and so does she."

"Enemies?"

"A sorceress, perhaps. Someone with the power to make her ill, to force a miscarriage."

"Are you suggesting that I—"

"No. But others have, including Taesara herself."

"The Queen has accused me of killing her child?"

"Not openly. Akmael would have her head for it if she did. But word has it from the castle corridors that this is what she believes."

"Her ignorance of our ways has persisted for too long. Someone must help her understand that a maga would never—"

"*You* would never. But there were many who fled from Kedehen's brutal wrath, and we would be fools not to suspect they are watching us still, hungry for vengeance, plotting to bring ruin upon the House of Vortingen and the people of Moisehén. Ensuring that King Akmael has no heir would be an excellent place to begin."

"Akmael has an heir. He has the Princess Eliasara."

"A girl cannot become a king."

"Just as a girl cannot practice magic?" Eolyn shot back.

"You seduced the Mage King to see that rule broken," Corey replied dryly. "I doubt Eliasara will have the same opportunity. Though it might be amusing to see her try."

Sir Borten halted his steed just then, and though he was some distance ahead of them, Eolyn was troubled by the thought that the wind might have carried more than a few words of their conversation to his ears. He studied their approach, sitting tall upon his destrier, the summer breeze sifting through his fine blond hair. Eolyn felt oddly self-conscious beneath his scrutiny.

"Why did you attack him last night?" she said in a low voice.

"Attack him?" Corey lifted his palm in a gesture of puzzled innocence. "He attacked me."

"There was no need for that flame, and you know it. If you had injured him, we would have been left without a swordsman."

The mage clucked his tongue. "Swordsman, indeed. That *swordsman* speared your brother once, and now it seems he wants to spear you. But he will bring you little pleasure, I can tell you that. A peasant's sword is a small and simple thing, blunt around the edges and disappointing in the thrust. What you require, Maga Eolyn, is a mage's staff: long and sturdy, magically cured, powerful to the touch, smooth in its finish—"

"Borten's sword cut your staff to the quick, Mage Corey."

Corey drew an indignant breath and let go a low chuckle. "The highlands of Moehn have put some spirit on your tongue. I am glad to see it. I wasn't going to hurt him, Eolyn. I just wanted to scar that handsome face a little. It would have served him right for courting my ward without permission."

"I am not your ward."

"You are my kin, cousin in the eyes of Dragon, and you carry the future of my Clan in your blood. You are not to waste your affections on the likes of that simple knight. Not when you have the Mage King at your beck and call."

Eolyn quelled a surge of anger, frustrated by the ease with which he could provoke her. She focused on the rush of the wind through fragrant grass, the bell-like melody of a field warbler, the heavy gait of her horse. She invoked the memory of Borten's embrace, the tender confidence of his kiss, the song of Aithne and Caradoc echoing through their newly discovered desire.

Sleep, Eolyn, he had said.

And she would have, wrapped in the warm sanctuary of his arms, had Corey not appeared with his rude reminders of the larger world.

"The path of a maga's heart is governed only by the Gods," she said, remembering the words of Doyenne Ghemena. "She must love as they command, with a ready spirit and an open heart. No amount of scheming or interference on your part will ever change that, Mage Corey."

"Love?" Corey responded with a confused frown. "When did I ever suggest we were talking about love?"

Chapter 23

Sir Drostan and his men broke camp as the sun spread its rosy light across the eastern horizon. They had left Rhiemsaven the previous day, and now followed a wide dirt road south along the Tarba River toward the Valley of Aerunden. The breeze was fresh, the sky clear, and the landscape wide open, with their visibility unfettered by woodlands or even an occasional hill. Reeds rustled in the wind. The river murmured at their side and sparkled like sapphires under the early morning sun.

Despite the bright summer dawn, something in the air kept Drostan on edge, like a faint stench of rotten flesh that assaulted his senses unexpectedly and vanished the moment he tried to identify its source. No bird sang, no fish leaped over the waters, no dogs barked in the distance. The whinnying of the horses was subdued. Even the ducks sat still, huddled near the river's edge, scanning their surroundings with nervous calls.

The tension brought back memories of the War of the Magas, when Drostan and his fellow mage warriors patrolled the countryside in a constant state of wariness, uncertain where the next deadly ambush waited, and what magic would be used to conceal it.

Drostan had sent scouts ahead of them. Now, he dispatched two more who took to the skies in the form of Hawk.

His plan was to ride as far as the Valley of Aerunden today, though they would not camp on the battle ground where the rebel Ernan met his defeat. In a place so recently visited by violence and death, the barriers between the world of the living and the world of the dead were thin and easily broken. Under the cover of night, the Lost Souls would drift through, drawn by Drostan's magic, and attack him in his dreams. While they did not have the strength to drag down a mage of his power, they could certainly give the old warrior a restless and difficult night.

A rider appeared on the road far ahead, a dark shadow approaching at a fast trot, dust kicking up under the hooves of his mount. When he recognized the man as one of his own, Drostan quickened his pace to meet him. The soldier carried a large ragged bundle in his arms, a boy in tattered clothes. His feet were blistered and bleeding; an unruly mass of hair hung over fierce brown eyes. Drostan would have thought him a half-wild orphan spat out by the nearby woodlands, had there not been a disturbingly familiar look beneath all that grime and sweat, and a hint of nobility in the lift of his young chin.

"The boy comes from Moehn," said the soldier who delivered him. "He claims to be a grandson of Feldon."

"Ah." Drostan recognized him now, though it took him a moment to place the name. This was the youth who had walked with him along the decrepit wall of Moehn. An undisciplined child who had spent his days in the streets with a loose following of ragged urchins, more intent on learning the arts of thievery than techniques of combat that befitted his station. "Lord Markl, if I recall correctly?"

"Yes, Sir." Exhaustion and hunger were plain upon the boy's face, yet he responded with vigor. "I've come to tell King Akmael that Moehn is under siege."

Drostan dismounted and helped the boy to the ground. "The King has been informed."

"How?" the boy asked, eyes wide with astonishment. "No one could have come faster than me. I rode without stopping from Moehn, I did, until my horse collapsed coming down the pass. Then I walked from there, and ran as much as I could, until your man found me."

"Word reached King Akmael by the gift of magic and the will of the Gods. We are the first to respond to Moehn's call for aid."

"You?" The boy assessed Drostan and his small company, doubt plain upon his brow. "Just you and these men?"

"More are to come."

"We'll need much more than this. I have to get to the City and speak with the King. How much farther is it?"

"Three day's ride on a fast horse," Drostan informed him grimly. "Longer, if you're walking."

Drostan led Markl, limping, to a large rock on the edge of the river and bade him to sit down. He signaled the healer Laeryon, who hurried forward to examine the boy's feet. Markl winced at the healer's touch and stifled a cry by biting his lip. Laeryon frowned, shook his head, and drew water from the river to begin washing and dressing the bloody wounds.

"He'll have to stay off his feet until they are healed," Laeryon said, "or they will fester and most surely be lost."

"Thirty men will not free Moehn," the boy insisted. "I saw the enemy's army. A thousand strong, it was. Maybe two. The King must send more, much more, and they must go up the pass *now* or everything will be lost."

"You saw their army?" Drostan received this claim with caution. A child prone to thievery would also be prone to lying.

"They marched into Moehn from the east, under flags of burgundy and yellow. Three miles long, the column was. Further than the eyes could see."

Drostan, who had been bending over to listen to the boy, straightened now and surveyed the landscape with a determined frown. Just to the west of the road he spotted a small rise.

"Bring the boy," he said to one of his men, and strode toward the grassy knoll.

Markl was gathered up and carried to the modest vantage point.

"How far away was the army when you saw it?" Drostan asked, indicating various landmarks within view. "From here to that fir, or to that stream? Show me."

Markl frowned. "Further than the stream. Almost to that patch of woods over there. That's what I'd say."

"And if you were to see that same army in front of us today, where would it start?"

"Down there," Markl pointed toward the south.

"Where, exactly?"

"At that big patch of grass."

Almost everything in front of them was either grassland or fallow pasture. Drostan did not allow his impatience at the boy's vague response to show. "Which patch?"

"The brownish part, with the yellow flowers."

"And where would it end?"

Markl jerked his head toward the north. "A mile that way. Maybe two."

"How far is a mile?"

"You don't know?"

"Show me."

Markl pointed to a distant stand of dead trees, leafless white trunks clawing their way toward the clear sky. "About that far."

Drostan sucked in his breath, troubled by the boy's account. If he spoke true, the threat was far greater than the old knight could ever have imagined.

"How wide was the column? How many men across?"

Markl shrugged. "Can't say, really. Wasn't close enough to see each man. Maybe about as wide as this road here. That's what it looked like, anyway."

"I see," Drostan murmured. What the boy described seemed well nigh impossible. How in the name of the Gods had the Syrnte dragged a force that large through the unexplored maze of the South Woods and into the heart of Moehn? "Now you must tell me: you said there were spearmen. Where in the column did the spears begin, and where did they end?"

Drostan's interrogation of Markl continued in this manner for the better part of an hour. The knight returned repeatedly to the same questions, asking them a different way each time, taking the boy to new vantage points, obliging him to use alternative landmarks, until at last he was satisfied with the relative consistency of the child's account. He then brought Markl back to the riverside, delivered him to Laeryon's care, and dispatched a messenger to the King's City.

It was sobering news at best, and Drostan felt a deep sense of foreboding as he watched its carrier race northward. Akmael, once Drostan's student and now his liege, had never confronted an enemy of this magnitude. Though Drostan had taught young prince well, and knew of no man more gifted in the arts of magic and war, the old knight feared for his King and for the people he was sworn to protect.

Instructing Laeryon to take the boy back to Rhiemsaven, Drostan mounted his steed and assessed the small company of men who awaited his command. A hundred more had been promised from the King's City, mage warriors among them, yet even so, it would be a paltry force given the scale of the Syrnte invasion. King Akmael would surely mobilize the royal army as soon as Markl's account reached him, but his liege would be long days in arriving.

Until then, the old warrior had no choice but to make do with what he had and stall the Syrnte onslaught at the Pass of Aerunden.

Chapter 24

"Mistress Adiana!" The girls squealed and ran toward Adiana, filling her arms with laughter. Only a few days had passed since she last held them like this, yet it felt an eternity. She drew a deep breath, inhaling their sweet aroma, and took each face in her hands.

"Catarina. Tasha." They had never appeared more beautiful than in this moment. Catarina was rosy-cheeked and full of bright giggles. Tasha tried to smile, though her eyes were haunted, no doubt the mark of Lord Mechnes's brutality. Adiana drew the girl close for a comforting embrace. "Where is Ghemena?"

"Don't you know?" said Tasha. "She ran away. They haven't found her."

Adiana's heart stalled in a mix of trepidation and hope. "When?"

"Our first morning here."

"More a fool, I say." Catarina twirled in a new gown, pink silks flaring around her ankles. "See what the San'iloman has given us? She says we are to live like queens."

Tasha was also dressed in a fine robe of pale blue, but she fingered the silver laces of her bodice, eyes downcast. "Ghemena wouldn't have any use for pretty dresses. She wants to be a maga." The girl bit her lip and added in a despairing whisper, "So do I."

Adiana touched Tasha's chin, compelling the girl to meet her gaze. "You are a maga. You must never forget that."

"They will make fine Syrnte witches, both of them." Rishona's voice, unmistakable in its seductive tenor, interrupted their happy reunion.

Adiana looked up, startled. She had not even noticed the San'iloman in all her splendor, having had eyes only for the girls. Rishona was even more spellbinding than Adiana remembered her, a melody of grace and womanly charm. She wore richly dyed silks that swirled around her shapely figure. Her ebony hair was braided and adorned with pearls; her throat and arms sparkled with jewels.

Lord Mechnes's warning about protocol returned to Adiana's memory, and she averted her gaze, cheeks flushing.

My Queen were the words that came to mind, but Rishona was not Adiana's queen. After some consideration the musician chose instead, "Most honored Queen."

Rishona laughed out loud. "Oh, for the love of the Gods, Adiana! You would think we had never been friends."

Catarina giggled. Even Tasha managed a shy smile, though she found Adiana's hand and clung to it tightly. Adiana glanced up, uncertain what to say or do. Rishona stood close, her perfume heavy with aromas of jasmine and night.

"I can only imagine the cruel jests my uncle must have played on you," the Queen said. "Tell me, Adiana, did he claim my guards would slay you if you so much as laid eyes on me?"

"In truth, yes," Adiana replied quietly.

"Well they might have, this morning while you were sitting amongst the other musicians. But I am the one who summoned you now, and I have given my men very explicit instructions regarding your well-being. No harm will come to you, sweet Adiana. So look upon me, and embrace me as your friend."

Still Adiana hesitated, for there was something in Rishona's tone that reminded her of Lord Mechnes in the moments when he thought he was being kind. She stiffened as Rishona drew her close and kissed her.

"I never imagined we would find you in Moehn." The Queen stroked Adiana's hair, holding her a shade too long. "I envisioned you making a fortune in Selkynsen, teaching music to the daughters of wealthy merchants."

"I came here to assist Eolyn."

"So I am told." Rishona withdrew, cupped Adiana's chin as she studied her bruises. "Did my uncle do this?"

Adiana nodded, wary of the tremble on her lip, shamed by the ease with which her captors could invoke tears.

"He has a strange way of showing his favor." The sympathy in Rishona's voice was tempered by an unsettling tone of curiosity.

"This was no favor. Lord Mechnes thought I knew where Eolyn was."

"Do you?"

"No." Adiana pulled away and sought Tasha's hand. "He claims you want her dead."

Rishona retreated a few steps. "War is a time of difficult decisions, Adiana. The maga poses a significant threat to our ambitions in Moisehén. Even so, for my part, I have long desired another destiny for her. You must remember that I loved her once, as did my brother. We treated her as one of our own, even offered her refuge among the Syrnte after Ernan failed. But she chose her path alongside the Mage King, and now all our visions coincide: Eolyn will not be swayed from her loyalty to him. So while I would prefer the maga to live, I have come to accept there is no other way."

"No other way?" Adiana responded in disbelief. "Is this the destiny of all those you once called *friend*, to die because there is no other way?"

Rishona's conciliatory smile cooled. She studied Adiana then regarded the girls with expressionless eyes. "I did not summon you here to question my judgment. Any other subject would have been sent from my presence and whipped for less than what you just said. But you are my friend, Adiana. I understand what you have suffered, and I can imagine the heartbreak and indignation you must feel. So I will tell you this: I have come to claim what is mine by right of birth. That is all. I would have seen this done through other means. Indeed, for years I fought to achieve it in way that would have kept all of you by my side, but this is the only path the Gods have left to me, and I must assume its burden."

"I pity you for your great burden then," Adiana spoke before she could check her tongue. "I can see how much it makes you suffer."

Rishona set her jaw and looked away. She signaled one of her servants, who brought a cloak and set it about her shoulders. "These days have been long and terrible for you. You need rest and proper food, before you can understand."

She gave each of the girls an affectionate touch on the cheek, then turned her attention back to Adiana. "My people have their orders. You are under my protection now. Stay here with the children, eat and drink as you please, rest in my bed until a proper place is prepared for you. No one will disturb you. If there is anything you want, you need only ask for it."

"Then I ask for our freedom."

A smile touched Rishona's full lips. "Freedom is not always desirable. Protection is better. Tonight we will celebrate our victory in Moehn. A suitable gown will be found for you. I would have you sit at my table and drink from my cup, as we did in the happier days of Corey's Circle. Afterwards, we will talk."

Rishona departed, surrounded by guards. In her wake she left a hum of activity: servants assembling furniture, airing linens, setting out food, dusting and adorning tables in her new pavilion. None of them paid notice to Adiana or the girls. It was as if the three of them did not exist. Adiana had the dismaying sensation that her situation had not improved in the least.

"Shall we play a game?" Catarina clapped her hands. "The San'iloman has been teaching us the most wonderful game, on a board of ebony with little figures of men and monsters. She says it is played by all the nobility in Ech'Nalahm."

But Tasha pulled Adiana close and whispered in her ear, "I don't like this place. Everyone pretends to be kind when in truth, they are selfish and cruel. Please, Mistress Adiana, you must take us home. I want to be with Maga Eolyn again. Please."

Adiana drew a breath intending to promise that she would, but then she held her tongue, though it broke her heart to do so. There would be no greater cruelty, she told herself as she wrapped her arms around Tasha, than to make this promise when she might not be able to keep it.

* * *

It was late when the guards woke Adiana.

She had fallen asleep with Tasha at her side, having succumbed to the spell of soft cushions in a low-slung divan. Tasha was groggy and her hair unkempt. Even now she clung to Adiana's hand as if resolved never to let go. Adiana rose quickly, pulling the girl up with her, self-conscious as always beneath the invasive gaze of Lord Mechnes's soldiers.

"Catarina," she called.

The girl looked up from happy contemplation of the eight-sided cards Rishona had left in her possession, each painted with strange and colorful symbols. "You and Tasha must remain here and look after each other, do you understand? I will return as soon as I can."

"The San'iloman has summoned all three," one of the guards said.

"The children, as well?" Adiana frowned and looked past the wall of their shoulders. Outside torches were lit, and the night was black. "But it is so late."

Their only response was grim silence. Adiana wondered why she insisted on questioning every order given her, when it was perfectly clear that as long as this nightmare continued, she would never be given a choice.

"But I want to go along, Mistress Adiana," said Catarina. "The San'iloman promised me there was to be music and dancing and much food."

"She'll turn us into food, I bet," retorted Tasha. "She'll throw us into an oven and roast us to crisp."

"Tasha," Adiana admonished. "You must not scare Catarina with such stories."

"I'm not scared," objected Catarina with a lift of her chin.

"Well, you should be!" Tasha shot back.

"Enough." Adiana smoothed Tasha's hair and kissed her on the forehead. "I will not have you two bickering like angry geese, not after all it has cost us to come together again. The San'iloman has summoned us, and we must go. That is the end of it."

She reached out to Catarina, and the girl took her hand.

A litter waited for them, draped in sheer silks as pale as a moonlit mist. The transport was elegant and luxuriously appointed, yet the sight of it made Adiana's breath stop short. Her heart pounded inside her chest, and her hands were suddenly cold with sweat.

The greater the kindness shown by these people, the more intense her suspicion.

One of the guards shoved her forward, and she climbed in with great reluctance.

"Mistress Adiana," Tasha murmured as she took a place next to her, "what's wrong?"

Adiana forced a laugh and shrugged her shoulders. "The chill of the night cuts deep when one has recently awakened. I should have had a cup of wine before leaving the tent."

"There's wine here." Catarina took the stopper off a silver flask and sniffed.

"I don't think you should touch that," said Tasha.

With an exaggerated sigh and a roll of her eyes, Catarina took a drink. She proffered the flask to Adiana, who shook her head, overcome by queasiness at the thought of imbibing.

"What do you suppose these are?" Catarina fingered several small baskets in front of her. A stifling aroma emanated from them, heavy with strange spices that reminded Adiana of the markets of Selkynsen. It made her dizzy.

"Leave that be," she said. "Remember what Maga Eolyn told you about unfamiliar herbs."

Catarina pouted but folded her hands and at last sat still in obedience.

Above them hung a small cage with a white owl that screeched and fluttered its wings as the litter was lifted and born forward. Fighting off a wave of nausea, Adiana studied the bird, certain she had seen this image before. In a dream perhaps, or a nightmare.

"Mistress Adiana?" Tasha's voice loomed then wavered and faded.

A low rhythmic thud sounded inside Adiana's head. She shut her eyes and pressed her palms against her aching forehead.

"Are you not well?"

"It is nothing." In truth she was succumbing to an inexplicable wave of panic. A shower of black spots exploded in front of her. "Do you hear something, Tasha?"

"What, Mistress Adiana?"

"Babbling. Like the hisses of a thousand snakes. Words I can't quite understand…"

A wintry chill invaded the marrow of her bones. A muffled howl tore through her with an agonizing pitch, like the desperate cry of a wolf caught in a hunter's trap. Ebony claws reached toward her, behind them gaping holes in ghostly and distorted faces. Adiana struggled to escape the phantoms, feeling like a fish caught in a net, except she was being dragged deeper into the darkest of all seas, rather than upwards, toward light and air.

"Help me," she whispered, but the current was too strong. Tasha's alarmed cries faded as Adiana was swept away on a river of shadows and terror. Tendrils of wispy fog reached toward her, snapping in her face like rabid dogs, wrapping around her limbs and throat, then slipping away and returning to grasp at her again. Moans of hunger droned in her ears. The discordant roar was driving her mad.

"Renate, please!" she cried out in desperation.

The old maga's voice replied in a hoarse whisper.

Music is your magic. Melody is your spell.

But what music could be found in this darkness? What melody in this awful chaos? Adiana forced air through her throat in an attempt to scream, but no sound fell from her lips. The tendrils caught upon her like thorny vines now, cutting into her ankles and wrists, pulling her against the current. A powerful stench invaded her nostrils, like the rot of a man many days dead. Violently she jerked away and found herself once again inside the litter.

The curtain of silk came into focus.

Tasha's voice sounded close by, calling her name in desperation.

A woman leaned over Adiana, caressing her hair, murmuring strange words in a comforting cadence. Her face was drawn and aged, her gray eyes lined with kohl.

"It has ended," she said. "Come, you can get up now."

"What has ended?" Adiana pushed herself to a sitting position. "What happened?"

The old woman watched her with a knowing smile. "Such beauty and power in your soul. They would take you without the San'iloman's leave, if they could."

Tasha slipped her arm through Adiana's. "No one is going to take her."

The old woman merely laughed. Her long hair was neatly braided and coiled. She wore a white robe with a jeweled belt, and a flowing cloak of many colors. Gold adorned her head and throat; earrings hung in a cascade of rubies over her thin shoulders.

"Who are you?" Adiana asked.

"I am Donatya, priestess of Mikata and servant of the San'iloman. You will come with me." She nodded to Tasha at her side and Catarina, who now slept in the litter. "The children remain here."

"No!" cried Tasha. "You will not separate us again."

Donatya narrowed her eyes and nodded to the guards that surrounded them.

One of the men pulled Tasha forcibly away from Adiana, another bound the musician's hands. Tasha fought against her captor, kicking, clawing and screaming, until Donatya stepped forward and slapped her hard across the face.

"Silence!" she said. "The Syrnte do not tolerate disobedient children. Any more fuss from you, and I will cut out your tongue."

Tasha whimpered and gave Adiana a pleading look.

"Be a good girl, Tasha, will you?" Adiana said quietly, fighting the terrible premonition that she would not see Tasha or Catarina again. "Take care of your sister."

Tasha shook her head in denial, biting her lip to keep from speaking. Her legs were bound and she was put back into the litter, the curtain closed behind her, while they led Adiana away.

There was music and song in Moehn that night, but not in this place. Donatya and the guards brought Adiana to small copse of trees well outside the ruined walls of the town. Adiana recognized the knoll. They had picnicked here on occasion with Lord Felton and his family, the adults sharing sweetmeats and bitter ale while the children tumbled in the grass. Ghemena had run wild with Markl and his motley street urchins, their laughter rising in giddy waves toward a bright summer sun. The happy memory ignited a sharp pain in Adiana's gut. Those days felt like a distant dream now. Perhaps none of it had ever really happened.

Torches illuminated their path. At the crest of the low rise was a large circle marked by a strange luminous wall. Inside the translucent blue flames Adiana saw movement. As they drew close, lumbering beasts came into focus, pacing on all fours, ebony claws on their long glowing limbs. They lifted their formless faces in unearthly howls. Adiana cried out in terror, recognizing the monsters from her vision. In their midst stood Rishona bright as the full moon, an obsidian blade lifted in one hand. At her feet, a girl heavy with child wept inconsolably, the tangled mass of her hair trapped in the unyielding grip of the San'iloman.

Adiana cowered, resisting the forward momentum of her escorts. Rishona struck with such speed, Adiana did not understand what had happened until a river of blood flowed from the girl's throat and she collapsed convulsing to the earth. The Queen stepped away from her victim, and the beasts fell upon their prey, ripping open her belly and consuming all they found within.

Adiana's knees buckled and she fell to the damp earth. Vomit spewed from her churning stomach. All power of movement abandoned her limbs. The guards took rough hold of her arms and dragged her to the edge of the circle, where the Queen stepped through the curtain of fire.

"What is this?" Rishona cast a disdainful look toward Adiana before assessing Donatya with a harsh gaze. "I have no use for this woman. I sent for the children."

Donatya responded with a respectful bow, then drew close to the Queen and whispered in her ear, all the while keeping a hawk's eye on Adiana. Rishona's expression softened as the priestess spoke. A smile touched her lips. When Donatya finished, the San'iloman looked upon Adiana as if seeing her for the first time.

"Sweet Adiana," she said, "who would have foreseen that you would be the bearer of such a great gift?"

Taking hold of the musician by a fistful of hair, Rishona pulled her toward the circle. With her hands bound and useless, Adiana kicked and screamed, digging her heels into the earth and refusing to be ready quarry, until a mailed hand came down hard on the side of her head, sending stars through her vision and renewing the taste of blood on her lips. She lost her footing and was dragged inexorably forward. Darkness spun around her. Thunder ran through the earth. She heard shouts of men and the clatter of metal. Violent hands, familiar in the cruelty of their grip, tore her away from the Queen and threw her to the ground, well outside the wall of flame.

"You do not have leave to make use of this woman!"

Adiana spat blood out of her mouth, gasping for each precious breath. An unsettling scent filled the air, of spices and death and burning fields.

Mechnes, she thought. *That voice belongs to Lord Mechnes.*

"I do not require your leave, uncle," Rishona said. "The creatures have called for this woman. They hunger for her like they hunger for no other soul in this province."

Mechnes's tone was low and full of menace. "Prisoners and slaves do not choose their meals."

"The more magic we give them, the better they will be able to serve us. And she," Adiana felt Rishona's predatory focus, "is a vessel of Primitive Magic."

A tense silence followed, broken by Mechnes's audacious laughter. Adiana heard the approach of his heavy gait and winced as he lifted her face to the torch light.

"A vessel of Primitive Magic." There was amusement in his eyes, a sardonic grin on his face. Adiana thought the Gods especially cruel in that moment, that they would give this evil man such a handsome countenance. He released her as suddenly as he had taken hold of her. "I do not require a demon to tell me that. You, Rishona, have the young magas, and any other woman or child of this province that you desire. Those creatures will be satisfied with what we offer, or they will remain forever in their cold prison."

"Uncle—"

"Take this woman to my quarters." Mechnes told one of his men. "She is to be bathed and bound in the usual fashion, and left undisturbed until I return."

"I am your Queen!"

Rishona's angry declaration brought all movement to a halt. Looking up from her miserable state, Adiana saw Lord Mechnes and the San'iloman, eyes locked on each other and jaws set, their rage hot and foul like sulfur put to flame.

Without shifting his gaze from his niece, Lord Mechnes said in deliberate tones, "You have your orders, man. Do as I say."

Adiana was pulled up from the ground and thrown over a broad shoulder. As they carried her away, she caught Rishona's expression wavering in uncertainty for only a moment.

The Queen straightened her shoulders and said to Donatya, "Bring me the girls, then. And make haste. We cannot leave this portal open much longer."

Moments passed before the meaning of these words hit Adiana.

"No," she said as if coming out of a trance. Then louder, "No! Not them. Not Catarina and Tasha. Take me instead!"

No one paid her any heed. The soldier who carried her continued his steady pace away from the circle of fire. Frantic, Adiana looked around as best she could, trying to remember where they had left the litter, hoping to catch a glimpse of the children.

"Tasha!" she cried. "Catarina!"

Their voices came to her as if from a great distance, anxious and garbled.

"Stop!" Adiana wailed, all her fear and fury channeled into this one desperate entreaty. "Oh, for the love of the Gods, stop! You cannot permit this. Take me! Spare the girls, I beg you."

"Silence that woman!" Mechnes's command cut sharp through the stygian night.

A soiled rag was stuffed into Adiana's mouth, forcing her to breathe through her nose in short ragged puffs. Tears burned in her eyes. Every muscle cramped. Her entrails revolted as if about to be torn from her body. With bound hands she beat against her captor's back, but each blow fell impotent. Exhausted by the horror of her helplessness, she paused and listened again for the girls.

So few sounds came to her now. The steady thump of her captor's gait. The hiss of torches. The distant music and laugher that floated toward them from the town. The labored rhythm of her own breath.

Sweat soaked her bodice and formed rivulets that ran down her strained neck. She tried to look back toward the circle of fire, but already they were unbearably far away, moving at an angle that did not permit her to see.

Please, she begged, hoping the Gods would hear her silent prayer, *spare them this. Let me go in their place. Please…*

Catarina's and Tasha's screams ripped open the night, shrill with terror, cut short by the bitter silence of death.

A tremor shook the earth, accompanied by the deafening roar of those bloodthirsty beasts. The soldier lost his footing, stumbling and cursing as Adiana slipped from his grasp. She did not feel the impact of hitting the ground, but remained limp and numb to the world around her as the soldier recovered his balance, hauled her back onto his shoulders, and continued stoically in the direction of Mechnes's tent.

Chapter 25

Eolyn stood, searching the shadow-cloaked wood, eyes alert, breath shallow, hand firm on her oak staff. The crickets chirped their quiet rhythms, but the trees had ceased all movement. Not even their leaves rustled in the dark.

Borten stirred. Reluctant to surrender the watch entirely, he had slept at her side. Standing up, he unsheathed Kel'Baru, a sliver of moonlight catching the long blade. Several paces behind them, Mage Corey and Mariel were deep inside their own dreams.

"What is it?" Borten's whisper was barely audible.

"I'm not certain." A feeling, like a breath of wintry air, had raised the fine hairs on her arms.

Eolyn remembered a time not so long ago when the night forest was a place of warm mysteries to be explored with happy abandon. Now she had grown wary of this midnight realm, whose power to conceal could favor them as easily as it might betray them.

Mist floated, delicate and gray, just past the broad trunks in front of them. A hollow wind moaned through the trees, followed by the rustle of stiff bushes. The shrill call of a spotted owl pierced the heavy silence. Borten stepped forward and assumed a middle guard, both hands firmly on the hilt of Kel'Baru.

"Perhaps we should warn Corey." Her words stalled as the mist was set into motion, swirling in a small vortex that coalesced into a ghost-white beast.

The Naether Demon sprang for Eolyn.

Lunging into its path, Borten swung low and sliced through its luminous flesh. The black maw contorted in an anguished howl. The demon stumbled backwards and charged again, ripping open the knight's leg with an ebony claw.

Ehekaht, faeom dumae!

The thunder from Eolyn's staff threw them apart. Borten recovered and drove Kel'Baru into the demon's torso. The beast fell while the knight withdrew the blade, now dark with oily sludge. A second demon sprang out of the shadows and pummeled Eolyn into the ground, knocking the staff from her grip.

Ehekaht, she gasped. *Soeh mae.*

A desperate spell invoked on instinct, but it worked. A ward sprang up. The demon raged over her like a winter storm, claws tearing at the magic shield, maw yawning like the abyss of the Underworld. Eolyn strained against the force of its hunger, uncertain how long her power would hold. An ancient curse thundered through her awareness.

Saenau
Revoerit
Nefau

Eolyn beat back a wave of nausea. Darkness swallowed the light. The creature tumbled away as if toward a precipice, dragging her with it until the claws slipped and the forest came back into focus. She found herself on her knees struggling to regain her breath.

Borten helped her to her feet.

Corey held her staff in both hands, aiming the crystal head at the demon as it retreated. A dark cloud flowed from the crystal, barreling toward the beasts and cloaking them in shadow. They cowered together and beat at the air, filling the night with agonized howls.

"Eolyn!" Corey's neck strained with the force of his effort. "I need a white flame!"

Recovering her focus, Eolyn summoned the purest fire known to Dragon.

Ehekaht. Aenthe rehoert!

A white-hot shaft of light crackled from the maga's palm and hammered into the demons, igniting them in cobalt flames. Corey and Eolyn sustained their magic as long as they could, drawing on each other's power, until the fire faded and Borten strode forward with Kel'Barú. The knight severed their heads and began to hack their bodies to pieces.

Corey set aside the staff. Sweat beaded his brow. He put his hands on Eolyn's shoulders and searched her eyes with great intensity. "Are you all right?"

"Yes." She fought to steady the tremor in her voice. "I'm winded, that's all."

Corey nodded before moving toward Borten and their fallen attackers.

"Where is Mariel?" she asked, and the girl appeared.

They clung to each other, Mariel weeping, Eolyn murmuring words of relief and comfort, while Corey squatted next to the chunks of glowing flesh. He passed his hand over them as if studying coals from a fading fire. Vapor rose from the remains.

"As cold as ice," he said in wonder. Then he stood and examined Borten's arm and leg, both drenched with blood.

"It is nothing," said the knight.

"Right you are, again." Corey fingered the area around the cut in his arm with care. He cast Borten a disparaging glance. "Remarkably."

"Corey, please." Eolyn extracted herself from Mariel's hold. "Why must you be so disagreeable even now?"

"Disagreeable?" The mage lifted his hands in a gesture of innocence. "All I meant is that monsters of this sort, fresh from the Underworld, might carry dark magic that could seep into the simplest of wounds and kill a man. We wouldn't want Borten to suffer a miserable death from poisoning by Naether Demons . . . Would we?"

Eolyn accompanied Borten to a nearby stone. The knight sat down while she tore back the bloodied fabric that covered his wounds.

"Patience, Eolyn," said Corey. "The man is yet weary from battle."

Eolyn ignored the mage. The claws had slashed deep into Borten's flesh, but there was no sign of dark magic, and the flow of blood was already beginning to slow.

"Mariel, bring that flask of water at the base of the tree, would you?" While the girl did her bidding, Eolyn opened her medicine belt and set aside willow, arnica and foxes' clote. "I must find more herbs in the morning. This is all I have, and the dressing should be changed every day."

Borten put his fingers under her chin and lifted her face to his. A smile touched his lips, but his eyes had hardened. "I can collect my own herbs, Eolyn, and dress my own wounds. You have the means to escape, and you should do so now. Every moment you remain here is a wager against your own death."

They were wise words, laden with concern for her well-being. Why then did it hurt so much to hear them?

"It is only another day's ride," she said. "Then I will fly to Selkynsen, and Mariel can—"

"What if those creatures reappear tonight, and in greater numbers?" Borten's tone was impatient, bordering on angry. "What if the Syrnte find us tomorrow?"

Eolyn accepted the flask of water from Mariel and began washing Borten's wound with more vigor than was necessary, or kind. "I have made my decision. I do not wish to speak about it any further."

"Eolyn." Corey's voice cut sternly between them. "Stand up, would you? And step away from the knight."

"Oh, for the love of the Gods, Corey!" She sat back on her heels, exasperated. "Don't you start."

"I am not trying to intercede in your lover's quarrel. Stand up, I say. Now."

His ominous tone sparked renewed fear, and Eolyn obeyed. Mariel backed away a few steps, a cautious look on her face. Borten watched Corey with a wary gaze while fingering the hilt of Kel'Barú.

The mage approached Eolyn, eyes narrowed and focused not on her person, but on her aura.

"What is that?" He spoke slowly, reaching out as if to touch the ethereal colors that defined her spirit. "That shadow . . . it was not there before. It looks as if someone punched a hole in your life force."

His words trailed off into unspoken thoughts. The mage turned back to the slain Naether Demons, now no more than a loose collection of glowing puddles that diminished even as they watched.

"And the shadow fades as our attackers disappear from this world." He paused, consternation filling his countenance. "Did this happen to you last time they attacked?"

"How am I to know, Corey? I cannot see my own aura."

"Yes, of course." He nodded. "But the Naether Demons can. They see it from their realm and follow it likes moths to a flame, or wolves to the feast. Driven by hunger toward a power that can at last break open their prison of a thousand years."

Eolyn shook her head, though trepidation had lodged in her heart. "You are speaking nonsense, Corey. My aura holds nothing that would not have been offered by any maga or mage in all the centuries since the Naether Demons were banished. Indeed, your magic is of a stronger class than mine, and therefore more attractive to them, by the same argument."

"My magic is not stronger than yours, but even if it were, this has nothing to do with the pull of our magic. It's not only that they can see you Eolyn. You are giving them a door."

Eolyn caught her breath as the meaning behind his words became clear. Her hand went instinctively to the silver web that rested at the base of her throat.

"What does he mean?" Mariel's voice shook. She stepped close and took the hand of her tutor.

"Any place in which souls are torn from their bodies through violence offers them a path to our world." Eolyn did not look at Mariel as she spoke. "My soul was torn from my body and cast into the Underworld with the curse of Ahmad-dur. Akmael restored me to life, but the breach between this world and theirs remains. It follows me wherever I go."

"No," Borten objected. "That does not make sense. It's been years since Tzeremond cast that curse. If what you are saying is true, they would have come long ago."

"They have not had assistance until now," replied Corey. "The Syrnte are feeding them magic, and with each meal they grow stronger."

Borten stood and scanned the area around them. No one spoke for several moments. The knight drew a decisive breath, strode to Eolyn, and strapped Kel'Baru around her waist.

"Borten, what are you doing?"

He took hold of the silver chain and lifted it over her head, pressed the medallion into her palm. "Go to the King. Place yourself under his protection. There is nothing more we can do for you here."

"But I can't—"

"He is right, Eolyn," said Corey. "The safest place for you is in the City, with Akmael and all his mages."

"If I return now, I would be taking this danger into the heart of the Fortress of Vortingen."

"We cannot be certain about that," Corey said. "The ability of these beasts to find you may be tied to the proximity of the Syrnte. But even if it weren't, you are not the only one who carries this burden. Akmael also descended to the realm of the dead. The Naether Demons may be stalking him even as we speak."

Cold terror took hold of Eolyn.

Borten set heavy hands on her shoulders, forcing her to meet his gaze. "If the King is taken unawares, if he is slain, we are ruined. He has no heir. Moisehén will collapse into civil war, and all the Syrnte will have to do is wait until we've ravaged our own fields and destroyed our own people, before claiming what little remains."

Eolyn broke away from his grip. "I know, Borten! Do you think I cannot see what this means? That I do not fear for him, for our people? My heart weighs so heavy that I can hardly bear to carry it. I understand I must go back. It's just that I. . ." Her voice faltered. The memory of Borten's kiss returned fresh as a summer breeze, painful as a twisting knife. "I want everything to be different."

Borten's expression softened and his shoulders deflated. He studied her with a hint of sadness in his eyes.

"I would have a word alone with Maga Eolyn," he said.

Much to Eolyn's relief, Corey gave no disparaging remark or scowl of displeasure.

"Come, Mariel," was all he said. "Say farewell to your tutor."

Mariel was biting her lip and blinking back tears. She flung her arms around Eolyn. "Tell me we will see each other again. Tell me no harm will come to you."

"Remember what I've taught you, Mariel," replied Eolyn, for she would not make false promises in uncertain times. "Do as Borten says. If the year should pass and I have not returned, petition for your staff in the spring. You are a maga in the tradition of Aithne and Caradoc. Dragon will look after you, and give you a tutor."

Mariel sobbed while Eolyn kissed her cheek and withdrew.

Mage Corey placed a reassuring hand on the girl's shoulder then approached Eolyn. "When you arrive at the City, you must seek out High Mage Thelyn. Ask him to show you the royal library, and to take you to Tzeremond's quarters."

"Tzeremond?" Even now the mere mention of that wizard's name could make Eolyn's heart skip a beat.

"He had a collection of books, ancient and precious. Annals of women's magic, works handwritten by the great wizards, magical secrets gathered from distant places. We know this library was hidden somewhere in his chambers, but we have never been able to decipher the ward. You must find the entrance, Eolyn. Instinct assures me there are weapons within that can be used against the Naether Demons."

"I see." She nodded. "I will do my best, Mage Corey."

"I dare say your best can save this kingdom." His expression was a rare mix of sympathy and admiration. He paused before adding, "There is one more thing I would ask of you. Leave your staff with me."

Eolyn hesitated. Doyenne Ghemena had told her never to leave her staff in possession of another mage, lest its power be used as a force of destruction. "I don't think that would be wise, Mage Corey."

"Borten's sword will not help us if the Naether Demons should reappear, and the Syrnte have their own magic. I can do much without a staff, but it will be better for us if I have one."

Eolyn looked to Borten, but he only shrugged. "I do not know the implications of leaving your staff behind. It is your decision, Eolyn. And if Mage Corey uses it to fly away, well, perhaps that would be better for everyone concerned."

Reluctantly, Eolyn retrieved the staff from where it lay. Despite her uncertainty, she would go with greater peace of heart if they had this instrument to protect them. She proffered the polished oak to the mage, who set both hands upon its smooth surface. They stood for a moment, eyes locked on each other and staff held between them, while their magic met and resonated in a low hum.

"I entrust you with this instrument, Mage Corey, that you may use it to defend those I love, whom I leave under your protection." She pulled the mage closer and added in a low menace, "If any harm should come to Borten or Mariel through fault or failure of your own, I swear to the Gods I shall kill you the next time we meet."

He smiled. "I will miss you too, Eolyn. And do not worry about your precious knight. His selfless dedication to your well-being makes him more valuable to me than you might imagine. I promise not to hurt him . . . much."

"Curse you, Corey!" She tried to wrest the staff from his grip, but Corey held firm.

"It was a jest," he said. "You have nothing to fear, Eolyn. Your student and your lover are safe with me."

Eolyn examined his face and the subtle shades of his aura, searching for any sign of deception, but found nothing. Surrendering the staff, she stiffened as Corey embraced her and kissed her on the forehead.

"Remember what I told you about the Queen. Be cautious. Be prudent." He released the maga and turned to her student. "I've a few spells to teach you, Mariel, that you may need in the coming days. Why don't we start now, and leave Borten and Eolyn to whatever intimacies the moonlit wood inspires."

The two of them departed, the sound of damp leaf litter beneath their feet fading with each step.

In the silence that followed, Eolyn could not bring herself to look at Borten. She studied the silver web in her hand, the jewel that bound her to Akmael, the gift once meant as a sign of his abiding love. The knight stepped forward and enclosed her hands with his.

"It seems only a few days have passed since I truly saw you for the first time," she said. "Now I don't know if we will ever meet again."

The thought brought on a renewed wave of grief that she warded off by embracing him, inhaling his aroma of loam and crushed leaves, now mingled with the disturbing scent of fresh blood.

He released her, his expression grave. "Forgive me, Eolyn, for never having spoken to you about your brother's death."

She shook her head to dismiss his words. "It does not matter. Ernan chose his own fate. I have come to accept that now. And you and I, we have built a different life since then, in a new world."

"We cannot erase the past, Eolyn. It lives with us whether we speak of it or not."

Eolyn managed a smile of amusement. "You sound like my Doyenne."

"Your brother died valiantly, determined to defend you until his last breath. I knew not who he was, only that he would slay the King if I did not stop him."

"One of them was destined to die that day." Ernan's rebellion had been a confusing time of conflicting desires. In truth, Eolyn did not care to be reminded of it now. "You slew my brother and saved our King. Therefore I must forgive you in one breath, and thank you with the next."

"That cannot be easy for you."

"No," she admitted quietly. "It is not."

He studied her as if seeking to engrave her image in his mind. "After your brother perished, the King entrusted you to me. I remember that moment as if it were yesterday. It was the first time I ever held you in my arms."

"Borten, please—"

"You were spent and cold," he insisted, "your robes charred and your skin tinged with a bluish cast that made you seem more dead than alive; and yet, I thought you the most beautiful woman I had ever seen. Such is the power of your magic, your valor. You were the maga who escaped all the pyres of Moisehén, and returned to challenge the Mage King. You had lost your battle, Eolyn, but you had won his heart."

"I do not wish to speak of these things now."

"He loved you then, and he loves you still. Any fool can see that."

"Akmael has his Queen and his kingdom. I am not bound to him."

"He is the King."

She bristled at the finality in his voice. As if a handful of words decided everything. "I am a High Maga. I choose the keeper of my heart. I, and no one else. Not even the King."

"Do you?" He spoke as if directing the question more to himself than to her. "Do any of us really choose when it comes to love?"

His musings confused her. "The Gods are offering us a gift. To refuse would be an insult to them."

"The Gods have given us their gift, now they are taking it away. Fate is leading you back to the Mage King. I feel it with all my heart, though it fills me with despair. There is no future for me along the path you must take."

Her breath came up short, and her voice shook with anger, desire, denial. "So that is all, then? Our companionship, our affection, our kiss? It all simply ends here?"

He did not retreat from her challenge, but stepped forward and took her face in his hands. "I have watched you build your school and forge a new life out of ashes. We have spoken, argued, shared meals, fought at one another's side. I—a humble knight from Moehn—have fancied myself wealthier than the Mage King himself, for the Gods had granted me what he so coveted. Every single day I woke up in anticipation of seeing you. Always I have loved you, Eolyn, but to stand between you and my liege would only put us both in danger."

"I don't understand what you are talking about."

"Akmael is a good king, but he is a man like any other. He showed me great mercy once, when his father perished at the point of my lance. He will not indulge me again, should I return this favor by taking away someone else whom he loves."

"That is utter nonsense! Akmael would never—"

"That is an illusion you harbor because of his great kindness toward you," Borten said. "Many would say he has been too kind to the maga from Moehn. Never let him think you have played him for a fool."

She drew a breath to protest, but he silenced her with an ardent kiss, fingers intertwining in her thick tresses. He rested his forehead against hers. Cheeks flushed and lips burning, Eolyn traced the lines of his face with trembling fingers.

"Borten," she murmured, confused beyond thought by the force of her desire.

"Go now." His voice was hoarse. "Go, before I beg you to stay."

"Why would fate be so cruel as to inspire this love in the moment when we must say good-bye?" She sought his lips again, and he granted a tender kiss before releasing her and retreating several steps. The tension in his face had diminished. Compassion mingled with sadness in his eyes, but his stance was firm.

"Go," he said quietly.

She let the silver web slip from her palm and held it suspended from its delicate chain.

Ehekaht.

The amulet began to spin on its axis.

Elaeom enem.

The spell was breaking her heart. She held onto Borten's image even as the forest melted around her, a gloomy vortex that consumed everything and left her in momentary darkness.

The floor materialized cold and hard beneath her feet. A familiar and comforting aroma enveloped her, of stone and earth and timeless magic. Walls appeared, curtained by shadows. A solitary candle illuminated a small table. Pale moonlight streamed through arched windows and silhouetted Akmael, who stood with his back to her, looking south over the city.

Once not so long ago, Eolyn had thought she would never again set foot in this place where she had first given herself to the Mage King following the defeat of her brother. Nervously she glanced at Akmael's bed, and was surprised not to see Taesara's figure tucked under the covers, until she remembered the curious habit kings and queens had of not sharing their private chambers.

She hesitated, the silver amulet warm inside her grip. It would be a simple thing to return to Moehn, and to Borten, in this moment. Perhaps Akmael would not even notice she had been there.

The Mage King's shoulders stiffened. He adjusted his stance and cocked his head, as if sensing the presence behind him.

"Akmael," she said.

He spun around, knife in hand.

"It is me. Eolyn."

She heard his sharp intake of breath. "Thank the Gods!"

Akmael swept her into his arms and covered her face with kisses. Eolyn sank into the sweet familiarity of his embrace, the aroma of his skin, the memories of happy adventures in sun-dappled woods.

"We have lost so much." She pulled away, searched his eyes in the dark. Her knees felt weak, and she struggled to calm her pulse and regain her breath. "Moehn is overrun, and the Syrnte are summoning the Naether Demons back to our world."

"Naether Demons?"

"I have seen them. One in the South Woods, and two just now, about a day's ride from the Pass of Aerunden. High Magic will deter them, but the only weapon that can slay them is this." She unfastened the belt that held Kel'Baru and proffered the sword to Akmael.

He unsheathed the blade, holding it to the moonlight as if greeting an old and not entirely welcome acquaintance. "So I must wield the Galian sword if I am to confront the Syrnte. Let us hope, then, that it will listen to me now."

Eolyn's heart contracted with the memory of how Kel'Baru had failed her brother. "It will heed you, my Lord King. I will do everything in my power to make it so."

A smile touched his lips. Akmael sheathed the sword and set it aside.

"There is more—" she began.

He hushed her with a kiss.

"Please, my Lord King. I must tell you—"

"Eolyn, my love." He took her face in his hands. Strong hands, tempered by magic and made for war. Hands that sparked the ache of desire with nothing more than the familiarity of their touch. "Tomorrow, we will prepare for our battles. Tonight I want only to be with you."

His lips found hers again, and Eolyn surrendered to their insistence, closing her eyes, shivering as he freed her body from the stifling bonds of her tattered dress. The Mage King lifted Eolyn up and delivered her to the heat of his bed. What small voice of protest sounded inside her heart was silenced by the overwhelming need to drown in this intimacy, to fly on the wings of Dragon and forget the cares of the outside world.

She drank deep from the cup of their shared desire, and when the ecstasy was complete and their passion spent, she lay awake in Akmael's arms, listening to the steady beat of his heart. The Mage King shifted in his sleep, tightening his embrace. Eolyn pressed her lips to his warm chest, succumbing to the deep sense of security she felt at the center of his keep.

As she drifted toward slumber, her thoughts returned to Borten, to the time they had shared, the sweet discovery of his kiss, the sadness of their parting, the life they would never know.

"I love you," she murmured on the edge of her dreams.

Though she was no longer certain for whom the words were intended.

Chapter 26

Mechnes's gait was quick, his temper raw. For all her wanton beauty and womanly elegance, Rishona could act like a witless princess of six summers when the mood struck her. Once they had satiated the Naether Demons and returned to her pavilion, the Queen's fury had exploded like quickfire. Mechnes had settled the argument with a violence rarely directed at his niece, beating the rage out of her until she turned on him like a lynx in heat, desperate with an old and familiar hunger. The moment filled him more with mirth than desire. He had mocked her advances and then abandoned her, leaving the San'iloman alone to contemplate the bitter truth of her dependence on him in all things.

Torches illuminated the starless night. The rhythm of the camp had lowered to a pulsing murmur, characteristic of the brief period between when the men finished with their whores and gaming, and when they rose to begin a new day.

He found the peace of his tent refreshing. Two servants stepped forward as he entered, with a washbasin and towel that he used to cool his face and neck.

"The woman?" he said.

They nodded toward the back of the pavilion, where his bed was partially concealed by sheer drapes and illuminated with candles.

Adiana lay asleep, bound hand and foot.

Contemplating the landscape of his next conquest, Mechnes removed his belt and undid his doublet. Her shapely ankles were just visible beneath the hem of the light cotton shift that revealed so well the graceful curves of her body. Her eyes were swollen from the force of her tears; her face marked with exhaustion.

Behind him the servants poured wine, laid out food and set fresh water on a small table near the bed. He allowed them to assist with his outer garments, then took a seat while one of them knelt to remove his boots. Goblet in hand, he sent them away. The tension was fading from his shoulders. The candles exuded a sweet aroma of summer sage and purple anise.

Mechnes took a drink, reclined his head and closed his eyes, listening to the troubled murmur of Adiana's dreams.

He saw a woman consumed in flames, a man beheaded in a town square. Adiana ran from those deaths through mist-filled alleys, calling the names of her precious girls, terrified by the silent pursuit of a formless enemy.

"Jonaias," she murmured fitfully. "Jonaias. . ."

The nightmare faded, and began again.

Mechnes released her visions and opened his eyes.

A kinder man would let her sleep off the fatigue and shock, but the Syrnte Lord had never found much use for kindness, though in recent days Adiana's intriguing beauty had left him unusually benevolent. He had refused to cripple her fine hands, and protected her from the basest instincts of his men. He had given her a place of honor among his own musicians, and tonight he had saved her life. Tomorrow, his dear niece Rishona, in her murderous rage, would likely poison the lovely musician from Selkynsen. After that, Mechnes would be left satisfying his needs on servants and whores, some already well-used by his men.

He set aside his wine with a decisive grunt. It was time to claim his due.

"Adiana."

She started, opened her eyes then closed them tight as if to shut him out.

"Look at me."

Her eyes were reddened, her cheeks splotchy as if plagued by a fever.

He sat next to her, using a damp cloth to refresh her face. "You should procure, not to weep so much. The effects are unbecoming on a face as fair as yours."

A dry laugh burst from her lips. She looked away. When she spoke, her voice quivered with anger. "The well of my tears may be deep, Lord Mechnes. But you are the one who keeps dipping your cup. Bring those children back to life, and I will be most glad to stop weeping."

He set aside the cloth, laid a tender hand on her cheek. "There is something I would ask you, Adiana, and you must answer truthfully."

She set her jaw, kept her eyes averted.

"In these days past, have any of my men done you harm? You may answer without fear of reprimand or punishment. If one of them has violated my orders, I will have his head."

"You have done me harm." She met his gaze. "Perhaps you could demand your own head."

Mechnes appreciated her unflinching humor. It set her apart from so many others, who simply wept or raged their submission. He shifted his position to tend to Adiana's bound feet. Loosening the leather cord wrapped around her ankles, he ran his palm over the smooth surface of her skin, the elegant curve of her calf. "Truly you are beautiful. Even the slave markets of Ech'Nalahm rarely see a woman so finely wrought."

The binding fell way, and he brought her foot to his lips. Her momentary resistance aroused him, as did the taste of her skin, the rose-scented oil that mingled with her own sweet aroma. When his hand strayed toward her knee, she jerked away and curled into herself like an injured pup.

He settled beside her, found her hands and began to untie them. Her limbs were pliant, emptied of any desire to fight. But Mechnes would have more from her than mere acquiescence.

"Who is Jonaias?" he asked, stroking the silky strands of her luxuriant hair.

Surprise crossed her face, though she managed to hide it with a look of disdain. "I thought you could see all the threads of my past."

"His face was hidden in your dreams. Who is he?"

Something broke in her expression, giving Mechnes a glimpse of the vulnerability he sought, the reluctant recognition that there was no one left to her save the Syrnte Lord.

"He was my father's steward," she confessed, her voice reduced to a murmur, her gaze distracted by images from the past. "When my parents died and I ran away to the piers, he came after me. He took me away from that life, and gave me a place in his home."

The revelation moved Mechnes. "You were calling for your champion, then."

"Why do you pretend intimacy with me?" The challenge in her sapphire eyes was firm but without fire. "Do what you came to do. It does not matter anymore."

"I pretend nothing." He took her delicate hand in his. "I intend to pleasure you."

"A whore does not feel pleasure."

Mechnes caressed her fingers with his lips, found the place on her wrist that made her shiver. "Then you have never been the whore of a Syrnte Prince."

"You…" She struggled with some impossible thought that darkened her features. "You murder those children, and then speak to me as if. . . What vile place did you come from? How is it possible to live as you do, without soul or sentiment?"

"This is sentiment." Loosening her shift, he exposed the creamy rise of her breasts. "Though you may not recognize it as such. I have seen many slain, Adiana: valiant men and beautiful women, innocent children swept away by forces beyond their control or understanding. I learned long ago not to regret their passing. The best way to honor our dead is to embrace the life that is left to us."

"This is no life." Her voice was barely audible, and she lay still as a mouse under the paw of a cat.

"Ah, no? What is it then that you have clung to with such ferocity these past days? Of all those we found in that little school, you are the only one that remains. The only one clever enough to have sought refuge under my wing."

"I sought no such thing."

"It is with admiration that I speak. Be true to yourself, Adiana. You have never felt more alive than now, with death crowding close, showing you time and again its brutal face."

"You know nothing of what I feel!"

He hushed her and placed his fingers upon her brow, compelling her eyes to close. "I know the way you perceive the world shimmering around you. Even now you hear the pulse of this camp, the murmur of my men. Every smell, every sound, every sensation calls to you, because you have looked into the eyes of death and survived. You cannot shut out the comfort of this bed, the heat of my touch, the scent of our desire."

His hand passed from breast to belly, and drew back the folds of her skirt. She reared against him, but he immobilized her, taking his time to explore the secrets of her womanhood. Fear and longing, shame and desperation fought for control of Adiana's countenance. He could feel the sweet ache of all her wounds reopened, the intensification of the void that drove her toward experience, sensation, satiation. A flush of heat blossomed between her thighs. Mechnes sustained a tender but insistent touch, teased her breasts with tongue and teeth, until at last she arched her back and shuddered, a choked sob breaking upon her lips.

He withdrew his hand, the evidence of her need glistening on his fingers.

"The Gods take you!" Tears streamed down her face, and she beat at his chest with tight fists. "May they take you and tear you limb from limb."

"Be careful what you ask, Adiana. Who will protect you and comfort you, if I am gone?"

"I will not forget those girls," she said between gritted teeth. "I will never forgive what you did to them."

"I have no need for your forgiveness." He rent her cotton shift in two and settled his weight upon her. "As for what you remember and what you forget, that is your decision."

Chapter 27

When the dream world at last released Eolyn, golden light slanted into the King's chambers at a sharp angle, cutting through the shadows and leaving bright replicates of tall windows at even intervals along the stone floor.

Embarrassed at having slept so late yet reluctant to leave the comfort of Akmael's bed, Eolyn yawned and stretched. The covers were soft, impregnated with his magic and the compelling aroma of their shared love. Stories stirred in her memory, old legends told at the fires of her village, of princesses who had slept for a hundred years, hidden away in the quiet refuge of their bedchambers at the heart of some old castle.

"I would sleep a hundred years," she murmured to whatever Gods might be listening, "were I given the opportunity in this moment."

Akmael was nowhere to be seen. Eolyn vaguely recalled him rising before dawn, the warmth of his lips upon her temple, the blanket he had tucked around her shoulders before he departed, bidding her to sleep and closing the door softly behind him. It seemed like another dream, the most pleasant in a very long while. Indeed, she could not remember the last time she had awakened so well rested.

She sat up, and was startled by a sudden movement in a dimly lit corner, a girl rising from a wooden stool. She had pale cheeks and wore a plain dress; her hair was tucked carefully under a beige cap. She gave a brief curtsey, eyes alert and hands clasped tightly in front of her.

"Who are you?" Eolyn asked.

"Milady Maga Eolyn." Again the girl curtseyed. "I am Yessenia. The King requested that I tend to you when you wake."

"Tend to me?"

"Yes. That is, if it please you, Milady Maga Eolyn."

"I see." Eolyn had grown up tending to her own needs, and could not understand the feigned helplessness of royals when it came to bathing, dressing, cooking and eating. But young Yessenia looked so eager in her hopes to please, and in truth Eolyn did not know where to begin if she wished to find a wash basin, food, or a fresh set of clothes. So she nodded and said, "Very well. But please, call me Eolyn."

"As you wish, Milady Eolyn."

"No." Eolyn rubbed the bridge of her nose, feeling a heavy weight settle behind her eyes. She did not belong in this place. She never had. "Just Eolyn, please."

"I can't do that!" Yessenia's eyes went wide in her round face. Then she lowered her gaze and curtsied again. "I mean, forgive me, milady, but it wouldn't be proper, calling you by name."

Eolyn drew a breath and studied the stone walls, wishing they would fade for just a moment and reveal an ancient forest draped in emerald moss, illuminated with diffuse golden light, and beyond the massive trees, a river with crystalline waters flowing over smooth boulders, where she and Akmael would play until the sun sank low and twilight called them home.

She shook off the vision and gave Yessenia a sympathetic smile. "Then you may call me Maga Eolyn. But please, not milady."

"As you wish, milady. Oh, I beg your pardon." Another curtsey. "Maga Eolyn."

The morning meal—or rather, midday meal—had already been laid on a polished oak table: bread and Berenben cheese, fruits, meats, and sweet mead. Yessenia wrapped a warm robe around Eolyn's bare shoulders as she sat down to abate a now ravenous hunger.

While the maga ate, the servant diligently coaxed all the knots out of her copper tresses with a wide-toothed comb. More servants appeared with pitchers of fresh water and a large shallow basin. After finishing the meal, Eolyn accepted Yessenia's offer to assist her while bathing, and luxuriated in the feel of the servant's hands rubbing soap over her tired limbs, of the cool water running through her hair and down her back.

The undergarments and dress they brought were simple but finely woven, the skirt and bodice a deep shade of blue. After a moment, Eolyn recognized the gown. It was one of several left behind years before, when she had refused Akmael's proposal and embarked upon her journey south. The realization that he had kept it all this time surprised and moved her in ways deeper than she cared to admit.

Yessenia took much time and great care with Eolyn's hair, weaving a string of river pearls into an elegantly piled braid. The extravagance made the maga uncomfortable, but she did not protest, because Yessenia's touch relaxed her, and she liked the whisper of the pearls. Stones born of water and life, theirs was a happy and quick song, never bogged down by the slower rhythms and deeper moods of their more ancient and ponderous kin.

Once she finished, Yessenia stepped away to admire her work. "Have you nothing else, Maga Eolyn?"

Puzzled by the question, Eolyn frowned and shrugged.

"Other jewels," Yessenia explained, "to grace your appearance."

"Oh." Eolyn's hand rose to the base of her throat. The silver web had slipped from her fingers last night, somewhere between Akmael's kisses and his bed. "Yes, I have a necklace, but I don't know what became of it."

A brief search revealed the amulet on a small table next to the bed. Yessenia furrowed her brow, as if it were not quite what she had in mind.

"It was a gift from the King," Eolyn said. "I assure you it is most appropriate."

"Of course." Yessenia nodded with a sudden smile. She fastened the clasp behind Eolyn's neck, then retreated and gave a brief curtsey. "Is there anything else you desire, milady? Beg your pardon. Maga Eolyn."

"No. Thank you." Eolyn's hands worked restlessly against each other. She glanced around the room, at Yessenia's expectant pose, uncertain what to do next. "Where is the King?"

"He meets with his advisors." She gestured to the wide heavy door that led to the rest of his apartments. "He asked that you seek him out, when you are ready."

The maga nodded and started toward the door, but Yessenia ran to open it. Eolyn paused at the muffled sound of men's voices floating down the passageway.

Be cautious, Corey had warned. *Be prudent.*

"Is there another entrance?"

"Another?" Yessenia looked as if she had just been asked to solve an impossible mystery.

"Yes. Some other way that I might enter the King's audience chamber. A servant's route, perhaps."

"It would not be proper for you to enter like a servant."

"But I can't. . ." Eolyn bit her lip. She knew not who waited in the presence of the King, but if she entered like this they would all know she had come from his bedroom.

"Is the Queen with him?"

"No, Maga Eolyn." Yessenia arched her brow in a conspiratorial expression that seemed incongruous on her innocent face. "The Queen is indisposed."

Of course, Eolyn thought. The miscarriage. The need to visit Taesara, attend to her illness and comfort her mourning, surged in Eolyn's heart, though she knew after everything that had come to pass, that would not be possible. Drawing a deep breath and straightening her shoulders, Eolyn started down the hallway, conscious of the lift of her chin and the soft rustle of her skirts.

Her entrance into the council chamber brought all conversation to a halt.

More than a dozen men were gathered around the long table that occupied the center of the room: noblemen in elegantly embroidered doublets, knights in armor, and High Mages in flowing robes of forest green. Eolyn recognized several of Tzeremond's old adherents, among them, gracious old Tzetobar, the long-faced Lord Herensen of Selkynsen, and Corey's friend High Mage Thelyn. These same men had sent the magas and all their allies to the pyres. They had forced Doyenne Ghemena into hiding, imprisoned Briana of East Selen, and erased centuries of proud history. They had tortured Eolyn's mother, sentenced her to death, and watched her burn. Now all the laws that had once prohibited women's magic were lifted, yet here Tzeremond's disciples stood watching her.

Perhaps they were waiting for the maga's next mistake.

"Maga Eolyn." Akmael, standing at the head of the table, acknowledged her presence.

Eolyn bowed. "Forgive me, my Lord King, for interrupting this audience."

"This is no interruption. We are all most anxious to hear more of your trials in Moehn." Akmael extended an arm toward her. His face was expressionless, as was his custom when he met with his men, but Eolyn could see in the softening around his eyes that her appearance pleased him. "Come."

She approached, occupying a space created by shifting bodies.

"High Mage Tzetobar." She nodded to the rosy-cheeked mage across the table, who even in the most serious of moments managed a kind spark in his blue eyes. "It is good to see you again."

"I assure you, Maga Eolyn, the sentiment is most heartily shared," he said.

"And you, High Mage Thelyn. Lord Herensen." Eolyn met the eyes of each man in turn, greeting all assembled, apologizing to those whose names she did not remember, and making note of new faces that had appeared.

"This is Lord Penamor." The King intervened when she came to a man at the far end of the table. "The new ambassador from Roenfyn, and uncle to the Queen."

Eolyn hoped her expression did not betray the quickening of her heart. Penamor was a tall man with stiff shoulders, a narrow face and shrewd eyes. His wore a slate gray cloak, and his doublet bore the sigil and colors of his king, a sheath of silver wheat on a sage background.

She nodded. "Well met, Lord Penamor. Welcome to Moisehén. I regret that we must receive you under such trying circumstances."

"As do I," he replied with a cold unblinking stare.

"Maga Eolyn." Akmael drew forth a large map of the southern provinces and laid it out for her to see. "We have received word from Sir Drostan. He means to stall the advance of the Syrnte at the Pass of Aerunden. Our hope is that he can hold them until the army arrives."

"You will meet them in Aerunden?" she asked.

"We march at dawn."

Eolyn frowned and studied the map, troubled by this news for reasons she could not quite capture. The men resumed their conversation; their talk of arms, supplies, and levies like the murmur of a stream behind her thoughts, until the danger she sensed unfolded like a dark rose in her mind.

"That may not be wise," she said.

Everyone looked at her as if they had already forgotten she was there. Eolyn bit her lip, uncertain whether she should have spoken at all. She glanced around the table until her eyes met Akmael's.

"Please, Maga Eolyn," he said. "Speak."

She drew an unsteady breath. "My Lord King, it has been but three years since you met Ernan's forces in the Valley of Aerunden. Many people died that day; the curtain between the world of the living and the world of the dead is still thin. If the Syrnte intend to summon Naether Demons on the battlefield, then that valley could be the ideal place for them to do so."

There was a shifting of feet and a clearing of throats, accompanied by looks of doubt, curiosity, and scorn.

"I dare say the Maga Eolyn has a point," said Thelyn with a lift his dark brows.

"Yes," agreed a mage warrior called Galison, a fair-headed man with a broad face. "But the Syrnte have taken control of the upper reaches of the pass. We cannot, at this juncture, hope to push them back into Moehn. Not without incurring great loss. So enter the Valley of Aerunden they must, and when they do they will summon their Naether Demons whether we meet them or not."

"Well said, Galison." The King studied the map in front of him while the men nodded and voiced their concurrence, only to fall into renewed silence when Akmael asked, "What, then, would you recommend, Maga Eolyn?"

She faltered under expectant gazes. "Well, I . . . I'm not certain, my Lord King. There is much we do not yet know about the Naether Demons, or the power the Syrnte hold over them. I would think their time in our world is constrained by the integrity of the breach they use to enter it, and the potency of the magic given them. So, while the Syrnte may be able to summon Naether Demons in the Valley of Aerunden, I do not believe they could travel far from the place where they emerged, except perhaps by some extraordinary magic, a power beyond anything we have yet conceived."

"They may well have that kind of power," said Sir Galison.

"I don't believe so," Eolyn replied.

"Why not?"

"Well…" Eolyn paused, for her initial response had been based more on instinct than on logic. "If the Syrnte had magic that formidable, they would not need to summon Naether Demons. They could simply crush us, and be done with it."

"Maga Eolyn." Thelyn addressed her now, long fingers working against his staff of polished cherry wood. "I understand it was Mage Corey who was sent to retrieve you. Why is he not here?"

"This device," she touched the silver web at her throat, "can only carry one practitioner at a time. Mage Corey insisted I use it to return to the King."

"Where did you leave him?"

"Just south of the Pass of Aerunden."

"He could fly out, then," Thelyn concluded. "Cross the mountains into Selkynsen, and be in Rhiemsaven by the day after tomorrow."

"I am sorry to say that is not his plan," Eolyn replied. "Corey intends to help Sir Borten look after my student Mariel. They will find a way out of Moehn together if possible, and see Mariel safely into hiding if not."

"We have need of him." Thelyn turned to the King. "There is no one who knows more about Syrnte magic than he."

"If there is anyone who can escape an occupied province, it is Mage Corey," Lord Herensen said drily. "Survival is that man's greatest talent."

"But will he escape in time to be of assistance to us?"

"Mage Corey understands the gravity of the threat we face," Akmael said. "If he sent Maga Eolyn in his stead, it was with full confidence that she would be as great an asset to our efforts as he, if not greater."

"Mage Corey asked that you take me to Tzeremond's quarters, Mage Thelyn," Eolyn said, "that we might decipher the ward to the Master's library. Corey is convinced Tzeremond had records that can help us defeat the Naether Demons."

"We've been trying for years to open up that library," said one of the other High Mages, a bent old man with a thinning beard and gravelly voice. "It is impossible. The Master wanted no one to enter, before or after his death."

"Every ward can be unraveled," Eolyn countered, "even one cast by Master Tzeremond."

The statement was met with grim faces and a shaking of heads.

"We must try," she insisted. "It could be our only hope."

Their murmurs of objection continued, but Akmael cut them short. "High Mage Thelyn, you will accompany Maga Eolyn and assist her with this task. Anything you find that can help us must be communicated to me at once."

"As you wish, my Lord King." Thelyn bowed, and Eolyn thought she caught a wink in his eye.

"Maga Eolyn," Akmael continued, "you have shared very useful information and insights, but you have yet to answer my question."

"My Lord King?"

"What do you recommend with respect to the Valley of Aerunden?"

Again Eolyn frowned, searched her thoughts, put them in order. "I would send mages at once, as many as possible, to begin sealing the breaches that remain in the valley. It will not be enough, of course. There isn't sufficient time, as you well know; closing all those doors requires planting new life, allowing it to grow and thrive. But there are wards that could block the way temporarily. We can at least make the task more difficult for them."

"What if you are wrong, Maga Eolyn?" Sir Galison challenged. "If the Syrnte are able to march forth from Aerunden with an army of Naether Demons, what then?"

It was Herensen who stepped forward and said, "Perhaps there would be a way to harry the Syrnte, to force them out of the valley before they make camp, so they do not have the opportunity to work their magic there."

"Harry them, or lure them forward." Akmael clasped his hands behind his back, brow furrowed in concentration. "To cede another inch of land after they have taken Moehn and the Pass of Aerunden seems foolhardy at best, and yet. . . If we are to be truthful with ourselves, we must consider the fact that we do not even have reliable information regarding the size of their army, only the account of an injured and frightened boy. By letting the Syrnte march north towards Rhiemsaven, we would give our scouts the opportunity to better estimate their numbers, men and demons alike."

"My Lord King," objected Galison, "I urge you not to consider—"

"I will consider it, Galison." Akmael responded in a way that put an end to all discussion. "Though I have not yet made my decision. Mage Seldon?"

"My Lord King." The mage who stepped forward had a ruddy face with a bulbous nose and a thick yellow beard.

"See to it that thirty mages are dispatched at once. They are to ride to the Valley of Aerunden with all haste, and there set to work sealing whatever breaches they can find. You must also send a message ahead of them to the magistrate in Rhiemsaven, that he may put his own mages to the same task."

"As you wish, my Lord King."

"With all due respect, King Akmael." Lord Penamor's angry interjection brought all movement to a standstill. The ambassador gestured toward Eolyn. "This is unacceptable. A woman sitting at a war council? Her advice heard and heeded?"

Akmael let the question hang in the air before responding in even tones. "You would do well, Lord Penamor, not to question who sits on my council."

Silence followed, electric and heavy.

"My Lord Penamor," High Mage Tzetobar interjected with conciliatory tone, "this is not just any woman. She is a High Maga, trained in the tradition of Aithne and Caradoc. The only one left to our people. Her knowledge is vast as it is unique, and as well respected as any High Mage."

"She alone among us has met with the Naether Demons," added Thelyn. "And if I understood my Lord King's recounting of her tale, has already defeated them. Twice."

"It is true." Eolyn spoke quietly in response to Thelyn's questioning look, conscious of Akmael and Penamor, whose gazes remained locked, their stances tense as stags preparing to charge. "Though I would not have overcome them without the assistance of Sir Borten and Mage Corey."

"You must tell us what spells were used, what proved most effective."

"Why of course, Sir Galison."

The charged silence between Akmael and Penamor choked off her words. Resentment billowed like an angry storm over the council room. Eolyn's skin prickled, as if lightning were about to strike the table in front of her.

"That is enough for one morning," Akmael said tersely. "You have your orders."

Penamor was the first to leave. The others broke off in twos and threes, conversing quietly as they departed the King's presence, some with more haste than others.

Thelyn made his way toward Eolyn, circling the large table and slipping through the moving bodies. He had not aged in the least since Eolyn last saw him; a handsome man, always meticulously groomed, with a thin dark beard that enhanced the angle of his jaw. His cherry wood staff was adorned with a crystal head of andradite.

"Maga Eolyn." He bowed when he reached her side. "You must be very worried about your ward, the young Ghemena."

Ghemena. Eolyn brought a hand to her forehead and rebuked herself silently. In truth she had not thought about her student all morning. Such was the spell of the Mage King; even her wits had remained in his bed. "Yes, of course, Mage Thelyn. Where is she?"

"She has been entrusted to me. Had I known you were returned to us, I would have brought her with me this morning. As it is, she is studying magic under the tutorship of Mage Veroden, along with other children of her age."

"Other girls, studying magic? Here in the City?"

"No, not girls." He smiled. "There are no girls studying magic here. Or rather, there weren't, until yesterday."

"This is most irregular," Eolyn said doubtfully, "to have a girl studying among mages."

"Perhaps." Thelyn shrugged. "Or perhaps the first mistake of our predecessors was to separate the boys from the girls."

"High Mage Thelyn." Akmael's stern command interrupted their conversation. "You are dismissed as well."

"Of course, my Lord King." He bowed in deference, then said to Eolyn, "I will take advantage of this brief respite to bring Ghemena to the castle. She will be delighted to learn you are safe and well."

"Thank you, Mage Thelyn. I am most grateful."

He nodded and was gone.

"All of you as well," Akmael said to his servants, "leave us."

They disappeared without word or sound, closing the heavy doors behind them.

"My Lord King," Eolyn turned to Akmael, "there is something of great importance we have not yet—"

In a few long strides, he closed the distance between them and cut her words short with a kiss, heated, insatiable, so that she gasped for air when his lips released hers and then coursed without reprieve down her neck.

"My love," she murmured, wrapping her arms around him, overcome by the sudden ecstasy of his touch.

She intertwined her fingers in his hair as he lifted her up on the table, pushing back her skirts until he found what he sought. His thrusts were demanding and deep, tinged with anger; she clung to him with vigor, muffling cries of pleasure and need against his shoulder, dizzy with his voracious desire, until she heard his groan and felt his release shudder through her.

"Akmael," she murmured, feathering his neck and face with kisses. "My love."

They remained intertwined, their breath keeping rhythm with the fading pulse of his heat inside of her. Akmael's brow was damp, and Eolyn's dress suddenly stifling. His fingers sank into her hair. Gently he pulled her head back to expose the arch of her throat, caressing it once again with his lips. Loosening her bodice, he bent to taste the salty dew that had gathered between her breasts. How had she had ever found the strength to walk away from this?

"By the Gods, you are magnificent," he whispered.

Tears threatened to spring from her eyes. *No, my Lord King,* she wanted to say. *I am not as you say. I am the greatest fool that ever lived.* But she spoke no words, only held him close and kissed him again.

Gently he withdrew, and watched her while she straightened her skirts and smoothed her hair.

"No," he said, when she began to tighten the laces of her bodice. "Leave that as it is, for the moment."

A flush rose to her cheeks. Eolyn nodded, and Akmael helped her to her feet.

"You angered Lord Penamor," she said.

"He angered me. It is not his place to tell me how to run my council."

"It is not the running of your council that has upset him. I should not be here, Akmael. Not like this. When the Queen hears of it, she will surely—"

"The Queen is my concern, not yours." He traced the line of her cheek with his fingers, let them settle on the hollow of her throat where the silver web rested. "I cannot bear to be without you any more. Stay with me now. Promise you will never leave again."

Words failed her. She nodded, though her heart remained uncertain, and let him gather her in his arms.

"Akmael," she said inside his embrace, "the windows the Naether Demons use to find our world, we carry one, you and I, wherever we go. Our journey to the Underworld has left us vulnerable. They can find each of us directly, if they have sufficient magic to cross the barrier."

He stiffened and pulled away, searched her face with serious eyes. "You are certain of this?"

"Mage Corey saw the signature in my aura after their most recent attack."

"Then we must find a ward capable of sealing a breach woven through a living soul." His tone was pensive, troubled. "Perhaps such secrets can also be found in Tzeremond's library."

"That is my hope, though you have not given me much time if we are to march at dawn."

He cast her a puzzled glance, and gave a short laugh. Dark eyes sparking with amusement, he took Eolyn's chin in hand. "My love. *We* are not marching south tomorrow. I am marching south, with my men. You will remain here, in the safety of this fortress."

She hesitated, burdened by the sudden shadow over her heart. "We must remain together."

"Our love has weathered greater divisions and harsher conflicts than this."

"I am not talking about our love!" Eolyn caught her breath at the hardening of his countenance. "No mage or maga has confronted a threat like this for generations. Every instinct I have is now telling me we will not vanquish the Syrnte or their Naether Demons if we are not at each other's side. Akmael, my love, if you go forth alone tomorrow, I fear you will not return."

The smile that touched his lips did little to sooth the premonition of terror and loss that had gripped her heart.

"I will hardly be alone." He took her face in his hands, kissed her forehead. "The strength of your sentiment moves me. You must know it is my greatest pleasure to be in your presence, and I would have you with me at all times were it possible. But I have experienced the fear of losing you in battle once. I will not suffer that torture again."

"Akmael, please—"

"No," he hushed her by setting a finger to her lips. "I am making enough decisions in this campaign on a foundation of uncertainty. I will not add risking your life to the list. If in your study of Tzeremond's collection, you find evidence to support this concern of yours, dispatch my messengers. Should I find your letters convincing, I will send for you."

"I will not sit here twiddling my thumbs while the fate of the kingdom rests in the hands of some messenger."

"You are not to leave this City," his tone was stern, unflinching, "unless in the company of an armed escort appointed by me."

"But I don't need an escort! I can use the silver web—"

"No. For the love of the Gods, Eolyn. I am going to war, not to a summer festival. There is no telling what circumstance you will meet if you to attempt to use this magic to find me. If you travel toward Rhiemsaven, you will do so by land in the company of trusted warriors chosen by me, and me alone. Do you understand?"

Eolyn met his stare, jaw set. "Yes, my Lord King."

Although it was one thing to understand his will, quite another to acquiesce to it.

Chapter 28

Adiana was dragged from Mechnes's bed in the predawn hours, a fresh dress pulled over her head, a worn cloak thrown about her shoulders. Groggy, muscles aching from exhaustion and misuse, the musician from Selkynsen was ushered outside Mechnes's pavilion by a plump sour-faced matron, who ordered her to wait next to a pair of mules. The animals blinked at her, tearing mouthfuls of hay from dirty bales and flicking away flies with restless tails.

As always, guards accompanied her; two this time, their gazes more lascivious than ever, so that Adiana began to wonder whether she was the morning meal promised them. She shivered, pulled the cloak tight about her shoulders, but to no avail. It was not the breeze that chilled her; it was the icy void that had consumed her heart.

The camp was dissolving into a rising cacophony of activity. Tents were being struck amidst the shouts of men and clatter of tools. Horses whinnied and stamped. Bustling servants emptied Mechnes's pavilion of its furnishings, pulled stakes from the mud, let the brightly colored canvass flutter to the ground. Adiana could not see the Syrnte Lord, but she heard his voice, commanding and impatient as he drove an entire army toward a unified rhythm, an ominous requiem that heralded death for her people.

At last he appeared some twenty paces away, surrounded by officers with whom he was engaged in vigorous conversation.

Adiana's gut tightened with something that felt like need, but which she chose to recognize as fear.

A polished breast plate covered his chest; a cloak of burgundy and gold hung from his broad shoulders. In the crook of his arm he carried a helmet, the other hand rested on the hilt of his sword. His dark brow was furrowed, the set of his jaw grim. Each word he spoke came sharp and quick. Men nodded and took their leave; others stepped forward with attentive expressions.

No one questioned his will.

The cadence of Mechnes's orders stopped when the San'iloman rode into their midst. Everyone responded with deep and sustained bows, some on their knees, save Lord Mechnes who remained standing and met her with a direct gaze.

Rishona sat tall on a chestnut mare, chin lifted, face masked by a sparkling veil. She wore a breastplate and cloak to match her uncle; her skirt was draped over the horse's back in a swath of burnished gold. The jeweled scimitar at her belt seemed more adornment than weapon.

For several moments, Queen and General watched each other in silence.

Then Rishona extended a hand toward Mechnes.

He stepped forward, touched her gloved fingers with his lips.

Quiet words were exchanged between them. Mechnes nodded and summoned his horse.

Adiana's heart stuttered in panic, though she did not understand why until she heard the dry chuckle of the guard behind her. He stepped close and took rough hold of her arm, ignoring the growled objection of his companion.

"You're a pretty whore to have caught the general's eye," the guard said. She cringed at the stench of sweat and grime on his clothes, the stink of last night's ale on his breath. "But you'll be alone now, won't you?"

She could not think to respond before he was wrenched away and a warm spray of blood wet her cheek. The assailant fell to the ground, clutching a crimson river that pulsed from his throat. His partner watched with dispassionate eyes, a grimace on his weathered face as he cleaned his knife. Then the killer set his gaze on Adiana, a lewd invitation in his gape-toothed grin, until the smile was startled off his face and he dropped to his knees.

"Lord Mechnes," he said, eyes downcast.

Adiana spun around.

The Syrnte general studied the scene with narrowed eyes and a stormy countenance.

"Forgive me," the guard continued, "I did not think. . ."

The man looked from the general to Adiana, his expression one of anxiety and fear. At their feet his companion convulsed then lay still. The man bent his head again, stared resolutely at the ground.

"Mercy," he said quietly.

Adiana could see his worth extinguished in Mechnes's eyes.

"It is too early in the day to be losing men," the Syrnte Lord muttered, but drew his sword nonetheless.

"My Lord Mechnes, please!" She took hold of his arm, then let go at the angry heat of his sudden glare. Her hands burned where she had touched him, yet the rest of her body felt cold as a winter night. She backed away, averted her gaze. When at last she found her voice, it was reduced to a murmur. "Too much blood has been shed on my account. Please, let this man be. He did not lay a hand on me."

Adiana closed her eyes, keenly aware of Mechnes's stance, the way he savored the power he held over life and death. Moments passed while she braced against the sickening sound of metal opening up flesh. Canvas fluttered, crates fell loud upon carts, soldiers grunted and officers bellowed long calls demanding order. The air after all these days still smelled of fire and charred wood, of triumph and defeat, of revelry, suffering, and blood. Always blood, eternal blood. Hot scarlet rivers let loose upon the earth, drying into bitter ochre stains that riddled the soul, exuding an acrid vapor that permeated the camp and made Adiana sick to her stomach.

"Please." She clutched at her abdomen, fighting the surge of bile in her throat. "Let him be, or end it now."

Mechnes said nothing, and sheathed his sword. The sound hit Adiana like a breeze from the South Woods: fresh, unexpected.

"Get out of my sight," he said to the guard. "Do not disappoint me again."

The man scuttled away.

Lord Mechnes produced a clean rag and began wiping the blood from Adiana's face, his touch rough but not unkind. His eyes met hers in ephemeral moments as he worked. When he finished, he stepped away.

"You need rest," he said. "There'll be little of that to be had today."

Adiana watched him in silence. The air had taken on a strange resonance. The sounds of the camp faded into the background; the soldiers and beasts of burden blurred as Mechnes's face became ever more vivid, dark hair softened by strands of gray, face marked by the scars of his many battles, stone blue eyes that knew not love or compassion. He had destroyed her life, raped her spirit, gutted her soul. There should be nothing left of Adiana, and yet here she was standing before him, her gaze steadfast.

For the first time in days Adiana felt no fear.

Perhaps, in truth, she no longer felt anything at all.

A shrewd smile played upon Mechnes's lips. He reached forward, touched her chin. "You have pleased me, Adiana of Selkynsen. You will not be left behind."

He departed as suddenly as he had arrived, issuing a few short barks that left Adiana in the company of a new set of guards. One of them bade her to sit as the sour-faced matron brought a bowl of lukewarm gruel and a cup of watered wine. Adiana lost sight of Mechnes, though she could see the parting and shifting of his men as the Syrnte Lord approached his mount. The San'iloman sat on her mare, back erect, still as a heron at the water's edge. Though the shimmering veil concealed the true direction of her gaze, Adiana sensed the bite of Rishona's envy, sharp as her obsidian blade.

Mechnes climbed on his steed, drew his sword, and saluted his queen. Shouts of allegiance and victory thundered across the camp. Flags floated high in the early morning breeze; horses pranced impatiently to the ring of metal and the chink of mail. As the royal guard fell into formation around the Queen and her General, the clouds in the sky ignited with the brilliant colors of the waking sun.

The march toward Moisehén had begun.

A maga should not be sad when the sun rises, Eolyn had once told Adiana. *A maga celebrates the dawn and partakes in its joy.*

But Adiana had never been a maga, and now she never would be. She had become a woman of no consequence, a wicked man's whore.

Adiana was loaded onto an oxcart with the rest of the food and the equipment. The column snaked ahead of them, though half the camp, it seemed, had yet to begin its march. The cart creaked and rocked as oxen pulled it onto the road. Behind them Moehn came into view, charred walls hung with bold Syrnte colors. Shirtless men labored to refortify the town, tearing down what was too weak to restore, laying barriers of heavy stone behind rows of sharpened stakes. Above them soldiers stood on mounds of rubble, scanning the landscape, watching as their comrades fell into stride and the column flowed inexorably north and west.

Every rut in the road jolted Adiana. The canvas on which she sat was lumpy; the objects beneath it hard and unyielding. Yet the discomfort did not ward off the great weariness that pressed down upon her. She closed her eyes, surrendered to sleep, and did not wake again until she heard the girl's happy laughter and lyrical voices, the sound of their feet pounding against the earth as they ran toward her.

Mistress Adiana!

Adiana bolted upright, hand gripping the rim of the cart, heart leaping inside her chest. With anxious eyes she searched the train of carts and mules, the servants and slaves who walked among them, the men on horseback that surrounded them.

"Tasha?" she called. "Catarina?"

No one responded.

The plump matron, who rode at the head of the cart, glared over her shoulder.

A pair of oxen nearby announced with long protesting lows that they had decided not to continue. The driver shouted and whipped their flanks with a willowy switch, until at last the beleaguered animals bellowed and reluctantly pulled forward, cart groaning behind them.

Adiana secured her unkempt hair behind her ears and pulled the hood of her cloak over her head to hide from the unrelenting sun, from the guards who watched her with serpent eyes.

"Forgive me," she murmured.

The girls did not answer. Even Renate no longer whispered inside her head. Nor did Adiana expect to hear them, to feel their presence as anything more than a lingering torment, ever again. She had given herself with abandon to their murderer, sinking toward oblivion as a drunkard drowns in his wine, without thought or care for those he loves, certain that dawn will erase all memory, until the morning light breaks through a colorless sky and he finds himself alone with his pain.

Adiana's hands felt numb despite the warm summer day; her bones ached as if with a fever. She tried to lay down on the lumpy canvas, but the moment she closed her eyes Mechnes was upon her, pitiless hands wringing pleasure from every contour of her body, drinking the nectar of her womanhood as if she were nothing more than a ripened plum crushed in his grasp.

Shuddering in disgust, Adiana sat up, tucked her knees tight to her chest and took to staring at the dirt road as it rolled beneath the cart like a dusty river, long straggling ruts broken by sharp-angled stones, ever different yet always repeating. The rhythm comforted her, lulled her until the mind was drained of all thought and she could almost convince herself she was alone in a formless world.

The sun was high when the caravan came to a stop. Riders slid off horses and carts. Those who had been walking wandered a little ways off the road, some finding places to sit. Flasks of wine and water were uncorked, food was produced from hidden places and gnawed or chewed upon. One of the guards offered Adiana water, which she accepted with wary gratitude. The matron gave her an apple, scowling as if she were sacrificing a meal fit for a king.

Adiana slid off the cart as well. The ground swayed beneath her feet before becoming firm and steady.

The earth is the source of a maga's power, Eolyn used to say, *the fountain of all her courage.*

She walked several paces without realizing it and then stopped herself. Glancing around she saw the guards had followed her. They watched with hooded eyes, alert yet somehow distant. They made no comment or rebuke, so she turned and continued, conscious of their heavy footfalls while she wandered onto the grass beside the road.

The landscape of Moehn, despite all the horrors visited upon it, had not changed. The grassy hills spread low, seeming to rise and fall in an almost imperceptible breath as they stretched southward toward the distant smudge of the Paramen Mountains. The crops were densely cultivated, though each field had been invaded by at least one scraggly tree. Lord Mechnes would be pleased, she thought with a contradictory mix of pride and melancholy, when he saw just how bountiful this land could be.

It occurred to Adiana that she might never lay eyes on the province of Moehn again; that wherever this war was leading, it would not bring her back here. Not that there would be anything to come back to except sadness and loss, bitter memories of the joy and friendship she once knew, of the people she betrayed.

She took off her shoes, pressed her feet against the soft verdant blades, prodded at the herbs with her toes until one pricked back. With a sharp gasp, Adiana knelt down. She recognized the rosette, and she pulled it, roots and all, out of the soil.

The flower was deep maroon with a speck of gold at its heart, the leaves purplish-green and spiny, the roots a blood-stained ivory. Adiana swallowed hard, cradled the plant in her hands as if it were a most precious jewel, feeling the Gods had finally smiled upon her. She might not have the strength to avoid Mechnes's bed, but this much she could do. She could reject his seed. Eolyn had taught her how.

"What is that?"

The man's voice startled Adiana. She jumped to her feet, clutching the plant to her breast though the leaves stung her fingers. Kahlil studied her with dark eyes framed by heavy lashes, a frown upon his full lips. Behind him stood the ever-watchful guards.

Adiana lowered her eyes to the crumpled plant. "It's . . . an herb my mother once used for tea. I thought perhaps it could help me sleep at night. I have not been sleeping well, of late."

Kahlil set his jaw, extended his hand. "May I see it?"

Adiana hesitated, for she had no way of knowing whether he would recognize the medicine, and if there was one thing men found intolerable, it was the thought of a woman rejecting their seed at will. Yet to keep the plant from him would only arouse suspicion.

Reluctantly, she handed it over, hoping that what Rishona had said during her time with the Circle was true, that the herbs of Moisehén were different from those used by the Syrnte.

Kahlil took the plant by the roots, twirled it slowly in his hands. Carefully he broke off the tip of one of the leaves, crushed it, sniffed it then touched it to his tongue. With a grimace he spat it out. "It is very bitter."

"Yes," Adiana stumbled over her words. "The infusion softens the taste, and it is mixed with other herbs and sometimes sweetened. With honey."

Kahlil nodded slowly, staring at the plant. "My sister had a taste for bitter herbs."

"Your sister?" In all the years they had played music for Mage Corey, Kahlil had never mentioned his family. "I did not know you had a sister."

"She died." His eyes met hers, though they seemed absorbed by some troubled memory. "She, and the man she loved."

"I'm sorry." Conscious of the guards nearby, Adiana stifled the impulse to give him a comforting touch. "I'm very sorry."

He shook his head, drew a breath as if to release the memory. "It happened a long time ago."

Still he did not return the plant. Adiana glanced at the ground beneath them, surreptitiously searching for another, though she had little hope of finding one.

Bloodswort is a lonely herb, Eolyn had said. *It hides from many eyes, including our own.*

"I have spoken with Lord Mechnes," Kahlil brought her focus back to him. "He has given permission for you to sit with us when we rehearse. That is, if it be your will."

Adiana did not like the sound of her laughter. It was high pitched and broken, the laugh of a madwoman. "He said that? If it be my will?"

"No. . ." The frown on Kahlil's face deepened. There was a sympathy in his eyes that she despised. As if he could understand. As if anyone could possibly understand. "No. This is what I say: If it be your will, Adiana. We would be honored to have you sit with us."

By the Gods would the tears never stop? She turned from him, so he would not see her wipe the sting out of her eyes. "I cannot make music anymore. This is no place for music, and there is no melody left in my soul."

For a long time, Kahlil said nothing. Then he stepped close and said in a low voice, "All of us live at the mercy of gods and kings. But as long as we have music, we have our freedom. They cannot touch us inside our songs. You knew this once. You must remember it now."

Her throat constricted painfully.

He offered her the wilted plant. "Promise me this will not kill you."

"Kill me?" She glanced up at him in surprise. "No, it won't kill me. Well, it might, if I were to take enough. But I'm far too cowardly to kill myself."

"Cowardly?" He furrowed his brow, as if that were the last word that would have come to mind. "You said it is mixed with other herbs. What else do you use?"

"Angelica," she murmured, looking away. "Coltsfoot. Hemlock. But this is the most important."

"Then I will find more of these plants for you." When she did not respond, he added, uncertainty in his voice, "Shall I send for you, then, when we rehearse?"

Adiana shrugged and turned her back on him, looking southeast toward where Eolyn's *Aekelahr* once stood, to the place where all her instruments had perished in flames, their ashes scattered by a cruel and unforgiving wind.

Chapter 29

Taesara's uncle stormed in unannounced, scattering servants and ladies like a fox among chickens. "Get out! All of you."

The Queen's attendants departed with startled faces and murmured protests. Only Sonia remained at her side, clasping Taesara's hand with the clawed grip of a small bird.

"A bolder harlot I have never seen!" Lord Penamor rumbled, his footfalls heavy on the stone floor as he paced in front of them.

Taesara shifted her position against the pillows, but there was no escaping the persistent cramp in her lower back. She forced calm into her voice. "So it is true. Sonia heard the whispers of the servants this morning. It is said the witch appeared last night and stayed with him until dawn."

"Those eyes of hers, like smoldering coals of midnight lust." Penamor's words dripped with venom, but his gaze seemed caught inside a forbidden thought. "She distracts every man in her presence, yet the King allows her to stand among us as an equal, as one of his own counsel, professing folly as if she knew anything of war."

"It has long been said that he is much taken with her."

"Taken." Penamor snorted. "Bewitched, more like. That woman who should have burned with the rest of the magas."

"She is not a maga," the Lady Sonia volunteered beneath her breath. "She is nothing but a common witch."

"Witch. Maga. Sorceress. Harlot." Penamor spat out each word with vigor. "They are all the same."

"Not the same." Sonia's voice gathered strength. "A true maga would not have seduced a king."

A scowl crossed his face. He jabbed a finger at Sonia while addressing Taesara. "Why did this woman remain when all were told to leave?"

"Because I bade her to remain, uncle," said Taesara. "Sonia has studied the magas, as you well know. I thought her knowledge might be of use to both of us, under the circumstances."

Penamor pinned the lady-in-waiting with a hard gaze. "Do you have a curse we can use to rid ourselves of this witch?"

Sonia pursed her lips, glanced at the Queen.

"Well?" Penamor prompted.

"I do not pretend to know their spells and potions." She lifted her chin. "What I offer is some insight to their history and teachings."

The ambassador eyed her with contempt. "The Mage King is siring a bastard on that whore even as we speak, and you would give us a history lesson."

"Uncle!"

"I say only what needs to be heard, Taesara. What have you done these past years, with all your beauty, all your grace? After the many sacrifices your father made to secure this marriage, have you nothing more to show for your kingdom than this? A scrawny girl, a dead prince, and a whore in your husband's bed."

"I will not stand for this!" Anger rose hot in Taesara's throat. "Our family was mad to think I could appease the Mage King. Needlepoint you taught me, and riding. Charity and stylish dress. Songs and clever dialogue, demure dances and quiet obedience. These were the tools, you said, that would win the love of a king. But this king does not love me. He loves only that woman, who brings him the two things he desires most: magic and war."

"A king's greatest desire is a son," said Penamor. "Give him that, and he will love you."

"It is too late." Her heart contracted painfully at the certainty in her own voice. "Indeed, there was never a hope to begin with."

"Curse you, Taesara!" He pounded his fist on a table. "I will not listen to this nonsense. You will find a way back into his favor and deliver him a prince."

She frowned and turned away. The last of her son's blood had not yet drained from her womb, and already they demanded she conceive another. What a bitter duty that was, to suffer under the Mage King's weight, longing for a tenderness that she knew would never come, stifling cries of pain so as not to displease him. And the silence that filled her chambers after he left: dark and impenetrable like his heart, comforting only in its capacity to hide her tears.

"My Lord Penamor," Sonia volunteered quietly, "already my Queen has suffered the worst of losses at the hands of this woman. If you have any love for your niece, you must surely see that—"

"Love for my niece?" Penamor strode toward them, stood over the bed much like the King had on the day of her miscarriage, an ogre ready to strike at the slightest provocation. "My love and my duty are for my kingdom, the security of which rests on my niece's capacity to please the Mage King and to prevent him from siring a bastard sorcerer with that shameless witch."

Taesara studied him a long moment, her stare unblinking, a wintry calm overtaking her.

"Get out," she said.

Penamor's eyes widened. "What?"

"Leave my presence. Now." When he did not move, she added, "Or shall I call my guards to escort you?"

Penamor set his jaw, sent Sonia a viperous glance, and returned his gaze to the Queen. "I only say what you must hear."

"Leave!"

He lifted both hands in a reluctant gesture of appeasement and departed.

Sonia rose, closed the door behind him, and turned to the Queen. Though not an attractive woman, the Lady Sonia knew how to present herself. Today she wore a teal robe with ivory trim that offset her neatly bound dark hair. Her carriage was always impeccable, one of quiet dignity.

"It was unwise to dismiss him so," she said.

Not a rebuke or impertinence, simply the reflection of Taesara's own thoughts; something for which Sonia had shown a gift ever since she came into the Queen's service.

Taesara rubbed her forehead, searching for a clear thought, a path through this haze of mounting fear and desperation. "Do not call the others back yet. I would have a moment's peace."

"As you wish, my Lady Queen."

She closed her eyes to ward off the dizziness.

"Shall I serve you a cup of tea?"

"Yes."

Sonia's skirts rustled as she moved about the room, her slippered feet hushing the echoes of Penamor's indignant rage. The cup she brought warmed Taesara's chilled hands; the aromatic brew soothed and awakened her senses. Sonia blended herbs in ways that always refreshed Taesara, no matter what her mood. As the Queen drank, the lady sat at her side, a frown on her pug-nosed, freckled face.

"What are we to do, my Lady Queen?"

Taesara drew a deep breath. "We must find a way out of here before death takes us all."

"Flee?"

"And take Eliasara with us."

Sonia frowned, shook her head slowly. "We cannot leave Moisehén without Lord Penamor's sanction and protection."

"I have a handful of guards who are loyal to me. None would stop us if we left the castle—"

"But all would take note."

"We could find away to depart without fanfare, then descend to the piers and travel by boat down river. We'd be in Roenfyn before anyone—"

"Even if we secured safe passage, and escaped the pursuit of the Mage King's men, your father would not receive us should we depart like thieves in the night."

Taesara set her cup aside. Her stomach revolted against the truth. Fear pricked at her neck. Sonia was right. King Lyanos would declare her a disgrace to his house and kingdom.

"That witch took my son." Her voice trembled as she reached forward and wrapped her hand around Sonia's wrist. "She will kill my daughter. With the princess gone, there will be nothing left to protect me from the Mage King's cold ambition. I, too, will die in this place, at his hands or at hers. Why can my uncle not see this?"

"Perhaps Lord Penamor shares your concerns, but is reluctant to admit them. The future of Roenfyn weighs heavy on his heart. If we leave the Mage King alone with this mistress, they will breed more of their kind. Roenfyn will be trapped with the Galian wizards on one border, the Mage Kings of Moisehén on the other. The day they decide to contest our lands, our people will be slaughtered between them."

Defeat settled heavy on her shoulders, and Taesara sank back into her pillows. "I am but one woman. I cannot stand in the way of such terrible forces."

"You are a Queen."

"A queen with no defense against a maga's curse."

"She is but a sorceress," Sonia corrected quietly, "and in the King's eyes, she is first and foremost a woman."

Taesara cast her lady a sideways glance. "What do you mean by that?"

"She has captured his heart." Sonia shrugged. "Someday, she will break it."

Taesara laughed out loud. "More likely he will break hers."

"She will betray him with another man. It is simply a matter of time."

"Only a fool would cuckold the Mage King."

"Witches are fools when it comes to love. That much is clear in all the annals."

Taesara studied Sonia's face, wary of the promise of triumph that glinted in her hazel eyes. "You truly believe she will betray him?"

"It is rumored she had many others before she came to the king's bed. Why should that change now?"

A shiver coursed through Taesara at the memory of all those stories: hapless youths overcome in moonlit fields, troubadours who worked in Mage Corey's Circle, rebels who fought against the Mage King. Men and women alike. Some whispered that even Mage Corey had found entertainment in her pleasures. And only the Gods knew how many nobles and peasants had surrendered to her wiles these recent years in Moehn.

"Rumors," she said nonetheless, for in her clearest moments all the gossip seemed little more than ephemeral tales spun to shorten dull winter nights. "We need more than rumors to turn the Mage King against her. Even if all they say is true, it matters not how she conducted herself before now. What the King will mind is how she conducts herself from this moment forward."

"History breeds suspicion," Sonia insisted. "It was Kedehen's suspicion that condemned Briana of East Selen to the tower. If we are clever, my Lady Queen, the Mage King's suspicion will condemn Eolyn to the pyre."

"He would not listen to me, no matter how irrefutable the evidence. He would first condemn me for having questioned her at all."

"I have considered that, my Lady Queen." Sonia nodded thoughtfully, and it occurred to Taesara that the lady-in-waiting had considered a great many things in recent days. "What I suggest is that we keep your person separate from the entire affair. With your permission, I would bring this proposal to Lord Penamor that he might appoint trusted informants to aid in our cause. When the time comes, accusations could be brought forward in such a manner as to avoid implicating you or your father's house."

Sonia's scheming amused Taesara, though her smile was sad. "It is sweet and loyal of you to think of all this, my dear Sonia, but I would rather you convince Lord Penamor to help me escape."

The lady pursed her lips, dark brows coming together in a pronounced frown. Retrieving Taesara's empty cup, she rose to refresh the Queen's tea. When she returned, her aspect was pensive, her words slow and careful.

"I will do whatever you ask of me, my Lady Queen, but I beg you, do not underestimate your power in this moment. The people of Moisehén have come to love you. The peasants see you as you are: good, generous, and compassionate. The noble families are careful in their loyalties, but wary of the Mage King, and they admire your beauty and graciousness. Even among the class of mages you have made friends. There are very few in this kingdom who desire a return to the days of Kedehen. They do not want another witch in the King's bed, much less on the throne. Many will support you, if we stand against her."

"It would not be enough." Taesara tugged at her fingers, panicked by the thought of remaining in the same city with that terrifying woman. "Even you have said none can exceed her power save the Mage King himself. However many allies I have, they cannot protect me or my daughter from her curses."

Sonia took both the Queen's hands in hers. In her steady gaze, Taesara caught a glimpse of the core of this faithful servant, solid and immutable as if taken from some secret place deep inside the earth, tinged with an ochre flame of determination.

The anxious flutter that plagued Taesara's heart stilled.

"The Gods will protect you, my Lady Queen," Sonia assured her. "The Gods always protect the good and the righteous."

Chapter 30

In the evening, Eolyn accompanied Akmael up the narrow winding stairs of the southeast tower to walk the ramparts. The breeze was warm, the stars just beginning to ignite in the darkening sky. Torches hissed and flared in response to the shifting wind. Thin smoky plumes rose from their flames, carrying the sharp aroma of burning pitch and charred wood.

Eolyn kept close to her King, hand resting in the crook of his arm as they matched each other's stride along the stone walkway, sentries greeting them along the way. The heat of his presence sustained her, invoked a sense of constancy in the midst of so much turmoil. She sensed the power of Vortingen's mountain rising through Akmael's core like a slow river of molten rock, timeless and indomitable. Eolyn wondered why it had taken so many generations for the mountain's influence to awaken magic in this line of Kings, who had since the time of Vortingen lived in this citadel. Perhaps there were others before Akmael's father, princes and princesses who longed to pursue the traditions of Aithne and Caradoc, but who turned away from the call of the Gods and allowed their desires to be buried in time and silence.

Akmael paused and set his gaze past the City toward the horizon, already lost in the gathering dusk. Eolyn suspected his thoughts were upon Rhiemsaven and the narrow road that wound from there toward the Pass of Aerunden, where the Syrnte awaited him.

He rested his hand upon hers. "Apartments are being prepared for you here, in the East Tower."

"Your mother's prison?" The words escaped her lips before she considered their consequences, but even as he tensed into a brief silence, she felt no desire to retract them. Briana had died in that tower, and Eolyn's mother had been captured there and sentenced to a bitter fate.

"I am not incarcerating you," he said in terse tones. "Those apartments are spacious, and well-appointed. Protected by powerful magic. It is the most secure place in this keep; indeed, in the entire kingdom. You will want for nothing, and you will be safe until I return."

"I see." Eolyn withdrew gently, let her hands rest upon the smooth stone parapet. "It is most generous of you, Akmael, but it would be better if I stayed in the Mage's Quarter. Thelyn has already agreed to help me find a place there—"

"I will not have it."

She bristled at the finality in his tone. "I cannot remain in the castle. Ghemena needs me. She was devastated when she learned I would not stay with her tonight; and she is furious with me for not returning at once to Moehn to search for Tasha and Catarina."

"Those girls are beyond your help now."

"I know. But Ghemena does not understand this. This is not the moment to abandon her to the company of mages and strangers. She needs something of the past to hold her steady, and a maga as her tutor, that she might direct her energies toward the future."

"Then she may stay here with you, in the East Tower."

"Akmael, you cannot expect—"

"Eolyn." He took her by the shoulders with a grip so firm it threatened to bruise. The action startled her into silence. "Why must our parting be marred by argument? Tomorrow I leave this fortress to meet a formidable enemy about whom I know distressingly little. The future of this kingdom—of our people—weighs heavy on my heart. Give me at least this much peace: Let me depart knowing that you are well cared for, and safe."

She held his gaze for a moment, then lowered her eyes and nodded her assent. "It will be as you wish, Akmael. I will stay in the East Tower, and Ghemena with me."

His hold on her relaxed. "Thank you, Eolyn. You will be content, I promise you."

Taking her hands in his, he brought them to his lips. "Your aura grows ever brighter as the shadows deepen. It is extraordinary in its colors, so richly hued."

Desire flushed through her. So many years she had known him, yet the passion he inspired continued to fill her with awe and uncertainty. She received his kiss and returned it, an ardent promise of the pleasures that awaited them in the intimacy of his chambers.

"Enough conversation." He placed her hand in the crook of his arm. "We will descend at the next tower and return to my quarters. Tzetobar waits for one last audience before I depart. This night promises to be far too short."

He paused to study her again. A frown crossed his brow, sending a chill down Eolyn's spine.

"What is it, Akmael? What do you see?"

"Your aura. It has changed."

Subduing a wave of panic, she anchored her spirit to the mountain's core. They had left everything behind in Akmael's chambers: his staff, her sword, all the instruments of their magic neglected in a moment of carelessness. "A shadow? A place of no light? It is a sign that the Naether Demons are coming."

He made no move, but simply stood in front of her, immutable as a wall of stone.

"Do you understand what I am saying?"

"It is not a shadow I see."

"Akmael, please—"

"This thread is too beautiful to be a herald of those monsters." Stepping close, Akmael ran his hand just over her hair as if sifting through wayward currents of light. "I have never noticed it before. It is of purest silver, thin like the sharpened edge of a newly forged sword, shimmering like water reflecting the sunlight. It disappears, then flickers back into brilliance."

The pounding of Eolyn's heart faded until all she could hear was the sound of her own tremulous breath.

This cannot be, she told herself. Not here. Not now.

"Why does this trouble you?" he asked.

Long ago, Doyenne Ghemena had taught her how to recognize the transformative moments of a maga's life. Each one left a particular signature on the aura: the first kiss, the rites of Bel-Aethne, the impact of death, the discovery of love. The emergence of new life. In recent days she had wondered, worried, as the rhythm of her body strayed from that of the moon. There could be many explanations for the lack of synchrony, terror and tragic loss among them. Now, with what Akmael had described, there was no longer any doubt in her mind.

"It is a child." Her whisper was barely audible, yet seemed to echo off the castle walls and city roofs. "It is our child, Akmael. Yours and mine."

For what seemed an eternity he said nothing, dark eyes fixed upon hers, countenance strange and inscrutable. "I had thought that magas had ways to avoid—"

"We do. I just couldn't. Gods help me!" She covered her face with her hands. What had she done? The country was at war, and she was with child. The King's child. Bastard, they would call it. A crucible for even more division and strife. "Forgive me."

"Forgive you?"

"I never intended for this to be your burden." She had conceived in a time of peace, in another world already so obliterated Eolyn wondered if it had ever truly existed. Her daughter was meant to grow up among Eolyn's sisters in the quiet province of Moehn, with picnics by the river, forays into the South Woods. Magic and friendship gracing her life. Violence and warfare a distant reality, the concern of others. Her existence would never have come to Akmael's attention, and even if it had Eolyn would have said. . .

What would she have said?

That the father was Borten, or the mother Adiana. She would have said the newborn was abandoned as an orphan at their gate, wailing her distress on a frigid night. She would have said…

Akmael, this beautiful child is yours.

Because she understood in this moment, with utmost clarity, how impossible it would have been to lie to him.

Akmael wrapped his arms around Eolyn, pulling her so close she was scarcely left room to breathe. "You ask my forgiveness when you have brought me the greatest of all joys."

Tears stung her eyes as she felt the intensity of the emotions coursing through him. She feared all that Adiana had prophesized would now come true, and she pleaded silently to the Gods that they would not give her a son.

"Come, now, my love," he murmured. "It is time for us to rest."

"But Akmael, we must speak about this. It is most unexpected, and we cannot—"

He silenced her with a tender kiss. "Do not be anxious about our son, Eolyn. His lineage is strong, and his destiny is great. He will have the protection of his father, the Mage King, and the magic of his mother, High Maga of Moisehén. This prince—this child, the fruit of our love—will wear the crown of my fathers. And none shall stand in his way."

Chapter 31

At dawn Eolyn accompanied the King's procession down the long winding road from the castle to the central square, then through the City to its massive gates. Trumpeters and drummers headed the column, followed by a company of mage warriors. The King and his guard rode beneath flags of the royal house, the silver dragon of Vortingen undulating against a purple night. Behind Akmael's guard came the High Mages of the Council, Eolyn among them. The mages bore richly embroidered cloaks of forest green, against which Eolyn's burgundy robes, though less intricately adorned, contrasted brilliantly. Representatives of the noble households of Moisehén followed, each bearing his own sigil in an explosion of color that was muted by the onset of infantry and cavalry carrying more purple flags at the rear.

The people swarmed the streets and hung from windows and balconies. Their aspect was grim but hopeful. Old men shouted encouraging words, children offered trinkets of luck to the soldiers, women cried out to the Mage King, pleading protection for their husbands, sons, and brothers. Flowers were showered upon the King's retinue, delicate blossoms of hawthorn and rosemary for courage and guardianship. When recognition of the Maga Eolyn spread through the crowd, lilies and primroses were strewn in her path.

Just outside the city gates waited the bulk of Akmael's forces, assembled in long columns and rows, the size of which made Eolyn's breath come short. Years before she had seen the Mage King's army arrayed against her brother's men, but it seemed much larger now, more formidable and fearsome than ever before.

Akmael raised Kel'Barú high, blade shining like the ivory moon. The soldiers responded with a deafening roar of allegiance.

Rarely had Eolyn felt so far removed from the moment in which she first met this Prince of Vortingen, a lanky and uncertain youth lost in the lush corridors of the South Woods. Magic had seemed an innocuous game back then, as natural to him as it had been to her. Now the words of Doyenne Ghemena echoed ominously in her heart, and she understood the trepidation of the magas who had risen up against Akmael's father.

Mixing magical power with royal power is dangerous. You cannot have that much dominion in the hands of one family.

Now the course charted by Kedehen and honored by his son would continue in Eolyn's child who, boy or girl, carried royal blood and magical power. The thought provoked a slight flutter in her womb, and the maga set a hand upon her abdomen to calm the movement.

At the Mage King's command, the royal guard parted, opening a path between him and the High Mages. Tzetobar led the council members forward to meet the King, Thelyn at his right hand and Eolyn on his left. Akmael and High Mage Tzetobar entered into a long ritual exchange that symbolized the transfer of certain powers over affairs of the City in the King's absence.

The rosy-cheeked diplomat had been informed of Eolyn's situation in private council the night before. A new will had been drawn up in which the King recognized Eolyn's son as his own. One copy had been left with Tzetobar, the other with Eolyn, each bearing the seal of Vortingen.

"He is a man of utmost discretion," Akmael had assured her. "He has served my house well and always acts in the best interests of the kingdom. If anything should happen to me, you must depend on him. You and the prince will be in capable hands."

Eolyn did not share his confidence. She felt only confusion and uncertainty, the troubling sensation of being dragged forward by currents beyond her control. Adiana's warning tormented her. *The Queen and all her offspring, and all those loyal to them, will hate him and wish him dead and see it done before he is old enough to understand his own power.* How was she to know, so recently arrived to the City, who was loyal to the Queen and who was not? And how would Tzetobar interpret the best interests of the kingdom, if Akmael were slain and the Syrnte marching toward the City?

An intense longing for the return of Mage Corey surged in her breast. No one knew the murky labyrinth of politics in Moisehén as well as Corey, and no one would be more devoted to the protection of this child, who for him would be much more than a prince of the line of Vortingen. Boy or girl, the infant was Corey's long awaited heir to the Clan of East Selen.

Another roar from the people startled Eolyn out of her reverie. The King and Tzetobar had finished their dialogue. Akmael's eyes now rested upon Eolyn. Out of respect she lowered her gaze, the stillness of her body a rigid mask that concealed a burning desire to embrace him—and love him—one more time.

"Maga Eolyn." He drew close on his mount, and she lifted her eyes to his. They had murmured their tender farewells in the predawn hours; his kisses coursing over her face as she breathed in his essence of ancient stone and timeless magic, of leather and mail and the inception of war. "You have your charge. See it done. I will be looking for your messengers in the coming days."

"Yes, my Lord King. I will not disappoint you."

A smile touched his lips. It was a rare expression for such a public event, and it vanished as quickly as it had appeared. He saluted her and the rest of the High Mages, then signaled his mount to turn away.

"My Lord King!"

Akmael halted at the plea in her voice. Though she had spoken out of place, there was no consternation in his aspect, only patient expectation. With a nod he bade her to continue.

"Return to us." Her voice broke over the words, and she struggled to steady her heart, to subdue the sting in her eyes. "You, and all your men. Do not let the women of your city mourn their husbands. Do not let them raise their young in solitude."

He studied her, an odd set to his jaw, uncommon compassion in his eyes. The breath of dawn swept across the field of soldiers, its soothing whisper reflected in a host of fluttering banners, in the hush of grass at their feet. A horse whinnied, another stamped. Metal clinked against metal, leather rasped against mail. Still the Mage King held Eolyn in his gaze, as if she were the finest of treasures, a ribbon of beauty woven unexpectedly into the otherwise crude fabric of life.

"War leaves many widows, Maga Eolyn," he said at last, his tone subdued, "but I will do my best to bring these men home, and leave no one unaccounted for. As for the woman to whom I am bound—the true Queen of Moisehén—she will have me at her side when this conflict is over. On this, you have my word."

With that he departed, riders assembling behind him, spears and flags raised as they began their journey south.

The mages and noblemen separated. Those charged with attending the city—Eolyn, Tzetobar, and Thelyn among them—moved to the side of the road so that all who were to accompany the King might pass.

They spent the better part of the morning watching company after company join the column, imparting blessings and invoking wards to protect man and beast. When the last regiment of cavalry fell into place, camp followers forming a ragged tail behind them, mages and maga passed back through the city gates and journeyed up the winding road to the castle.

In the front courtyard they were met by servants and stable hands. As Eolyn dismounted she noticed Taesara and her ladies gathered on one of the high balconies. The Queen's face was pale, her aspect weak. She did not acknowledge the arrival the mages and nobles, but kept her gaze directed resolutely toward the south, where Eolyn imagined she could still see the long snaking column of Akmael's army as it receded from the City.

One of her ladies—a dark haired woman—watched Eolyn instead. Her chin was lifted, her eyes narrowed. An unsettling look of amusement and triumph played on her thin lips. More than malice, Eolyn sensed from the woman an intense anticipation, as if she suffered from an unbearable thirst that was about to be quenched.

"Maga Eolyn?" Thelyn appeared at her side.

A shiver ran through Eolyn, and she broke away from the wordless exchange with that woman, grateful for the High Mage's distraction.

"I thought we might, after a brief repast, continue our work in Master Tzeremond's quarters."

"Of course, Mage Thelyn. I was thinking just the same."

They had visited the wizard's rooms the day before, but there had been little time for more than a cursory tour of the labyrinthine apartments. Thelyn had assured her little had changed since Tzeremond's death. Years had passed, yet no one seemed anxious to occupy the the Master's dwelling or raid its artifacts. Eolyn could see why. Tzeremond's spirit still lingered in that place. At times his form melted out of the dank shadows, only to vanish again when she spun, startled, to confront him. And the piercing gaze of his amber eyes seemed to follow her every step, raising the hairs on Eolyn's neck, making her arms tingle with anxiety.

Today when she arrived after a modest meal, the mood of the place was somewhat improved. Thelyn must have spoken with one of the stewards, for Eolyn found servants busy removing dust sheets from the simple furniture and scrubbing the neglected stone floors. A number of windows had been opened, bringing in fresh air and allowing the midday light to chase away shadows and ghosts.

Amidst the bustle Thelyn waited, polished cherry wood staff in hand. He greeted her with a bow of respect and said, "You have not brought your staff, Maga Eolyn. May I suggest we send for it? This will likely be an arduous task, requiring the channeling of much energy."

"I understand, Mage Thelyn, but unfortunately I no longer have my staff. I left it in the care of Mage Corey, and so must proceed without it."

Thelyn straightened, cocked one brow in surprise. "You entrusted your staff to Corey?"

"Yes." Eolyn pushed away the doubt that still haunted that decision. It was far too late for regrets now. "His staff was damaged when he arrived in Moehn. So I offered him mine, that he might better protect my ward Mariel."

"I see." A bemused frown crossed his face, followed by a shrug. "You are braver person than I, Maga Eolyn. Though if Mage Corey were to honor anyone's confidence, I daresay it would be yours."

Eolyn was not quite sure how to respond to this.

"Let us proceed, then." Thelyn gave a sweeping gesture toward one of the darkened narrow corridors. "Ours is a formidable charge, and the war will not wait."

Chapter 32

Mage Corey, Borten, and Mariel turned northward after Eolyn's departure. They abandoned their horses, travelling on foot to avoid being too conspicuous. Mariel's dark tresses were shorn and her dress exchanged for a loose tunic and trousers that concealed her budding figure. The costume worked an unexpected magic on the girl's spirit. The haunted look left her emerald eyes. There was a new set to her shoulders and added energy in her step. She rarely lagged behind now, and at the end of each day she took out her knife and practiced throwing it at targets that the mage obligingly selected.

Late on the third day of their journey, Corey and Mariel were following a small stream through a narrow valley when Borten descended from a nearby ridge, a dark scowl marring his countenance. He stopped in front of them and assessed Mariel sternly.

"Stay here," he said. Then to the mage he barked an equally curt order, "Come with me."

Corey bristled, but repressed the desire to respond in kind. He had not seen the knight so grave since the last time the Naether Demons attacked. They climbed the steep slope, leaf litter crunching under their feet. The late afternoon light sliced through thin trunks of birch and alder. Near the top, Borten signaled the mage to get down, and they approached the ridge on hands and knees. Below them stretched a broad grassy valley where a road followed the glistening course of the Tarba River. On that road, an army marched westward under banners of scarlet and gold.

Corey shook his head in dismay. "Could the Gods have granted us any better luck?"

The snap of branches nearly bolted the mage out of his skin. Borten spun into a ready crouch, knife in hand, but it was only Mariel watching them with worried eyes.

"I told you to stay below." The knight's rebuke was delivered in soft tones.

"I don't want to be alone anymore."

She dropped onto her knees and crawled until she lay beside Corey. Her aroma of oak leaves and loam proved a pleasant distraction.

"What's happened?" she asked, then gasped when she saw the Syrnte army.

"We are too close. They will break for camp soon, and send out foragers." Borten drummed his fingers against the damp earth. "We will find a concealed place in which to spend the night. Then we will head east until we have a greater chance of crossing the road unnoticed."

"I can invoke some additional wards once we've settled," offered Corey. "They will not hide us entirely, but they can divert the unsuspecting."

The knight nodded, rose to his feet, and started back toward the stream, signaling them to follow.

* * *

Compared to East Selen, the forests of Moehn were dizzying in their summer activity. At night frogs, crickets, cicadas, and other unnamed creatures burst forth in raucous song. Corey might have found their cadence soothing, were it not for his wary attention to any sound that might indicate a Syrnte patrol, or worse, the Naether Demons.

Beside him Mariel slept, her quiet snore falling into easy harmony with the insects that ruled the night. The light of a waxing moon fell in speckled patterns across her heart-shaped face and shorn hair. One hand lay in a covetous grip over the hilt of her knife.

Corey looked up through the thicket of branches that concealed the little hollow where they lay, a damp depression surrounded by rocky walls, carpeted with spongy moss and rotting leaves. Somewhere nearby Borten was keeping the first watch, but the knight's vigilance, no matter how dedicated, could not calm Corey's mood.

Curiosity nipped at his heart, restless like a magpie in search of shiny objects hidden beneath dull tones of the readily apparent. He glanced once more at Mariel, laid his hand upon her forehead, and murmured a short spell to ensure a deep and dreamless sleep. Then, centering his spirit and calling upon the powers of the earth, Corey assumed the shape of Fox.

Sound illuminated the darkness. Corey's sharp ears detected the scratch of a cricket's legs, the rumble of a mole beneath the earth, the scuffle of a sleepy thrush shifting its position on a branch. Flattening his tail and lifting a paw, he turned his ears forward then back, until he caught the steady resonance of Borten's breath some twenty paces away. Having determined the position of the knight, Corey crept off in the opposite direction.

The mage retraced their path along the stream, trotted over the ridge, and picked his way down the slope beyond. At the edge of the young wood, he settled on his haunches and wrapped a soft tail around his feet, his eyes fixed on the west, where the fires of the Syrnte camp dotted the grassy vale.

After indulging in a meticulous grooming of his paws, Corey lifted his snout and listened again. The valley was rife with voles digging up roots and chewing on sedges. Nervous squeaks floated low over the ground, carried away by the slightest breeze. Their sweet smell of oil and salt made Corey's mouth water. His stomach gave a plaintive plea. He trotted forward a few paces and crouched, tail extended behind him as he gauged distance with scent and sound.

The rodents within striking range ceased all movement, but Corey could smell each one, and the occasional shiver or muted alarm call betrayed them. He did not delay his decision, but sprang into the air and pounced on the nearest, which squirmed and squealed its distress even as Fox scooped it up and snapped the delicate bones in a few hard chomps. Warm blood wet Corey's tongue and then the vole was gone, carried whole down his throat and adding a satisfying weight to his belly.

Leaving the other voles in peace, the mage continued in the direction of the Syrnte, keeping just inside the line of trees. He did not intend to wander close. There would be dogs to pick up his scent, servants anxious to protect their masters' chickens, men with more than a passing interest in securing a fine pelt. But much could be heard and smelled by Fox from a safe distance, and what Corey sought was a familiar voice, or a whispered spell. Something that might afford an insight into the magic upon which the Syrnte now depended.

He trotted toward the flickering torches until the muffled din of the camp blossomed into a rich tapestry of discrete noises: lowing oxen and stamping horses, taunts of men well into their drink, the hiss of a soldier relieving himself, the high-pitched laughter of a whore. A strand of melody separated itself from the midnight hum, reaching toward him with haunting intensity.

May the Gods spare the leaves from touching you as they fall
Lest their delicate blades be turned to ice. . .

The fur on his neck rose. He gave a short gruff bark. Corey recognized the song, a daring verse attributed to Lithia, lover of the Mage Warrior Caedmon and one of the great magas who endured the long war against the People of Thunder.

May the rain cease drenching your body
May the earth stop kissing your feet. . .

The music tightened around his throat, a trapper's noose pulling him forward like the sirens of Antarian legend. Just outside the flickering arc of light cast by torches, he paused, heart palpitating against his ribcage, head low to the ground, back arched and tail tucked between hind legs as he paced, studying the camp with wary eyes.

May the Gods erase your constant gaze
Your precise words
Your perfect smile. . .

Spying a corridor of shadows he slipped into it, moving stealthily between stacks of crates and untended carts, heeding the sound of footsteps and shying away from the mangy stink of dogs.

May they extinguish you without warning
In a burst of flame
In an explosion of ice. . .

At last he drew near. Creeping underneath another cart, Corey lowered himself on his furry stomach and scooted forward. A table well-lit by numerous torches came into view, laden with food and drink, occupied by boisterous men. Next to it, a small group of musicians. Among them, his sweetest voice, his finest music: Adiana.

If all this should fail then let death take me
So as not to see you always

Everywhere
In each moment
In all my visions. . .

Her face was discolored from bruises, eyes glittering like stone. Yet her song was as impassioned as ever, meticulously executed through its climax. At the table's head sat a powerfully built man who watched her with a predatory gaze. The others kept to their drink and conversation, while a handful of willing whores provided welcome distraction.

The closing cadence was met with hearty applause, soon silenced by their imposing leader, who announced the end of the meal. Officers, servants, women and musicians took their leave. Only Adiana remained seated with back straight and eyes downcast, hands folded on her lap, hair a river of burnished gold in the flickering light.

"Come," he said, and she obeyed.

Accepting the cup of wine he offered, Adiana drank not as a woman savoring its sweet bite, but as one intent on losing herself in a misty stupor. The man pulled her into a rough embrace, loosened her bodice, assailed her soft flesh until she gasped and melted into him, the emptied cup slipping from her fingers, her aura a violent tempest of remorse, desire, revulsion, desperation.

A yelp escaped Corey's throat, and he scuttled backwards into deeper shadows, until the undisturbed rhythm of the camp assured him no one had heard. He flinched at the sound of plates and cups clattering to the ground, followed by the Syrnte commander's feral groan. As Adiana's cries began to pierce the night, Corey rose, shook the dust out of his fur, and sneezed.

Without looking back, he departed the camp along the same shadow-filled path through which he had come.

In the morning, flame throated warblers, yellow breasted thrushes, and black tailed chickadees summoned a reluctant sun. With stiff muscles and bleary eyes, Corey abandoned the post he had taken over from Borten and wandered down to the stream to refresh his face and fill his water skin. Mariel and the knight emerged from their resting place as the mage climbed back up the bank.

Wary of the proximity of the Syrnte, they took their meager breakfast of tart summer berries in silence. Corey prepared tea to warm their hands and bellies. Mariel finished her meal first and unable to contain her restlessness, stood and started throwing her knife.

"Your tutor is also skilled with the blade," Corey commented. "Did she teach you?"

"Yes." Mariel extended her hand toward the beech where she had just embedded the blade. With a brief spell, she called the knife back to her grip. "Maga Eolyn taught me how to use the knife, and with any luck, Sir Borten will teach me how to use the sword."

The knight sputtered over his drink, but he smiled, wiped his mouth on his sleeve and said, "If that is what you wish, Mariel, then we may start today, once we have put some distance between us and that army. I'm certain the Maga Eolyn would be pleased."

"No, she would not." Mariel's tone was neither insolent nor argumentative, simply subdued with truth. "But I suspect even Maga Eolyn has come to realize, as I have in these days recently passed, that one cannot live in this world without preparing for war."

They continued east as Borten had proposed, keeping to the narrow valley with its clear bubbling stream. Squirrels chattered from low perches. Once in a while a crow cawed from some solitary branch. Corey could see from the darting of Borten's eyes and the grim set of his mouth that the animal's attention made him nervous. While the mage shared his concern, he found some comfort in the knowledge that the Syrnte were not very gifted when it came to the language of woodland animals. What were obvious signals to Corey and Borten might well pass unnoticed, even by a skilled Syrnte scout.

By midday the sun had warmed the forest, though its light barely penetrated the broad leaves of oak and elm that dominated the grove through which they were passing. Corey's gut tightened with a sudden spasm, as if someone had fastened a rope around his entrails and was pulling them out. He would have blamed the vole he swallowed the night before, but he knew better. Coming to a halt, he watched Borten and Mariel ahead of him. Then he looked back at the path they were leaving behind.

"Well." He drew a deep breath, patted his stomach, his medicine belt, the hilt of his knife. "I suppose this is as far as I come today, then. Mariel!"

The girl stopped at his call, regarded him with a questioning gaze. Corey strode forward and handed her Eolyn's staff.

"Be a good maga and return this to your tutor when you see her again," he said. "Return it whole, or she will surely blame me for any damage it has suffered."

"I don't understand—"

"And you, Borten." Corey took the knight's arm in his. "I'm loath to admit it, but you're a good man. A worthy servant of the King and a skilled protector of the magas. Keep this one safe, as I would very much like to see her again."

"What are you up to?" he said suspiciously.

"I am…" Corey cleared his throat, unaccustomed to uncertainty, to the nervous flexing of his hands. "It would seem I am going back. Yes, that's what I'm going to do. Go back, and follow that army."

A ring of metal, and Corey found the point of Borten's sword at his throat.

"It seems that you are not pleased by my decision."

"I would be most happy not to have you with us, Mage Corey. But if you are captured—or worse, turn yourself over willingly, something I would not put past you—what they learn from you may well destroy us. I will slay you before allowing you to return that way."

Corey glanced at Mariel, who watched them wide-eyed. He drew a resigned breath. "Adiana is with them."

"What?" Mariel's exclamation startled a small flock of birds out of a nearby fir.

"Hush, child!" scolded Corey, "or they will find us yet."

"How do you know this?" demanded Borten.

"I went there last night as Fox. I did not intend to enter their camp, but on a whim I wandered inside, and saw her."

"Why didn't you tell us?" Mariel's tone was distraught, angry.

"Because I thought it best that you—especially you, young maga—did not know." He met Borten's gaze. "She's been claimed by one of the officers, a man of very high rank, though not nearly high enough, I'm afraid, to deserve her."

Borten lowered his sword, although the doubt in his expression was undiminished.

"If you had told us, we could have..." Mariel paced beside them, hands working as if to extract words from the air. "We could have rescued her somehow, brought her with us! We could still bring her with us. She might know where Catarina and Tasha are, and we could all be together again. Whole. A coven, like before." She halted, eyed both of them with determination. "We must go back. We have to set her free."

"Oh, for the love of the Gods, don't be a fool," said Corey. "Even if there weren't an army surrounding Adiana, by now that Syrnte commander has bound her mind to his. In the moment she sees someone she recognizes, he will know. That person will be captured, tortured and slain."

"But the girls—"

"The girls are dead."

Mariel stared at him dumbfounded, eyes watering as if he had slapped her in the face.

"I saw it in her aura." Corey assumed a more gentle tone. "Everything once dear to Adiana is gone. The girls are beyond our help, Mariel, and so is she."

"Then why return?" Borten asked with narrowed eyes.

"Because I cannot. . ." Corey faltered. A self-deprecating laugh escaped his lips. Who would have thought he would succumb to such sentimentality? "I cannot find it in my heart to leave her. During Ernan's rebellion, when I was arrested in Selkynsen, Adiana was the only one who came after me. Somehow she convinced Khelia and Rishona to give her a band of warriors that I might be rescued. It was a fool's mission, and lucky for her by the time they arrived in Selkynsen I had long since been taken to the King's City. Otherwise she would have died in the attempt to free me, and I helpless to do a thing about it. When they missed their opportunity, Adiana sent the warriors back to Ernan and traveled alone to Moisehén. There she waited, day after day, night after night, certain that on any given morning I would be publicly beheaded or burned. She waited because she did not want me to die alone, without a friend nearby."

Mariel's brow furrowed, and she shook her head. "Mistress Adiana often told stories of the rebellion, but that was not one of them."

"Likely it displeased her to learn afterwards that I was not languishing in some rancid dungeon, but rather housed as the King's guest in the sumptuous apartments of the East Tower, a willing traitor to Ernan's cause. I myself never heard this story from Adiana's lips. It was Renate who told me. I did not understand how much her devotion had moved me until now." He looked at Borten. "Adiana is suffering a torturous dismemberment of the spirit at the hands of the Syrnte. I may not be able to save her, but I can bear witness to her fate as a friend, and stand nearby when she meets her darkest hour."

For a long moment no one said anything. Insects buzzed through the humid air, leaves rustled in the breeze, a chipmunk scampered past their feet. Mariel turned her back on the men and drifted to a nearby elm, where she leaned against the trunk and watched the wood beyond in silence. Borten sheathed his sword.

"Go then," he said. "May the Gods be with you."

Corey nodded, let his gaze linger on Mariel's slender back before starting on his way.

He had gone some thirty paces when Mariel's shout stopped him. The girl came running and stopped breathless, tears streaming down her cheeks. She thrust the staff into his hands. "Take this."

"Mariel, I cannot risk—"

"Please. The forest tells me you will need it more than I."

"I see." He doubted her story, but could not deny the sense of security he found in the resonance of the smooth oak.

"You must tell Adiana—" A sob cut short her words. Drawing a shaky breath, she straightened her shoulders, wiped away the tears. "If you can find a way, please let Adiana know that we are with her. We are always with her. Our love for her will never end."

Corey wrapped his arm around Mariel and pressed her tight against his chest.

"This," he murmured, setting his lips upon her forehead, "is why the Magas will not be vanquished."

Chapter 33

Ehekaht rehoert aenre!

Fire flared through Eolyn's veins and burst from her palms in twin shafts of red that pummeled the stone wall in front of her, only to be thrown back in a cloud of suffocating heat that expanded relentlessly until the maga, unable to withstand the blaze any longer, released her spell with a cry of frustration.

Hair singed and robes smelling of smoke, she stalked forward and beat her fists against the cold rock, before sinking wearily against its unflinching face, cursing Tzeremond and the spell that transcended his death.

"It's hopeless," she moaned. "Nothing will break it."

High Mage Thelyn stepped close, his aspect one of curiosity as his hawkish nose following the hairline cracks between the well-fitted blocks.

"You mustn't despair," he said. "Every mage in the City has tried his hand at this. You have only just started."

Despite the complex layout of Tzeremond's quarters, the High Mages had long ago determined where the secret library must lie. A careful mapping of the apartment had revealed the existence of a room near its center with no visible entrance. It was here that Eolyn and Thelyn had focused their exhaustive efforts.

"It's been three days already," Eolyn said. "Three days is too long."

By now Akmael would be approaching Rhiemsaven, and only the Gods knew how much time he would have between there and his first confrontation with the Syrnte.

"We must look elsewhere for our answers," she concluded.

"Where else? The libraries of East Selen? We'd waste at least a quarter moon just getting there and back." Thelyn stepped away from his perusal of the cracks in the wall. "It's remarkable. Common hammers and maces shatter upon touching this. Even a red flame cast with all the fury of a High Maga cannot leave a scar." He paused, thoughtful. "I would very much like to have this ward. Let us hope it, too, is somewhere inside."

Eolyn groaned in frustration, let her head fall back against the wall, and covered her face with aching hands. Her shoulders were stiff, her stomach sour from having channeled so much destructive energy without the aid of a staff. They had tried every conceivable trick in their attempts to unravel the ward. She knew no spell more aggressive than the flame she had just cast.

"Would you deny me your knowledge even now, Tzeremond?" She turned her ear to the rough stone, half hoping it would yet provide a hint of an answer. "Our country is under siege, your King in danger. I know you have no love for me, but it is said you once loved our people. For their sake, please. Let the echo of your voice return."

The stone remained silent.

Eolyn ran her fingers through her hair in dismay. It was no use. The power of the mountain would not be broken here.

Thelyn clucked his tongue. "Perhaps we should rest. Return later this evening, or tomorrow."

Muffled laughter followed his words, the belabored wheezing of an old crone.

Eolyn straightened, glanced down the darkened corridor that led to the other rooms. "Did you hear that?"

"What?" asked Thelyn, voice subdued with expectation.

Again the unrestrained chortle of an old woman in a fit mirth. It was coming from inside the wall.

Don't try too hard, child, she cackled, *or you'll break your teeth!*

Eolyn gasped and pressed herself against the stone.

"Impossible," she whispered.

"What?" Thelyn insisted. "What did you hear?"

Shaking off her doubt, Eolyn rose, set both hands upon the wall, and drew a long breath, intent upon acting before reason undermined instinct. The invocation fell from her lips as more of a question than a command.

"Ghemena?"

Again, the wall responded with silence.

Blood rose hot to Eolyn's cheeks. She felt like a fool. "You are right, Mage Thelyn. We should rest, for I am at my wit's end, and subject to the whims of a woman gone mad."

Thelyn drew a breath to respond, but was interrupted by a thump from within the wall, followed by the scraping of stone against stone. A long slow hiss of air was released into the room, like the sigh of a weary lover, carrying the stale odor of used wax and dusty parchment.

Eolyn retreated from the open doorway, wary of what it might reveal.

Thelyn, on the other hand, laughed out loud, strode forward, and extended his arm into the space beyond, allowing it to be swallowed by inky shadows. "Three years and countless mages, when all we needed was a maga with the right word. Corey will be overcome with envy at not having been here to witness it."

"But I don't understand."

"Nor do I. Why would your student's name hold the key?"

"Not my student. My tutor, the woman who adopted me. Ghemena of Berlingen."

Thelyn's countenance lost some of its levity. He raised his brows, looked toward the doorway.

"Ah," he said.

"Ah?" Eolyn repeated, bewildered. "Is that all you can say? You knew him better than I could have ever hoped to, surely you must understand this mystery. What does it mean?"

Thelyn let go a slow exhale. "I would conjecture that it means the old wizard was a young man once, and like any mage subject to the whims of *aen-lasati*. Doyenne Ghemena would have been a worthy choice for his discerning temperament. From what I know of her reputation, she was one of the few of their generation who matched him in skill and knowledge."

"Impossible. He hated the magas, all of them."

"Did he? I've never been entirely certain, myself. Don't misunderstand me, Maga Eolyn. Tzeremond never lost the opportunity to remind us of the ruin the magas brought to Moisehén, and he undertook the duty of destroying them with genuine determination. He was absolute in his devotion to magic, to his people, and to his liege. He spoke nothing of his own needs and desires, so that most came to believe he did not have any. But every mage has a heart, or so Caradoc taught us, and thus we must surmise that Tzeremond loved someone once. Ghemena of Berlingen is as likely a candidate as any I can imagine."

"He ordered her abbey destroyed! Berlingen was razed, and all within murdered."

"No, in fact." Thelyn leaned upon his staff. "That is a story I can tell. Kedehen wanted Berlingen obliterated, for he was certain the abbey had given refuge to the magas during the war, and thought it a nest of sedition. Tzeremond argued against the strike, out of concern—as the story is told—for the treasures held in its library. Though given what we've just witnessed here, perhaps he was worried about more than the burning of books. Kedehen ignored Tzeremond's counsel, as you well know. And Berlingen is no more."

"She despised him." Eolyn shook her head, unable to reconcile this version of history with everything Ghemena had taught her. "She blamed him for everything. The deaths of the sons of Urien, the crowning of Kedehen, the start of the war, the persecution of her sisters, even her own exile. Never once did she even hint that they might have…"

A shiver ran through Eolyn, like the icy caress of a winter wind. For an ephemeral moment, the cottage of her childhood took shape around her. She felt the warmth of blankets and furs, and inhaled Ghemena's sweet aroma of old age and quiet places.

He was handsome, if you can believe, with a unique color to his eyes, a piercing amber brown that could leave a young maga like me very unsettled.

Words uttered one Midwinter's Eve, a few sentences lost in a long night of storytelling.

"Ghemena detested Tzeremond and everything he represented." She looked up at Thelyn, as if he might hold the key to the mysteries of the Doyenne's heart. "She never could have loved him."

The mage studied Eolyn with an odd expression, as if she were a misplaced piece of some curious puzzle. Then he shrugged. "Perhaps Tzeremond's affections were not returned. Though as you must know, Maga Eolyn, it is one of the continuing mysteries of Primitive Magic, how many are driven to despise the very people they once loved. Of course, now that both of them have been delivered to the Afterlife, we will never be certain what really happened."

Eolyn wrapped her arms around her shoulders, a chill still fresh on her skin. How many more secrets had Ghemena kept from her?

With a brief invocation, Thelyn ignited an amber glow in the crystal head of his staff. He nodded toward the library. "Shall we?"

They stepped into the room together, pausing just beyond the doorway while their eyes adjusted to the dim light.

"We will have to send for candles," Thelyn observed.

Even as he spoke the shadows lifted, revealing a windowless room in somber shades. Shelves lined the walls from floor to ceiling, and on these lay countless tomes, scrolls, and loose sheets of paper neatly stacked under polished stones. What space was not occupied by books was filled with artifacts of magic. Eolyn recognized certain tools hailing from places as far away as Galia, Antaria, the Paramen Mountains, and the lands of the Syrnte. Interspersed among them were even stranger objects of enchantment, the origins of which she could not place.

Thelyn had lapsed into a reverent silence.

Eolyn left his side and wandered into the room, skirting tables laden with bulky piles of books until she came to a broad desk. She laid her hand upon its smooth surface, a single wide plank cut from the heart of an ancient oak. On it sat his quills, a dry inkwell, more stacks of paper and books. One volume lay open, the richly illustrated page marked with a charcoal ribbon.

At her feet, an ironwood box carved with strange symbols. Before considering the consequences, Eolyn bent to open it, but found nothing inside except an empty sheet of dark silk. She stood again, holding the musty cloth in her hands. A sense of mourning crept into her heart. There was anger here, and great sorrow.

"Something was destroyed in this place," she murmured. "Something very valuable."

"Let us hope it was not what we seek," replied Thelyn.

Eolyn scanned the long shelves, warped under the weight of Tzeremond's massive collection, and let go a heavy sigh. "I thought the difficult part would be getting in here, but look at this. It would take years to read through it all, and we have at most days. How will we even know where to begin?"

"I will send for scribes and mages to assist us in reviewing these volumes," Thelyn assured her, crossing into the room and taking a place at her side. "In the meantime, I think we can find the answer to your question by considering another: What was the last spell that Master Tzeremond cast?"

Eolyn blinked and met his eyes. "The one he used against me. Ahmad-dur."

A grin broke wide on Thelyn's face, and despite the thread of horror that always returned with the memory of Tzeremond's attack, Eolyn found the mage's satisfaction contagious.

"Of course!" She reached for the open tome, heart leaping with renewed enthusiasm. "Let us start, then, where Master Tzeremond left off."

Chapter 34

Sir Drostan walked the length of the hastily constructed fortification at Sevryn's Point. The rugged abatis seemed to writhe under the shifting torchlight. The night air was cool, yet heavy and still. Soldiers lay awake, breath shallow and bodies restless. Above them a band of misty white stars divided the black firmament. Far below, the unseen Tarba River cut through the steep gorge with a muffled roar.

"Any sign of our scouts?" he asked when he reached the far end.

Theoryn, a long-faced man with sober eyes, shook his head. "No, Sir Drostan. Gaeoryn and Eldor have not returned."

Drostan grunted his displeasure. The two mage warriors were young and able, recently recruited from the province of Selen. They had departed at sunset, assuming the shape of Owl in order to spy on Syrnte activities. "They've been recognized."

"They are not long delayed," countered Theoryn, his tone more one of hope than of argument. "The Syrnte have not detected any of the others in recent days. Why should these two be caught now?"

"The Syrnte have held Falon's Ridge with but one regiment of soldiers. Now it is different." Earlier that day, the invading army had emerged from the heart of Moehn and made its vast camp at the head of the pass. Drostan's blood had run cold upon hearing his scouts report the numbers. He had sent messengers at once to Rhiemsaven, knowing his small contingent would soon lose their tenuous hold at Sevryn's Point and be forced to surrender the valley below. "We must assume there are witches among them who can recognize a mage's aura. If we are lucky, Georyn and Eldor are dead. But the Syrnte are a clever enemy, and may well have trapped them alive. Call the men to arms. I want two more scouts half way up the pass, no further than—"

A flare of diffuse jade light interrupted his words and illuminated Theoryn's scarred features. Drostan's muscles tensed as he looked toward the head of the pass. A curtain of fire was wrapping around Felon's Ridge. Undulating shafts of amethyst and malachite caressed the night sky, drawing in a vortex of lightning-tipped clouds that had not existed until this moment.

The forest held its breath.

The voice of the river was extinguished.

Drostan's hackles rose; a cold wisp of the Underworld wrapped tight around his gut. He unsheathed his sword, drew a breath to alert the men, but no sound fell from his lips. Along the length of the abatis the soldiers of Moisehén stood frozen, entranced by the display of otherworldly magic.

A deafening scream sounded from the high ridge and sent the forest into mayhem. Birds flew squawking from their sleepy perches, fawns hidden in glades bawled for their mothers, trees creaked and groaned as if death were being drawn up in excruciating threads through their roots. Drostan's men covered their ears and cried out; many fell to their knees or stumbled, confused and oblivious to the weapons at their sides, to the duty in their hearts.

"Order!" roared Drostan, his voice suddenly and inexplicably recovered. "Order, I say! To arms!"

The mage warriors were the first to return to their senses. They rallied the men, casting wards to deaden the impact of the unearthly howls. Those posted on the flanks set the crystal heads of their staffs aglow and gathered nascent, multi-colored flames in their palms. Some shapeshifted into wolves and slipped silently into the forest on either end of the abatis, where trees clung to a treacherously steep grade that Drostan hoped would discourage the Syrnte from any approach except along the road. The soldiers jostled each other as they formed ranks, until all stood with swords drawn and faces alert, eyes shining in the torchlight as they fixed their gazes on the shadowy road.

Absolute silence followed, as portentous as the screams that had invoked chaos moments before. At the head of the pass the eerie curtain of fire persisted. Troubled by the rattling shiver of the trees and the icy mist that rose off the ground, Drostan anchored his spirit near the heart of the mountain.

Ekahtu. Sepuenem al melan dumae, Erehai abnahm al shue.

The earth trembled as if under the charge of a thousand horses. Drostan scanned the area below Falon's Ridge, but all was shrouded in darkness. Every sound, every instinct indicated the Syrnte were fast approaching, yet they were not using torches.

"Mages," he called. "*Aen ehaen!*"

The warriors sent forth amber arcs that ignited shrubs and trees, illuminating the road some thirty paces ahead. High branches roared in protest, leaves and needles hissed as the fire converted them into floating ash.

"*Rehoernem enem*!"

Before the blazing trees could be brought down, a horde of Naether Demons leapt out of the darkness. The monsters cleared the abatis with a single leap, long limbs outstretched as they barreled into the center of Drostan's line. The men scattered in terror while their companions were captured and rent limb from limb. Demons flew at Drostan and his mages with nightmarish ferocity, black claws eclipsing the light of the burning trees. In their cavernous maw Drostan glimpsed the desolate depths of their prison, a realm of spent magic and slow decay.

He ducked as a demon passed over him, landed, and spun around. The beast reared up with luminescent arms outstretched and sliced at the knight's head. Drostan evaded the blow and charged forward, sweeping low with his sword. The blade sank into the belly as if swallowed by viscous fluid. The creature cried out and stumbled back, arms flailing while shadows oozed from the wound. The knight watched aghast as the flesh became whole.

The Naether Demon charged. Drostan sprang to one side, his sword connecting with the demon's shoulder and severing its arm. With a piercing howl the creature tumbled away, leaving the amputated limb convulsing at Drostan's feet.

Naeom anthae!

White flames sprang from Drostan's staff and consumed the ebony-clawed arm. The knight sprang upon the crippled beast, striking at head and limbs, scattering the pieces, and igniting them with magic.

"Dismember them with steel!" He shouted to the mage warriors nearby. "Burn the remains."

Word spread. Drostan moved among his men, urging them on as they hacked and flamed their enemy. With growing confidence they gained ground, until a second pack of Naether Demons leapt over the abatis, bringing a fresh wave of terror.

The largest fell upon Drostan, pounding him into the ground, slicing open armor and ripping apart the flesh exposed. The knight cried out as pain seared through his torso. Sword and staff were knocked from his grasp. Invoking a ward, Drostan crawled out from under the beast, clawing a path over roots and leaf litter. The protection did not hold. Frigid claws drove deep into Drostan's thighs. The creature dragged him off the ground and flung him against a large trunk.

Stunned, Drostan fell to the ground. Each gasp burned through his ribs as he forced himself up against the old tree. Blood ran hot down his back and legs. Violent tremors coursed through his arm, yet Drostan's staff responded to his call, flying into his grip just as the Naether Demon sprang.

Ehekahtu, faeom dumae!

Power thundered from his core, throwing the Naether Demon off its feet. Drostan sank to his knees, dizzy from the force of his spell and the rapid loss of blood. The forest wavered on the edge of his awareness.

The Naether Demon recovered its footing to confront him again. Beyond it, all semblance of order had disintegrated. Dozens of men lay dead. A handful of mage warriors yet stood their ground, but too many had fallen, and others screamed in torment as the demons tore open their breasts and consumed their hearts with bloody vigor. Already they were overwhelmed, and Drostan had no way of knowing how many more of these beasts the Syrnte held in waiting.

"Retreat!" The knight's voice was hoarse, but it carried over the chaos and was echoed by the few remaining men. "To the valley, and from there to Rhiemsaven!"

Soldiers fled on foot or horse. Mage warriors brought down the last of the burning trees and called upon the shape of Owl to make their escape. Only Drostan remained, his legs weak and his magic spent.

The Naether Demon crouched in front of him, rocking with patient rhythm. More of its kind flocked around them, the promise of death glowing in the black pits of their eyes.

Ehekatu, faeom shamue.

Ambling forward, the Naether Demon pinned the knight to the trunk by his throat. Drostan's breath was choked away in a knot of unrelenting pain. Shadows interrupted his vision. The beast stripped off his breastplate, trembling with a malevolent and hungry purr. Drostan closed his eyes and reached desperately into the heart of the old tree at his back.

Ehekaht, naeom enem.

The Gods responded. Tendrils of the oak's powerful spirit slipped into Drostan's veins, replenishing the breath he was being denied. As the demon's icy claw scored his breast, Drostan became one with the forest. His flesh did not open but was transformed into a rugged layer of crusty bark. His trunk expanded, trapping the Naether Demon's claws and swallowing its arm. The beast howled piteously.

Drostan's branches groaned, twisted, and fell upon the Naether Demons, entangling them in a net of woody vines, lifting them toward the unforgiving heavens. The tree shuddered under the weight of so much death, living wood turning black as it struggled against its prisoners.

Unable to bear the load, Drostan's trunk split with a thunderous crack. The mammoth oak fell, crown roaring down through the canopy and onto the road, where it crashed into the blazing trees left behind by the mage warriors. Branches and leaves ignited in an instant, consuming the demons in their fiery grasp.

Drostan's spirit slipped from the oak as its wide trunk crackled and steamed. On the other side of the abyss, he heard the call of his brothers and sisters long departed, beckoning him toward a quiet place where weary warriors could at last find their rest.

Chapter 35

The Syrnte marched triumphant into the Valley of Aerunden under a sky feathered with low-lying clouds that flew swiftly east. The banners of their army snapped in the harsh wind, bright flames of scarlet and gold that defied the darkening heavens and filled the narrow plain with color and movement.

Mechnes's appetite for conquest gnawed inside of him like a restless beast. To the north lay the army of the Mage King, and beyond whatever bloody fields he brought with him, the greatest riches of this kingdom: the precious mines of Selkynsen, the iron hills of Moisehén, the rivers of magic that ran beneath Selen. Mechnes could taste it all on the winds that coursed through this valley, and it made his mouth water.

His men were in good humor. They had suffered few casualties these past weeks, and the San'iloman's extraordinary power over the Naether Demons had seduced them into an illusion of indestructibility. They shared laughter and ribald jokes as tents and pickets were raised, and bowed in reverence whenever Rishona passed among them.

Mechnes decided to indulge their happy mood for one more day.

As twilight descended over the valley, he responded to the summons of the San'iloman and assembled with his officers at the summit of a low ridge on the southern edge of the valley. The grassy knoll was fringed by young trees and afforded a generous view of the landscape. It was here that Rishona had first summoned a Naether Demon to consume the soul of the wizard Tzeremond; and here that the Mage King and High Maga had descended into the Underworld, an action that would eventually spell their doom.

On a makeshift altar, Rishona and her priestess Donatya gave offerings of thanks to the Gods of the Syrnte, burning aromatic leaves and letting the blood of small creatures that squealed their anguish while Donatya sent her shrill howls toward the heavens.

Mechnes puffed out his cheeks in a slow exhale, convinced that if the Gods existed, they would strike down this hag for assaulting their ears with her butchered hymn. He drummed his fingers on the hilt of his sword, and tempered his impatience by letting his gaze linger on Rishona's snow white gown, admiring the way its sheer fabric clung to her breasts and thighs. The sweet music of Adiana's distress floated through his mind, a constant provocative melody that accompanied him always, even when she was not near.

He would have those two together someday, Adiana's hungry surrender woven richly through Rishona's aggressive desire, their hair intertwined in splendid ribbons of gold and ebony. His loins stiffened at the thought, and a wry smile touched his lips.

When at last the hag finished her cawing, twilight had deepened into a starless night. The San'iloman and her general mounted their horses and processed down from the ridge, guards and officers falling into position around them. Wherever they passed they were greeted with shouts of adulation and victory.

Upon arriving at Rishona's ample pavilion, the San'iloman dismissed all their attendants, servants included. Numerous candles infused with aromas of honey and jasmine cast their flickering light over her wide bed, at the foot of which was a small table lavishly set. Wind battered the tent, lifting the skirts of the canvas and sending short gusts of air swirling at their feet, causing Rishona's dress to ripple over her creamy skin. She lifted the sparkling veil that concealed the discoloration of her face, lingering evidence of the bruises she had received at his hand in Moehn. Bidding the Syrnte general to take his seat, she served him wine and food, her demeanor one of deference, her smile gracious and pleasing.

"Today we have come full circle." Rishona removed her slippers as she took her seat, indulged him with a flash of her dark eyes. "Here in Aerunden, I watched Ernan meet his defeat, and my brother flee as a coward. Now I have returned with you: your courage, your leadership, and your magnificent army. You brought us a great victory in Moehn. Soon victory will also be ours in Moisehén."

"Our march through Moehn was little more than a pleasant outing for these men who call themselves soldiers," Mechnes replied, his tone decidedly sober. "The Mage King awaits us on the road to Rhiemsaven. With any luck, by tomorrow my scouts will tell us where. He will not surrender so easily."

Rishona shrugged, sipped her wine. "He is young, and yet new to war. He will be no match for your forces."

"I am not such a fool as to underestimate him. Mark my words, Rishona, this royal progress you have so enjoyed is about to become a cruel and bloody campaign."

"My Naether Demons will—"

"—make little difference at this point. They attack only at night. And they are disorganized, unreliable. They fight their own battle, not ours."

"Their battle is our battle."

"For the moment. They are useful pets, when they obey your command. But have you considered the possibility that one day they will not?"

"Of course, Uncle. I am not such a fool, either. Donatya and I are prepared to send them back to their cold prison, and close the door behind them forever. But even if such a day should come, I suspect it is still far off. They have, after all, done everything I've asked them to do and without hesitation."

"They did not kill the maga."

"Twice they found her, twice they failed." She responded not with indignation, but with a humble voice and steady nod. "Their failure was also mine. I sent them too soon; they did not have sufficient magic. Now they have grown in strength. I could feed them again and send them after her tonight if you like. But the Mage King is now within their reach. I suggest we prepare the Naether Demons to strike directly at him."

Mechnes paused over his wine. "You truly believe they can slay him?"

"Oh yes. They hunger for him more than any other. They know—as do we — that with the Mage King destroyed, all of Moisehén will fall to its knees, its magic unraveled from north to south, and east to west."

Once they claimed Moisehén, there would be little to stop the Syrnte expansion toward the west. Roenfyn would fall within a season. From there, they could take the fiery lands of Galia, or send their armies south toward the misty shores of Antaria.

"What if they are together, Mage King and High Maga, as we suspect?"

"The task will be made more difficult, but not impossible." Rishona picked up a plum, bit into it thoughtfully, full lips lingering on the juicy pulp. "Not if we make the proper sacrifice."

Mechnes gave a low chuckle, accompanied by a look of warning and admiration. She did not flinch beneath his gaze but stood, approached with a sinuous stride and knelt at his feet, pulling the pins from her dark hair so that the ebony tresses tumbled over her shoulders. With a gentle touch she began removing his boots.

"You want Adiana," he said.

"I do not want her, uncle." Setting aside the boots, she sat back on her heels, hands folded in her lap, eyes downcast so that her lashes shown dark against her cheeks. "Not so much because she pleases you, but because I once called her friend. Would that the Gods had given me another path, but they did not. Adiana is the single richest vessel of magic that we took in the highlands of Moehn. The Naether Demons assure me that with her, they can destroy the Mage King before we ever meet him in battle, and the Maga as well, if she is at his side."

Mechnes leaned forward, touched her chin with his fingers. "You should not believe the promises of those beasts."

She smiled, took his hand and pressed it to her lips. "I do not trust them without reservation. I only tell you what the Naether Demons have told me. It is for you to decide, in your wisdom, whether to heed their words."

Drawing close, she ran her palms along his thighs. There was a youthful eagerness to her actions, reminiscent of the days when she first discovered the meaning of desire in his bedchambers. "Yet I can say this: to this day they have not deceived me, and I have no reason to believe that they are deceiving me now. We can claim our victory over the bodies and blood of a thousand soldiers, or we can grant the Naether Demons this one small sacrifice, and be rid of the Mage King forever."

She laid her head upon his lap, set to work on the lacings of his breeches. Mechnes played idly with a lock of her hair, took a thoughtful drink from his cup.

"You think to bewitch me," he said. "Like you did that witless brother of yours. Like you did to half the court at Ech'nalahm."

Her laugher was light, musical. Rishona rose on her knees, brought his lips to hers. She tasted of sugared plums and smelled of wanton desire. “I would not pretend to bewitch you, uncle. I wish only to please you, as you have always pleased me.”

Chapter 36

Eolyn lifted her head from its resting place on the tomes she had taken from Tzeremond's library, and realized she had fallen asleep. Words from the carefully transcribed history had followed her into her dreams, images of ancient magic and brutal monsters, violent battles and frigid Underworld prisons. All of them scattered under the insistent pounding at the entrance to her chambers.

Shaking off the drowsiness, she rose, crossed the antechamber, and laid her hands upon the sturdy wooden door. "Who calls at this hour?"

"The King, my lady." It was Tibald, the captain of her guard, his gruff voice muffled by the barrier that separated them. "The King's messenger has arrived from Rhiemsaven."

With a whispered spell, Eolyn undid the ward that protected her residence in the East Tower. She lifted the bolt and peered into the darkness beyond. Tibald's lips were set in a grim line over his chestnut beard. Behind him stood half a dozen other men at arms, faces expectant under the light of the flickering torches. One of them proffered a folded piece of paper bearing the seal of Vortingen. Eolyn accepted the missive, surprised by how heavy it felt in her hand. She bade them to wait, stepped back into the antechamber, and broke the seal.

Maga Eolyn, Akmael had written in his own hand. The paper bore traces of his essence, the ink an imprint of the weight of his grief. *It is with deep misgivings that I place this burden upon you, but the hour is late, and I have no other choice. You must come to me now. The Syrnte have taken Aerunden with their Naether Demons, slaying almost all who protected it. Sir Drostan was among the fallen.*

Eolyn drew a sharp breath, knowing how deeply Akmael would feel the loss of his beloved tutor and trusted advisor. Though she had not known Drostan well, he had always treated her with kindness. There had been an aura of timelessness about him, of invincibility.

While the mage warriors I have are able men and loyal of heart, they do not know these creatures, or the Underworld realm from which they came. I need your power and your wisdom at my side.

"I'm not ready," she murmured, looking at the stack of books that had consumed every thought, every moment, since Tzeremond's library was revealed to them. She had read much, and learned much, but she had not yet found what she sought.

Or if she had found it, she had not yet recognized it.

"What has happened?" Ghemena wandered in from the bedroom and stood beside the desk, hair disheveled, nightshift crumpled beneath a blanket wrapped around her thin shoulders. She studied Eolyn with a sleepy frown.

"I must leave the City at once, Ghemena."

"You're going to Moehn?" There was doubt in her eyes, but hope in her voice. "You'll bring them back then, Tasha and Catarina and Mistress Adiana?"

"No." Eolyn shook her head.

"That's from the Mage King." The girl pointed accusingly at the letter. "You're going to him! Why? Our sisters are in danger."

"The entire kingdom is in danger, Ghemena, and my skills are needed to defend it."

"Why should you waste your skills on defending him and his mages?"

"Ghemena—"

"They burned the magas!"

"That is not entirely true—"

"Yes it is. That man's father burned them all, except for the one on whom he forced his seed to make the Mage King. You know this, and still you act like he is more important than any maga, more important than our entire coven!"

"Our coven could not have existed without his protection."

"This is not protection." She pounded a fist against the table. Her cheeks were flushed and wet with tears. "He keeps you like a caged bird while Tasha, Catarina, and Adiana perish in Moehn."

Eolyn set the letter aside, taken aback by the intensity of Ghemena's resentment. She took the girl gently in her arms, wiped the tears away, smoothed the hair from her face. "Dear Ghemena. I know how hard our many losses have been for you. Everything is so complicated and difficult in times of war. When the Syrnte invasion is turned back, and our land once again at peace, you and I will have a long talk about everything that has come to pass. Gods willing, we will be reunited with our sisters then."

"What if we never see them again? What if they're dead because we didn't go back?"

"Then we will sing the songs of passing, weep for the loss of their friendship, and start over. There are many able women in Moisehén, new sisters whom the Gods will guide to a path of magic, together with us."

"None of them will be like Tasha, or Mistress Adiana. I promised Tasha we'd go back for her."

"Not all promises can be kept, Ghemena. Especially in times of war."

"This promise *must* be kept! It's Tasha we're talking about."

Eolyn let go a slow breath, uncertain how to respond. A memory of Corey's words came to mind, uttered in the bitter days following her brother's defeat. "I won't ask for your forgiveness, Ghemena. I only hope you will someday come to understand why I made the choices I did."

"I think you're making these choices because he's cast a spell on you." Her words sprang out in angry hiccups.

Eolyn could not help but smile. "You think so?"

Ghemena nodded fiercely.

The maga touched her nose and kissed her forehead. "Then you must invent a ward to break the Mage King's spell. Now go ready your things. I can't leave you alone in this castle."

This brought a smile to her face. "I'm going with you?"

"No. I will leave you in High Mage Thelyn's care until I return."

The smile was instantly replaced by a scowl. "Him?"

"I'm afraid there's no one else, for the moment."

"But I don't like him."

"Why not? Has he been unkind to you? Has he mistreated you in any way?"

"No. But he's a man."

"Oh, Ghemena." Eolyn lifted her palms in frustration. "Half the adults in this world are men. Sooner or later you must to learn to like at least one of them."

"I liked Borten well enough," she replied sullenly, "but you abandoned him, too."

With that she stomped off, ignorant as to how deeply her words knifed Eolyn's heart. Remorse and raw uncertainty flowed from the wound, along with the bittersweet memory of Borten's kiss.

They would live, Eolyn reassured herself. Borten and Mariel would reach his family's estate, and there they would be safe.

"My lady?" Tibald called her attention back to the task at hand. His massive frame almost filled the doorway. Behind him she could see the other men, all of them waiting for her instructions.

She rose, blinked back the sting of regret. "Please advise the members of my guard. We depart within the hour."

Fresh horses waited for them in the outer courtyard, still shrouded in the dark of predawn. Eolyn mounted together with Ghemena and nodded to Tibald, who barked orders to open the gate. As she spurred her mare forward, Eolyn glanced toward the high windows of the Queen's apartments. They were dimly illuminated from inside, and a shadow passed along the balcony just as Eolyn's view was blocked by the high arch of the castle portal.

They rode down the winding road toward the City in silence, hooves clattering against cobblestones, the chink of swords and mail falling into rhythmic accompaniment. At the city square, they turned down the wide avenue that led to the Mages Quarter.

The people of Moisehén were just beginning to stir. Candles flickered on the window sills. An occasional clatter of pots sounded from a back entrance, accompanied by the shrill voice of a woman harrying her children out of bed. Eolyn breathed in aromas of steaming tea and fresh bread, interrupted by the disagreeable smell of a man relieving himself in a corner. She heard the snoring of a drunkard in an alley, passed an ox driver muttering curses as he coaxed his beasts of burden into wakefulness.

Their arrival at the Mages Quarter was announced by the refreshing fragrance of silver linden, whose leafy branches cast wide arches over well-kept streets. High Mage Thelyn's residence was dark, and his servant reluctant to call the master from his sleep.

Eolyn's insistence in the name of the King did little to persuade him, but when Tibald stepped forward with sword drawn and stormy countenance, the young man hastened to comply.

Thelyn's sleepy eyes opened wide upon seeing her and the King's escort. He asked no questions but beckoned Eolyn and Ghemena inside, bidding the men-at-arms to remain at his door.

"I leave for Rhiemsaven at once," she said.

"I surmised as much." He looked down at Ghemena, who clung to Eolyn's side and fixed him with a dour stare. "And this one stays with me?"

"If you would be so kind."

"Of course." He instructed a servant to prepare a room. "Ghemena, go with Mikahl. He will see that you have everything you need."

She hesitated, cast a final pleading look at Eolyn, who bent to give her a hug.

"Do as High Mage Thelyn says, Ghemena. And pray to the Gods, that they will not keep me away from you for very long."

Mikahl took her satchel and her hand. The two disappeared down one of the long corridors, Ghemena dragging her feet. Thelyn ushered the maga into a small antechamber, where he invoked a sound ward around them.

"Have you found anything else in Tzeremond's collection?" he asked in a low voice.

"No. I am sending some of the most detailed accounts to Rhiemsaven, that I might continue to study them there, but it's all just histories. Events. I fear I will be of little use to the King, but he has called and I must answer his summons." The memory of her descent into the Underworld crept unbidden into her shoulders, and she shivered. "I don't even have a staff to reinforce my magic."

He nodded grimly. "There is much a High Maga can do without a staff, but when meeting the enemy, in particular an enemy such as this, it is a necessary tool."

"You think I was a fool to leave mine with Mage Corey," she said. "So do I."

An amused smile touched his lips. "Not a fool, just remarkably trusting. I may have a reward for your trust, Maga Eolyn. I've a mind to grant you the opportunity to ignite Corey's envy."

She frowned in puzzlement. "How would his envy serve me?"

Thelyn stepped away with a bow of deference, and ran his hand along the stone wall toward the southeast corner of the cramped space. Murmuring a spell, Thelyn drew back the stone as if it were a thin curtain. Behind the illusion stood a staff of rowan, aged and polished, with a head of crystal amber. The High Mage took it up with both hands and proffered it to the maga.

Eolyn recoiled in a serpentine instinct, her spirit rooting to the ground, energy surging toward her fingertips. "I know this staff. It was used against me."

"To cast the curse of Ahmad-dur," Thelyn confirmed. "It remains the most powerful staff in the kingdom, though its master is no longer with us. I believe it would be your best choice now."

"I cannot use this instrument. It would defy everything I try to do."

"I beg to differ, Maga Eolyn. You see, I have been plagued by a certain curiosity in recent days. Tzeremond allowed you into his library. You, and no one else, were given the cipher for his ward. This is a great puzzle to me. Given all Tzeremond's dedication to eliminating the magas, given everything he taught his followers regarding the dangers of women like you, why reach across the chasm that separates us from the Afterlife in order to touch your awareness? And why now?"

"You read too much into this, Mage Thelyn. My deciphering of the ward was mere coincidence; a memory that came in the right moment, the lucky instinct of a weary maga—"

"With all due respect, Maga Eolyn, do not insult our dead brothers and sisters by denying their power to speak to us when the desire moves them and the need is great."

Unable to counter his words, she studied the staff in his hands.

Eolyn's mother had reached out to her when she was a girl lost in the South Woods, and Doyenne Ghemena in more subtle ways in the years since her death. Even the Mage King Kedehen had allowed her a vision of his boyhood dreams, right here in Moisehén, on the ramparts of the fortress.

Why was it so difficult to imagine the wizard Tzeremond might do the same?

"Rishona summoned a Naether Demon to consume him," she said. "He would not have survived to enter the Afterlife. It's impossible for him to speak to any of us now."

"The Syrnte Witch wished him and all his magic destroyed," Thelyn agreed. "Yet if you but lay your hands on this staff, Maga Eolyn, you will realize she did not succeed. Tzeremond's spirit must have found a way to escape the Naether Demons, for his magic cannot live in this world unless it also survived in the next."

Eolyn hung back in doubt.

"All I ask is that you test its magic," Thelyn said. "If the staff does not please you, you need not take it."

Hesitant, she stepped forward, laid a palm on the polished wood and closed her eyes to listen to its quiet hum. The feel of Tzeremond's magic surprised her. She expected anger, aggression, resentment; but all she detected was discipline and focus, the stalwart dependability of a well-rooted tree.

When she opened her eyes, Thelyn had stepped away and the staff lay steady in her hands. The mage studied her expression a moment and shrugged.

"He was not a bad man," he said, "just bad for some."

She gave a short laugh of disbelief, tears stinging her eyes in an intense surge of emotion. She remembered the fiery destruction of her village, the brutal death of her family, the years of exile, fear, and hiding that had culminated in the heartbreaking war against Akmael.

And at the center of it all, Tzeremond.

Was it truly possible that her enemy in life could become an ally in death?

"You will take it, then?" Thelyn asked.

"Yes." She pulled the staff close to her breast. "Thank you, Mage Thelyn. It is a most generous gift."

"I do this not for you, but for our people," he said, "and it is not a gift."

"I understand." Eolyn smiled. "It will be returned to you then, when this war is done."

He nodded and escorted her to the door. The guards waited, torches in hand. The sky overhead had already brightened with the tenuous light of predawn.

"Our liege has granted me means of magic to reach him," she said to Tibald. "I will use this spell now. You and the other guards will remain here. I thank you, in the name of the King, for your service."

Tibald nodded. "As you wish, Maga Eolyn."

Eolyn stepped away and withdrew the silver web from its resting place over her heart. A breeze whipped at her cloak and sent leaves scuttling across Thelyn's courtyard. Candles now illuminated every window of the High Mage's household. She felt many eyes upon her, curiosity and anticipation sparking the brisk morning air. Eolyn's shoulders stiffened under the unwarranted attention, and her focus broke when she began the invocation. In that moment she realized that even during the recent years of freedom, she had remained accustomed to practicing magic with discretion, in quiet moments hidden from public view. To have so many witnesses to her power, especially men such as these, still felt dangerous, unwise.

Reminding herself that Tibald and the other guards had been appointed by Akmael to protect her, she drew a breath, anchored her spirit, and started again.

The world shifted, faded, and then returned.

Rain wet her face and cloak, enveloping her in a light but steady curtain of gray that dewed her lashes and blurred her vision. Low and distant thunder was quickly overwhelmed by the sudden whinny of horses, the stamping of hooves, the startled shouts of men. Swords rang from their sheaths. Wary of the threat of death, Eolyn sank to her knees, head bowed, hands gripping the staff of Tzeremond, keeping still as a cornered fox while blades hissed in menace and rivulets of water pooled on the muddied ground beneath her.

A sharp command from Akmael, and the weapons receded. She heard him dismount, recognized the weight and rhythm of his gait. Still she did not dare look up until he stood before her and bade her to rise, offering his gloved hand. She accepted his assistance, met his gaze.

"Maga Eolyn," he said.

"My Lord King."

They had lived this moment before, it seemed, years ago when the Lost Souls were crowding around them, and magic and hope had all but failed. They had touched one another in just this way, seen each other as if for the first time. Power had coursed between them as it did now, reigniting their spirits, breaking open the dark vault of the Underworld, allowing Mage King and High Maga to return to the realm of the living.

He glanced at the amber crystal set upon its rowan pillar, furrowed his dark brow. "I recognize this staff."

"High Mage Thelyn has entrusted it to me," Eolyn said, "that I might use it to defend our people."

Akmael nodded, a hint of tenderness in the stony set of his eyes. He laid a hand on her cheek, pressed warm lips against her damp forehead. "At last you have arrived. Eolyn, my love. My warrior queen."

Chapter 37

A throaty gargle startled Adiana out of her sleep. She looked around disconcerted. Everything seemed unfamiliar, and disturbing dreams clung to her awareness. She could not remember where she was.

A flurry of black and ivory feathers lunged at her, wings beating in her face. With a sharp cry, she scrambled backwards, her retreat cut short by a crate. Before her stood a magpie, its feathery coat black as a starless night, downy breast white as snow. It strutted a few jerky steps, hopped onto her lap and looked at her first with one amber eye, then the other. Talons pinched her legs through her worn skirt.

"Shoo!" She swatted at it with her hand.

The bird squawked and fluttered a few paces away. It bent to the ground, flipped a stone, straightened, and watched Adiana again.

"Cursed vermin!" A rock flung by one of the guards skidded across the dirt, just missing the magpie. The bird opened its wings and leapt cawing toward the heavens, diminishing quickly into a small shadow against a slate sky. The guard drew close, spat at the ground where it had stood and muttered, "They're bad luck, those birds."

He cast Adiana a greedy glance, and turned his attention elsewhere.

A flash of incandescence against the russet folds of her skirt caught Adiana's eye. It was the broken wing of a Mersien butterfly, adorned with intricate looping patterns of pale green and glittering silver. Adiana picked up the delicate wing with care, awed by this unexpected manifestation of beauty in a world that had become so harsh and ugly. She and Tasha had chased these butterflies at the height of spring, their laughter floating free across the open fields of Moehn. The memory brought tears, followed by a rueful smile. It seemed funny somehow, that she had not yet run out of tears.

"You're the laziest whore I've ever seen." The fat matron stood over her, hands on her hips, a scowl fixed on her chubby face. Gertha, she was called. Or at least this was the name Adiana heard when others spoke of her.

She did not wince at the matron's words. A whore was what she had become, and when she was not playing music or serving Lord Mechnes's needs, she felt idle and useless. "If you wish to give me some task, I would not complain. I can wash and cook, sew and mend—"

"And roughen up those lovely hands of yours? Lord Mechnes would have my head for it. Besides, you'd sooner fall asleep than scrub pots or mend shirts."

"I have not slept so easy of late," Adiana said. "I would welcome the distraction."

"You've been sleeping well enough since we arrived in this place. Haven't stirred from that spot since yesterday afternoon."

Adiana scrambled to her feet, slipping the butterfly wing into her pocket. Soldiers moved about with bold purpose, shouting at each other and exchanging broad grins as they sharpened their weapons and tended the horses.

"That long?" she asked, confused. "I've been asleep that long?"

The matron chuckled derisively.

"He didn't call for me," she realized, fear pricking her heart. "Last night he did not call."

"Now don't you worry your lazy whore's head." Gertha folded her flabby arms, studied Adiana with narrowed eyes. "If Lord Mechnes had lost interest, half the army would've rutted with you by now. No, you're still his prize, and off limits to the rest. I've got orders to see you cleaned up, so the General can hear you play tonight."

She winked, and gave a lewd toothless grin.

As evening fell, Adiana was delivered to Lord Mechnes's tent bathed and perfumed, hair brushed until it shone then braided with blossoms of purple aethne gathered from the nearby woods. The dress they had given her was clean but simple. Its sheer fabric did little to ward off the chill, leaving her with a sense of raw exposure that made her cheeks flush in the presence of the men, though all save Mechnes did not allow their gaze to linger on her for more than a moment.

Kahlil and the rest of the musicians did not speak as she took a place next to them, but this no longer mattered. Their habit of silence had become as much a fixture in her life as Mechnes's insatiable desire. She picked up a psaltery, tuned it, and when Idahm marked the pace of their song with the slow beat of his drum, began to play.

It was a somber dinner, devoid of the raucous merry-making that had characterized these gatherings ever since their departure from Moehn. No other women were present. Food and wine were pushed to the edge of the table to make room for maps splayed across its center. The officers did not sit but rather stood restless, some pacing momentarily before returning to the fold, all speaking earnestly, emphasizing words by jabbing at the maps or sweeping their palms in wide arcs across the painted landscape.

Adiana did not understand their discussion, and in any case paid it little heed, absorbed as she was by the spell of her own music, its gentle caress and comforting embrace, its kind invitation to a place of forgetfulness.

At length the debate died down, and then finished altogether with a monologue by Lord Mechnes, to which the officers responded with brief nods or short bows before taking their leave.

Men and musicians at last dismissed, Adiana set her instrument aside and waited.

Lord Mechnes indulged in a slow walk around the long table, ignoring her presence as was often his habit, while studying the map with a shrewd gaze, fingers drumming against the hilt of his sword. When he returned to the head of the table, he took a seat, served himself a cup of wine, and directed his attention to her.

"Play," he said.

She chose the lute this time, interpreting a song Kahlil had taught her years ago, one evening when Corey's Circle was resting from its long journey between Moehn and Selkynsen, right here in the Valley of Aerunden. It was a mournful tune, and she was not certain of the meaning or pronunciation of all the words, but this was the melody stirring inside her heart. She gave it all her voice and passion, though her ribs were still tender at every breath and her spirit shivered under the weight of the general's presence.

When she finished, he said nothing. The silence grew long and uncomfortable, until at last she lifted her eyes and found him studying her as if she were a sculpture he had just commissioned, or a foal recently produced by one of his mares.

"Why that song?" he asked.

"It is the one that came to me, Lord Mechnes." He had never posed such a question before. "That is all."

"Do you know its meaning?"

"I believe it is a love song. That is what Kahlil said, when he first taught it to me."

"Ah." He leaned back in his seat, loosened the lacings on his doublet. "Are you in love, Adiana?"

"I have never been in love, Lord Mechnes." Her gaze was steady, her tone tinged with defiance. "And by the mercy of the Gods, I never will be."

Chuckling at this, he set aside his wine. "Well said, Adiana. Well said, once again." He leaned forward, the mirth draining from his features. "You found a jewel this afternoon, one of emerald and silver that you slipped into your pocket. Not wanting to be parted from it, you then tucked it into the sash of the gown you now wear."

Adiana nodded, no longer surprised that he should know these details, that he could see pieces of the world through her eyes.

"Show it to me."

With some reluctance she surrendered the butterfly wing, laying it carefully in the rough palm of his hand, fearful it might disintegrate at his touch. He picked it up with thumb and index finger, bade her to sit at his feet while he examined the wing with a suspicious frown.

"The magpie gave you this?"

"The magpie?" The suggestion caught her off guard. "No. The bird was there, but it did not give me this. Perhaps it spied the wing on my lap and wanted to steal it." Her voice trailed off into confusion. Why would he think such a thing?

"The magpie might have been one of your friends," said Mechnes. "The Maga Eolyn, perhaps?"

"Eolyn?" Her laughter was dry. "That was not Eolyn."

"Why not? I have heard your magas and mages can assume the form of many forest creatures."

"Yes, but they shapeshift into animals compatible with their character. The magpie is a bird of cunning and thievery. It is not like Eolyn at all."

"One of her companions in magic, then. A mage, sent to rescue her friend."

Adiana shook her head and looked away, wishing for a spell that could erase the vividness of his presence, this constant smell of sweat and leather, blood and war. Melancholy weighed on her shoulders, crept into her voice. "No one is coming to rescue me, Lord Mechnes. I am well forgotten by those who might have once called me their friend."

His rested his hand heavy on her head, stroked her hair, lifted her chin. She despised the compassion she saw flicker behind his eyes. It was like a cruel note of hope in an otherwise vicious song.

"Why do you believe no one will come for you?" he asked.

"Those who were not crushed during the invasion of Moehn are now gathering to the Mage King. Eolyn, all the mages, the noble families, and their men-at-arms. They see the Syrnte army at their doorstep, and they unite with one purpose: to defeat you. Even if they knew of my capture, they would not waste time mourning it. They will not sacrifice a single man to take me from your side, for they know the challenge that waits when your armies meet, and they cannot waste able mages on inconsequential matters. I was once worth much to my friend Eolyn, but that worth amounts to nothing when weighed against the fate of this kingdom."

An odd expression crossed his countenance.

"Does it?" He spoke as if to himself. "Amount to nothing?"

The uncertainty in his voice unsettled her. She averted her gaze.

He released her chin, refreshed his wine, and nodded toward the bed. "Go. Ready yourself. I leave tomorrow, but we have yet a generous night ahead of us."

Adiana obeyed, letting the dress slip from her shoulders as she took refuge beneath a soft blanket. She lay awake watching the Syrnte commander lost in thought. He ran his fingers idly over a map at his side, drank absently until at last he tipped the cup and found it empty.

Hunger flared in his eyes.

With sudden decisiveness, Mechnes sprang upon her, tore back the covers, and dragged Adiana into a vortex of unyielding passion.

Adiana met the Syrnte commander's desire with equal ferocity, refusing to let this night be anything less than luminous. Not because she wished to please him, but because she felt the beady eyes of death upon her, its sharp beak anxious to pluck at her flesh, its feathers of snow and shadow beckoning toward a final embrace.

When Mechnes released himself inside of her, his roar was one of rage and triumph. Adiana's body shuddered with forbidden ecstasy. He caught her in a bruising hold, breath hot upon her skin, voice hoarse in her ear.

"No one shall have you as I have had you," he vowed. "No one."

In the morning, when the sun's first light broke over the Valley of Aerunden, Lord Mechnes began the long march north with his officers, his guard, and the greater part of his army.

Adiana was left behind, surrendered to the will of the San'iloman.

Chapter 38

Akmael's army plodded beneath gray and weeping clouds. By mid-afternoon, the rain relented somewhat, and while the sun did not yet show its face, the sky brightened and steam began to rise from the horses and the cloaks of their riders. Scouts returned from the south and spoke at length with Akmael and his officers. The mood of their brief deliberation was grim; jaws set and eyes hardened as all spoke in subdued but earnest tones. At Akmael's command, they continued another half a league before reaching a campsite along the Tarba River.

While the men began setting picket lines, pitching tents, and digging latrines, Eolyn was asked to accompany the King, his officers, and his mages, in order to survey the ground where Akmael intended to halt the Syrnte advance. It was a broad plain sloping downward from a low ridge, flanked on the west by the steep banks of the Tarba and on the east by a young but dense forest. The terrain would give them an advantage, Akmael told her, and this was one of the reasons why he had decided to wait for the Syrnte here.

At the crest of the ridge, Eolyn dismounted with the rest of the mages. The King and his men completed their rounds on horseback, while she and her fellow practitioners walked barefoot, listening to the hush of the wind over damp grass, the quiet turnover of the earth below their feet. They sent their spirits toward the core of the long plateau. Eolyn could tell from the slow pace of its heart that this was the root of an ancient mountain range, worn to its foundations by time and forces beyond her ken.

One of the mages drew close, a portly man with a jovial face, a bulbous nose, and bushy white eyebrows who introduced himself as Echior. "We met once, in a hamlet of Moehn. Not that I would expect you to remember an old man like me, but I certainly would never forget a young woman like you."

Eolyn had to study him a moment before the memory coalesced in her mind: a village wedding that had piqued her curiosity, a conversational mage with keen blue eyes who had filled her with trepidation.

"You could have trusted me then, you know," he said, "though you were wise not to."

"You were the one who told me about Mage Corey," she realized.

"Yes." He gave an energetic nod. "You found him, then?"

Eolyn smiled. "I did."

They searched the low-slung ridge alongside the other mages, until they found what they sought near the river bank: a small rise that could serve as a focal point from which magic would be sent across the plain, strengthening the resolve of Akmael's soldiers even as they plunged into the terror of battle. No sooner had they cast their first circle than the King and his men returned. Akmael dismounted to inspect their work. Expressing his approval with a brief nod, he instructed the mages to establish a second circle to the west, near the forest. Eolyn was then obliged to return to the camp at the King's side while the mages continued surveying the ridge, or headed for the forest to gather branches of oak, rowan and alder in preparation for the sacred fires to come.

"You must be weary," Akmael said as they rode together. "Ours has been a long journey today, but yours the longest of all."

The comment took her by surprise. She did not feel tired in the least. "I am well enough, my Lord King. There is no place for weariness on the eve of war."

"Well said." His gaze never left the landscape, and Eolyn could feel him register every dip and knoll, every stray tree and solitary rock. "We must speak of the Naether Demons."

"I fear I do not have much to say yet."

"We must speak, nonetheless. This evening, we will sit with the chief officers and High Mages, and you will share everything you know."

"As you wish."

"There is something else." He reined in his steed. "Did Borten instruct you as I commanded?"

Eolyn's throat constricted. "My Lord King?"

He gestured to Kel'Barú, strapped to his side. "Did he teach you how to use this sword?"

"Well," she stumbled over her words, "yes, but—"

"Show me."

"My Lord King, we only started a few weeks ago, and I have not touched a weapon since I escaped Moehn."

"All the more reason."

Akmael dismounted, beckoned her to follow. He unsheathed Kel'Baru and gave it to her before procuring another blade from one of the knights. The men gathered around them in a loose circle, some dismounting, others remaining seated on their horses, all of them watching with expressions of amusement, curiosity, doubt.

Eolyn balked in anticipation of their ridicule. "Please, Akmael—my Lord King—this is a pointless exercise."

In a single stride he was upon her, his blade a deadly flash that gave her no time to think before deflecting its descent. Metal sung against metal, the blow reverberated through her body, causing her to lose her footing and stumble back on the slick grass. She recovered breathless and frightened, never having imagined he would strike with such force.

"Ground yourself," he said. "You do not have my strength, but you have your magic. Use it."

The severity of his tone squashed the anxious protest of her heart.

Eolyn drew a breath and pressed her feet firm against the damp earth, the weight of inevitability settling on her shoulders. Kel'Barú hummed in her grip as if awakened from a deep sleep. Its whisper invoked images of battles long forgotten, of those who had fallen under its blade.

"Good," Akmael said, though he corrected her posture and the placement of her feet. "Again."

Eolyn struck without hesitation, but her renewed resolve did her little good. There was not a guard or a counter she chose that met with his full approval, and she died a dozen times during their brief parry. Even so, the men did not jeer. When the ordeal at last ended, Akmael simply nodded and said, "It is a start."

He returned his sword to its owner, then sheathed Kel'Barú.

"I will not be putting you in the vanguard, Maga Eolyn." This provoked laughter from the men. "But you will have this weapon at your disposal, and you must use it with confidence should the need arise."

Eolyn nodded, tight-lipped, the blood having drained from her face. They returned to their horses. As Akmael prepared to assist her in mounting, a tremor shook her body. Smoke and flames clouded her vision, blades swinging through chaos, the bodies of children slaughtered, the twisted corpse of her father. Her knees failed, and she would have sunk to the ground had the King not caught her by the elbow.

"Eolyn," he said, voice laden with concern.

"You held back." She recovered her balance, looked up at him, pleading. "Do you think I do not know? You held back. If anyone should ever attack me in earnest, I will never be able to—"

"The sword is not your only defense."

"But it is a man's first weapon."

"Eolyn." He took her face in his hands. "This will not depend solely on you, and certainly not on your ability to handle a sword. There are men assigned to your protection, under orders to take you north to Rhiemsaven, and from there to the King's City, should the tide turn against us in battle."

"I will not desert you."

He warmed her lips with a tender kiss, set his hand upon her belly. "What you carry within is much more important than any battle we might wage together. The destiny of my fathers will be undone if you are snatched from the world of the living. Promise me you will protect yourself at all costs, even if it means leaving me to my death."

"For the love of the Gods, Akmael, you cannot ask me to—"

"Promise me."

The rain had returned, a slow mist that wet her cheeks and chilled her bones. She longed for a warm fire on a quiet hearth, for the stars that hung over Ghemena's cottage, for the fireflies that danced in the summer meadow.

"You could have come to my world," she said quietly. "You could have left all this behind and stayed with me in the South Woods instead."

A melancholy smile invaded his eyes. He studied her a long moment. "Could I have?"

Pain lodged in her throat. She looked away. "Every moment we are together, we are preparing to be apart."

"Every moment we have been apart has brought us back together. We must have faith in that now."

"Then why do you speak of these things? Of your death, of me fleeing to the City?"

"Because it is a foolish king who does not recognize his own mortality. A greater fool still, the king who loses his determination to live. I will do everything in my power to win this war, and my power is great. But their power…" He glanced south, toward the ruinous Pass of Aerunden. "Their power may be greater, and the Gods may have their own plans. We must be cautious, and we must be brave." He set his eyes upon hers, expression resolute and filled with respect. "You have always been both."

Eolyn held his gaze. Acceptance began to take root in her core with the steady vigor of a young oak. This was her place: at his side, on the eve of war.

She nodded and mounted her horse, the ache in her heart receding under the inexorable tide of fate.

Chapter 39

In the Valley of Aerunden, the San'iloman's camp was charged with excitement. From the confines of her tent, Adiana heard a marked crescendo in the shouts of men and servants, the movement of feet, the whinny of horses. The girl who brought her daily meals appeared, cheeks flushed with anticipation.

"Lord Mechnes' messenger has arrived from the north," she said brightly. "They have sighted the armies of the Mage King, and will engage with them on the morrow, or the day after. Victory is at hand, everyone says so. The Lord General has never lost a battle, and the San'iloman will send her creatures after the Mage King tonight."

The girl skipped out of the room, leaving Adiana staring at a plate of food for which she had no appetite.

Adiana had understood her fate from the moment Lord Mechnes turned her over to Rishona, giving strict orders that no man lay a hand on her. She had wanted to scream at his hypocrisy. Why did it matter, with her world obliterated and her death warrant signed, whether she were raped once or a hundred times?

Yet she had held her tongue and stifled her rage, silence and the illusion of calm having become her only refuge. When he set lips upon hers to say farewell, she had surrendered to the sickening pleasure of his touch.

At night when she lay down to rest, she felt the iron confines of his embrace, tasted the bitter salt of his sweat. On the rare occasions that she managed to sleep, her dreams always led back to him.

Such was the power of Syrnte magic: even in his absence, Mechnes had her ensnared, his insatiable hunger intertwined with the music of her mind; her shame, desire, and fear interwoven with his bloody ambitions.

Could they ever be parted, or were their spirits so tightly bound that he would follow her into the Afterlife, tormenting her with this revulsion and need for the rest of eternity?

Adiana shuddered at the thought.

No, she reassured herself. Death would be her escape, and soon Rishona would open that door.

Later that afternoon, servants came for her. They bathed her, dressed her, brushed and plaited her hair as if for preparing a maiden for a wedding. Adiana let them do as they pleased, no protest on her lips, no resistance in her heart.

She had only one misgiving: She would never know the fate of her people. Had Eolyn survived? And what of Mariel and Sirena? What of Borten and that new guard, the burly and unkempt man whose name Adiana no longer remembered? Did anything remain of the dream they tried to build in the highlands of Moehn? A shard of women's magic that could sustain the tradition of the Magas?

"Eolyn, my friend, you often told me the dead can assist the living," Adiana murmured as they adjusted the lacings of her dress. "If this is indeed true, and you remain in this world, then I will find a way to help you."

The sun had long disappeared behind the western hills when they bound her wrists and led her up a long winding path to a grassy knoll overlooking the narrow Valley of Aerunden. Torches lit their way under a starless sky.

The San'iloman waited for her in a simple ivory gown. A circlet of gold and rubies adorned Rishona's dark hair, which tumbled freely down her shoulders. Beside her the priestess Donatya held a satin pillow on which rested the obsidian blade.

Rishona greeted her prisoner with a deep bow. "Adiana, beloved sister, it is in this place that the defeat of the past will be transformed into the victory of tomorrow." The San'iloman lifted her arms and spoke to all those assembled. "This woman's life is the final and greatest sacrifice we will make on this campaign. Honor her. Honor her, I say! For it is by her magic that the people of Moisehén will at last be freed from the treachery of the Mage Kings. It is through her death that glory will come to the Syrnte."

Soldiers and servants went to their knees in reverent silence. Only Rishona remained standing, triumph illuminating her face. She stepped toward Adiana and continued in gentle tones, "Do not fear, my beloved sister, for my blade is swift and true. Death will embrace you with the sweetness of a summer breeze. I swear to you by all the Gods I serve, no one will forget what you gave for your people, and for mine. After this night you will be remembered forever."

Adiana was caught between the urge to laugh and the need to vomit.

Yes, she thought, I will be remembered. Remembered as prisoner, slave, and whore to the vilest people to have ever claimed the Syrnte crown.

Rishona clapped her hands and everyone rose. The San'iloman and her priestess lifted their voice in song. Fire ignited along the rim of a wide circle marked by pungent herbs, forming an iridescent curtain of sapphire and amethyst, shot through with gold and viridian.

Adiana had never been one to pray to the Gods, but she did so now, begging for a speedy death. She called to Renate, Tasha, and Catarina, pleading that they deliver her from the labyrinth of the Underworld, and receive her with friendship and forgiveness in the Afterlife.

Rishona passed through the curtain of flame as if gliding on air. She took a stance at the center of the circle and chanted in an ancient language unknown to Adiana. The obsidian blade glinted in her grasp. Thunder rumbled beneath the earth. The hairs on Adiana's neck rose, fear surged down her spine. When the San'iloman extended her arm toward the prisoner, her face was pale as the moon, her eyes glassy and black.

The guards shoved Adiana forward.

She stumbled through the curtain of fire. The flames were cold and left her unscathed. Sound was muted within, and a stench of death and decay rose from the damp earth.

Panic overtook her. Adiana turned to flee, but the curtain roared with a gust of scalding wind that threw her off her feet. She landed hard, bruising her elbows. The leather cords drew blood from her wrists.

Rishona caught her by a fistful of hair and with inhuman strength dragged Adiana to the center of the circle. Lifting high the obsidian knife, the San'iloman chanted while the ground rippled with restless fury.

Blind terror consumed Adiana. Caught in Rishona's pitiless grip, she kicked and shrieked and wept for mercy. Lightening crackled at the edge of the circle, and snaked toward them in undulating rivers.

Rishona paused in her song, knife suspended at her victim's throat.

Adiana ceased her cries, paralyzed by the frigid sting of the San'iloman's blade.

Before them hovered three serpents, scales glowing like a thousand stars. Their forked tongues flickered in fiery sparks. They recoiled, heads lifted, ready to strike.

Adiana sensed uncertainty in Rishona's stance.

The San'iloman's grip loosened, the blade strayed from Adiana's throat. In that instant the snakes sprang forward, hissing past Adiana and striking the San'iloman. Two latched onto her wrists, the third sprouted wings leapt toward her neck. Rishona cried out and slashed at the attackers with her blade, severing heads from necks and letting go a thunderous curse.

Lightning inundated the circle. Air began to move in a vortex that quickly gathered speed.

Horrified, Adiana scrambled away. Wind stung her eyes. Explosions of fire and sulfur choked off her breath. Just as she reached the sapphire curtain, a wall of yellow flame cut across her path.

"Adiana!"

Her name was a howl on the wind, and yet the voice sounded impossibly familiar. Spinning around, she saw Mage Corey, his countenance infused with deadly intent, a shaft of yellow flame bursting from his palm.

"Stay where you are," he commanded.

She obeyed, watching in bewilderment as he completed another circle of flame within the first that had been cast by Rishona.

Behind him two mage warriors were locked in struggle with the San'iloman. Wind and light twisted in a turbulent maelstrom. Those within could barely be seen. Curses imploded inside Adiana's head. Her ears rang and her body ached, and she begged the Gods to stop them all before this terror obliterated her.

Corey strode into the fray, power crackling from his staff. A glowing carpet spread over the ground and the serpents reappeared, not three this time but dozens. Rishona's blade struck rapid and furious, but each writhing body she severed was regenerated. Heads grew tails and tails sprouted heads.

The San'iloman's arms flailed in an ever more desperate attempt to defend herself, but she was trapped in a voracious net of light. The stench of burnt flesh impregnated the air. The screaming wind transformed into a mournful gale, and then was silenced altogether. Rishona sank to her knees, convulsed, and became still. Her arms fell limp at her side, her shoulders sagged. She hung her head in defeat.

The snakes dissolved, though the glowing net from which they had arisen still hummed over the earth.

Cautiously, Corey approached the San'iloman.

Rishona lifted her eyes to the mage. Recognition and surprise filled her countenance, followed by affection and sorrow.

"You," she said quietly.

Corey accepted a sword from one of his companions.

"Yes, me," he said, and hacked off her head.

Scowling, the mage strode to Adiana and cut the cords from her wrists.

"Find the King," he told the mages, "and tell him all that you have seen."

They shimmered, transformed into owls, and escaped on silent wings. One of them carried off Rishona's head, blood-matted hair entangled in its talons.

"What?" Adiana gasped for breath, tried to recover her composure. "Why are you here?"

"Because of you." He surveyed the wall of fire that still protected them, blood and sweat beading his brow. "And I am not likely to let you forget it."

Adiana heard shouts of consternation. A spear flew through the fire and grazed past Corey's shoulder. He went to his knees and pulled Adiana down with him.

The ground lurched. Howls erupted from the bowls of the earth, followed by a belligerent pounding beneath their feet.

"I fear this is going badly," he muttered.

The ground caved in at their feet. Corey rose and with a thunderous curse sent a bolt of white light into the trench. Screams of rage and agony burst from the shadows below. The mage hauled Adiana to her feet and pulled her away.

"Those demons are coming," he said, "and I do not have the means to stop them."

Another spear hissed past from outside the circle. The trench spewed forth a shower of rock and grit, followed by an ear-splitting shriek.

"Don't leave me here," Adiana begged.

"I will not abandon you, but to take you with me involves a great risk."

"Greater than this?"

Corey set his lips in a thin line. "Perhaps. Do you trust me, Adiana?"

"No."

He wrapped his arm around her so that she felt the length of his staff at her back. "You always were the clever one. Remember this: Your sisters love you. As do I."

Corey planted his lips upon hers. Startled, she pulled away, but the mage held fast. His kiss erased all shame, all regret, all her miserable failures; fusing past, present, and future into a single flash of light.

Hope ignited in Adiana's heart, along with the memory of what it meant to live in a world of innocence, a place of limitless possibility.

Then she was falling away from him, collapsing in on herself. Adiana's limbs shrank and changed form. The wall of fire roared to greater heights as she fluttered helpless to the ground. She clutched at the grass only to realize she had no fingers, struggled to stand on legs that bent in awkward directions. In terror and confusion she cried out to Mage Corey, but all that escaped her throat was an anxious repetitive chirp.

Wind buffeted her feathers, giant talons seized her body. The ground raced away just as the dark hole disgorged a herd of Naether Demons. They leapt through the ring of fire and seized all within reach, tearing them limb from limb. Screams of anguish filled the night, and then slowly faded into the distance.

The light from the torches disappeared among twisting branches and dense foliage.

The air felt cool upon her face. The tranquil sounds of the forest soothed her spirit. Shadows enveloped Adiana's awareness. Memories slipped toward sweet oblivion, flowing down a darkened path until all that was left was a single melody, a melancholy warble, a sequence of crystal clear notes easily scattered by the careless wind.

Chapter 40

Mechnes sprang from sleep, knife in hand and eyes alert. He detected no movement in the shadows, not even a lifting of the canvas by the passing breeze. An eerie quiet had settled over the camp, muffling the snores and murmurs of men, the footsteps of passing guards and the spitting hiss of bright torches. Beyond these sounds, on the edge of Mechnes's awareness, flitted an ephemeral whisper, a simple and repetitive string of notes.

The Syrnte Lord closed his eyes, bent upon drawing the timorous song from its hiding place. Time and again the notes slipped from his grasp until at last they skittered beyond reach, leaving a silent void, like the cavity that remained when the roots of a tree were torn from the earth.

His head began to ache.

The melody, he was certain, had been Adiana. Or what was left of her.

Shaking off the disturbing image of the musician's last moments, Mechnes rose and splashed cool water on his face, then called for his steward to assist him with his armor.

Outside a damp gray curtain of fog shrouded the light of predawn. The camp stirred with the impatient calls of his officers, the grunts of awakening men, the rasp of leather and the chink of mail. Mechnes mounted his horse and cantered to the line of pickets that faced north toward their enemy.

"What have you to report?" he demanded of the men on duty.

"Nothing, milord," answered their captain. "They have not stirred in all the night."

Mechnes received this news with grim countenance. Could these creatures of the Underworld be subtler than he thought? Capable of finishing the Mage King while passing unnoticed?

He turned to the officers that accompanied him. "Form the infantry in the usual manner. Tehmad, you will take three companies of armored horse to our right flank. When our archers begin to shoot, sweep away their cavalry and cut down the enemy mages. Athenon, command our left. Use your horse to drive the enemy into the river. I will command two companies in the reserve and bring them to support the first success. Mage King or no, we attack as soon as this accursed fog burns off."

The sun rose restless and hot as the Syrnte army formed on the field of battle. Vapor lifted off the grassy earth, rising toward the heavens, forming white billows that sailed eastward in silence. Wind gusted across the field, stirring up aromas of wet grass and flowering chamomile. Mechnes inhaled the sweet fragrance, invigorated by the thought that it would soon be salted with sweat, blood, and death. It was here on the verge of battle that he always felt the most alive, overlooking the abyss where thousands of fates would intersect and no amount of Syrnte magic could unmask the future that waited on the other side.

The ground was damp but tractable, sloping gently up toward a ridge that was occupied by a scattered line of mage warriors, with companies of horse on either flank. The numbers were few, but more men might well be hiding behind the ridge.

The Mage King appeared at the crest, mounted on a large destrier and accompanied by a small contingent of knights. At his side, a woman in burgundy robes, the crystal head of her staff glinting in the newly revealed sun. Mechnes would have laughed at the Mage King's folly of bringing a woman to the battle field, but his amusement was undercut by the echo of Rishona's voice, a prophecy told long ago when they first conceived this campaign.

The Mage King's power is complete only with the Maga at his side; and the full potential her magic realized only in his presence. She is the one we must slay first, before all others.

"That one," he said to his officers, "is dangerous."

"The woman?" Tehmad did not bother to hide the doubt in his voice.

"She is the last of the High Magas. It may well have been her magic that caused the Naether Demons to fail. A sack of gold for the man who brings her to me, dead or alive."

The Maga separated from her liege, taking a small number of mages with her. They, in turn, divided into two groups that took positions at the rear of the cavalry on each flank.

The King and his guard rode down slope, flags lowered in an appeal for parley.

Mechnes shook his head in dismay. Why waste the morning with talk when the crux of the matter was best decided by fighting?

"Come," he said to his men nonetheless. "Let us indulge this young warrior with a friendly chat before we deliver him to his fate. Perhaps the ground will dry a little more as we speak."

They met in the center of the field. For all Mechnes had heard about the Mage King's formidable magic, he found the regent unimpressive. Not a single scar marked his bearded face, and his level gaze appeared untested by the harsh choices of campaigning. Mechnes had skewered countless young commanders like this one, men who believed they had come to battle for honor, not for blood; innocents brought down in short order, and sentenced to slow agonizing deaths as the Syrnte Lord took possession of all they once held dear.

"If you have words for me, Prince Akmael, then be quick with them. The day has begun, and my men are impatient for their kill."

The young King blunted the sting of Mechnes's taunt by holding his silence. He studied the officers who accompanied the Syrnte commander, then scanned the troops assembled behind them.

"You are not welcome here, Lord Mechnes," he said. "I bid you to return with your army to the land of the Syrnte, and leave the people and provinces of Moisehén in peace."

"Peace is what we intend to bring." Mechnes lifted his arm in a conciliatory gesture that was not without a hint of mockery. "This kingdom has been at war with itself for two generations because your father, the usurper, murdered his siblings and took that which was not his. Today we will put an end to this struggle. Tamara-Rishona, daughter of Joturi-Nur and of Feroden son of Urien, San'iloman of the Syrnte and rightful Queen of Moisehén, has returned to assume the throne that is hers and become a true steward of her people."

"A woman cannot claim the Crown of Vortingen."

"This woman will claim whatever she pleases."

The Mage King nodded to one of the men at his side, who produced a blood-stained bundle and unfurled its cloth, allowing the contents to tumble to the ground.

Mechnes faltered when he recognized Rishona's severed head, her blackened eyes staring blankly at the sky, fair skin transformed into a sickly gray, blood-matted hair splayed against the pale green grass.

His vision blurred.

There was another woman with my Queen, he thought. Her eyes as blue as the sun-lit sea. Was she still?

Laughter tumbled from Rishona's lifeless lips, but it was not his niece's laugh, it was Adiana's.

No one is beautiful when they are dead.

Mechnes shook off the vision, annoyed that the musician's fate should yet trouble him.

If she had survived, he would find her.

The Syrnte horses whinnied. Several of his men reined back a few steps before Mechnes halted their startled retreat with an angry shout and a lift of his hand. He shifted in his saddle, lips twitching with barely suppressed rage, fingers curling into a tight fist.

"Tehmad," he barked, "retrieve our Queen."

The officer dismounted, gathered Rishona's remains and wrapped them with reverence in his own cloak.

Mechnes clenched his jaw, gaze honed to kill as he directed his fury at the Mage King. "You are not worthy of the crown you wear, Prince Akmael, for only the most depraved of men would so defile a creature of such beauty. I do not know by what black arts you slew the San'iloman, but the arm of her vengeance still lives. You and your men will die here today. The women of Moisehén will become our slaves; their children will be given in sacrifice to the goddess Mikata. Your queen," he glanced toward the red-clad figure on the ridge, "and your maga will be mine to use as I please before delivering them to the cruder appetites of my men. Your daughter, the Princess Eliasara, will be thrown from the ramparts of your fathers' fortress. Your lands will be ravaged, your people destroyed and the last of your seed obliterated for this crime you have committed against my people and my blood."

He spat on the ground, turned and unsheathed his sword.

"For the Queen!" he roared to those who awaited his command. "For Tamara-Rishona, the San'iloman. For the glory and vengeance of her people!"

His officers repeated the call, and together they galvanized the men, who responded with rabid shouts and raised swords, spears beating against shields, feet stamping upon the earth, until the very heavens trembled with the thunder of their wrath.

Chapter 41

Eolyn dismounted and removed her shoes. The cool grass and the calm pulse of the earth seemed incongruent with the tension that sparked the air, the knowledge that the sweet smell of this summer morning would soon be tainted with violence and death. She took her place at the center of a circle of eight High Mages, each man occupying a cardinal point twelve paces away from her. They had chosen this position with great care, in accordance with the oldest traditions of wartime magic. Its confluence of energy allowed access to the deeper forces of the earth and connected many points along the ridge and slope.

From here they could see the full extent of the battlefield, illuminated in the gold-green hues of the rising sun, the massed forces of the Syrnte a black shadow across its face. Eolyn had never witnessed such a great and terrible army. Men stood under flags of burgundy and gold, shoulder to shoulder like stones that would not be moved. What she remembered of her brother's troops seemed ragged by comparison, and the forces Akmael had organized to defeat Ernan those four years past, small and inconsequential.

Akmael's army was larger now, but not as large as this. The greater part of his men lay in wait behind the ridge, out of the enemy's sight. Victory, Akmael had told her, would depend upon the surprise and speed of their attack.

"Maga Eolyn," one of the High Mages prompted her, "it is time."

Eolyn nodded and wrapped her hand firmly around Tzeremond's staff, connecting to the steady pulse of magic that lived in its heart.

Ehekaht, she said, and the High Mages joined in the chant,

Ehekahtu

Naeom avignaes aenthe

Sepenom avignaes soeh

Renenom ukaht maen
Evenahm faeom reohoert
Ehekaht, Ehukae

Each staff emitted a low hum as its crystal head ignited with the sacred fire of Dragon. Maga and Mages synchronized the energy of their staves before sending tendrils of their spirits like fine roots toward the heart of the mountain. From here, they wove a net of magic that bound all the warriors of Moisehén: spearmen and archers, knights and mage warriors, that latter adding strength to the spell with their own potent resonance. At the center of their collective, the Mage King's spirit intertwined with Eolyn's, the magic of each feeding into the other, building like an intense sapphire flame that illuminated the very portals of death, driving the Lost Souls and their terrible hunger further into the shadows of imagination.

Eolyn drew a sharp breath, understanding for the first time that this was why he had summoned her: to invoke the magic that they had discovered when Tzeremond banished her spirit from the world of the living, a power that bound them and kept the Underworld at bay. Akmael intended to use it as a barrier between now and the hereafter, between life and death, between victory and defeat.

She started at the blast of horns and opened her eyes to see the Syrnte advancing up slope, an aggressive march that unsettled the bowels of the earth. Eolyn fought to quell the fear inside, an insidious twinge that threatened to burst into panic with each step that brought the Syrnte closer to the ridge. The net woven by the circle of mages shivered under the weight of their march. The links between each man tightened, and the army tensed as a single entity: a dragon perched upon a cliff ready to strike, its scales forged from mail and metal; its fiery breath held in the staves of mage warriors; its serpentine gaze delivered through Akmael's eyes, sharp and calculating, attentive to experience, reliant upon instinct. In silence they waited, their focus absolute, until all Eolyn could hear was the fall of the enemy's feet, the calls of their officers, the labored breath of each man.

Akmael chose his moment. The trumpeters threw open the gates of war. Mage warriors sent bellows of fire against the Syrnte, searing shields and flesh, forcing them to halt. Shouts of panic and pain afflicted the enemy ranks, lines wavered despite the harried reprimands of officers and the repeated wail of their horns.

Again Akmael's trumpets sounded, and the men of Moisehén rose as one, sprang over the ridge and plummeted toward the Syrnte lines, their roar the synchronized voices of ten thousand men, spears extended like claws as they descended upon their prey.

The panicked Syrnte fired ragged volleys of arrows into the mass of attacking men, bodkin points piercing mail, the cries of the fallen silenced as the soldiers who followed trampled them down. The opposing lines clashed with a deafening force that reverberated across the field, metal singing against metal, splintering wood, hewing limbs.

Eolyn detected the vortices of the Underworld as they bloomed underfoot, relentless holes that dragged the fatally wounded toward cold silent depths. Every soul that slipped away was like a splinter driven into her spirit. How much of this brutal torrent her magic could bear, she did not know.

Yet she had Tzeremond's staff in her hand and his mages in her circle. She held the Mage King in her heart and the South Woods in her soul. She had the memory of her coven and her stubborn dreams of peace. What power she could draw from all this she resolved to give to her people today, to stand or die with these men-at-arms, defending until her last breath the heritage of Moisehén and the magic that made them whole.

Chapter 42

The Mage King did not charge with his spearmen.

Mechnes, a wolf hard upon the scent of his prey, tracked Prince Akmael as he rode behind the lines, along the crest, and toward the river. The Syrnte infantry were driven down slope, but the Mage King's weaker flank had begun to cede ground under the pressure of Barathamor's horse near the river. The destruction of Akmael's cavalry on the right flank could expose his foot soldiers and turn the battle back in Mechnes's favor.

Seizing the opportunity, Mechnes unsheathed his sword and spurred his reserve into action.

"I want the Mage King's head," he cried, "and the Maga's corpse. All other plunder is yours. To victory!"

His men echoed the shout, their canter gathering into a gallop. Mechnes pulled ahead to lead the wedge that drove hard into the melee, seeking to separate the Mage King's horse from his infantry. He split the skull of a stray foot soldier, releasing a warm spray of blood to whet his appetite before bearing down on one of the mounted men.

Sword met sword in a vicious song as Mechnes forced his opponent back. The horse whinnied in protest under its besieged rider, who struggled to repel each savage stroke. His shield splintered under Mechnes's relentless pounding, his blade failed to penetrate the Syrnte Lord's rapid counters. When the man's strength gave way and his guard faltered, Mechnes plunged the blade into his torso, relishing in the sound of metal parting mail and ripping through flesh. The wounded rider tumbled from his mount.

Mechnes spat, wheeled his horse around, and chose his next kill, a sallow-faced youth who had lost his helmet. Blood streamed down the boy's face from a cut over his eye, but he was quick with the sword, deflecting a blow meant to sever his neck, and counterattacking with skillfully delivered strokes. When the blade slipped from the youth's hand, he seized Mechnes's sword arm, muscles bulging on his neck as he struggled to keep the Syrnte Lord's blade from slicing open his face.

Mechnes grinned at the youth. "First battle, lad?"

"And your last, milord." The boy spoke between breathless grunts and shoved his shield at Mechnes in an attempt to throw him off balance. Knocking aside the attack, Mechnes released his knife and drove it into the boy's throat, twisting until blood spurted hot from the wound. The young knight managed a few feeble blows before succumbing to a fit of choking. Mechnes threw him aside with disdain.

The grass was now slick with blood, and the invigorating taste of salt and iron hovered about the field. Mechnes saw flames exploding amidst his men, and heard furious roars as Akmael's Mage Warriors shapeshifted into bears. Yet the Syrnte had been prepared for these tricks, and the cries of his men rang out in relentless chords of triumph, while the silver and purple banners of the Mage King fluttered and fell back, their hold increasingly uncertain against the renewed determination of the Syrnte army.

The horns of Moisehén blasted from the ridge.

"Form ranks!" Mechnes thundered, indicating the crest where a fresh flood of spearmen appeared led by the Mage King. "Form ranks!"

His trumpeters repeated the call as Mechnes disengaged from the melee. Other riders gathered to him, but too few and too slowly. The new line of warriors pounded forward, thrusting spears at rider and horse, shouting threats of death as they stabbed both men and mounts.

Mechnes parried their wooden shafts, and injured any soldier that came within reach, but the Mage King's reserves were skilled and pressed forward relentlessly. The animals whinnied in protest, nostrils flared and eyes crazed with fear. They shied away from the spearmen, rearing and prancing in circles.

"Curse this madness!" Mechnes reined in his mount and urged the beast backwards, anger running hot through his veins. The horses were useless against these foot soldiers, and the battle was slipping from his grasp. "Hold your ground, men! The Mage King is within reach."

He spotted Prince Akmael just beyond the line of spears, mounted on his horse and galvanizing the soldiers. Hungry for the royal bastard's blood, the Syrnte Lord spurred his horse back into the fray, coming head to head with the spearmen and taunting their front line.

"You think you are soldiers? You are nothing! Cowards and women, all! I am Mechnes, Lord of the Syrnte and Prince General of the San'iloman. I will have your heads, all of you, and the entrails of your king!"

A soldier with a weathered face and steady hands lunged toward Mechnes, separating himself from his comrades, ignoring the reprimands of his officer. Bloodlust and ambition burned in his eyes as he thrust his long spear at the Syrnte Commander.

"You think yourself the Mage King's hero?" Mechnes laughed and drew back as his quarry followed, spinning on his horse, sweeping aside the spearhead with his shield. "Every army has a fool like you."

The man lunged again, slipping on the bloody remains of an unfortunate soldier, and Mechnes responded with lightning speed, sword slicing through leather and mail to tear open his chest. The man stumbled back, determination overcoming surprise as he tried to regain his stance. Adjusting the grip on his spear, he attacked once more, but the thrust was weak. Mechnes struck, cleaving the man's skull and snatching his spear as he fell.

Sheathing his sword, Mechnes let the dead man's weapon settle in his grip as his mounted warriors continued to cede ground to the Mage King. The spear was not well balanced for throwing, but no matter. The Syrnte Lord had made use of poorer weapons under more difficult circumstances. He eyed his target, now pulling to the front of the line, urging the men forward with vigorous shouts and raised sword.

Mechnes waited with predatory patience.

The Mage King spotted the Syrnte Lord and spurred his horse to close the distance between them.

Mechnes stood in his stirrups, drew back his spear arm, and breathed a short prayer to the silent heavens.

"If there be Gods, let them favor me now."

He released the spear. It sailed in a straight line toward the Mage King, hit the regent and toppled him from his horse. Shouts of consternation overtook the ranks of Moisehén, and their lines buckled against the Syrnte.

Chapter 43

Eolyn cried out as pain seared through her. She clutched her shoulder, dizzy and nauseous, fighting for each breath, arm numb from shock.

The mages who had been holding the circle with her ceased their chanting and watched with confused and wary expressions.

"No," she murmured, blinking back the haze as an icy finger of dread wrapped around her heart. "Akmael..."

She abandoned the circle and ran down slope. A mage warrior assigned to Eolyn's guard intercepted her.

"Milady!" He caught her arm, bringing her momentum to a sudden painful halt. "You can go no further."

She shook him off, eyes fixed on the battle. "Where is he? Where is the King?"

Below, chaos was taking hold. There was no sign of Akmael, only his rearing horse, frightened and trapped inside a mass of fighting men. The two armies writhed together like giant serpents in their death throes.

A triumphant howl echoed across the field. "Slain! The Mage King is slain!"

Horns sounded, and the Syrnte let forth a deafening roar of victory. Men began to break away from the ranks of Moisehén, an ominous trickle that preceded frenzied retreat. The rout, Eolyn knew, would be merciless.

"Milady." The mage warrior demanded her attention. "We must leave now."

The rest of her guards had gathered around them, some already mounted, one of them with her mare in hand.

"He is not dead." Eolyn took her horse by the bridle and pressed her forehead against the flat of its snout, whispering words of encouragement in a language learned long ago.

"Gods grant that you be right, but it changes nothing. The battle is lost, and I have my orders."

"Your orders are to protect me." She mounted, Tzeremond's staff in hand, Kel'Barú at her hip. "Protect me then, as I ride to the aid of our King."

She spurred her horse into a gallop, charging downhill toward the heat of the fray, ignoring the guards' shouts of consternation. Stragglers who had begun their retreat paused at her passing, watching the maga's descent with bewildered expressions. On the edge of the battle she reined back, nostrils flaring at the sting of blood, stomach roiling at the sight of so many mutilated men.

"Gods help me," she murmured, invoking the spirit of her dead mother. "Beloved Kaie, Maga Warrior, woman of my blood, give me strength."

The guards were approaching, hooves pounding against the earth while they shouted their demands to halt. Eolyn did not look back, but waited, measuring the pace of their pursuit. Just before they reached her position, she spurred the mare forward again, forcing them to follow.

She kept her eyes on Akmael's horse as they plunged into a river of death. The cacophony of metal and men driven mad overwhelmed her senses. Turbulent currents of fighting impeded her pace and threatened to drag her down to a bloody death. The guards managed to surround her, defending her with sword and shield, their entreaties for retreat silenced by the will to survive. Under their protection she pushed forward, conserving her magic as much as she could while invoking quick and scalding flames to fend off her attackers.

At last a path opened between her and Akmael's horse. She sprang forward, breaking free of the circle of guards and invoking the speed of the wind.

She did not see the Syrnte warrior until it was too late. His sword flew from his hand, a flash of deadly light that sank deep into her horse's neck. The animal reared, throwing Eolyn as it crumpled to its knees screaming. She hit the ground hard, bones cracking upon impact, breath knocked from her lungs. Gasping, she scrambled to regain her footing, limbs throbbing with pain, tears threatening to blur her vision. Somehow Tzeremond's staff remained in her grip, and she used it to steady her spirit, to reach for the power of the earth.

A Syrnte soldier rushed her with sword raised, but his advance was stopped short by a shout from the man who had brought down her horse. That man approached now, triumph in his gate, his blood-spattered face twisted into a malicious smile.

"Maga Eolyn," he said, pausing at a distance. "I am Lord Mechnes. Do you come to reclaim the body of your dead King, or to pay homage to your new master?"

"A maga has no master." Her voice was hoarse, and she fought to still the tremor in her hands. "Save the Gods who rule her heart."

"I will take your heart then." He accepted a sword from one of his comrades. Eolyn remembered how swift and sure the first had flown from his grip. "Though I may be obliged to cut it out."

Kel'Baru shivered at her side, restless in its hilt, eager for this man's blood. She ignored the temptation of its call. To go after this man with a sword would be the greatest of all her follies. Instead she adjusted her grip on Tzeremond's staff, focused on the steady hum at its core.

"You are finished here, Lord Mechnes," she said. "In the name of the King, I bid you leave these lands. You and all your men. I will not ask again."

"It is your King who is finished, maga. I rule Moisehén now. And I bid you, set aside your staff and kneel before me, or you will find this sword lodged between your pretty breasts."

Maehechnahm, she replied, *arrat saufini*

Tzeremond's staff jumped at her call, an ominous surge of power.

The man flung his sword in a sure straight path.

Ehekaht neurai!

Lightning tunneled from the earth and travelled through the rowan staff, bursting from its crystal head in an explosion of white fire that lanced at Eolyn's opponent and threw him to the ground, trapping him in a luminous net. Eolyn clung to Tzeremond's staff, channeling all power of life and limb into its deadly fire, bracing for the impact of the Syrnte sword in desperate hope that her enemy would perish before his blade parted her sternum. Fire crackled over his body and he screamed in agony, but Eolyn did not relent until his cries faded and the stench of burnt flesh filled the air.

Eolyn released the curse. Her hair was singed. The palms of her hands were blackened and raw. Her ears rang. She coughed and gagged and drew a rattling breath. Running a sore hand over chest and abdomen, she found herself whole and unharmed. The flame had deflected Lord Mechnes's sword, which lay useless on the ground, blade tarnished, leather wrappings of the hilt melted away.

Warily she approached her victim, remembering the last time she had attempted this curse, how Tzeremond had survived its impact and risen again, vanquishing the maga and banishing her soul to the Underworld. Drawing Kel'Baru, she held the faithful blade in front of her, stepping close and setting the tip of the sword at Mechnes's throat.

The man wheezed, sputtered, and lay still. He turned his head as if to look at her, though his soot-encrusted eyes had been burned white by the curse. He lifted a trembling hand toward her face.

"Adiana." His voice was reduced to a ragged whisper, tinged with mirth and melancholy. "I knew it would be you."

"What?" Eolyn's bewilderment gave way to realization and then horror as his limbs went limp. She let go of the sword and fell to her knees. Taking the Syrnte warrior by the shoulders she shook him and slapped him across the face. "No! You cannot die. Not until you tell me what you have done with her!"

Eolyn beat her fists upon the dead man's chest, tears streaming down her cheeks, imploring him to speak until rough hands took hold of her and dragged her away.

"Maga Eolyn." The man repeated her name, holding her gently by the shoulders until her ravings ceased and she looked at him as if awakening from a dark and terrible dream. It was one of the guards, face bloodied and dripping with sweat. He regarded Eolyn as if seeing her for the first time. Releasing her abruptly, he backed away, head bowed, a mix of respect and fear in his eyes.

"Look, Maga Eolyn." He gestured down slope. "Look at what you have done."

Along the length of the field of battle, the last of the Syrnte fled before the banners of Moisehén. Stragglers were being hacked down, scattered bodies looted by the King's soldiers.

Eolyn turned away from the slaughter, bile rising in her throat. In war, even victory seemed an ugly thing. "Where is the King?"

The guard nodded grimly in the direction of a group of knights and soldiers. Akmael lay splayed on the ground at their feet, surrounded by the corpses of men who had tried to protect him.

At last unhindered, Eolyn rushed to his side. Her heart stopped at the sight of his face, ash-gray and steeped in death, the skin around his lips and eyes a sickly blue. The spear that had brought him down had since dislodged, whether during the fall from his horse or by his own hand she could not know. Blades had pierced his armor, and the lacerations had produced copious amounts of blood. Though the flow appeared to have stopped, Eolyn knew from his drenched tunic, and the dark and sticky pool beneath him, that he had already lost too much.

"Akmael." She knelt beside him, removed his gauntlets and took both hands in hers. His fingers were stiff and cold as ice. She felt for his pulse and after a long agonizing moment found it, fainter than the whisper of falling snow.

"Send for High Mage Rezlyn." She loosened the straps on his armor that she might expose the wounds and bind them. "And a litter for the King."

Chapter 44

Akmael was borne with reverence back to his tent, where High Mage Rezlyn and Eolyn stripped him, removed shards of metal and grit from his wounds, and washed them with wine and water. They applied poultices of yarrow, vervain, tormentil, and fox's clout. Rezlyn's expression was somber as he worked, and there was a haunted look to his eyes, as if he were reliving a terrible memory.

"What is it?" she asked when they finished binding the wounds. "What do you see?"

Rezlyn shook his head, hand hovering over the gash left by the spear. He spoke low that the others in the tent might not hear. "I see his father."

With a sharp intake of breath, Eolyn turned to Rezlyn's table of herbs and extracts, began gathering the ingredients for an infusion of ironwort and blood thistle.

"That was more complicated than this," she said. Kedehen had died from a spear wound, a mass of splintered wood that had taken out his eye and penetrated his skull, festering for days before releasing the old King from his agony. "Nearly impossible for anyone, mage or maga, to clean and heal. There was little you could have done, save wait for the Gods to make their choice."

Her hands shook, vials slipped from her fingers. A violent spasm coursed through her womb and she sank to the floor trembling. Cold sweat broke on her skin.

Rezlyn was at her side in an instant. "Maga Eolyn!"

She struggled to speak, each breath cut short by a new wave of pain.

"Please," she managed through frightened gasps, "please, Mage Rezlyn, ask them to go. Everyone."

The mage sent away the servants, knights, guards, and nobles who had been watching their work with anxious eyes. Then he returned to Eolyn and wrapped his cloak around her shoulders.

"You have asked too much of your magic today. You must rest, Maga Eolyn. Allow me to care for the King. I will prepare an infusion to calm your spirit."

"Mage Rezlyn." Eolyn clutched at the healer's arm, gave him a pleading look. "I am with child. The seed has just taken root, and I fear it is too young, too delicate to survive the curse I cast today. Ahmad-kupt…"

His eyes widened in realization. "It tries to claim the life inside of you." Rezlyn rested a hand upon her abdomen, listening with his touch, attempting to sooth the battle within. "The child's father is a warrior."

"How do you know?"

"Because he fights." Rezlyn's glance strayed toward the King. "He has sounded his battle cry through your pain. A meeker baby would slip quietly away, and you would not have known until morning when the blood of his defeat stained your bed."

Renewed spasms coursed through her.

"We will start with the root of winter sage to cleanse you of the curse, salvia to calm the muscles of the abdomen, and juniper and rosemary to protect the child." Rezlyn helped her up and guided her toward the King's bed.

"I am of no use to Akmael like this," she protested. "I would rather rest elsewhere than be an invalid at his side."

"It is his son that is in danger, is it not?"

Eolyn opened her mouth to object, bit her lip and looked away, unable to voice the lie.

"The son's spirit can help the father, just as the father's spirit can help the son," said High Mage Rezlyn. "This is powerful magic, and we cannot deny it to them."

She met his eyes, a challenge overriding the tremor in her voice. "You must not tell anyone."

Rezlyn responded with a gentle smile that enhanced his many wrinkles. "You need not worry, Maga Eolyn. If there is one thing I have demonstrated during my years of service to the House of Vortingen, it is my capacity for discretion."

Chapter 45

The Lost Souls of the Underworld dragged Eolyn down into their midst, the thousand tentacles of their thirst penetrating her spirit, seeking the life within. Eolyn clung to the world of the living on a thin thread of winter sage, the bitter root spooned into her mouth by High Mage Rezlyn, whose face appeared distorted and blurred in the dim candlelight whenever she surfaced from her nightmares. She took the magic he gave her and wove it around her unborn child, interlacing the ephemeral fabric with fresher aromas of rosemary and juniper, all the while beating off the Lost Souls until the protective cloak gathered strength, and the decaying spirits who sought her baby withered at its touch, at last slipping away toward eternal darkness.

At dawn she awoke exhausted.

Every muscle in her body ached, but the spasms had passed, and she could feel the child alive inside her womb. Mage Rezlyn brought her another infusion and examined her carefully. Bruises had bloomed purple and black over her ribs.

"I must have cracked them when I fell from my horse," Eolyn said. She had not even noticed the pain until now.

Rezlyn shook his head. "The Gods must favor you, Maga Eolyn, to have allowed you to charge into that melee, and come away with only this." He produced a linen bandage that he used to wrap her torso.

"Let me tend to the King," she said.

"The child is still delicate. Too much exertion could yet do harm."

"No task heals us better than the task of healing others."

Rezlyn's eyes warmed at the words of Aithne and Caradoc. "Very well. But when I order you to rest, Maga Eolyn, you must rest."

Akmael hovered between this world and the next, his skin translucent, his body cold and unresponsive. Eolyn kept a close eye on his wounds, changing the poultices and applying fresh bandages several times a day. On the third day after the battle, the High Mage Rezlyn inspected the laceration left by the spear, and on finding it clean, decided to have it cauterized. Akmael's body convulsed at the touch of the hot iron, a reaction that worried Eolyn but seemed to please the court physician. The stench of burnt flesh brought back unwanted memories of the curse of Ahmad-kupt, and when they applied the iron a second time, Eolyn turned away, eyes watering. Once they had sealed the wound, new poultices were prepared using fennel, elecampane, and Berenben cream to heal the blistering skin.

When they finished wrapping the bandages, Eolyn closed her eyes and set her hands upon Akmael, her spirit seeking out torn tissues and splintered bones, weaving what she could back together with her magic. It was exhausting work, and she could keep it up for only short periods of time before the flame of her magic wavered and Rezlyn withdrew her hands, breaking her focus and reminding her she also had a child to protect and heal.

He brought another cup of ironroot tea, and Eolyn delivered the infusion to Akmael's cracked lips in small spoonfuls.

"He lost too much blood," she said, "and these infusions, I fear, are not replacing it rapidly enough."

"Healing must obey the pace of the earth," Rezlyn replied.

Eolyn bristled at the echo of Doyenne Ghemena's words. "Why, then, is the pace of the earth so slow?"

A commotion outside the King's tent distracted them from their conversation. Raucous shouts and laughter filled the air, the sounds of men meeting in friendship. Mage Corey strode in, sunlight following him in a luminous cloud. He greeted Rezlyn with a hearty embrace, and turned to Eolyn, who set aside the cup and flew into his arms. He had washed recently and donned fresh clothes, but the smell of Moehn clung to him, of earth and crushed oak leaves, of pine and sweet herbs. It made Eolyn's heart ache for home.

Corey's silver-green eyes sparkled. "I never thought I'd receive such a greeting from you, Maga Eolyn."

She flushed and withdrew. "I never thought I'd be so glad to see you, Mage Corey. You must tell me of Mariel and Borten."

"They are alive and well, or were the last time I saw them. I have no reason to believe they have come to any harm. I suppose we shall know soon enough, with Lord Herensen on his way to chase the last of Syrnte out of Moehn. Ah!" He proffered the staff he carried, of polished oak and water crystal. "This, I believe, is yours. It is a fine instrument, Eolyn. Thank you for entrusting it to me."

Eolyn's heart swelled as she accepted the staff, her magic reconnecting with the familiar resonance of the South Woods. "Corey, the mage warriors who brought Rishona's head to Akmael spoke of you. They said they met you at the head of the Pass of Aerunden, and that you had followed the Syrnte army for days."

"It is true." He grinned. "I have become an honest hero."

Eolyn drew a breath, but the question faltered on her lips. "Perhaps you have heard I slew the general who commanded the Syrnte army."

"Yes, of course. Very impressive, but I assure you, the San'iloman was the more prestigious kill. You haven't bested me, Eolyn. Not yet."

"No." She held up her hands, trying to stay his humor. "Please, Corey. That is not what I meant. When he died, Lord Mechnes mentioned Adiana with his last breath, and I thought... I thought perhaps you had seen her. And the girls, Tasha and Catarina?"

Her voice trailed off at the change in his expression. She had never seen him like that, without even a hint of levity in his eyes.

"The girls are dead, Eolyn," he said. "I am sorry."

Eolyn beat back the rush of pain unleashed by these words, focusing on the one name that still held hope. "And Adiana?"

Corey regarded her in silence. "Adiana is beyond our reach, for the moment."

"Then she is still a prisoner of the Syrnte? Perhaps we can send word to Lord Herensen, and he could—"

"No." He waved her words away. "No, Eolyn. She is not with the Syrnte. She is safe, but her situation is complicated. I think it best that we do not speak of it now."

"But how can you—"

"No." He took her chin in his hand. "Look at you, Eolyn. How long have you have been carrying the weight of this kingdom on your shoulders? Your magic is spent and your aura faded. You must recuperate your strength, and bring the King back to our people. When these tasks are finished we will speak at length, and you will know the fates of all your sisters."

The maga drew a breath to protest.

"That is my final word," Corey said, and Eolyn understood from his tone there would be no more argument.

Reluctantly she returned to Akmael's side, troubled by Corey's unyielding silence, by the dark riddles that lurked behind his words.

Chapter 46

Eolyn took to sleeping at Akmael's side every night. No one questioned her decision to do so. His hands had grown warmer, but still he did not respond to her touch. Time and again she searched for him in her dreams. He eluded her like a shadow flickering on the edge of awareness.

At last one night she found him. Not Akmael the man, but a boy lost in the black forest, crouched beside a gnarled old tree, peering anxiously into the endless gloom.

I must find my mother, he said. *She left long ago and never returned.*

A woman's voice floated from the other side of the formless woods. Akmael sprang to his feet and ran toward it.

Eolyn cried out and caught his hand, pulling him back from the darkness, but the boy wrenched free of her hold.

I must find my father, he insisted. *He waits in the halls of my ancestors and has prepared a place for me.*

Many voices were calling to him now, old and young, woven together in a single tapestry of timeless song that settled in the high branches and glowed like an ivory moon. Akmael began to scale one of the giant trees.

There is light in the South Woods. Eolyn followed him in desperation. The shadowy branches slipped from her grasp and she lost her footing on ephemeral holds. *Light, and magic. A river with sparkling fish and trees that reach toward the sun.*

I have no need of such things. Truth waits for me, there. He nodded toward the luminous orb. *Truth and peace. The spirits of all those who have gone before. I will not delay any longer.*

Eolyn grasped Akmael's ankle, finding it surprisingly solid to the touch. The tree hissed and shivered, attempting to throw her from its nebulous trunk. *There is a child whom we have not yet met. He waits on the riverbank.*

Akmael paused in his ascent. *What child?*

Can you not hear his voice?

The trees wavered in a breeze that could not be felt.

Laughter slipped through the darkness, soft and high-pitched, and faded away.

The cloud of Akmael's uncertainty grew. Eolyn leapt upon it.

Come with me, she said.

He watched the orb above them, longing in his stance.

Your ancestors will wait.

Reluctantly he set his gaze upon her, ebony eyes in a pale dispassionate face.

I do not remember the way, he said.

Then let me show you.

Light began to filter through the forest as they walked hand in hand. The herbs at their feet drew color from the earth, sprouting flowers of ruby and amethyst. The trees solidified into twisting branches of crusty bark, adorned with emerald leaves and opal blossoms. The river murmured their names, and they paused on its banks, watching the flow of the water rise until it caressed their bare feet, cool and soothing, ever full of life. On the other side floated a silver star, formless and vibrant like the lanterns of the Guendes that once guided her home.

Eolyn awoke.

Daylight filtered into the tent. Akmael sat in the bed next to her, idly stroking her hair. His convalescence had left him pale and gaunt, but he was alive.

"High Mage Rezlyn has told me of all you did on the day of the battle," he said, "of how your courage inspired my men."

She could not find a voice to respond. Rising, she touched his face, struck with wonder. Akmael took her hand in his, pressed it to dry lips.

"Foolish woman," he murmured, but his tone was one of gentle admonishment. There were tears in his eyes. "Never disobey me again."

Chapter 47

Taesara studied her face in a mirror that had been crafted by the silversmiths of Antaria and gifted to her by the noble house of Velander on the occasion of her marriage to the Mage King. A finer mirror could not be found in all of Moisehén, yet the Queen longed for a cleaner image, something that reflected the warmth of her cheeks and the curve of her brows, something that made her look alive, not etched from stone.

She set the instrument aside. "This will not do. I never know what he sees when he looks upon me."

"He sees great beauty, my Lady Queen." Sonia was putting the finishing touches on Taesara's hair, tucking stray locks into the elaborate weave of her golden tresses, adorned with silver ribbons and sapphire crystals.

"Beauty is not enough." Taesara rolled these words on her tongue, their flavor new and bitter. She stood abruptly and distanced herself from Sonia, smoothing the folds of her purple gown, fingering the braids of her hair.

"Trust me, my Lady Queen," said Sonia. "Men are hungry after war. Your beauty will be enough."

"Not with that witch at his side."

"Even if he slept with a thousand harlots from here to Rhiemsaven, it would not matter. You are his Queen. Give him your adoration, grace him with your beauty, and he will come to you. Tonight."

Taesara shivered at the thought. How could something so distasteful for a woman be so sought after by men, and so necessary for bearing children?

Horns blasted from the towers of the fortress. Taesara's belly tightened like a fist.

"That is the third call, my Lady Queen."

"I know!" she snapped.

The lady stiffened and bowed in deference. "There is little time left, if it still be your will to meet the King before the gates."

Taesara's will or not, it had to be done.

Lord Penamor waited for them in the antechamber, wearing the colors and sigil of Roenfyn. He assessed his niece with a sharp gaze, eyes lingering on her exposed hair. The blood rose to Taesara's cheeks. It felt vulgar and unclean to forego a cap and veil, but Sonia had insisted this would arouse the Mage King's appetite. *You may not be able to match the maga's witchery,* she had said, *but you can make use of her tricks.* Taesara fully expected her uncle to disapprove, but after a moment he merely snorted and gave a shrewd smile.

"Only a fool would not want you," he said.

"My Lord King is not a fool," Taesara replied. "My Lord King is bewitched."

His lips thinned into a straight line, a note of sympathy flickered behind his hardened eyes. They had made their peace following his outburst in her chambers, but that had not lessened Taesara's burden. She had to bring the Mage King to her bed soon, and conceive him a son, or all would be lost.

"What you need is a smile, to complete your charm." Penamor touched her cheek. "Come, Taesara. It is not as bad as all that. You have two kingdoms at your feet, and the beauty of the Gods in your face. That peasant whore has nothing but her miserable spells and foul potions."

"The Syrnte have handed her the kingdom," Taesara replied. "The people worship her now. The stories we've heard—"

"Lies and deceptions, all invented to make her into something she is not."

"Invented? An entire army witnessed—"

"Tales of war are always exaggerated. Even if there were some substance to what they say, it does not matter. Every lie can be made a truth, and every truth a lie. All it takes is patience, persistence, and a few well-placed words."

Taesara held her uncle's gaze. She could find no flaw with his reasoning, and this realization at once troubled her and gave her hope.

"My Lady Queen." Sonia spoke with urgency. "Please, we must leave at once."

A festive atmosphere greeted the Queen's entourage as they descended from the castle. Laughter and song, improvised music and dance, followed them from the central square to the city gates. The happy shouts in praise of Queen Taesara lifted her spirits, though the cobblestone streets were not nearly as crowded as she expected. When they reached the entrance to the City, Taesara saw why: The people of Moisehén had rushed forth to meet their King, in a rapturous tide that had flooded the fields beyond the city walls with a sea of celebration.

Taesara had thought her heart could not sink lower than it had in days recently passed, when the maga's curse had stolen away her unborn child. But she was not prepared to see the witch riding in triumph at the Mage King's side, receiving the enthusiastic adoration of their people. Women and children crowded toward the maga, showering her with white lilies until her arms overflowed with fragrant blossoms. Men lifted cups overflowing with ale. "Long live King Akmael!" they cried, and intermingled with this came the equally passionate declaration, "Gods protect the Maga!"

"May the demons take her," muttered Penamor.

Taesara spurred her horse forward, obliging the guards to open a path toward her liege. The people seemed intent on keeping her away, and desperation mounted with every moment that separated her from the King and his mistress. At long last the fact of her royal presence rippled through the chaos, and the people parted to make way.

Urging her mount into a canter, Taesara closed the distance until the Mage King's imposing gaze settled upon her. She stopped abruptly, praying the insecurity that plagued her every breath did not show in the set of her shoulders or the lines of her face.

"We welcome you, my Lord King, on this most happy day," she said.

The King nodded, first to her and then to Penamor at her side. The war had left his face thin and without color. Food, sun, and sufficient repose would change that, Taesara knew, but nothing would ever diminish the darkness of intent behind those stony eyes, an ominous look that made her shiver from the very first day she had met him, and that had intensified during his confrontation with the Syrnte.

"Thank you, Taesara," he said. "Lord Penamor."

"On behalf of Roenfyn, I congratulate you, King Akmael," said Penamor. "Please know that my liege is most ready to offer any assistance you require, as peace and order are restored to your lands."

"King Lyanos' offer is most gracious," the King acknowledged.

Taesara hastened to brighten her smile, trying to awaken his warmth with an expansive gesture of her arm. "Shall we continue to the City, my Lord King? A feast awaits us in the castle hall. Food, drink, well-deserved rest and revelry for my beloved husband and his loyal men."

The maga, seeming to at last understand she was not welcome, signaled her mount to move aside, but the King raised his hand to stop her.

"Maga Eolyn, have I given you leave to go?"

"No, my Lord King." The witch had the presence of mind to appear abashed. She met the Queen's stare, and then looked to the King. "I meant no insult. I simply thought—"

"This victory is yours as much as it is mine," he said. "We will ride through the City gates together."

Taesara felt a tremor at the base of her spine, a knot of anger that threatened to explode in screams of rage. She tightened her grip on the reins.

"Of course, Maga Eolyn," she said, forcing her smile. "My Lord King is right in this as he is all things. We have heard many tales of your heroism during the battle against the Syrnte. We must let the people pay you due homage."

If the Mage King appreciated Taesara's dignified surrender, he made no indication. The maga did not meet Taesara's eyes as they rode past. A bold harlot she may be, thought Taesara, but not bold enough to gloat in her victory.

As Queen's entourage fell into place behind the King's guard, Taesara's uncle drew close. "You are not to allow her to sit at his side during the banquet."

Taesara shrugged. Always she had found her uncle's demeanor intimidating, but in this moment, he only amused her. "She will sit at his side, uncle. And sleep in his bed. Tonight and every night, for many years to come."

"Do not speak like that," he insisted between gritted teeth. "We are far from finished with this matter. I will not see you further humiliated. King Akmael knows the consequences should he so much as dare…"

Taesara shut out Penamor's words.

She drew a deep breath, watched the waving flags and raised spears, let the shouts of the people fade into the background. Her anger was dissolving under an unexpected lightness of being. The burden of the Mage King was being passed on to that woman, and Taesara was surprised to discover she no longer cared. She wanted nothing more of this violent man, of his strange kingdom, of these terrible sorrows.

She would take Elisiara away from this place. Roenfyn might judge Princess Taesara unfit to marry again, but they would give her refuge nonetheless. She and her daughter could devote their lives to a quiet cause among the Sisters of Humility, or the Servants of the Poor.

No longer would they be plagued by the ambitions of men and sorcerers.

No longer would they live in fear of the poisonous reach of the Witch of Moisehén.

"Taesara!" Her uncle's harsh rebuke broke through her thoughts. "Are you listening?"

The world came back into focus: the chaos of voice and song, the stench of horse and sweat, the heavy gait of a thousand men, banners of silver and purple fluttering in the wind.

"Yes, uncle," she said. "I am listening."

But his words no longer held any power over her.

Chapter 48

"There will be war."

Tzetobar's words hung over the High Mages assembled. They had arrived in secret, transformed into creatures that slipped unnoticed through the night, their gathering protected by formidable wards.

Corey studied them all, trying to divine the thoughts behind each countenance.

"Roenfyn's soldiers are inferior to ours," Thelyn said smoothly, "and they have no magic. King Lyanos will be especially wary, now that that we have defeated one of the greatest armies of the eastern kingdoms."

"They could ally with Galia or the kingdoms of the Paramen Mountains." Old Tzetobar drew a wheezing breath and rubbed his forehead. "There are still many exiles who wish to avenge Kedehen's legacy and claim this kingdom as their own."

"Roenfyn fears Galia as much as they fear us, perhaps more," Thelyn countered. "I find it difficult to imagine they would grant Galian wizards safe passage across their lands."

"That still leaves the Mountain Warriors," interceded Sir Galison, "some of whom supported the insurgent Ernan."

"I suspect the Mountain People have lost interest in our affairs," Corey said. "They united with Ernan because of their desire to see women's magic restored. That goal has been achieved."

"Women's magic has not been restored," Rezlyn's voice was somber, his aspect grim. "The bans were lifted, but no exile has returned despite the King's generous invitation. After four years, we have but one High Maga and two young girls who cling to her shadow. A tenuous spark at best."

Corey shrugged. "We have made an honest effort."

"The Mountain People will judge by our successes," replied Rezlyn, "not by our efforts."

"Success will come." Tzetobar lifted his hands to stall their argument. "Maga Eolyn will start a new *Aekelahr* inside this City, with our full support and the protection of the King. That was decided long ago. What is under discussion here is whether she should be granted the Crown as well."

After a long uncertain silence, Sir Galison asked, "Do we have a choice?"

Corey allowed himself a dry laugh, though no one seemed to share his amusement.

"We may not have a choice," said Tzetobar, "but we can still be the voice of prudence."

"At what cost?" Thelyn gestured to include everyone present. "Look at us. There are more High Mages in Moisehén than there have been in a generation, and yet our numbers on the Council dwindle. Will he throw us out as well, if we oppose his desire to anoint a new Queen? And if he does, who then will be the voice of prudence when the Mage King seeks to use his power in ways that are truly unacceptable?"

"This is unacceptable," interjected Galison. "Dissolving the contract with Roenfyn is an insult to Taesara and her people."

"Perhaps." Thelyn sat back, eyeing the younger mage. "Though Roenfyn is hardly our greatest threat."

Corey rolled his eyes. "Spare us your riddles, Thelyn. We have no time for them."

A smile touched Thelyn's lips. "I merely repeat what I have already said to the company here assembled, what I concluded from my study of the annals recovered from Tzeremond's library. If the Naether Demons now have the power to escape their confinement with aid, as Corey suspects they do, then our best hope for protection is a perfect integration of male and female magic, a true resurrection of the traditions of Aithne and Caradoc."

"It is one thing to espouse the integration of male and female magic," Galison countered, "quite another to commit the folly our King proposes. And there is another consideration of greater importance: This kingdom hangs on a precipice until a prince is born. Queen Taesara has proven her fertility, and her fidelity is without reproach. The same cannot be said of Maga Eolyn."

"Eolyn cannot be bound to any man," Corey agreed. "The path of Aithne is incompatible with the burdens of a Queen of Vortingen."

Tzetobar cleared his throat and exchanged a cautious glance with Rezlyn.

Corey pinned them both with a hard gaze. "What? What is it that you have not shared with us?"

"You must understand, Mage Corey." Tzetobar assumed a conciliatory tone that only raised the mage's ire. "We have both been under oath, I to the King, and High Mage Rezlyn to Maga Eolyn, whom he tended after the battle at Rhiemsaven."

Realization hit Corey like the cold wind before a violent storm. He stood, fists clenched. "By the Gods. She is with child?"

"The King's child," Rezlyn said, "by her own admission."

"She lies," Galison said.

"Eolyn does not lie," replied Corey, though the maga's tryst with Borten sprang fresh to his memory. "That is one vice the maga has not yet learned."

"The King has written a new will," Tzetobar said. "It was drafted before he departed for Rhiemsaven, one copy left in my care, the other with Maga Eolyn. He recognizes her son as his own and names him heir to the throne of Moisehén."

The air, already warm and humid, became stifling. Corey moved to a nearby window, craving a fresh breeze and the soft sounds of the night, but both were muted by the wards that protected their conversation.

Darkness shrouded the City.

Corey struck his fist against the sill.

Curse you, Eolyn.

How could a woman so adept, with such remarkable talent and strength of spirit, be so foolish when it came to matters of the heart?

"If that child is born a bastard," Corey said, "it will tear this kingdom apart."

No one questioned his conclusion.

Tzetobar and Rezlyn, the oldest among them, met Corey's gaze with haunted eyes. They had lived through the collapse of the Old Orders and the brutal purges that followed. Thelyn and Corey had survived the war as children and grown up navigating the labyrinthine politics of the aftermath. Galison had come of age in a time of cautious hope.

For all of them, war against another kingdom—even a weak and insignificant one such as Roenfyn—was a danger best avoided. But war amongst themselves? That was unspeakable, a horror that must never be suffered again.

"All of you act as if this is a regrettable circumstance for which we will pay dearly," said Thelyn. "Yet I say it is an opportunity. It would be most strategic to position the maga as close to the Mage King as possible. Let her give him his prince. King Akmael respects Maga Eolyn, even heeds her advice. We can take advantage of this by ensuring that her counsel systematically reflects our own."

Galison snorted. "And how do you expect to accomplish that?"

"It may not be as difficult as you imagine. Maga Eolyn has shown unfailing respect and a willingness to cooperate with us all. Tzetobar, Rezlyn, myself, and other mages have established a positive rapport with her, one that is not burdened by rancor or past resentments. And there is a brother among us—" Thelyn cast a meaningful look at Mage Corey. "—who holds her ear like no other."

Corey chuckled and clapped his friend on the shoulder as he reclaimed his seat. "You amuse me, Thelyn. I appreciate your faith in my silver tongue, but Eolyn is as stubborn as Aithne herself. She has never had any patience for my wisdom."

"She will learn patience," said Thelyn, "if she is made Queen."

Corey held Thelyn's gaze. Beneath all of this, there was a deeper ache that plagued him, a nameless regret that struggled to rise above the talk of war, intrigue, and the uncertain future of magic. He swallowed the bitter taste on his tongue.

"I hope you are right, old friend," he said. "I hope you are right."

Chapter 49

Late afternoon sun cut through the windows of the East Tower, illuminating Eolyn's chambers in ribbons of burgundy and gold. Enchanted by the warm colors, the maga caught the strands in her fingers and showed Ghemena how to weave them into butterflies of light. The girl learned the game effortlessly, and together they danced in a cloud of fluttering sparks until a guard interrupted their laughter to announce the unexpected arrival of Mariel and Sir Borten.

The young maga rushed into her tutor's arms, shedding tears of joy while Eolyn kissed her face and gave thanks to the Gods. Ghemena squealed as Borten lifted her high, swung the girl around and caught her in a bear's embrace. His face was weathered but otherwise unchanged. When he set Ghemena down and turned to Eolyn, the same deep kindness glowed steady in his blue eyes. Eolyn shifted awkwardly on her feet, embarrassed by the realization that she did not know what to say, where to begin even, given all that had come to pass.

Borten took her hand and touched it to his forehead.

"Maga Eolyn," he said.

"Sir Borten." The formality felt appropriate and yet misplaced. Eolyn remembered well the desire behind his touch, the heat of his kiss, and the heartbreak of their parting. It all seemed a strange dream now, an ephemeral moment that had slipped away with the shadows of the night. "How very good it is to see you again."

"We've heard everything about the battle." The summer sun had colored Mariel's face so that her green eyes looked more enchanting than ever. She wrapped her arm around Eolyn's waist. "Everyone talks about it everywhere we go. Is it true what they say, that you slew the Syrnte General and won the battle all by yourself?"

Eolyn laughed. "No, Mariel. The stories exaggerate. All of us defeated the Syrnte together. The Mage King and his army, the men who protected me, and without Tzeremond's staff, I might have never—"

"You must not understate your achievements, Eolyn," Borten said quietly. "Without your magic, this kingdom would have been lost."

Eolyn blinked and glanced away. Images of the world they once knew flooded her heart: the *Aekelahr* and its fragrant garden, her small library and the humble stables, spring in the South Woods, Summer Solstice in the town of Moehn. All of it destroyed in the space of a few weeks. "My magic was not enough."

"Sir Borten is teaching me how to use the sword!" Mariel announced.

Eolyn caught Borten's eyes with a smile. "Is that so?"

"I've learned so much already. I want to show you, Maga Eolyn, and then we can practice together."

"She is a good student," said Borten. "I hope you do not object."

"Object?" Eolyn replied. "No, of course not. It is the King who might object. He granted me permission to use Kel'Barú, but the edict that prohibits magas from learning weaponry still stands. I will speak to him, however. I want Mariel to have these skills, and Ghemena as well. All of my students who are so inclined must be allowed this privilege."

Ghemena clapped her hands in glee. "We'll start over now, won't we? The four of us will go home together, and we'll find more sisters, and everyone will have staves *and* swords!"

Her declaration was met with awkward silence. Eolyn drew the girl close. "Perhaps, Ghemena, in time. There is so much yet to be decided."

"Moehn has hard months ahead of it," said Mariel. "No one knows where the food will come from. The Syrnte did not leave much behind."

"Ours are a hearty people. They are not unused to hardship," Borten replied, "and there is yet time for a second harvest. We will survive the winter and rebuild in the spring."

"You will go back soon, then?" Eolyn asked.

"I have decided to petition for stewardship of Moehn. Feroden's family was destroyed, save for young Markl, whom I hope to take on as my ward. The rest of our nobility are in shambles. The people of Moehn have no one to lead them—no one capable of leading them—in times like this."

"You would be a most worthy choice, Sir Borten," she said, though it saddened her to acknowledge this. Without Borten she would have few friends in the City, no one in whom she could completely trust.

"Thank you, Maga Eolyn." He cleared his throat and glanced away, a frown upon his brow. "Your return to the highlands would be most welcome. With your power to heal, to lead, to give people hope—"

The guard returned, announcing the arrival of High Mage Thelyn, who swept into the room wearing the full regalia of his station, a staff of polished cherry wood in hand.

A knot of doubt settled in Eolyn's gut, but she greeted the Council Member with a gracious smile and introduced him to her companions. The mage took her hand and bowed, lifting her fingers to his forehead.

"It is done." He straightened. "Taesara is no longer Queen of Moisehén."

"I see." Eolyn did not know how else to respond. The heavy weight of Borten's silence settled on her shoulders.

"How can that be?" Mariel asked, eyes wide and uncomprehending. "Our Queen is no longer a queen?"

"The King has made it so, and his decision has met with the Council's approval," Thelyn replied. "He requests to see you at once, Maga Eolyn. It is my honor to escort you into his presence."

"What for?" Ghemena demanded.

Thelyn arched one brow, amusement in his dark eyes. "We do not question the King's will, young Ghemena, but if you must know, he is poised to offer Maga Eolyn the highest honor conceivable for a woman of Moisehén. I suggest that we do not keep him waiting."

"But I don't understand," said Mariel. "Maga Eolyn, I thought you and Sir Borten—"

"Mariel." Borten's reproach was quiet but firm.

Mariel bit her lip and stared in confusion at the floor.

"I think you should leave." Ghemena took a stance between Eolyn and the mage. "I think you should go away right now and never come back!"

"Ghemena, please." Eolyn drew the girl away, stroking her ash blond hair. The decision had come so quickly, more quickly than she had ever thought possible. And to have it announced in this of all moments, when what little was left of her family had just been restored to her. "High Mage Thelyn, you must have patience with us. While this news is not entirely unexpected, it is . . . unsettling. I need a moment with my students. You may wait in the antechamber. I will be with you shortly."

Thelyn's gaze flicked toward Borten then back to Eolyn. He gave a stiff bow and left the room, shutting the door quietly behind him.

"We should run away," Ghemena said, "before the Mage King casts his final spell and makes you his slave forever. We can hide in the South Woods, and Borten can protect us. No one will find us there."

Eolyn gave her a gentle smile, saddened by the direction the girl's imagination had taken. "Ghemena, you know such spells do not exist, not in the traditions of Moisehén."

"That man is not part of our traditions."

"The Mage Kings are a new tradition," Eolyn replied, "one sanctioned by the Gods for two generations."

"Does this mean you aren't coming back to Moehn?" asked Mariel. "You're going to stay here now? Forever?"

"You cannot say yes to him!" Ghemena's face was red with fury.

"This is Maga Eolyn's decision, not yours." Borten's words came sharp.

Ghemena looked at him as if she were betrayed. "But she—"

"You have said enough. Maga Eolyn understands your concerns, and High Mage Thelyn is right. It is not wise to keep the King waiting." Borten regarded Eolyn, his expression strained between determination and resignation. He gave a bitter smile. "It seems the Gods have brought us back together for the simple purpose of finishing what we had already ended."

"Borten, I—"

"No." He lifted his hand to stop her. "No more words. Go, Eolyn. Go and meet your destiny."

She hesitated, knowing that if she turned away from them now, all hope of recuperating the world they once knew would be forsaken.

"Ghemena," Eolyn began, but the girl turned on her heel and stalked over to one of the broad windows that faced south. There she curled up on a chair, hugged her knees to her chest, and stared wordlessly at the landscape beyond.

Lips drawn in a thin line, Borten went to comfort her.

Eolyn drew her older student close and spoke in gentle tones. "Mariel, you must understand. To turn away from this path would be a betrayal of my own destiny."

"Your destiny is to abandon us?" Mariel's eyes were damp, her fingers cold.

"I am not abandoning you. I want you and Ghemena to stay with me, to complete your instruction, and to petition for a staff. If the Gods grant your petition, I intend to teach you the ways of High Magic, just as I would have in Moehn. We can establish a new coven here, within the walls of this city."

"It won't be the same."

"No, nothing will ever be the same again. The war saw to that."

"Please don't say that," Mariel whispered, tears streaming down her cheeks. "We've travelled so far, and I thought that once we were together again, once we went home. . ."

Eolyn drew her into a tight embrace, heart breaking under the burden of her own doubts.

"We are together again," she said. "That is what matters most."

Chapter 50

High Mage Thelyn led Eolyn through winding corridors and inner courtyards, until they emerged along the northern flank of the castle wall and paused in front of a simple wooden door.

Eolyn drew a breath of surprise when she recognized it. "But this is—"

"—the entrance to the Foundation of Vortingen, yes."

"I thought women were not allowed."

"Anyone is allowed, if the King wills it. In the time of Urien, the magas in his favor came to this place to celebrate the High Holidays. All that ended with Kedehen's reign, of course, but Briana was brought here to consummate the union between the House of Vortingen and the Clan of East Selen. King Akmael has not granted this privilege to any woman, not even to Taesara of Roenfyn, until today."

Thelyn signaled the guards to retreat a short distance, invoked a sound ward, and continued in quiet tones. "Forgive my boldness, Maga Eolyn, but you must understand that we are in a grave moment. While not without precedent, the King's decision has been a difficult one, unacceptable for many, though now it will be obeyed by all. Your part in this matter has not been inconsequential—"

"My part? I was not even asked—"

"You will be asked, now. I feel compelled to warn you that any answer other than one that meets with the King's pleasure cannot be considered. I say this for your good, and for the good of all our people."

Eolyn stared at him, indignation rising in her veins. "I assure you, Mage Thelyn, I am quite capable of making my own decisions."

"Then I trust you will make a wise one." Thelyn opened the door and stepped away. "You must enter alone. I cannot follow."

Eolyn slipped into the dark corridor, passing her fingers along the cold wall as she walked. Powerful currents of magic pulsed inside the rock, sparking at her touch. Eolyn wondered what secrets the coarsely hewn stones would reveal if she closed her eyes and surrendered to their will.

Without warning the passage opened onto a wide grassy knoll. Scattered trees lined the cliff edges. At the center, a circle of pale monoliths reached toward the sky. The clouds were beginning to burn with vermilion-pink tones of sunset. Akmael stood among the long shadows, contemplating a low-slung outcrop of granite. A tongue of silver flame flickered idly over the palm of his hand. He looked up as she approached.

"Eolyn," he said. "At last."

Humbled by the grandeur of the place, Eolyn paused just outside the circle. She could feel the spirit of Dragon, still breathing fire into the heart of Vortingen's mountain.

"Come." Akmael extended his hand. "I want to show you everything."

Eolyn removed her shoes. Side by side they walked along the cliff edge, grass cool beneath her feet, the landscape illuminated in the copper shades of late afternoon. Toward the east, rolling hills led to the dark forests of Selen. Westward over fields and pastures lay the distant wastes of Faernvorn. In the north, Eolyn could just make out the stoic gray face of the Eastern Surmaeg.

"It is said that when Dragon first appeared to Vortingen, he flew from the north. The crown he brought was retrieved from the highest reaches of the Surmaeg. Messenger landed here." Akmael indicated the spot, unmarked saved for a ring of fragrant purple Aethne. "Vortingen had recently defeated the People of Thunder, and his ferocity in battle was legendary. Nothing could stay his blade or instill fear in his heart. Yet when the wind from Dragon's wings threw down the trees, when the mountain thundered beneath his feet, when Dragon's fiery breath broke open the night, the Warrior Chief fell prostrate and wept."

Flames danced behind Akmael's dark eyes, every gesture was filled with excitement. Eolyn had not witnessed such carefree enthusiasm since he was a child in the South Woods.

"Dragon set his scorching breath upon the mountain's face, and when the ground was burned away Vortingen saw this slab of granite." Akmael led her back among the monoliths. "In it was revealed all the lands that would come under our stewardship:

Moisehén, Moehn, Selen, and Selkynsen. As the kingdom was consolidated by Vortingen's heirs, monoliths were brought from each of the four provinces to complete this circle and keep watch over the territories given to the descendents of Caradoc and Aithne."

He paused, a frown furrowing his brow as he studied the stone map. "Perhaps we have not always fulfilled our duty as the Gods envisioned, but it is a difficult task to maintain peace among a people so prone to war. I have been burdened by my father's legacy and uncertain at times how to continue. Eolyn." He took her hand and searched her face. "You never told me in what form Dragon appeared to you when you petitioned for your staff."

Eolyn's breath quickened. She hesitated, accustomed to guarding this secret deep inside her heart. "You never told me about your fast, either."

Akmael laughed. "I was quite prepared to do so, Maga Eolyn. There was nothing I wanted more than to boast about all my visions, but as I recall that was the day you threw me out of the South Woods and told me never to come back."

"I did no such thing," she countered. "You knew what the Doyenne had asked of me. I told you that you could come back when I finished my training in High Magic."

"And how long was that going to be? Five years? Six? An eternity, as far as this young prince was concerned." The amusement faded from his eyes. "Twice the Gods have asked me to wait for you, and twice I have failed. Their patience must be beyond measure, to have brought us back to this moment again."

"I don't understand."

He took Eolyn's hand and drew her close. "Tell me your story, Eolyn, for I very much wish to tell you mine."

"I expected a quiet creature." The words felt strange on her tongue. Perhaps they had been kept in silence for too long. "A marten perhaps, or a dormouse."

"I hoped for a bear, myself, or a snow tiger."

"I spent the night in Lynx's lair. As dawn broke, I searched every rock and crevice along the ridge, but found nothing. Not even an ant or a spider. I had never seen a place so devoid of life, and my anticipation faltered toward despair."

"The same happened to me," said Akmael. "I was terrified. I was my father's only son, after all. What would happen if the Gods refused my petition? How could I ever hope to wear the Crown?"

"Then I saw her, like jewel sailing above the fog that shrouded the forest."

"When his shadow passed over me, I understood."

Eolyn caught her breath.

"Why have we not spoken of this before?" she whispered.

He brought her fingers to his lips, breathed in the scent of her hands. "Tell me more."

They spoke together, phrases intertwining until their memories merged into a single song, a shared dream, an invocation offered to the heavens:

Her scales shone like crystal
His were obsidian, tinged with rose
Reflecting all the colors of the dawn
As if forged from a Galian volcano
She shattered the sword you had given me
He demanded a lock of your hair
And placed a shard at the heart of my staff
And embedded the silky strands in its crystal head
Because every heart must have a thread of steel
Because the roots of power are found in love
From the beginning she said
In the end he told me
That a new era would start with this journey
That my magic would be incomplete until I found you.

A mist clouded Eolyn's vision. The Mage King drew her into his arms, and she rested her head against his chest, listening to the steady rhythm of his heart.

Overhead, stars began to glimmer in the darkening firmament.

"Nothing more shall divide us after this day." Akmael's voice was husky. "Everything I once called mine I surrender to you: my heart, my magic, this fortress, the kingdom and people entrusted to me. The Gods appointed me as their steward." He set his lips upon hers, warm with the promise of pleasures to come. "But you, Eolyn, are the steward of us all."

Chapter 51

Guards escorted Mage Corey to the new Queen's apartments, a haven of light and color where living plants occupied every available shelf and table. Eolyn was seated with one of the ladies appointed to her service, a dark-haired beauty that Corey recognized as one of Herensen's many nieces. They made a lovely picture, the light from the windows painting a golden sheen around their heads as they studied a heavy tome on their laps. At their side stood Ghemena, restless on her feet, a scowl on her young face.

A warm smile spread through Eolyn's eyes as she stood to receive him. "Mage Corey. How good it is to see you."

"Thank you, my Lady Queen." Corey bowed low, touching her fingers to his forehead. The formality irked him. He would have much preferred the spontaneous embrace they had shared in Rhiemsaven, but he understood such effusive displays of friendship were no longer advisable. He turned to acknowledge the others. "Lady Vinelia, Maga Ghemena."

Herensen's niece responded with an elegant courtesy, but Ghemena refused to acknowledge his presence. Corey ignored the slight and instructed the servant behind him to place a large object covered in blue silk on a nearby table.

"I have brought something for you, my Lady Queen. A wedding gift, of sorts, but I would..." He faltered. As long as he had put this off, the task had not grown any easier.

Understanding filled Eolyn's countenance. She spoke quickly. "You would speak with me in private. Of course. Elia, please take Ghemena to the courtyard. Mariel will be having her lessons with Sir Borten at this hour. Perhaps Ghemena can join them. Inform the servants I am to be left undisturbed."

Lady Vinelia and Ghemena departed, the latter pinning Corey with a baleful stare.

Eolyn closed the book she had been reading, a compendium of the sigils of Moisehén.

"I should be teaching magic, not learning politics," she said.

"You will have your coven soon enough, safe inside this City. No one will burn your *Aekelahr* or scatter your sisters again," Corey replied.

"It will be more secure in some respects," she said, gaze turned inward. "Less in others."

Eolyn's aura had recovered its strength. The shadowy strand that had connected her to the Underworld was replaced by delicate threads of brilliant silver that wove through the rich colors, confirming the news Tzetobar and Rezlyn had shared, as well as the rumors now running rampant through the City.

"I would have expected Sir Borten to have departed for Moehn by now." Corey picked up an adornment from a nearby table on the pretense of studying its delicate art. "He seemed most anxious to assist his people the last time I spoke to him."

"The King favors Sir Borten's petition, but he has been reluctant to let him go. Akmael wants only the best men assigned to my personal guard, and there are few he believes he can trust as well as Borten."

Corey raised his brow at the irony. Stepping close, he invoked a sound ward and continued in low tones. "It would be best for you if Borten left."

"For the love of the Gods, Corey! I am not such a fool. I know what is expected of a Queen. Sir Borten poses no threat in that regard. Besides, the longer he delays, the more opportunity the girls have to consider—"

"Staying with you? That cannot happen, Eolyn. You must send Mariel and Ghemena away."

"Are you mad?"

"Mariel was a witness to your romance."

"As were you."

"Yes, but I know how to hold my tongue."

"Do you?" She pinned him with a sharp gaze. "In my experience, Corey, you always say whatever serves you in the moment it serves you best."

"It would not serve me to cast doubt on the paternity of your child."

"How did you—?" She waved away her shock. "You may put your fears to rest, Mage Corey. Sir Borten and I never had the opportunity to consummate our affection, thanks to your untimely appearance."

"My timely appearance, you mean." Corey searched Eolyn's face for any sign of deception. He would rather confront an army of Naether Demons than contend with the fury unleashed were Eolyn's child born with Borten's blue eyes and golden hair. "You should be grateful to me for that."

Eolyn shrugged, annoyance plain upon her face.

"I had thought perhaps you came today to share with me the fate of Adiana," she said tersely. "If your only purpose is to keep watch over my friendship with Sir Borten, then I can assure you it is unnecessary. You may go."

Chastened, Corey stepped away.

"Of course, my Lady Queen. My apologies." He cleared his throat. "We will speak of that shortly, but first I have something to show you."

With a respectful bow, Corey retreated to the table where the servant had left his package. He removed the silk cloth. Inside a large gilded cage fluttered a cream-colored sparrow with dark wings and a burgundy streak over her eyes. On her breast a golden mark, like a drop of pure sunlight.

"This is a Tenolin sparrow," he said. "It is a bird of special significance for me, one of the very few varieties in which the female also sings. They nest during the summer in the forests of East Selen."

Eolyn approached and laid her fingers on the cage. "She is beautiful, Mage Corey, but you have chosen a strange gift. A creature of the wild should never be caged. I am bound as a maga to set it free."

"That is my hope, but the breeding season is too far advanced. If we were to let her go now, she would have no mate or family, no one to show her the way south. We must keep her alive during the winter and set her free in the spring. I thought, given your gift with animals, I could ask you to watch over her until the snows melt."

"Of course, but I don't understand. How did you find her this far west?"

The mage forced out his breath, trying to relieve the painful constriction in his chest. "I did not find her, my Lady Queen. I made her."

The color drained from Eolyn's face. She covered her mouth and stumbled away, knocking a small table and sending its crystal adornments crashing to the floor. Her voice shook like leaves on an autumn wind. "This is Adiana?"

"Was." Corey frowned, unable to meet her eyes.

"Why would you do such a thing? Scatter her spirit to the wind?"

"There was no other way. I had to transform her, or leave her behind. Adiana would have been torn apart by the Naether Demons. I thought. . ." Corey shook his head. He had thought himself powerful beyond reason. Curse his pride. Curse the price she would pay for it. "I thought, given the time Adiana had spent with you, she would be more prepared."

"She was not a maga! Music was her magic. Music and friendship."

"I know. But she had strength, a resilience of a sort one rarely sees. I never expected her spirit to slip out of reach so quickly. I tried to bring her back, Eolyn. I used every spell at my disposal, but it was no use. It was as if. . ." Here Corey stopped. It was as if Adiana had not wanted to return, but he would not say this to Eolyn.

"She was my true sister, my friend in magic, and now I will never be with her again. Not here, not in the Afterlife." Eolyn sank to the floor. "I should have gone back."

"There was nothing you could have done."

"I abandoned her. I abandoned all of them. Look at what they suffered, what she's become because of me."

Corey knelt beside her. "You, too, would have been lost, or worse. Your sacrifice—their sacrifice—has saved us all."

"But at what price?" Her words came choked between anger and grief. "No, Corey. You are wrong. I have failed. Just as Briana failed her Clan, just as Renate failed her sisters. And now their punishment is mine. I am alone. Always in the end, alone."

She covered her face and surrendered to wretched sobs.

"Eolyn." He took her into his arms, uncertain whether she could hear him from inside that well of anguish. "You are not alone.

From the moment you first stepped into my tent all those years ago, you have never been alone. And I swear to you, dear Maga, as long as the blood of East Selen runs through my veins, you will never be alone again."

Chapter 52

Eolyn had not returned to Selen since the days of her brother's rebellion. She remembered its rolling landscape well: the slow climb into far reaches of the province, where the Clan of the East had thrived for generations until the War of the Magas culminated in their annihilation. The trees whispered with their lost voices; the wind spun ancient spells over hills painted with the first spring flowers.

As the Queen's procession drew closer to Corey's estate, dense woodlands replaced the open pastures. Eolyn welcomed the shade of the towering firs, the sweet perfume released as their horses trod upon the damp carpet of fallen needles. Long ago she had walked through these woods with Adiana; danced and sang with her at the festivals of Winter Solstice and Eostar. Those had been times of paralyzing fear and constant hiding, yet looking back Eolyn could only see the light and laughter of her friend.

Corey's manor looked just as she remembered, a rambling semicircular construction with thick timber supports and thatched roofs. At the center stood an ancient fir planted by the first mages and magas to settle the area. Eolyn was given a spacious set of apartments that befit her status. These she shared with her newborn son Eoghan, Mariel, Ghemena, and the Princess Eliasara.

The morning after they arrived, Mage Corey strapped Adiana's cage to his back and they left the manor together. The sun had not yet risen over the trees when they reached a woodland meadow where Corey spread his cloak on the fragrant grass. He assisted the Queen as she settled with the Prince. The girls ran off in search of mushrooms and winter berries. Young Eliasara waddled after them, her gurgles and laughter floating freely over the tall grass. It warmed Eolyn's heart to hear the child laugh, for she was on the whole a very serious girl.

"I don't understand why Akmael kept the Princess with us," she said to Corey. "He shows her so little affection. It saddens me."

Taesara's distress at learning her daughter would not be allowed to leave Moisehén had been terrible to witness. She had thrown herself at the King's feet, wept, and begged for him to reconsider, but Akmael received her entreaties with a stony countenance. His heart would not be moved.

"The King's decision was not made out of fatherly love." Corey began to secure the cage to a low-hanging branch with a piece of twine. "Eliasara is a hostage against the interests of her mother's family. King Akmael is wise not to become attached to her, as would be you."

"What do you mean?"

"What I mean, Maga Eolyn, is this: the one disadvantage of holding a card is that someday you may be forced to play it. That is something for you to remember, now that you are Queen."

"Are you suggesting he would use his own daughter as a pawn? Akmael would never be so ruthless."

"Akmael, perhaps not." Corey tightened the knot, checked that it would hold the weight of the cage. "The Mage King, however, will do whatever is necessary to prevent Roenfyn from raising an army against us."

Corey withdrew the silk cloth that concealed Adiana. She fluttered and sat still, peering at her new surroundings with something akin to curiosity.

"This is their last opportunity to say good-bye." Corey nodded toward the path the girls had taken. "Are you certain you do not wish to tell Mariel and Ghemena the truth?"

Eolyn shook her head. "It is better this way; better for them to live with the hope of seeing her in the Afterlife."

Prince Eoghan began to fuss, and Eolyn loosened her bodice, coddling the baby as she offered her breast.

"That is scandalous behavior, you know," Corey said. "Didn't anyone tell you that you should have a wet nurse?"

"I've enough silly rules to obey now," retorted Eolyn. "That one was too ridiculous not to break."

"Right you are." Corey sat on a nearby log and glanced around the meadow. The forest was tranquil, filled with the delicate dawn chorus that characterized these northern hills.

"What do we do now?" Eolyn asked.

The mage drew a breath and shrugged. "We wait."

The sun rose slowly behind the misty trees.

Bumblebees hovered over the field.

Eolyn and Corey fell into easy conversation, remembering with fondness the days of the Circle, the vivacious character and enchanting music of their friend from Selkynsen.

Little Eoghan nursed, dozed, and nursed again. He was a strong boy, healthy and whole, and Eolyn's heart swelled with gratitude every time she set eyes upon him. He had inherited his father's dark hair, and Eolyn wondered whether his eyes, now an amorphous gray-blue, would settle into the silver-green of his grandmother's Clan, or become dark like his father's.

At irregular intervals the girls appeared and dumped treasures of the forest into Eolyn's lap. She and Corey interpreted each one for them, according to their knowledge and training: this feather of the dwarf owl could grant protection from the hunger of the Lost Souls; that shard of glassy stone could dissolve a miscast spell; dew collected from the web of this spider could be used for diseases of the eye. The list went on and on, and Eolyn learned much from Corey, who knew these northern forests far better than she.

When Mariel appeared alone with a wreath of purple aethne, a cloud was cast over the Queen's contented mood. The young maga proffered the flowers to Mage Corey, a smile on her lips.

"I made this for you," she said. "If it pleases you, that is. It is a gift, from me and from the forest."

Corey accepted the fragrant blossoms and regarded her with a gaze that was more than kind. "It pleases me very much, Mariel. Thank you."

She let go a short laugh and ran off, leaving Corey to suffer under Eolyn's withering stare.

"What?" he said. "They are only flowers."

"Don't play innocent, Corey. You know what that means. Bel-Aethne is just around the bend, and Mariel has her eye on you. She has ever since she came back from Moehn."

"It is her decision, Eolyn. Who am I to refuse if she chooses me?"

"I will not allow you to jest about this."

"I do not speak in jest. Mariel is old enough to become a woman in magic. This is her year, to petition for a staff and to participate as she pleases in the first rites of Bel'Aethne. You cannot take that away from her."

"I do not intend to. But you…" Eolyn gave an exasperated sigh, stumbling over the unexpected muddle of her thoughts.

"I what?" Corey asked crisply.

"I don't know! It's just not right, somehow."

"Better a mage—no, better *this* mage, in whom you can trust—than some torpid fool who has no hope of understanding how sacred and important this will be for her."

Eolyn groaned. "I want what is best for her, Corey. I only ask that you consider—"

Adiana startled them both by bursting into song, a long sweet trill followed by a series of short pulsing notes.

Corey lifted his hand to silence Eolyn, and she bristled at his assumption that she needed the signal. From the edge of the meadow came the male's response, lilting high as if in challenge, then fading into its own slow staccato.

"There he is," whispered Corey.

Eolyn saw a rustle of leaves, followed by a flash of color between bushes. Her heart contracted painfully. She rose and entrusted her sleeping baby to Corey.

Adiana was fluttering restlessly inside her cage, lifting her voice in that beautiful song every time she paused on a perch. Eolyn's fingers lingered on the latch, desolation creeping into her spirit.

"Ah hah! Look, Eolyn." Mage Corey spoke like a proud father on his daughter's wedding day. "Now there's a handsome fellow."

The male had perched on a neighboring tree. He watched Eolyn and her prisoner with great intensity. His coloring was similar to Adiana's, save for the rust-colored cap that hooded his black eyes.

Eolyn undid the latch and reached inside the cage, catching the sparrow with a gentle hand. Sustaining the bird's legs between her fingers, she smoothed its soft feathers. Adiana trembled in her grasp.

"This is not the marriage I envisioned for you, my friend," Eolyn murmured. In truth, she had never envisioned marriage for Adiana, but only the Gods knew what might have happened if her coven had been allowed to remain in the highlands of Moehn.

Perhaps Adiana would have found a good man, someone to temper her cynicism and nurture her heart. She and Adiana could have raised their children together, travelling every spring to enjoy the sun-speckled shade of the South Woods. "It was a fragile dream we had, was it not?"

The sparrow chirped and fluttered her wings.

"But we lived our dream. For a few short years, the Gods were generous with you, and with me. Now they act on different whims, and we have no choice but to give them thanks for what we had and continue on our way."

"Eolyn." Corey's tone was gentle. He stood beside her now, the baby cradled in one arm while he rested a hand on her shoulder. "Adiana's suitor grows impatient."

She nodded, pressed her lips against the sparrow's soft feathers. "Go, then, friend and sister. Be at peace. Be free."

Eolyn released the bird.

Adiana flew to a nearby branch, settled, and began preening herself.

Mage and Maga backed away to a prudent distance. Eolyn took Eoghan into her arms, clutching him to her breast as if he were the one thread that could carry her through this moment, when the bitter losses of the past would be transformed into the uncharted paths of the future.

The male alighted next to Adiana and began his courtship, an elaborate ritual of song punctuated by short hops and buzzing wings that Adiana managed to ignore altogether, choosing instead to groom her feathers meticulously and look in any direction save his.

This behavior stretched on, the male's display becoming ever more frenzied and Adiana's disinterest ever more determined, until Corey threw up his hands and exclaimed, "Look at what she puts him through! How long must the male continue this foolish song and dance before she pays notice?"

Eolyn smiled. "Not long enough, Mage Corey. Not nearly long enough."

Adiana hopped to a new branch and cocked her head at the male as if expecting him to follow. He did. At last she lifted her voice in song. He joined her, trills and warbles interweaving until their voices sounded as one, the notes like crystal bells on the morning air, an exquisite mix of joy and heartbreak.

The girls returned from the forest and gathered around Eolyn and Corey, spellbound by this enchanting display. When the duet ended, Adiana flew off quick as the wind, the male half a breath behind her. Their rapid chirps lingering over the meadow as they dashed toward the heart of the forest, sparks of yellow and scarlet fading among the shadows of the giant firs.

Silence followed, and emptiness.

Eolyn kissed the baby's forehead, and discovered she was holding Corey's hand. Quietly, she let him go.

"You never told us she could sing like that," said Ghemena.

"I did not know," replied Eolyn. "I've never heard a Tenolin sing."

"But he has." Ghemena pointed an accusing finger at Corey. "And he didn't say anything."

"Would you have listened to me if I had?" countered Corey.

Ghemena pushed her lower lip out in a sullen frown.

Corey gathered up his cloak and shook it out. "Mistress Tiana has told me there will be sweetbread for our midmorning meal today. Who remembers the way back to the manor?"

"I do!" shouted Ghemena, and she was off.

Mariel followed close behind, sword on one hip, Princess Eliasara on the other.

Only Eolyn stayed as she was, Eoghan pressed tight to her breast, eyes fixed on the path Adiana had followed.

Corey drew near, set his cloak upon her shoulders. "Shall we, my Lady Queen? A warm meal awaits us at the manor, along with some mulled wine and afterwards, I would think, a well-deserved rest."

Eolyn smiled, grateful for his companionship, which despite their many differences had never faltered after all these years.

"Yes, Mage Corey," she said. Tomorrow they would start the long road back to Moisehén, where her future awaited in the arms of the Mage King. "I am ready."

About the Author

Photo by Julia Shapiro

Karin Rita Gastreich lives in Kansas City and Costa Rica. An ecologist by vocation, her past times include camping, hiking, music, and flamenco dance. Karin's first novel, *Eolyn*, was nominated for the 2012 Thorpe Menn Literary Excellence Award. Her third novel, *Daughter of Aithne*, is scheduled for release in 2015. Karin's short stories have appeared in *World Jumping*, also from Hadley Rille Books, as well as in *Zahir*, *Adventures for the Average Woman*, and *69 Flavors of Paranoia*. She is a recipient of the Spring 2011 Andrews Forest Writer's Residency.

Follow Karin's adventures into fantastic worlds, both real and imagined, at *eolynchronicles.blogspot.com* and *heroinesoffantasy.blogspot.com*. You can also join Eolyn on Facebook or follow @EolynChronicles on Twitter.

Find out how it all began.

Eolyn

By

Karin Rita Gastreich

One woman's journey determines the fate
of a millennial tradition of magic.

Sole heiress to a forbidden craft, Eolyn lives in a world where women of her kind are tortured and burned. When she meets the mysterious boy Akmael, heir to the throne of this violent realm, she embarks on a path of adventure, love, betrayal, and war.

Bound by magic, driven apart by destiny, Eolyn and the Mage King confront each other in an epic struggle that will determine the fate of a millennial tradition of magic.

"Vigorously told deceptions and battle scenes will satisfy fans of traditional epic fantasy, with a romantic thread."
-Publishers Weekly

HADLEY RILLE BOOKS

Exceptional titles in fantasy, science fiction, and historical fiction.

If you enjoyed *High Maga,* may we also recommend:

FINDER
by Terri-Lynne DeFino

NIGHTINGALE
by Melissa Mickelsen

POETS OF PEVANA
by Mark Nelson

WORLD JUMPING
Edited by Eric T. Reynolds

FIRE & SWORD
by Louise Turner

THE SONG AND THE SORCERESS
by Kim Vandervort

CPSIA information can be obtained at www.ICGtesting.com
Printed in the USA
LVOW06s1035300815

452091LV00024B/1248/P

9 780989 263191